The *Art* of MURDER

Michael White has been a professional musician, a science lecturer, newspaper columnist, science editor for *GQ* magazine and a series consultant for the Discovery Channel's *The Science of the Impossible*.

First published in 1991, he is now the author of 33 books, including the bestselling *Equinox*, *The Medici Secret* and *The Borgia Ring*. He has been shortlisted for the Aventis Prize and was awarded the Bookman Prize in the US for best popular science book of 1998 for his biography of Isaac Newton, *The Last Sorcerer*. He lives in Sydney, Australia, with his wife and four children.

For more information visit Michael White's website at www.michaelwhite.com.au

D1101986

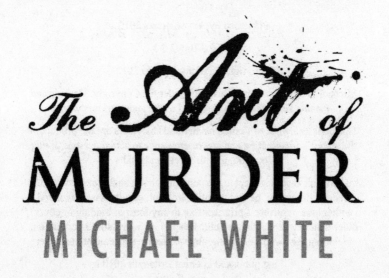

The Art of
MURDER

MICHAEL WHITE

arrow books

Published by Arrow Books 2010

2 4 6 8 10 9 7 5 3

Copyright © Michael White 2010

First published in Great Britain in 2010 by
Arrow Books
Random House, 20 Vauxhall Bridge Road,
London SW1V 2SA

www.rbooks.co.uk

Addresses for companies within The Random House Group Limited
can be found at: www.randomhouse.co.uk/offices.htm

The Random House Group Limited Reg. No. 954009

A CIP catalogue record for this book
is available from the British Library

ISBN 9780099551447

The Random House Group Limited supports The Forest Stewardship
Council (FSC), the leading international forest certification organisation.
All our titles that are printed on Greenpeace approved FSC certified
paper carry the FSC logo. Our paper procurement policy can be found at
www.rbooks.co.uk/environment

Mixed Sources
Product group from well-managed
forests and other controlled sources
www.fsc.org Cert no. TT-COC-2139
© 1996 Forest Stewardship Council
FSC

Typeset by SX Composing DTP, Rayleigh, Essex
Printed and bound in Great Britain by
CPI Cox & Wyman, Reading, RG1 8EX

'The creative process is a cocktail of instinct, skill, culture and a highly creative feverishness. It is not like a drug; it is a particular state when everything happens very quickly, a mixture of consciousness and unconsciousness, of fear and pleasure . . .'

Francis Bacon
(1909–92)

Chapter 1

Stepney, Wednesday 21 January, 8 a.m.

She came running down the street screaming at the top of her voice. As she ran, commuters heading for Whitechapel tube station moved out of her way thinking she was a madwoman. But she was not mad, she was simply terrified. She had just seen something that would make the strongest stomach somersault.

Her name was Helena Lutsenko, a Ukrainian immigrant. She had been in England for a little over six weeks and her English was limited to a couple of hundred words. In her petrified state, she could think only in Ukrainian. But even in her native language, there were few words to describe the horror of what she had just witnessed.

It was 8 a.m., halfway through the morning rush hour, and the Mile End Road in East London was awash with grey slush. It had snowed the previous night, and, as always in London, it had settled for about ten minutes before turning to a slurry unknown to pre-Industrial man: part water, part diesel, part city grime. The pavements were no better. The grey snow had been piled up to either side of a narrow footpath cleared for pedestrians, and although council road sweepers had been out since six,

1

throwing around sand and salt, the icy strip of pavement was treacherous.

Helena slipped and just broke her fall by grabbing a lamp-post. The shock forced her to calm down a little. She could do nothing in this state, she told herself. She needed to explain something, something desperate, something barely imaginable. And she needed to explain it to anyone who would listen. Anyone at all. Pushing away from the lamp-post, she took measured paces and deep breaths. Approaching a young man dressed in a business suit and carrying a briefcase, she began to articulate her horror, but the commuter speeded up instinctively. Helena walked up to a middle-aged woman talking into her mobile phone. The woman looked at her as though she were insane and shouldered her away. Just another East European beggar, the commuter thought, and sighed. Then a young couple turned a corner. They were well dressed but relaxed-looking, graphic designers or ad execs perhaps, definitely not bankers or insurance grunts. The woman was wearing a Comme des Garçons ankle-length coat; the man had a Louis Vuitton satchel slung over his left shoulder.

'Help me,' Helena said as clearly as she could. She stood in front of the couple, one palm held flat against the man's coat sleeve. He looked down at her hand, then glanced at the young woman beside him. She was ready to move on, but he was a little more patient.

'Please help,' Helena said.

The young man pushed a hand into his pocket and came up with a handful of small change.

'No,' she said, shaking her head. 'Not money. Come. I show.'

2

'What?' the young woman said suddenly and stared at the man. 'What does she want, Tom?'

Tom Seymour shrugged. 'Search me.'

'Please, come. I show.'

'Don't like the sound of this,' the young woman said, and took her companion's arm.

There was something about the desperate stranger that moved Tom. He seemed to know instinctively that she was genuine, that she needed someone. She was clearly terrified. He turned to the woman beside him. 'Trish, I think she needs help.'

'Yes . . . help,' the Ukrainian woman responded.

'Tom, you don't know her from Adam. She could be the front for a gang. Don't be a twat.'

He sighed. 'Yeah, you're right.' Then he tried gently to move Helena aside. 'Have to go,' he said to her.

Helena deflated like a balloon with the air sucked out of it and she burst into tears. Trish was already a pace away, but Tom hadn't moved.

'What's happened?' he asked.

Helena did not understand.

Tom put his hands out, palms up. 'What is it?'

'Man . . . dead,' she said, tears flowing down her cheeks.

Chapter 2

Helena took Tom's arm. Trish remained where she was, shaking her head, unsure what to do. In the end she simply said, 'I'll see you at the office,' and walked away.

Tom turned back just in time to avoid colliding into another commuter. He and Helena dodged to the right. He pulled his arm free. 'Where're we going?'

She looked round at him, but said nothing.

They turned a corner, right, off Mile End Road, down Vallance Road. Fifty yards further on, they swung another right into a narrow lane, Durrell Place. For the first time, Tom began to worry, began to wonder whether he had done the right thing after all. Then he saw a sign up ahead: *Berrick & Price Fine Art Gallery*. He recognised the name from an article in *GQ*.

Helena ran ahead. Tom caught up with her at the door to the gallery. The front windows stretched for about twenty-five feet. They were blacked out, with the name of the gallery printed in silver lettering across the glass in an eccentric font, a cross between Bank Gothic and Marlett, all block letters and narrow serifs. The door stood ajar. From inside came the faint smell of stale alcohol and incense.

'So, what's this all about?' Tom asked, dropping his shoulder bag to the ground at the gallery's entrance.

Helena simply pointed through the open door.

'Who are you?' he said.

Helena looked puzzled for a second, then tapped her chest. 'Me? Cleaner.' Then she pointed again. 'Man dead.'

'Dead? You sure?'

She nodded.

He thought about calling the police, but curiosity had already got the better of him. He had come this far, he thought to himself, why back out now? Some part of him was suddenly excited.

'Where?' Tom asked.

Helena just nodded towards the door.

Tom took a deep breath. 'Okay. You wait here.'

It was dark in the corridor, but an archway to his right led into a small room immediately behind the blacked-out windows. Bright halogen spots hung down in a cluster from the ceiling. Two walls were covered with vast canvases, blocks of pure colour, one a dark green, the other a deep purple. Under each stood a black leather and chrome sofa, original George Nelsons. Ahead was another archway that led into a much larger room, the display space.

Tom walked over to the second archway, hesitated for a moment and then stepped inside. This room was also brightly lit from rows of powerful halogens in the ceiling. In the centre of it stood some sort of installation, a tangle of plastic and steel, indistinct angular shapes bursting through a matrix of metal. Tom turned to his left and saw what he took to be another installation. He stepped towards it and froze. He felt the hairs rise on the nape of his neck. His mouth suddenly felt very dry and fear began

5

to ripple through the pit of his stomach. For several moments Tom Seymour could not fit what he was seeing into his image of the universe. It made no sense, it was a set of contradictions, what he was seeing clashed with the model of 'normal life' he had in his head. Then, as acceptance came, he felt his guts heave. Dashing back to the archway, he vomited as he ran, the spew landing on the expensive parquet flooring and slithering down his exquisite Yohji Yamamoto coat.

Chapter 3

Brick Lane Police Station, Stepney

Detective Chief Inspector Jack Pendragon had just switched on the coffee-maker on a counter at the back of his office when he heard a rap on the door. He could tell by the outline at the other side of the opaque window that it was his sergeant, Jez Turner. He turned back to fill the water container of the coffee machine, calling: 'Come in, Sergeant.' As he pushed a button the machine started its repertoire of sounds with a high-pitched whir followed by the crunch of beans being pulverised. Pendragon turned round to see an expression of excitement on Jez's face. 'Okay, what's the big news, Turner?'

The detective sergeant was twenty-three, tall and slim, with a taste for designer suits he managed to find at dramatically reduced prices and paid for by moonlighting as a DJ at a local club. Today he was wearing a dark blue, double-breasted Emporio Armani, a light blue shirt and a yellow tie held down with a slender gold tie-clip. With his hair greased back over his ears, his high cheekbones and large dark eyes, he looked like a 1920s gangster. 'Sir, just had a bell from the Emergency Call Centre. A murder just down the road in Durrell Place . . . an art gallery.

'Berrick and Price?'

'Dunno, guv.'

'Must be. It's the only gallery there,' Pendragon said half to himself. He grabbed his coat and scarf from a hook to the side of the office door and pushed past Turner into the hall.

There was a commotion at the front desk; a young man in a donkey jacket and calf-high Doc Martens was being restrained by the duty sergeant, Jimmy Thatcher. Another sergeant, Terry Vickers, was running towards them from a room down the hall. The young man tried to twist away from Thatcher, but the sergeant, a powerfully built cop who spent four evenings a week pumping weights at the local gym, was having none of it. As the restrained figure turned, Pendragon saw him head on. He had a web tattooed over his face, two blue spiders at each temple. The man was snarling and filling the air with expletives.

Vickers took only a second to reach them and yanked the man's right arm up hard behind his back, making him yell in fury. Between them, the two policemen dragged the tattooed man down the corridor towards the holding cells.

'Welcome to Wednesday morning,' Pendragon said to Jez as they sidestepped the two sergeants and their bundle of joy. The DCI's long face broke into a cynical smile.

As they went through the main doors to the station they were hit by a blast of freezing wind. 'Jesus fucking Christ!' Sergeant Turner exclaimed. Pendragon ignored him and gripped the collar of his coat tight about his face as he sped towards the nearest squad car. From behind them they heard the doors to the station swing open and close again and caught a glimpse of two other officers,

Inspector Rob Grant and his sergeant, Rosalind Mackleby, taking the steps down towards the parking bays.

Pendragon jumped into the driver's seat and turned the key in the ignition. A voice filled the car, reading a news bulletin on Radio Four. 'Weather conditions around the country have deteriorated dramatically overnight. Four inches of snow have fallen in some parts of the South East, and some of the worst of the weather has been in London after a blizzard swept over the capital in the early hours. The weather has caused serious disruption. All major airports have been shut down and . . .' Pendragon switched it off as Turner clicked in his seatbelt. The DCI reversed out of the spot and turned carefully in the snow. The wheels struggled to gain purchase, then he gently squeezed the accelerator.

Brick Lane had been transformed. Its usual drab greys and browns were smothered in white. 'Positively Dickensian,' Pendragon said to Turner with an edge of sarcasm. Cars with their headlights on and wipers snapping back and forth were moving as though in slow motion, and along the pavement marched figures bundled up in heavy overcoats and hats, hands in pockets, heads bowed to the wind. The falling snow was almost horizontal, carried through the air in powerful gusts.

Pendragon pulled the police car into a gap in the traffic and crawled along. They had the heater on 'Max' and the wipers cutting two semi-circular swathes across the windscreen. The car ahead stopped abruptly, red brake lights blazing in the driving snow. Pendragon put his foot to the floor, but the car just kept going. He turned the wheel and they slid sideways, finally stopping a few inches short of the kerb. The engine stalled. Pendragon pulled on the handbrake and turned the key. Nothing.

'Okay, let's go,' he said resignedly, and snapped the key from the ignition.

'Go where?'

'To the gallery, where else?'

It was only a short walk, but by the time they reached Durrell Place, Pendragon had lost sensation in his fingers and toes. He and Turner dashed into the entrance to the gallery just as Inspector Grant and Sergeant Mackleby's squad car pulled into the narrow lane behind them, sliding around in the powdery snow.

Pendragon stamped his feet and chunks of frozen slush fell on to the wooden floorboards. He opened his collar and looked up to see a pale young man, tall and wiry, clutching a leather bag over his left shoulder. He was sitting on a metal chair. Pendragon could see that his face was smeared with sweat in spite of the freezing cold. He was wearing a suit and an open-necked shirt. On the floor at his feet was a rolled-up overcoat. Beside the young man stood a woman: short, dark-haired. Probably in her mid-twenties, Pendragon thought, but she looked at least a decade older. East European features. She was dressed in cheap jeans and a drab brown coat that was far too flimsy for this weather. The man stood up.

'Detective Chief Inspector Pendragon.' The DCI nodded towards Jez. 'Sergeant Turner.'

The young man offered his hand. 'Tom Seymour.'

Pendragon turned to the woman. She was nervous, looking at the floor, raising her eyes but keeping her head down. 'Helena Lutsenko,' she said.

'So you made the call?' Pendragon asked, turning back to Tom Seymour.

He nodded. 'I was on my way to the tube station and this lady . . . Helena . . . stopped me and asked for help.' He wiped sweat from his forehead and blew air through his mouth. 'She . . . ah . . . led me here.'

'I'm cleaner,' Helena interrupted. 'I find dead man.'

'Okay,' Pendragon said, and glanced towards Turner to make sure he was taking notes. The sergeant had a pad and pencil in his hands and was writing quickly. 'Where's the body?'

Tom Seymour flicked a look towards the archway. 'Through there, in the main gallery.'

Pendragon turned to see Roz Mackleby and Rob Grant appear in the doorway. 'Ah,' he said. 'Sergeant Mackleby. I think these people need a cup of tea,' and nodded towards a door at the end of the corridor through which they could just see a rudimentary kitchen. 'Inspector Grant, come with us.'

The three policemen walked through into the reception area, ignoring the mammoth canvases and the expensive furnishings. Pendragon led the way under the second arch and into the main gallery. Surveying the far wall, he turned to his left and walked slowly across the wooden floor. A man was seated in a chair, hands in his lap. A pole had been placed behind his spine, keeping his dead body upright. He was wearing a black suit, white shirt and a red tie. On his head was a black bowler hat. Just under the rim could be seen a thin cord wrapped around the top of the head and tied to the pole. It kept his dead weight from falling forward. A hole seven inches in diameter had been

11

cut into the man's face. The hole was the depth of the head. Where his eyes, nose and mouth had once been was now a cylinder of air. It looked as if a massive cannonball had passed through the corpse's face. Placed at the base of the void was a polished green apple.

Chapter 4

Pendragon turned away and saw that Turner was as pale as death and Grant was doing his best to keep his stomach from embarrassing him. 'All right,' he said, his own face expressionless, only his dark blue eyes showing emotion. 'I want the building sealed off. And I do not . . . Sergeant? Are you with us?'

Jez Turner was transfixed by the sight in front of him, his face a blend of confusion and creeping revulsion.

'Sergeant!' Pendragon waved a hand in front of Jez's face.

'Sorry. Sorry, guv. It's just . . .'

'Put a call through to the station, inform Superintendent Hughes. Get outside! I want the whole lane cordoned off. No one in, especially the press. I want the media kept out of this for as long as possible, understand?'

Turner nodded and headed for the exit. Pendragon glanced at Inspector Grant and ran a hand over his forehead and through his short salt-and-pepper hair. 'We need Forensics here on the double. Put a call through to Dr Newman. And get Sergeant Mackleby to escort Seymour and Lutsenko to the station. We need statements ASAP.'

Inspector Grant stared fixedly at Pendragon and then left without a word. The DCI watched him cross the room and was about to turn back to the macabre sight when he saw Dr Neil Jones, the police pathologist, turn the corner under the arch and walk straight towards him across the wooden floor. Jones was short, pot-bellied and bearded. He was dressed in green plastic overalls to protect his suit and carried a grey plastic case in one latex-gloved hand. When Pendragon had first met him six months earlier, soon after the DCI had moved to his current job at Brick Lane, he'd thought Jones bore a striking resemblance to Gimli the dwarf from *The Lord of the Rings*, though he had never mentioned it.

Jones nodded to Pendragon and moved the Chief Inspector gently to one side so he could take a good look at the disfigured corpse.

'My goodness,' he said, as though regarding the football scores in the Sunday paper. 'How very unusual.' He ran a latex-covered finger around the inside of the huge hole where most of the man's face had once been. 'Well, he's definitely dead, Pendragon,' Jones remarked without looking up.

Pendragon ignored him. He was used to the pathologist's unconventional sense of humour and knew the best reaction was no reaction at all, just let the man get on with his job.

'I suggest you leave us two alone to get acquainted,' Jones added, nodding towards the corpse. Pendragon got the message and walked away towards the reception area. As he emerged from the gallery, he saw Inspector Grant trying to restrain a tall black man in an ankle-length oyster-coloured cashmere overcoat who was attempting to enter the reception area from the hall. 'Look, officer, it's *my* gallery, for Christ's sake!' the newcomer was saying. His voice was refined, educated. He towered over Grant by at least six inches.

'Inspector,' Pendragon said. Grant turned and, seeing his boss's expression, let the man pass. The DCI took a step towards the tall black man. 'I'm Detective Chief Inspector Pendragon. You're the gallery owner?'

The man stood rigid before Pendragon, searching his face intently. 'Jackson Price,' he said. 'I'm co-owner with Kingsley Berrick. What the hell's going on here?'

'Would you like to take a seat, sir?'

'No. Why?'

'I'm afraid there's some rather bad . . .'

'What's happened?' Price moved forward and, before Pendragon could stop him, passed under the arch and into the gallery.

'Sir. If you would . . .' Price was now three steps into the room and staring at the horrific sight close to the far wall. Then he simply sank to his knees, buried his head in his hands and started to rock to and fro.

Chapter 5

Five minutes later, Jackson Price was installed on one of the leather sofas in reception, nursing a mug of steaming peppermint tea. He hadn't said a word since entering the main room and was now staring fixedly into space. Pendragon was seated at the other end of the long sofa. He studied Price in profile. He was a handsome man: entirely bald, head smoothed to a shine; taut ebony skin; facial bones prominent but elegantly proportioned; eyelashes long. He had the air of an actor or an impresario. The two of them were alone in the reception area but nothing could be done about the occasional sounds coming from the gallery as Jones worked on the corpse.

'I realise this is extremely difficult,' Pendragon began. 'But . . . do you know the dead man?'

Price turned to him, his face fixed in a blank expression, as though still processing what Pendragon had asked. 'It's Kingsley Berrick,' he said at length, his voice a monotone. 'My business partner. He has a distinctive scar on his chin, just here.' He pointed to a region just below his lower lip, then looked away towards the huge canvases on the far wall.

Pendragon nodded. 'When did you last see him alive?'

Price turned back and seemed to unwind a little. He

took a deep breath and then a sip of the hot tea. 'Last night, at the private view.'

'Can you talk me through it?'

'It was a Luke Martin retrospective – these big canvases?' And he nodded across the room to a wall-sized expanse of turquoise. 'Some of the crasser journalists call him the "English Mark Rothko". Absurd, of course.' He sniffed and took another sip of peppermint tea. 'Anyway, it was a great success. The hacks claimed they loved it. We even had a couple of young royals here – admittedly from the wrong branch of the tree,' he added with a wave of his hand. 'A sprinkling of rock stars, old and young, and Casper Hammond popped in, en route to his hotel, straight off the plane from Hollywood . . . apparently. Best of all, everything was sold by nine o'clock.'

'And Mr Berrick?'

Jackson Price looked back at his tea, suddenly quiet. For a few moments it had seemed as though he had slipped into an alternate reality, one in which nothing terrible had happened. Now he was back confronting the grim truth. 'Oh, Kingsley was in a fabulous mood,' Price said quietly. 'He was terribly nervous earlier in the evening. But he always was a worrier. If I told him once, I told him a thousand times that worrying would be the death . . .'

'Mr Price, did Kingsley Berrick have any enemies?'

'Enemies?' Price shook his head. 'The very idea is simply preposterous, Chief Inspector. Everyone loved Kingsley.'

Pendragon decided to change tack. 'Did you see him leave last night?'

'Yes. As a matter of fact, I did. It was late . . . must have been oh, let me see . . . one o'clock? There were only a few of us still here. He left with Norman.'

'Norman?'

'Norman Hedridge, Kingsley's partner. Well, ex-partner. They're still friends, but no longer an item.'

'I see. And did Mr Berrick say where they were going?'

'Home.'

'And who remained behind with you?'

Price looked down at his cup again and took another sip before answering, 'Chester and Selina. Yes, that's it. Just the three of us.'

'Then?'

'Well, we stayed and chatted for a bit. Selina left before Chester. I set the alarm and went home.'

'Can anyone verify your movements after you left?'

Price looked startled for a moment. 'My mother was still up. I live with her.'

'She stayed up that late?'

'She's a worrier too.'

Pendragon paused for a beat. 'So how did the cleaner get in?'

'The cleaner?'

'The East European woman.' Pendragon paused for a second to recall her name. 'Helena Lutsenko.'

'Oh, right.' Price took a sip of tea. 'A couple of students live over the gallery. We pay them to let the cleaner in and out twice a week. I don't normally surface till at least ten.' He smiled for the first time, a big white slash across his face. 'Surely you don't think the cleaner . . . ?'

Pendragon ignored this. 'I'm grateful. It must be a

18

terrible shock for you. We will need to have a much more in-depth talk later . . . you understand?'

Price stared at him with his blank expression again. It looked as if he were about to say something, but then thought better of it. Opting to nod instead, he turned back to his tea.

Chapter 6

Pendragon walked into the corridor and headed for the gallery's kitchen. Mackleby and Grant were there with Tom Seymour and Helena Lutsenko. 'We'll need you both to come to the station to give a detailed report,' Pendragon said to the witnesses. Helena looked alarmed, but Tom Seymour simply nodded.

'I've called into work to tell them I'll not be in this morning,' he said.

'Good. Inspector Grant and Sergeant Mackleby here will escort you to the station . . .'

'But, sir, I do nothing!' Helena Lutsenko exclaimed, her eyes wide and dark with worry.

Pendragon found a brief smile from somewhere. 'Don't worry,' he said gently. 'We're not accusing you of anything.'

'But . . .' she looked panic-stricken '. . . my job . . . have to finish . . .'

Before Pendragon could say anything more, Roz Mackleby stepped in and placed her hand gently on Helena's elbow.

'Really . . . we won't bite,' Sergeant Mackleby insisted.

Pendragon spun round as Sergeant Turner appeared in the doorway.

'Lane's closed off, guv,' he said. 'And Forensics just called to say they're a few minutes away.'

'Good. Sergeant, I need you to get a complete list of who was here last night from Mr Price, and take a detailed statement from him. I want a full background on the event plus names . . . who showed, who didn't. Find out if anything unusual happened – everything you can get him to cough up. I'll meet you back at the station.'

'You're walking?'

'Need to clear my head.'

Before leaving, Pendragon turned back into the reception area, walked past Jackson Price and nodded to a uniformed officer posted at the archway to the main room. A police photographer was setting up a tripod and a digital camera a few feet from the murder victim. Jones was kneeling down in front of the dead man, peering into the gruesome void in his head and studying the apple.

'First impressions?' Pendragon asked.

There was an electronic whir from behind as the photographer ran off a couple of test shots.

Jones stood up. 'Well, it's a Granny Smith, Inspector.'

'Dr Jones . . .'

'Okay, okay.' Jones had his hands up. 'What can I say? Male, early to mid-fifties, average height, bit on the plump side. It's impossible even to guess at the cause of death before I get the body to the lab. I'd say he's been dead eight to ten hours, no more. The body's stiff from rigor mortis. No need for the truss. But obviously the body was put here when it was still relatively pliable.'

'All right. Forensics are on their way. I'll have the body released to you ASAP.'

*

Pendragon stepped out on to Durrell Place as Dr Colette Newman, Head of the Metropolitan Police Forensics Unit, emerged from a white van parked behind Mackleby and Grant's squad car. She strode towards him carrying a big plastic box similar to Jones's.

'Chief Inspector,' she said in her clipped, old-fashioned accent. Pendragon had first met Dr Newman the previous summer when they had worked together on a series of mysterious poisonings that had turned out to be the work of a crazed serial killer. She had been instrumental in piecing together some of the clues that had helped solve the crimes. A pretty blonde in her mid-thirties, Pendragon knew her to possess a keen intellect and a sharp wit. He had a lot of respect for her, and he liked her as well. 'Dr Newman,' he said. 'Sorry to drag you from your warm lab, but, well . . .' And he nodded back over his shoulder towards the gallery. 'This one should certainly pique your professional interest.'

'Oh, goody,' she said with a smile, and hurried past him towards the gallery door.

Pendragon had been only partially honest with Turner when he'd said he needed to clear his head. He needed to clear it of the horror, but he also needed to assimilate what he had just witnessed, to gather together his thoughts and begin to make some sense of it all.

It never got easier, he knew that. He had seen dead kids being dragged from lakes and old people sliced up on the swirly-patterned carpets of their tiny flats. No, it never got easier. Somehow, though, he had learned to deal with it;

to 'compartmentalise' as American psychotherapists would have it. But fancy words meant nothing unless he really could compartmentalise, and sometimes he could only just manage to keep it together in front of his junior officers.

In his twenty-five years of police service, Kingsley Berrick's was definitely the strangest murder Pendragon had seen. The body was what he had once heard described as a 'statement corpse'. Someone had not simply killed the man, they had wanted to present him as something else. He had seen immediately that the murder tableau was an imitation of René Magritte's famous painting *The Son of Man*, the classic Surrealist image of a bowler-hatted figure in a suit with an apple hovering directly in front of his face. But why had the murderer done it? And how? Answers to those questions would take a while to formulate, Pendragon knew that much.

The snow had stopped falling, but the recently swept pavements were now covered in a thin fresh coating that was starting to blacken and turn to slush. At the end of the narrow lane lay Vallance Road, usually a busy thorough-fare which today was almost empty.

At the junction with Mile End Road, Pendragon stopped at the lights. There were more pedestrians than normal, their cars left at home. The monolithic Victorian sprawl of the Royal London Hospital stood at the far side of the street. Snow had settled on the window ledges and the tops of archways leading through into its maze of interlinked buildings. But the white covering did nothing to soften the harsh lines of the place.

He turned right and merged with the other pedestrians,

wrapped up in Puffa jackets and anoraks, imitation Russian fur hats and Doctor Who scarves. He saw Grant and Mackleby's squad car turn out of Vallance Road and carefully negotiate the lights before slowly accelerating west, back towards Brick Lane less than a quarter of a mile away. He could just make out the backs of two heads in the rear seats, the unlikely pairing of Helena Lutsenko and Tom Seymour.

Chapter 7

Kingsley Berrick's ex, Norman Hedridge, proved extremely difficult to track down. Jackson Price had given Turner a phone number, but had warned him it wouldn't be easy to get the man to the station for questioning. It was only after Turner had called the number and been put through to a secretary that he discovered the stumbling block.

'Hedridge is an MEP,' he declared, walking into Pendragon's office. 'And he's in Brussels. Left on the early bird this morning.'

'Well, we'll just have to get him on to the first train back, won't we, Sergeant?'

'What's the problem? I heard the letters MEP.' Superintendent Jill Hughes was leaning on the doorframe, peering in at Pendragon and Turner. The DCI was at his computer, Turner had perched himself on the corner of the desk.

'Morning, ma'am,' Pendragon responded. 'Someone we need to question straight away. Maybe the last person to see the murdered man alive.'

Hughes had been brought up to speed when Mackleby and Grant had arrived back at the station half an hour earlier. 'You're talking about Norman Hedridge, I take it?' She held Pendragon's eyes with a steady gaze. She was a tough station commander, and, at thirty-three, one of the youngest Supers in the country. Guarded and occasionally aloof, she was nevertheless experienced enough to have nurtured a loyal and solid team at Brick Lane.

Pendragon nodded.

'I've already been on to the Commissioner about him.'

'You have?' Pendragon looked at Hughes and then at Jez. 'Get off my desk,' he snapped. Turning back to the Super, he said calmly, 'Well, that's good . . . isn't it?'

'Up to a point. Mr Hedridge is a friend of Commissioner Rampton, and . . .'

'Funny how they always are friends of someone, these VIPs,' Pendragon interrupted, and Turner gave a brief laugh.

Hughes glared back at them both and Turner altered his expression immediately. 'That's as may be, Chief Inspector,' she continued. 'All I'm saying is, tread carefully . . . please.' And she straightened up and walked away along the corridor.

Pendragon shook his head. 'The old boy network . . . never fails. Okay, Turner, so you got the guest list from Price?'

'I did. Over two hundred people attended. Old Kingsley Berrick was bloody well connected.'

'I'm sure he was. Two hundred guests? Well, we obviously can't interview everyone who was there last night, but Berrick must have had a close-knit group of intimates.'

'The gay art network?'

'For want of a better expression, Sergeant, yes.'

'And the starting point would be Norman Hedridge?'

'Indeed it would.'

It took until 3.30 for MEP Norman Hedridge to make it to Brick Lane Police Station. His driver dropped him and his lawyer at the stairs to the main doors where they were met by a constable and led along the corridor to Interview Room 2. Pendragon stood up as they walked in. Hedridge was an inch or so over six foot, big-framed, tanned, white hair cut into a fashionable, tousled style. He was wearing a Barbour jacket over a pin-stripe suit. The lawyer introduced himself as Maurice Strinner of Faversham, Strinner & Wrench. Pendragon knew the firm, the three partners' names were often featured in the news, famous for acting as solicitors to what had once been called 'the Establishment'. Strinner was a short man of forty-something. He had a bulbous, drinker's nose, watery blue eyes, a weak mouth. The lawyer turned to his client and introduced him as Norman Hedridge MEP. Pendragon shook hands with the two men and they all sat down. Turner came in then and pulled up a chair beside the DCI.

The atmosphere in the room was tense. Pendragon looked at Hedridge as the man stared fixedly at the wall between the two policemen, and it was at that moment he first put the face and the name together. Norman Hedridge . . . of course, he thought. The MEP had been a contemporary of his at Oxford. Pendragon had known Hedridge then, or at least known of him. Hedridge had remained totally unaware of Pendragon's existence, for theirs had been very different Oxfords. Pendragon had gone up on a

27

scholarship, which meant he had been at the bottom of the social pecking order, even in the early eighties when student life at the university was supposed to be cosily egalitarian.

The DCI had been born within half a mile of this station and had spent the first eighteen years of his life kicking around the local streets. When he had been noticed at school as exceptionally able academically, his headmaster at Stepney High had convinced Jack's parents to let him take the Oxbridge entrance exam. Hedridge, Pendragon knew, came from one of the wealthiest families in the country. His father owned vast tracts of land in Devon and Cornwall, and the Hedridges could trace their heritage back to a thirteenth-century baron who had stood beside King Henry III's son, Prince Edward, at the Battle of Evesham. Young Norman had been famous at Oxford for hosting flamboyant parties; leader of the in-crowd to which all the lesser aristos aspired to belong. Legend had it that after a summer ball at Christ Church, Norman had been found naked and unconscious in an inflatable dinghy circling the statue of Mercury, the centrepiece of the ornamental pond in Tom Quad. When one of the college Bulldogs, the university 'police', brought him round, they had fined him £50 on the spot. Apparently, his retort had been: 'I'll pay a hundred, my good man. It was worth every penny!' The Norman Hedridge now sitting before Pendragon was in nothing like so good a mood.

'DCI Jack Pendragon accompanied by Sergeant Jez Turner. Three-forty-two, Wednesday the twenty-first of January,' Pendragon intoned for the benefit of the digital recorder at the end of the table. 'Norman Hedridge MEP

28

has volunteered his time to answer questions concerning the recent death of Kingsley Berrick. He is accompanied by his lawyer, Mr Maurice Strinner.' He paused for a moment, waiting for Hedridge to engage with him. After a long pause, the man looked away from the imaginary spot on the wall and turned an imperious gaze upon him.

'Mr Hedridge,' Pendragon began slowly, 'you knew the deceased?'

'Yes, I did.'

'How would you describe your relationship?'

'We were friends,' Hedridge replied, giving the DCI a hard look.

'Friends? As in intimate friends?'

Hedridge didn't miss a beat. He simply turned to Strinner. 'I don't have time for this.'

'Chief Inspector,' Strinner began, 'my client is here to help with your enquiries. As far as we are aware he has not been charged or even accused of any crime. I fail to see the relevance of the question.'

'As both of you are aware, this is a murder investigation. Mr Hedridge is a known associate of Kingsley Berrick, and, according to a witness, left the gallery with the victim shortly before the murder took place. Indeed, Mr Hedridge may be one of the last people to have seen the victim alive.'

'I object to the implication,' Hedridge said coldly.

'I'm not implying anything.'

There was silence for a few moments. 'Mr Hedridge,' Pendragon began again, 'I am only concerned with solving this murder. I have no interest in your private life. But I feel that your relationship with Mr Berrick is pertinent to this enquiry. Because of that, I must be blunt. Were you and Kingsley Berrick lovers?'

Strinner immediately began to protest, but Hedridge stopped him with a raised palm. Then the politician looked Pendragon straight in the eye. 'No, we were not. And if any such accusation is made public, Chief Inspector . . .'

Pendragon had his own hand up now. 'You'll have me hounded out of the force? Blah, blah, blah. Do you think I haven't heard it before?'

Hedridge froze and Pendragon fixed him with his hardest stare, watching the other man's expression subtly reflect a series of emotions. After a moment, the politician broke into a politician's smile, one that stopped at the corners of his mouth. 'Very well, Chief Inspector. Very well.' There was a barely audible edge of acceptance in his voice. It was as though Pendragon had passed a test. 'Let us agree to avoid any hint of sexual reference, and I will agree to answer any reasonable questions you may put to me.' He stared at Pendragon with a look that suggested the DCI was never going to receive a better offer in his life.

'Talk me through the events of the evening, please.'

Hedridge looked down at the table for a moment, gathering his thoughts. 'I arrived late, about ten. I'd been at Westminster. There was still quite a gathering at the gallery. I had a chat with a few people I knew; drank a glass or two of champagne. Kingsley introduced me to a couple of artist friends. It was rather a jolly affair actually, and I lost track of the time. It got to about one o'clock and there were only half a dozen of us left. I admit, I was a little tipsy.'

'And then you left with Kingsley Berrick?'

'Yes, I did. I'd sent my driver home an hour or so earlier. We called a cab from the gallery. Kingsley lives . . . lived in Bethnal Green. I dropped him there and the cab took me home.'

'I see. That was the last time you saw Mr Berrick?'

'It was.'

'Can you recall the name of the taxi firm?'

Hedridge paused for a moment. 'Silver Cabs.'

Pendragon turned to the sergeant beside him. Jez Turner had already scribbled down the name.

'How long have you known the deceased?'

Hedridge took a deep breath, leaned his elbows on the table and clasped his hands together. 'Let me see . . . perhaps ten years. I met him by chance when the gallery was at its old site in Shoreditch. I bought a painting there, a Gary Heathcote. I was very grateful to Kingsley for that tip, it's shot up in value.'

'Was Mr Kingsley a popular man?'

'Not sure what you mean.'

'Sociable? A big circle of friends?'

'Well, yes, I believe so. I think it goes with the territory.'

'Any special friends?'

'I have no idea, Chief Inspector.'

'Would you consider yourself to have been a special friend?'

'Where is this leading?' Strinner interceded.

Pendragon turned to him. 'I'm trying to build up a picture of the victim's social circle. Does your client have a problem with that?'

Strinner looked at Hedridge, who sat staring coldly at Pendragon.

The DCI turned back to the politician. 'Let's put it another way, Mr Hedridge. Did Kingsley Berrick have any enemies?'

Hedridge looked a little startled for a moment. 'Not so far as I'm aware, Chief Inspector. We were friends, but I had no inside information about how he ran his business. I can honestly say we rarely discussed the commercial aspects of the art world.'

Pendragon paused for a moment and the room sank into a heavy silence. He glanced at Turner and noted that he was still scribbling diligently in his pad.

'My source suggests that your . . . relationship with the deceased had recently soured. Do you have any comment to make about that?'

'No.'

'Mr Hedridge, please don't insult my intelligence. My source referred to you as Mr Berrick's "ex".'

Hedridge gave him a fierce look and Strinner started to raise a hand.

'His words, not mine,' Pendragon added.

'Jackson Price, or "your source" as you prefer to call him, knows nothing about it, Chief Inspector.'

'That may be so, but for now I have to assume he does. And if he is correct, and you and Mr Berrick were . . . intimately associated and had only recently become . . . disassociated, that would have a bearing upon my investigation. Wouldn't you agree, Mr Hedridge?'

'Look, this is utterly ridiculous,' Strinner exclaimed. 'I'm sorry, but this line of enquiry is so far off beam as to be ridiculous. My client has come here to help solve your case . . .'

'That's correct,' Pendragon retorted.

'But the intricacies of my client's relationship with the murder victim . . .'

'Are entirely relevant, Mr Strinner. Come now, you know that as well as I do.'

Hedridge placed a hand on the lawyer's arm and gave Pendragon a pained look. 'I thought we had a deal, Chief Inspector.'

'The terms of a deal need to be clearly defined by both parties in advance, Mr Hedridge. You made a declaration of intent. I did not.'

Hedridge laughed briefly and turned to face his lawyer. 'Maurice, I think it's time we left.'

Chapter 8

'Well, that went well,' Sergeant Turner said sardonically as the door closed behind Hedridge and Strinner.

Pendragon shook his head slowly. 'Turner, when you are a grown-up copper, you might, if you're very lucky, begin to realise that what seem like the worst interviews often yield the most useful facts.'

Turner raise his eyebrows. 'Sorry I spoke.'

'Good.'

'But Hedridge was obviously lying out of his arse,' the sergeant added.

'About?'

'His relationship with Berrick.'

'Of course he was. Though, actually, Strinner was right. It isn't strictly relevant.'

'You sure, sir? Couldn't Hedridge have killed Berrick after a lovers' tiff?'

'Oh, come on, Sergeant. How often does a "lovers' tiff", as you put it, end with one of the "lovers" boring a huge hole through the other's head and propping them up in an art gallery as the centrepiece to a René Magritte-style tableau?'

'Not often, I s'pose.'

'Try "never". Or perhaps Berrick committed suicide?'

And Pendragon gave his sergeant a withering look. 'I think we'll find that the nature of their relationship was the only thing Hedridge *was* lying about. He was protecting himself – understandably. According to his file, he's married with two teenage children, and there's his political career to think about too. I knew he would clam up about his relationship with Berrick. I wanted to throw him off-kilter. Push him just far enough to let something slip.'

'Did he? I didn't notice.'

Pendragon was staring at the wall, lost in thought. 'No,' he replied absent-mindedly. 'No, he didn't. He's a politician, and a very clever one . . . Right, you can get busy, Turner,' he said, snapping back to the task at hand. 'I want you to check up on Silver Cabs. See if Mr Hedridge was telling us the truth about last night. I also want you to go through the entire guest list. Trace any connections between Kingsley Berrick and the names featured on that list, and then any links between Hedridge and those who were there last night. No matter how tenuous.'

'Well, sorry I criticised your interview technique, I'm sure,' Turner mumbled to himself as he walked off down the hall.

By the time Pendragon emerged through the main doors of the station it was dark outside, and it felt as though the temperature had dropped at least another five degrees. It wasn't worth bothering with a car; a fresh layer of snow had fallen, making the roads even more treacherous. Instead, he turned up his collar, plunged his hands into his pockets and headed through the gate on to Brick Lane.

The human tide had turned. All those people who had headed west into the city for their daily labours were now on the homeward journey, back to husbands and wives, curries and fish and chips, TV and Sky Sports, the pub and the bottle of chilled Pinot Grigio in the fridge, phone calls to Mum and Dad, a snooze in front of the box or ten pages of a paperback before bed, a freezing cold quickie under the duvet perhaps, and then sleep; ready for tomorrow's action replay.

The Milward Street Pathology Unit was only two hundred yards away. It was a single-storey red-brick building totally devoid of character. Thrown up in the 1950s, it was a monument to post-war austerity. Inside it was a little less austere. The hallway was painted a warm cream shade, and contained a cluster of chairs, a table with some two-year-old magazines on it, and a plastic palm in the corner. Pendragon strode along, ignoring his surroundings. He had been here on dozens of occasions, and almost every time the visit had involved his staring down at a corpse and receiving distinctly unpleasant information as to how the recently living person had become a dead one.

Jones saw him enter the lab and nodded before turning back to the latest arrival on the dissection table. The lab was a stark affair: whitewashed walls, scrubbed surfaces, and the irremovable stink of offal. Visible through an open door stood a wall of morgue drawers – the 'sunbeds' as the staff called them.

Jones looked up from the corpse. 'You're tired, Pendragon,' he observed.

The DCI shrugged and stared down at the almost

surreal form of Kingsley Berrick. He was naked, his body split and clamped open, red and grey, as dead as a carcass hanging in a butcher's window. He looked just like a thousand other corpses, except for the void where his face had once been, now backed by a circle of steel – the dissection table upon which his corpse lay.

'It's certainly a strange one,' Dr Jones said. 'I suppose you want the hows, wheres and whens.'

'The whos and whys would be good too,' Pendragon responded.

'Yes, well, that's your department. I've found a few answers to the obvious questions, though.' He pointed with a scalpel inside the huge hole in Kingsley's head. 'This all started post-mortem. He was killed by a needle thrust into the nape of his neck, here.' The pathologist turned Kingsley Berrick's body on to its left side and indicated a red dot on the back of the neck. He then rolled the corpse back and matter-of-factly lifted the dome of the dead man's head to reveal the brain. He removed this from inside the cranium.

'I've had a good poke around,' the pathologist went on. 'It's normal weight and in average condition for a man of Berrick's age. But look here.' He held the grey mass in his left hand and nudged a piece of tissue at the base of the organ. 'A hole,' he said. Placing the brain on a dish, he parted some folds. They could both see the red of a recent wound extending from the outer tissue of the brain almost to its centre.

'It was a fine needle, but a long one,' Jones said. 'Sank in at least fifteen centimetres. Passed through the cerebellum and on into the centre of the brain, coming to rest

37

close to the thalamus. Would have killed him pretty quickly – massive haemorrhage. As you can see, here.'

Pendragon had never become accustomed to the off-hand delivery style of pathologists, especially this one. But he had learned soon after meeting Jones that if he were to work with him, he would just have to blank out the man's seemingly ice-cold professionalism. Jones had mocked him for his squeamishness when they had worked together on their first case. After that, the DCI had developed a thicker skin.

'All right. Any thoughts on the hole?' he queried.

Jones returned the brain and closed the cranium. Then he ran the end of the scalpel around the inside of the opening in Berrick's head. 'It's a neat job. The hole is 12.1 centimetres in diameter, a fraction larger than a CD. It's more ragged at the back than the front, which implies to me that the killer used some sort of heavy-duty punch to smash out the centre of the hole. The head must have been clamped meanwhile. Look here, at the temples. Rectangular impressions in the shallow flesh. No bruising, which indicates it was clamped post-mortem.'

'Yes, but surely something so heavy-handed would have shattered Berrick's skull completely?'

'I thought precisely the same thing. But I learned two interesting things about the method our killer used. First, I found a few tiny specks of metal around the rim.' Jones walked over to a counter parallel to the dissection table. Returning, he held up a pair of microscope slides sandwiched together. With the light behind the pieces of glass, Pendragon could just make out a few particles of silvery material.

'This actually confused me even more for a time,' the pathologist went on. 'But then, as I was cleaning up the inside of the hole, I noticed a few dots of liquid oozing from the skin. Most of the interior of the hole here . . .' and he pointed to the opening '. . . has been cauterised. But a few bits have been missed. I tested the liquid.'

'And?'

'I was surprised to find it was hydrofluoric acid.'

'That's incredibly corrosive, isn't it?'

'You can say that again, Pendragon. But it makes sense.'

'Why. How was it used?'

'I'm not sure, of course, but the best scenario I can draw is that the killer placed a metal cylinder over Berrick's dead face and poured in the acid.' Jones placed his hands in a circle over the dead man's facial area to illustrate. 'This softened up the tissue, and, more importantly, made the bones of the face and skull malleable. This then enabled them to smash the hole through without shattering all the bones around the face. The hydrofluoric acid I found had leached out of the skin where the cauterising had not caught the flesh properly.'

'Good Lord!' Pendragon exclaimed, shaking his head.

'After making a crude hole, the killer would have tidied it up. There are a few marks . . . here and here.' Jones tapped the scalpel on the inside of the hole. Marks from a blade. The final task was to cauterise the opening.'

Pendragon felt a shiver of disgust pass through him.

'One very dispassionate murderer,' Jones added unnecessarily.

The DCI simply nodded. 'I can barely imagine what

sort of person we're dealing with here.' He took a deep breath. 'Any more accurate estimate for time of death?'

'Can't be precise, of course, but I would say most likely between one and two this morning. It's impossible to be sure how soon after death the mutilation was performed.'

Pendragon was about to ask another question when his mobile rang. He pulled it from his pocket, recognised the number on the screen. 'Dr Newman,' he answered cheerfully.

'Chief Inspector. We're just finishing up at the gallery. Can you spare ten minutes?'

'Certainly. Have you turned up anything?'

'Best if I go through it with you here.'

'Okay.' He paused to think for a moment. 'Give me fifteen minutes.'

'See you then.'

The crime-scene tape was still stretched across the entrance to Durrell Place and a constable in an overcoat stood in front of it, stamping his feet. Pendragon gave him a sympathetic smile as he passed under the barrier. Dr Newman was alone in the gallery, slipping out of her green plastic overalls as Pendragon walked in. Beneath them she was wearing a black knee-length skirt and a white blouse. Beside her on the floor was her case, opened out. Next to that lay a sheet of plastic with clear bags and a line of specimen bottles arranged upon it in two neat rows.

'You're on your own,' Pendragon observed.

'My team just left. They'll be back in the morning to finish up. It's been a long day.'

'Certainly has. So, what have you found?'

Dr Newman lifted one of the bags from the floor. The apple lay inside it.

'Ah, the Granny Smith,' Pendragon said, without expression.

Colette Newman tilted her head to one side and gave him a questioning look.

'Our friend Dr Jones. One of his little jokes. He made a point of identifying the apple before telling me anything else about the corpse.'

Dr Newman produced a half smile. 'We have a few prints on it, but I can guarantee they're from a local greengrocer. Anyone who could kill someone and set them up the way they did with Berrick wouldn't make such an elementary mistake.'

Pendragon nodded.

'That's confirmed by the fact that there are no prints on the chair and there was nothing on the body either. We managed to give it a thorough going over before it was moved over to Jones's lab. Has he turned up anything, by the way?'

'Berrick was killed by a long needle plunged into his brain. But Jones believes the victim's head was mutilated later, possibly using some kind of press.'

'Yes, I noticed the mark on the neck before the body was removed.' She lifted a bottle from the plastic sheet. In the bottom of it lay a tiny fleck of grey. 'The press idea makes sense. We found this, a sliver of steel. It's either from a knife used to tidy the hole or a punch of some sort. Before you ask, it's too small to help much, but we'll put it under the 'scope at the lab.'

'I don't suppose our killer left anything of themself behind?' Pendragon asked, without much hope.

'Sadly, no. I think they must have been wearing some sort of plastic suit.' She bent down to return the sample bottle to the sheet. 'But I've got at least one thing to show for eight hours' work.' Newman turned and walked towards the archway leading to the reception area. Pendragon noticed for the first time that a series of marker flags had been placed seemingly at random close to the centre of the room. He followed the Head of Forensics over to the first flag. Crouching down beside her, he could just make out some black marks on the wooden floor.

'Rubber,' she said without looking up. 'There's a line of these marks across the floor all the way from reception. They stop here.'

'From a tyre?'

'Correct. Or, more precisely, the tyre of a wheelchair.'

Chapter 9

Stepney, Thursday 22 January

Sally Burnside was an early-to-bed-early-to-rise type and she had a set routine. Up at 6.30 on the dot, out of the door by 6.40 and on her route around the Stepney streets. She rarely changed the course she followed: down Stepney Green, along the High Street, cut through the patch of lawn around St Dunstan's Church, and then west along Stepney Way before heading back east along Mile End Road.

This morning was no different, though she was annoyed with herself for leaving the flat five minutes later than usual, which meant she would either have to cut short the run or be late for the tube. The pavement along Stepney Green was completely clear of snow this morning. Rain in the night had washed away most of it and there had been no fresh falls. The roads were clear too, the traffic already building up.

St Dunstan's had looked unusually pretty twenty-four hours earlier, a patina of snow adding to the weathered beauty of its ancient stone. Now, the walls were rain-soaked, and puddles lay along the path from the gate. Sally sidestepped them; she was used to running whatever the weather.

She speeded up as she took the path around the side of the church. Ahead lay a short avenue of trees, set ten yards back from the road. She ran towards them, past a row of old gravestones. She had her head down for the first ten paces, but looked up as she approached a bend in the path. That was when she first saw something odd.

She kept up a steady pace but felt distracted, finding it hard to stay focused. What was that in the nearest tree? Five more strides and she was forced to pull up. She was not looking where she was going, it was getting dangerous. She slowed to a walk, hands on hips, trying to steady her breathing. She was ten metres from the tree now and the shape and size of the object were clearer.

A few moments later she was directly under the branches. She had stopped moving and was standing looking up at the thing above her head. It was an amorphous, flat object. For several seconds it looked something like a grey tarpaulin hanging over the lowest branch of the tree, about three metres above her head. Then Sally decided it looked like a giant pizza draped over the branch. It was largely grey, but there were streaks of red and white and random patches of black. She walked directly under the weird shape, looked up and moved her head to follow the leading edge of the thing to the point where it hung closest to the ground, a spot a couple of feet above the grass. Then she saw it, a thing so unexpected, she felt a sudden jolt in the pit of her stomach, a spasm that made her whole body tense for a second. Close to the edge of the object, embedded in the grey and red, was an eye staring straight at her.

Chapter 10

To Mrs Sonia Thomson
12 October 1888

Was I ever without malice? You may be surprised to learn that, until recent times, this was not a question to which I gave any thought. But now, as I write this account for you, dear lady, I feel compelled to ask it of myself. And I think the answer would have to be 'no'. I have always been wicked.

That is the honest truth and I never lie. Well, let me quickly qualify that. In this account of my experiences, I will tell the complete truth. I will not fabricate. All I write here is reality as I perceived it. I can promise nothing more.

But first we have to accept that there are many types of wickedness, do we not? There is the wickedness of those prosaic characters who stalk the nightmares of the innocent: the lumpen men, damaged or dull-witted individuals without finesse, devoid of any higher agenda. I would never put myself into that category, for I constitute a blend of wickedness with talent . . . great talent. It was only when I fully realised the extent and depth of that talent that I was able to channel my wickedness, and through this combination achieve greatness. But more of this later. Let me instead tell you the story of how I came to my great revelations, and how they secured for me my place in history.

Hemel Hempstead where I was born, William Sandler, on 10 August 1867, is a modest market town, genteel and pretty, and my parents' house, set among cornfields just beyond the jurisdiction of the town council, was a comfortable place in which to be raised.

It would be churlish of me to complain about the situation of my home, though everything else about it was bad.

The house was called Fellwick Manor. Built by my grandfather in the 1820s, it was a vast, boxy affair with too many windows, each a different shape and size from the rest. The architect appeared deliberately to have forsaken any of the Georgian taste for symmetry and proportion. It had ungainly, overbearing gables and a broad, squat porch. The bricks were too dark, the woodwork too light, and, to top it all off, a huge phallus of a chimney reared up from the back of the property above the kitchen. The house was set in three acres of prime Home Counties countryside, which was really its one saving grace. Otherwise, it was a typical monstrosity, built to impress, the thoroughly vainglorious trophy of a successful member of the mercantile class.

And my grandfather was certainly successful. He had been spat out of his mother's womb, the tenth of eleven children. All the others had wallowed in poverty, died young and vanished utterly from history. My father would never talk about any of his paternal relatives. He disowned them, just as my grandfather had done.

My father, Gordon Sandler, was a textbook example of the spoiled son of new money. Grandfather did all the work, made the fortune, and then his only son, my dear father, lived off it his entire life. Father was a husk of a man, tall and bone-thin, his face almost skeletal. He looked terrifying, even to me, his only son. I had only ever known him to be completely bald. He had black, piercing eyes, set too far back in his bony skull, and a black handlebar moustache. That was probably his only nod to fashion, yet it was an affectation to which he was entirely unsuited. My mother, Mary, was buxom, her hair perpetually scraped up in a tight bun. As a young woman she might have achieved an average prettiness, but the image I retain of her in my mind is all fleshy jowls and billowing black dresses. She scared me more than my father did.

Ours was an extremely religious household, though I myself could never understand what my parents saw to admire in God. My father was a lay preacher. With the fortune inherited from his father he had no need to make an honest crust: a full loaf was already provided. Instead, he gave himself over to the service of the Lord. Mother was equally pious, throwing herself into good works, helping the poorest of the local community – you can imagine the sort of thing.

There was no form of religious imagery displayed in our house. My parents were Calvinistic Methodists, a relatively new sect at that time. The only artistic expression of their religious fervour that they sanctioned was a tiny painting of Christ which hung in the parlour. In the hall, close to the front door, they displayed a framed letter from Reverend Griffith Jones, founder of the Order. According to family legend, my great-great-grand-father was Jones's right-hand man. Jones, I believe, had a lot to answer for.

My parents recognised quite early on that I was not inspired by the Holy Spirit in the way that they were. Indeed, I was a difficult child in almost every respect, and grew worse as each year passed. This was partly because of my own peculiar nature, but exacerbated by the fact that my parents responded to my stubborn, uncompromising personality in only one, rather unimaginative way – they regularly beat me to within an inch of my life.

It became something of a ritual. After committing an offence, no matter how minor, I would be summoned to my father's study. This was a very dark room on the ground floor, leading off the hall and facing south across the front garden, with a view of the road to Hemel Hempstead. However, I only knew this last couple of facts from my understanding of the geography of the house, for the curtains were always kept drawn in my father's study.

The walls were panelled with oak and the only illumination in the entire room came from a couple of gas mantles: one close to the door, and another, larger one, above Father's desk. The room was boiling hot in summer and freezing cold in winter. I often wondered how the bastard could ever do anything in his 'study', and then I would wonder what he needed a study for. He was not learning anything, he did not seem to work. All he ever did was read that damn book – you know the one I mean – in two parts, 'Old' and 'New'.

So, to the study I would be marched. Once I was inside, Mother would stand back against the door while Father questioned me. When I was very young, four or five, I would put up arguments in that infantile way. I would protest my innocence, try to offer mitigating circumstances. But after a time I grew to realise this was utterly futile because, no matter what I said, the outcome was always the same. Mother would lead me to the desk and I would be forced to bend over it with my trousers pulled down. She would pin my head to the desk top with her left hand and hold down my shoulders with the other. She always kept a crimson handkerchief tucked up her sleeve – the only concession to colour in her entire wardrobe. She wore black from head to toe, but that square of crimson cloth was concealed up her left sleeve. As she pinned me to the desk top, I could always see that handkerchief, clearly and close to. Then my father would take his cane from the cupboard next

49

to the door. I would hear it 'whoosh' through the air as he got the measure of it, and then the pain would slam into me like a steam engine. Afterwards we would pray together and I would be embraced and finally led from the room. 'There,' my mother would say as we crossed the hall, 'your soul will feel better now, William.'

I spent an inordinate amount of time alone. My parents did not like me mixing with the town children, and when I was not at my dame school I would sit in my room, staring out of the window, or walk through the fields and woods near the house. I was particularly fond of sitting by the river not far from the end of our huge, rambling garden. On my walks, I only rarely saw anyone else, and if I did encounter a group of children from school, they always ignored me.

I was eleven when I committed my first truly evil act. Up to that time I had been content messing around with small rodents and native reptiles. I liked to kill the creatures slowly, inventing new and evermore imaginative ways to do so. My favourite had been the time I crucified a rat which I caught under the bridge. I had devised a special trap which I laid with great care. The creature struggled to free itself from a net I had hooked up that was triggered to fall when the rat entered a small hole in the wall close to the waterline. Taking care to avoid the beast's sharp teeth, I managed to slip a cord around its neck. Later I ripped out its teeth using a pair of pliers I had stolen from my father's kit. The cross I had already prepared. I had even written a tiny INRI on a piece of wood tacked to the top of it.

But I did not consider killing animals, in whatever fashion, as actually being evil. That description I reserve for what happened one stiflingly hot day in August 1878. I remember it very clearly. It was the eleventh day of the month, and a day after my eleventh birthday. I had been down by the river. I was allowed to walk around the fields and copses far more freely now. I still rarely met another soul and still never talked to anyone, but I did have the sense of being allowed a little more independence by my godly parents.

On this particular day, I had been playing with a toy yacht I had been given for my birthday. I was trailing it through the current, secured to a long length of string. The boat had a single white sail that caught the breeze and propelled it through the murky brown water.

I was startled by the boy's sudden appearance at my shoulder. The first I heard of him was his voice.

'Lovely boat,' he said.

I whirled round, eyes wide with surprise, and he jumped back, equally startled by my reaction. I looked him up and down. He was tall – a head above me at least. I guessed he was about fourteen. He wore his sandy hair long, flopping into his eyes. He had a narrow face, almost ferret-like, and looked undernourished. He was one of the wretches from

51

the poor end of town, I surmised, no doubt a recipient of my darling mother's charity.

I turned back to the water and concentrated on guiding the boat to the rushes at the bank side.

'Can I 'ave a go?' the boy asked.

I ignored him.

'Can I?' he repeated, and stepped forward, tapping me on the shoulder.

I caught his ripe smell, a blend of sweat and soot, and felt a ripple of anger and disgust pass through me. I have always hated anyone touching me.

I turned to him and forced a weak smile. Then – I don't know why I did this – I handed him the end of the string. He clasped it in filthy fingers and beamed at me. 'Thanks.'

'What's your name?' I asked him.

'Fred.'

'Well, Fred, you know what to do?'

''Course. Fink I'm stupid? Nuffin to it. Just 'old the string and let the current carry it.' He took a couple of steps to the river's edge and we watched as the little yacht glided through the water. There was a narrow track beside the river and we trotted along it as the boat sailed on.

After a few minutes Fred seemed to have had enough. He stopped and leaned forward, taking deep breaths. He ran his free hand over his forehead and I could see he was sweating profusely. 'Blimey, it's 'ot,' he said, and lowered himself to the ground close to the track. Reaching into his pocket, he pulled out a small glass bottle and took a long draught from it.

I sat down beside him and he handed me the bottle. 'Blackberry juice. Made it meself earlier.'

I shook my head. 'No, thank you.'

'Suit yourself.' He took another mouthful and returned the bottle to his pocket. 'So where you from then?' he asked, turning back to me and squinting against the ferocious afternoon sunlight.

'I live up there,' I replied, and pointed back towards Fellwick Manor. We could just see the dark outline of the house.

'What? That bloody big place?'

'Yes.'

'Blimey, your parents must be fucking rich.'

I had never heard that word before. Had no idea what 'fucking' meant. I nodded. 'I suppose they are.'

'I'm just up 'ere for the day. From 'ackney. You know it?'

I nodded.

'Bloody 'orrible place. I love it 'ere, though.'

I looked away across the water. When I turned back, the boy had stood up and was running beside the river close to the bridge, clutching my boat to his chest.

'Don't launch it there!' I called. 'The current will take it under the bridge.'

'Let's go under with it,' he shouted back, still running.

'No, the rocks are too slippery. Keep the boat out this side. Take it over there.' I pointed towards the riverbank further along to our right.

Fred ignored me. Suddenly putting on a spurt, he leaped off the track and on to the patch of shingle leading under the bridge. A second or two later he had launched the boat. The current snatched it quickly and it was soon halfway across the river.

'Stop!' I shouted. 'It's too dangerous . . .' I saw the boy disappear into the darkness under the bridge and jumped down after him. I could feel fury at his selfishness mounting within me. I felt such intense hatred it drove me on. I thought nothing of the slippery stones underfoot.

My eyes adjusted quickly to the darkness. Here every sound was amplified, echoing around under the stone arch of the bridge. The place was rank with rotting vegetation and mould. 'Stop!' I shouted again, and my voice came echoing back to me. 'Come back.'

Then I heard a shrill cry, the sound of someone struggling to retain their balance . . . a loud splash.

I ran towards the sound and immediately saw the boy in the water. The river was deep here where the pillars had been excavated decades before. Fred's face was caught in a strip of light shining through the gloom between two metal struts close to the far side of the bridge. His eyes were wide with panic and he was floundering around in the water. The toy yacht appeared close to his shoulder and the string he had been holding a few seconds earlier was floating in the water, close to the edge of the rocks. I inched my way forward, taking great care with my footing, grasped the end of the string and pulled my yacht ashore.

'Help!' the boy screamed. I looked back and saw him struggling to keep his head above water. For a second he disappeared, then broke back through the surface and took a gulp of air. 'I can't . . . can't swim.'

I placed the boat carefully on one of the rocks and took two paces towards the water. A line of three black boulders ran from the edge of the shingle into the water. They were set about two feet apart. I knew I could clamber across them, I had done it before.

Fred was screaming now, overwhelmed with panic. His yells echoed around the stonework. I glanced over and saw him bobbing about still; he was kicking and moving his arms, trying to tread water, but he was tiring fast.

I reached the third stone. It was just a few feet away from the boy. I lowered myself into a crouch and leaned forward. I could see Fred's face more clearly now. His matted hair hung over his eyes. He was shaking his head and breathing fast. Then he saw me and held one hand above the water. I looked at his face and then at his hand. He seemed to realise my intent. For a second, there was answering viciousness in his eyes and his cheeks were sucked in, ready to denounce me. Then his expression changed. He fixed me with a look of despair . . . imploring, pleading.

I watched, not moving a muscle. I was transfixed, more excited than I had ever been in my life before.

I could have reached out my hand and grabbed him, but I chose not to. I watched as the last vestige of strength left him and he slipped under the surface of the water.

Chapter 11

Pendragon and Turner drew to a halt on Stepney High Street. The DCI flicked on the hazards, jumped out and led the way along the path as the sun started to come up. It cast a fiery red glaze over the gravestones. Shards of light were reflected in the east-facing stained-glass windows of St Dunstan's. As they rounded the side of the church they saw two men at the foot of an oak tree. Looking up, they could see the flat grey object draped over one of its lower branches.

'Fuck me!' Turner said under his breath as they approached. 'It's not until you actually see it, you can believe it.'

Pendragon averted his eyes from the monstrous thing in the tree and walked on, head down. Inspector Ken Towers was positioning a ladder under the tree, but it was proving difficult because the ground there was uneven. Beside him stood a man in a long black robe and clerical collar. He was in his early sixties, Pendragon guessed. He had a lined face and neatly cut white hair; bushy eyebrows, grey with a few flecks of black remaining. The DCI and Turner stopped beside the others, and for a few moments Pendragon silently studied the flattened shape hanging above them.

'Sir, this is the vicar . . . Reverend Partridge,' Towers said, nodding towards the other man.

Pendragon broke away from the weirdly fascinating sight and shook the cleric's hand.

'I don't understand this,' Partridge said, his face scrunched up like a cabbage patch doll.

'No,' Pendragon said soothingly and looked away for a second. 'Towers, who found the body?'

'A woman out jogging.' The inspector pointed to his left. An ambulance had pulled on to the path near the edge of the graveyard. Two women sat on its tailgate. One of them was a tall blonde, wearing knee-length Lycra pants and trainers, her hair pulled back in a ponytail. She was sipping from a white porcelain mug, a blanket wrapped about her shoulders, the corners hanging loosely over her front. Sergeant Roz Mackleby sat next to her, speaking softly.

Pendragon turned back to the scene under the tree. 'What exactly are you doing, Towers?'

'I brought out the ladder, Chief Inspector,' Reverend Partridge interrupted. 'I thought the poor soul should be brought down.'

Pendragon placed a hand on the cleric's upper arm 'That's very thoughtful of you, Reverend, but the Police Pathologist will be here soon. We should let him deal with it.' And he encouraged Reverend Partridge to turn away.

'Quite right. I understand,' the vicar replied woodenly as Pendragon walked across the grass, still with his hand on the older man's shoulder. The vicar was clearly in shock. 'I'll, em . . . I'll be in the vestry. Don't hesitate . . .'

'Thank you,' Pendragon said, and watched the man walk slowly towards the sanctuary of his church.

A small crowd had gathered at the other side of the railings to the churchyard, twenty yards away from the crime-scene. As Pendragon watched them, a patrol car pulled up next to the ambulance, and behind that came a grey four-wheel drive with Dr Jones at the wheel.

Pendragon called Turner over and they strode across the grass towards the new arrivals. The DCI waved to Jones as the pathologist clambered from his car and started to make his way between a couple of gravestones towards the tree. Pendragon and Turner waited for two uniformed officers to emerge from the back of the squad car and for Inspector Grant to come round from the driver's side. 'You two, get that crowd cleared,' the DCI told the uniforms, and indicated the gathering with a brief inclination of the head. 'Grant, I want this place sealed off. I want a screen around that tree. I don't want anyone without a valid reason for being there within a hundred yards of it. Turner, you come with me.'

They headed towards the ambulance. Sergeant Mackleby looked up as they approached and hopped down from the tailgate, her back straight.

'Relax, Sergeant,' Pendragon told her, and looked down at the young woman nursing her drink. She was staring at the ground. He glanced at Roz Mackleby, who raised her eyebrows. 'Sally Burnside,' she said quietly. 'Found the . . . er . . . body on her morning run.'

Pendragon sat down beside the young woman. 'Ms Burnside,' he said.

'Sally,' the woman replied, looking up suddenly. She

59

brushed a strand of blonde hair from her face and took a deep breath. 'I'm okay now.'

'Look, I think anyone would . . .'

'No, really, I'm good.'

Pendragon paused for a beat and looked up at Turner who had his notebook out. 'I'm DCI Jack Pendragon. I'm in charge of this case. This is Sergeant Turner.'

The woman glanced briefly at Jez and took another sip of her drink.

'Do you feel up to re-telling us what happened?'

'I told you, Chief Inspector, I'm fine.' Then she burst into tears.

The police officers were silent, letting the young woman cry it out. After a few moments, Roz Mackleby leaned in with a tissue. Sally Burnside took it and blew her nose. 'I'm sorry . . .' she began.

'There's absolutely no need to apologise,' Pendragon said, and waited for her to gather her thoughts.

'I was on my usual morning run. I almost always take the path through the churchyard.'

'What time was this?'

'Just before seven. I was a bit late this morning. I came round from there.' She pointed back along the path to where it curved close to one corner of the church. 'I saw this odd thing hanging in the tree. I couldn't make it out. As I came closer, I still had no idea what it was. It looked like a tarpaulin to me.' She paused for a second and took another couple of deep breaths. 'Then I realised what it was.'

'And you called 999 straight away?'

'Yes, I had my mobile.'

'The call was logged at four minutes past seven, sir,' Turner commented.

'Did you see anyone else in the vicinity?'

'No, no one at all.'

'Was that from the moment you ran into the church-yard? Think about it carefully, Sally.'

She shook her head. 'No one. There were people out on the street, around Stepney Way.' And she inclined her head in the direction of the main road. 'A couple of cars, but I can't remember anything about them.'

'No, that's okay.'

'But inside the churchyard, no. After I called the police, I went and sat on the bench over there. I couldn't see the . . . er . . . tree from there. I must have been in a state of shock because the next thing I knew two policemen were standing beside the bench.'

'All right, thanks, Ms Burnside,' Pendragon said, getting up and flicking a glance at Sergeant Mackleby, who resumed her place on the tailgate.

Pendragon and Turner walked back towards the tree. A screen was being erected and they could see Inspector Grant and two constables moving in on the rubbernecks.

Beneath the tree, Jones was staring up at the hideous corpse and shaking his head. 'Now I've seen it all, Pendragon,' he said, without taking his eyes from the object above his head. 'God only knows what you expect me to do with this.' Then he glanced round. 'You know that song, "Strange Fruit?"'

The chief inspector gazed into the branches. 'Yes, of course I do, Jones. Billie Holiday, based on a poem

61

by Abel Meeropol, about the lynching of two black men by the Klu Klux Klan.'

Jones was nodding sagely. 'Looks like someone's taken the idea a few steps further,' he said, his tone unusually serious.

Chapter 12

The digital clock on the wall flicked forward from 15.59 to 16.00 as Jack Pendragon walked into the Briefing Room of Brick Lane Police Station. The whole team had gathered there. Superintendent Jill Hughes sat in a chair at the front. Roz Mackleby and Rob Grant were at desks to either side of the room. Inspector Ken Towers sat a little behind Hughes, perched on the corner of Mackleby's desk. The three male sergeants, Turner, Jimmy Thatcher and Terry Vickers, stood in a ragged line, leaning against the back wall. Pendragon walked along the narrow space between the desks, edging past Towers and Hughes, and stopped in front of a smart board. A row of photographs had been stuck on to it. The first showed the body of Kingsley Berrick against the backdrop of a brightly coloured canvas. Beside this were a series of photographs of the body found that morning, hanging in the tree in the grounds of St Dunstan's Church. Under the picture of Berrick's corpse was a colour 10" × 8" portrait of the victim provided by the local newspaper, which had run a profile of the gallery owner two years before.

'You're all aware of the basic facts of the case,' Pendragon began without preamble. 'Two bodies in two days. The first found at Berrick and Price Gallery in

Durrell Place. The vic was Kingsley Berrick, one of the owners of the gallery and a well-known figure in the London art world. He was killed by means of a needle plunged into his brain.' Pendragon picked up a remote from a tray at the front of the smart board and clicked it. A picture from the Milward Street Path Lab appeared, a close-up of the back of Berrick's neck, the red puncture wound clearly visible. 'However, the killer did not stop there.' Pendragon clicked again, and a six-foot-square picture of Berrick propped up in the gallery appeared. There was a moment's preternatural quiet in the room. They had all seen this image before, but it still produced a potent effect.

'Second murder was discovered this morning.' Pendragon clicked the remote again and the image of the completely flattened body draped over the branch of a tree lit up the screen. A few clicks of the remote showed the hideous thing from half a dozen different angles. 'Absolutely no idea of the cause of death, of course, nor the identity of the victim. Forensics will be working around the clock.'

For a moment, no one spoke. Then Terry Vickers broke the silence. He had his arms folded across his chest and was staring fixedly at the smart board with his head tilted slightly to one side. 'I just don't get how these murders could 'ave been done, guv. I ain't seen nothing like it.'

'I agree, Sergeant. It beggars belief.'

'Yes, but these murders *have* been committed, haven't they?' Superintendent Hughes said matter-of-factly. 'So what has Jones found? And Forensics?'

Pendragon turned back to the board. 'Let's consider the Berrick murder first.' A morgue picture of the gallery owner's body appeared. 'The opening in his face was definitely made post-mortem. Jones believes it was done with some sort of mechanical punch or press.'

'Nice,' Towers muttered.

'Dr Newman has confirmed that the man was murdered at least an hour before he was placed in the tableau. She's found no useful prints and suspects the murderer wore protective clothing.'

'A thorough job,' Hughes commented, sitting up in her chair and leaning forward. 'Do Forensics have any idea if we're dealing with a single murderer?'

'Can't say for sure,' Pendragon replied. 'But Dr Newman found these.' An image of the tyre track on the gallery floor replaced the morgue shot on the smart board. 'I'd been wondering if there was more than one killer involved, but this suggests otherwise. Black tyre rubber from a wheelchair.'

'So you're suggesting that our killer dispatches Berrick with a needle in the neck. Smashes a six-inch-wide hole through his face and head, dresses him up and then transports the body to the gallery and across the room in a wheelchair before setting him up,' Jimmy Thatcher declared. 'A bit much, ain't it, sir?'

'Well, yes, it is, Sergeant,' Pendragon retorted. 'But you have before you the end result. If I hadn't seen it myself, I would have thought it pretty far-fetched too.'

Hughes was staring at the smart board, rubbing her chin with the fingers of her right hand. 'Okay, it's a working theory, Pendragon,' she said. 'Until we have a better suggestion, we'll assume that's what happened.' She half turned in her chair. 'What would you like to do next?'

'First, check out CCTV footage from the neighbourhood. See if we can get a car reg, or anything else to give us a lead. It's obvious the killer is using some specialist equipment. They must have a work space and access to equipment. It'll be a slog but we have to follow any leads we can in that direction. Turner, what have you got so far from Jackson Price?'

Jez pushed himself off the wall and drew his notebook from the pocket of his jacket. 'The guest list reads like a *Who's Who* of the London Cool Brigade,' he began. 'Super models, rock stars. It was obviously a big do and our vic was extremely well connected. I spoke to Mr Price. He was helpful, but I can't say I gleaned much from him. He gives the impression it was all happy chappies at the gallery. He and Berrick were apparently best buddies.'

'Yeah . . . bet they were!' Towers declared.

Thatcher and Vickers sniggered. Pendragon glared at them and they looked at the floor. 'Go on, Turner.'

'The evening went smoothly, apparently. Which I think is pretty bloody surprising considering all the towering egos gathered under one roof.'

'What about the cab company?' Pendragon turned to the others then to explain that Norman Hedridge claimed he had dropped Berrick at his flat and hadn't gone in with him.

'The company traced the driver for me. I spoke to him on the phone and he checks out Hedridge's story. According to the log in his car, he dropped Berrick at his flat in Bexley Road, Bethnal Green, at one-seventeen a.m.

He then took Hedridge to an address in the Barbican. Hedridge paid the fare for both him and Berrick using a credit card. That's logged at one-twenty-nine.

'All right, I want you to keep working the angle. We know Berrick and our charming MEP Mr Hedridge were . . . intimate at one time. Pay Price another visit, probe a bit deeper.'

'You think this has something to do with the gay scene, Pendragon?' Hughes asked.

'I think it's a possibility.'

She nodded. 'And what about the second murder? Anything yet?'

The image of the second victim returned to the screen. 'The victim's body has been completely flattened. Dr Jones has emailed over some preliminary data.' Pendragon picked up a folder from the desk nearest the smart board and glanced at the first page. 'Body is an oblong, 3.5 metres long by just under 2.25 metres at the widest point. It has been flattened to a surprisingly consistent thickness of between 2.3 and 2.4 centimetres. There are a few recognisable anatomical structures.' He pointed to the image on the board. 'A row of ribs here, a section of intestine there. And an eye . . . here. This murder would seem even harder to enact than the first. I've spent half the day trying to work out an MO. Then, just before coming in here I received two calls that helped answer a few questions.' There was an expectant hush.

'Dr Newman called first. Her team found some tracks near the tree and a mud trail that leads away around the graveyard and out across Stepney Green Park to a footpath. Unfortunately, the tracks have been chewed up, so they don't offer any detail. But then the second call came in. It was from the duty officer at Leytonstone Police Station. A member of the public phoned in to say they had some information about the incident at St Dunstan's this morning.'

'Information?' Grant said.

'The witness is a shift-worker. He claims he was walking by the graveyard at about five this morning when he saw someone using a cherry-picker. There was a tarpaulin screen obscuring half the tree. The witness assumed it was the council chopping down a dangerous branch . . . which I suppose is understandable after the weather we've been having. He thought no more about it until his wife told him something had happened in the church grounds. Reckoned someone had hanged himself.'

'A cherry-picker?' Sergeant Mackleby said. 'So that's where the tracks in the mud came from?'

Pendragon nodded and turned to Towers. 'Inspector, I want you and Vickers to check out any CCTV footage you can find. There must be cameras on Stepney Way. Any images of that cherry-picker could be worth their weight in gold.'

Towers nodded.

'Anything else from Forensics?' Hughes asked.

'Dr Newman has promised to rush through a DNA analysis. I'm hoping to hear from her within the hour,' Pendragon replied. He flicked off the smart board and perched himself on a table to one side of the screen. Folding his arms, he said, 'There's obviously a very clear connection between the two murders.'

'There is?' said Sergeant Vickers from the back of the room.

'Famous paintings,' Superintendent Hughes said quietly.

Vickers turned to Thatcher next to him and shrugged.

'The murder scenes are tableaux.' Pendragon stared at the blank faces of the Vickers and Thatcher.

'René Magritte?' Turner said, whirling on his fellow sergeants. 'Duh!'

Hughes caught Pendragon's eye and he allowed himself the faintest of smiles.

'The first murder scene was contrived to copy a famous painting, *The Son of Man* by the Belgium Surrealist René Magritte,' Pendragon said. 'It depicts a man in a black suit and bowler hat with an apple in place of his face. The second murder is another staged affair: *The Persistence of Memory* by Salvador Dali.'

'Is that the one with the floppy clocks?' Inspector Towers asked. 'My sister had a poster of that on her bedroom wall years ago. I always hated it.'

'It's all pretty bloody weird, if you ask me,' commented Sergeant Vickers, who had moved forward to sit on the edge of a desk across from Towers.

'It is,' Pendragon replied, looking around the room. 'It's bloody weird, but it's real and the connection is irrefutable.'

'So the murderer's a nut?' Rob Grant said.

'Depends how you define "nut", Inspector,' Pendragon retorted, growing a little irritable. 'The point is, the killer has a personal agenda. There's absolutely no chance of a coincidence here. Killings like these are carefully planned and meticulously staged. But, most importantly, they are statements. Our killer is not just disposing of people. He's making a point, a very serious point, and if we're to have any hope of catching him, we need to understand that point, PDQ.'

'Before he strikes again,' Hughes added, and an icy silence fell across the room once more.

Chapter 13

Pendragon's phone started ringing as he reached the door to his office.

He put the receiver to his ear and heard Dr Newman's voice.

'Chief Inspector, I have some news for you.'

'Good news, I hope.'

'I've got a DNA match for our second victim.'

Pendragon pulled over a pad from the top of a pile of paper at one side of his desk. 'Fire away.'

'A man named Noel Thursk. Had a record. Suspected of fraud five years ago. The case went to court. He was acquitted. Address recorded as number seventeen Trummety Street, Whitechapel.'

'I'm most grateful,' Pendragon replied. 'Good work, Doctor.'

'Glad to help.'

Pendragon was staring at the wall as Jez Turner tapped on the office door and popped his head into the room. The sergeant had to clear his throat before the DCI broke out of his reverie. Turner stepped in and threw himself into a chair facing the desk.

'Forensics have a match on the DNA from the body in the churchyard,' Pendragon told him.

'Wow! That was quick.'

'A man named Noel Thursk. Ring any bells?'

Turner was silent for a moment, looking vacantly at the mess on Pendragon's desk. 'It does actually,' he said. 'Can't think, though . . . hang on.' He came round the desk and started tapping at the computer keyboard. He soon had a list of names on the screen. 'I emailed this to you earlier. It's the guest list from the private view at Berrick's gallery.' Turner ran the cursor down the screen and stopped about three-quarters of the way through, over the name Noel Thursk.

'Well, I never,' Pendragon said. 'Time we had Mr Jackson Price pay us a visit, don't you think, Turner?'

Jackson Price sat stiff-backed in the chair in Interview Room 1, hands in his lap. 'Look, Chief Inspector,' he said earnestly, 'I want to help you, I really do. I just don't know how.'

'Well, look at the facts, Mr Price. During the past thirty-six hours there have been two murders. Both victims were linked to you and the gallery. Both were at the event two nights ago. We need to establish any further links that we can. Did you know Noel Thursk well?'

'I've been acquainted with him for a long time, but I couldn't say I knew him well. I don't know whether anyone did.'

'Why do you say that?'

'He was something of a loner. A rather private man.'

'He was a writer, yes?'

72

'He was originally a painter. Still dabbles, so I understand, but he decided, oh . . . at least a decade ago, that he couldn't keep going and started to write about Art instead. Had a column in the *Evening Standard* for a long time, but parted company with the paper. I remember there was some big row and he was shown the door.'

'When was this?'

'A couple of years ago. He freelances now. Or, at least, he used to,' Price added grimly. 'And I heard he was writing a book.'

Pendragon looked up from where he had been contemplating a blank notepad in front of him. 'A book?'

Price shrugged. 'Isn't that what journalists do if they hit the skids?'

'Any idea what the book was about?'

'None whatsoever, Chief Inspector. As I said, Noel was rather a private man and I didn't know him well.'

'You said he was a loner. Did he have *any* close friends?'

'Not that I know of.'

'What about Kingsley Berrick? Was he not a friend?'

'Oh, he knew him, of course. Thursk had made himself a fixture within the Art community. Part of the job description really, isn't it?' Price gave the policeman a blank look.

Pendragon was about to respond when his mobile rang. He recognised the number. 'Turner,' he said.

'Guv, you have Jackson Price there?'

'Yes.'

'I've just interviewed Selina Carthage. She was one of the last to leave the party on Tuesday evening. You know, one of the guests who stayed a while with Berrick, Price and Hedridge?'

'Yes.'

'She confirms that Hedridge and Berrick left together. She then went home. She lives in one of those posh places in Moorgate with a doorman downstairs. He confirms she came in around one-forty-five. Anyway, Ms Carthage reckons there was a bit of scene at the private view.'

'Can you be a little more specific, Sergeant?'

'There was a gatecrasher. A guy called Francis Arcade, would you believe?' Turner sniggered. 'A bit of a lad, apparently. Well known as a trouble maker.'

'Okay, thanks, Sergeant. Where are you now?'

'Off to see the last geezer who hung back at the gallery, a bloke called Chester Gerachi. Why is it all these arty types have such weird names?'

Pendragon ignored the question and closed his phone. 'That was my sergeant,' he said, turning a hard gaze on Jackson Price. 'Tells me there was a gatecrasher at the private view. You failed to mention that.'

Price showed little reaction, simply shrugged. 'I hardly thought it was important,' he said evenly. 'It was just Arcade. He is never welcome, but almost *de rigueur*, Chief Inspector. A private view would hardly be up to scratch if he didn't stick his nose in.'

Pendragon gave him a puzzled look.

'Francis Arcade's a joke,' Price went on. 'I'm surprised he doesn't hire himself out as a party entertainer, a performance artist.'

'So, what happened?'

'What happened? Mr Arcade showed up about ten-thirty. He hadn't been invited, naturally. He was turned away, but wouldn't take no for an answer and forced his way into the room. It was dreadfully dull. He should change the script a little.'

'What happened then?'

'Oh, he grabbed a drink, threw it over someone. Standard stuff. I was all for letting him stay. In a way, that's the last thing he would have wanted. Would have defused things. But . . .'

'But?'

'Kingsley wouldn't have any of it.' Price's voice dropped almost to a whisper.

'Mr Berrick intervened?'

'Well . . .'

'Either he did or he didn't, Mr Price.'

'Yes, he intervened. He and Arcade traded insults and then Kingsley took his arm. It looked for a moment as though it might turn really nasty, but then someone else took Arcade's other arm and the stupid kid just went limp . . . sort of gave up. Made his point, I suppose. They led him outside, and that was that.'

'Who was the other person?'

Price stared at the floor unable to look Pendragon in the face. 'I think you know, Chief Inspector.'

Chapter 14

To Mrs Sonia Thomson
13 October 1888

My mother died after a deliciously protracted illness. I was thirteen. I remember sitting with her in the darkened room directly opposite the top of the stairs in the east wing of the house. I grew fascinated by her physical degeneration. I had no emotional reaction to it whatsoever, but carefully catalogued each increment of her descent into Hell. For I was sure that if there were such a place, she would be heading that way. In fact, I took great pleasure in terrifying her with prophecy when we were alone together in that room. I spun such a tale of her sins . . . amplifying her every bad deed, convincing her utterly that she was destined for the eternal fires, that the flames would be lapping around her very soon. I recall standing outside the door and listening to my father's pathetic attempts to calm her down and his lame efforts to make her believe that she would be going to Heaven, that the Lord would forgive her sins. She could never mention to him what I had said, of course, because I had convinced her that if she did say anything, she would merely be compounding her own guilt.

But perhaps the most satisfying moment came when I managed to steal the crimson handkerchief she'd so cherished. She held it in her right hand where it lay outside the bedspread. My father and I were sitting on opposite sides of the bed, the curtains drawn tight shut. A single feeble lamp burned on a cabinet to my side of the room. The room stank of illness. I remember eyeing that handkerchief, waiting for the moment I could make my move, for I knew my unbeloved mother was close to death. I wanted to prise the scrap of crimson from her living fingers.

Then my moment came. Father left the room briefly. I stood up quietly and walked over to where my mother lay. I slipped the handkerchief from between her enfeebled fingers, thrust it into my pocket and returned to the chair just as Father stepped back into the room. The horrible woman died that night. I celebrated by taking the hand-kerchief down to the river and burning it in the silvery moonlight.

I have a certain Dr Egbert Farmer to thank for facilitating my eventual escape from Hemel Hempstead. Dr Farmer was my headmaster, and it was he who first took notice of my emerging artistic talent. He was a ridiculous, fat man with an absurd sense of self-importance, but he was also one of those individuals who felt the need to encourage those he believed to be talented.

I had conceived a great love for drawing, and later painting, which was my only release from the strictures of my unhappy childhood. My walks and adventures along the river and my occasional dalliances with the Lord's furred and feathered creations held limited charms, which I quickly outgrew. For a long time the incident with the boy from London loomed large in my mind, as you may appreciate. I relived the experience over and over again, my memory of it fresh and powerful. I could recall every fine detail of that hour by the river. I learned that his stinking body had been washed up downriver two days later. I would have given anything to have seen his corpse, but of course that was not possible.

I often sketched Fred, the drowned boy. I spent long hours struggling to bring to the page his expression of terror, the pleading light in his eyes as he slid away from this world. I fantasised about the look of him as he drifted under the water carried by the current, his head battered against rocks, his face cut by rushes, and I tried to visualise his bloated, green-tinged form as his parents would have seen it after he was fished from the river.

Needless to say, these were not the pictures Dr Farmer saw. By the time I was sixteen, I had quite a decent portfolio of conventional pieces, and I had entered a landscape in a school art competition. When I won the prize, it seemed to be the first time anyone at school even noticed I was there. Before then, I had been little more than a shadow. Even

Father took some notice when he heard of my success. Until then, he had not shown the slightest interest in my efforts but merely scoffed at the very idea his son should be interested in something so meretricious as art.

As a consequence, my father was quite bemused when Dr Farmer wrote to him inviting us to meet him. We dutifully went along to tea at the headmaster's cottage not far from the school, and when the good doctor explained to my father that he thought I was the most promising young artist he had ever seen, and that he believed I had a chance of a scholarship to study Fine Art at Oxford, Father was struck dumb.

He himself was not in the least bit academic, but he held Dr Farmer in high regard. Farmer had been an Oxford man himself and had once been something of an ambitious young fellow. Sadly for him, he had been wounded in the Crimea and never regained his health. He came from a wealthy family with connections who had secured him a teaching post in Hemel Hempstead, and when the former headmaster, Mr Bathurst, had died back in the late sixties, the good doctor had succeeded him in the post. And I'm grateful he did or else I might never have achieved the wonders for which I am now infamous.

On my first view of it, Oxford was shrouded in rain. The carriage taking me from the railway station rattled over cobbles and splashed through muddy puddles swamping Botley Road. It travelled past

79

Northgate, on to Turl Street, and pulled up outside my new home, Exeter College. I was in reflective mood, paying little heed to my surroundings. It was only the next morning when bright sunshine lit up my meagre room that I felt I had actually arrived.

My dear lady, to whom I have promised to tell only the truth and only the relevant details of my tale, I will not bore you with the minutiae of my introduction to university life. We have all heard such mundanities before, have we not? Let us not waste time, but instead move straight on to the meat of the story. If you'll excuse the pun.

Since my earliest childhood, I had, as you know, led a solitary existence, and so being thrust suddenly into a community like the University came as something of a shock. I quickly realised that I could spend my three years there in one of two ways. I could remain isolated, a misanthrope, or I could make a performance of it. The first path was more in keeping with my true nature and was seductive to me, but I also knew that I would gain far more from the experience of being a student at Exeter College, Oxford, if I . . . how should I put it? . . . partook fully of it.

I found I was rather a good actor – something of a natural mimic, in fact. I learned to disguise my voice and adopt different personae. I experimented with sartorial styling, facial hair, dyes and postures. I actually enjoyed it. And, I have to say, I'm quite a handsome fellow. I have fashionably long hair which is dark blond. I have a strong, intelligent face and large blue eyes. My lips are perhaps my least attractive feature, they are slightly too thin, but I have a manly chin, a powerful neck and broad shoulders. I'm several inches above average height, and of muscular build. But, more important than my physical appearance, I succeeded utterly in taking on the role of someone devoid of any anomalies of character, which meant I was readily able to make friends with others of my own age. I knew these were not real friendships, these people were mere stage props to me. Some may even have been fellow thespians – who could tell?

One such associate was Winston Merryfield, a medical student at Lincoln College. I can't honestly remember how I first met the man, and really it does not matter. I liked the sharpness of his mind. He was something of an old-fashioned intellectual type, always reading weighty German novels in the original language and extolling the virtues of his favourite composers. I hate music, always have done, and Merryfield's insistence that I attend the concerts he so loved tested my acting skills to the limit. But I thought from the off that young Winston would be a useful person to know, so with him I made a special effort.

One of the things I learned early in my university career was that there is a very important link between art and medicine. This is a fact many people ignore. As a student of Fine Art I was taught the rudiments of anatomy in the belief that it would facilitate a more realistic rendering of the human and animal form. That is an important area of expertise for the artist. Indeed, the Renaissance painter Leonardo da Vinci wrote about it. But the teaching of anatomy for painters is, well, let us say, less than comprehensive. And, as you know of me already, dear lady, I have always been inquisitive when it comes to bodies, dead or alive.

Merryfield was delighted when he learned that I was happy for him to bore me with his intellectual posturing, and even more so when I told him one evening, after a particularly tiresome performance of a plinky-plonky Mozart concerto at the Sheldonian, that I wanted to know more about human anatomy than I could gain from my own courses of study.

'My dear Sandler,' he replied with characteristic enthusiasm, 'that really is a very easy matter to resolve.'

'What do you mean exactly?' I replied, leading him on.

'Are you tired?'

'No.'

'Well then, why waste a moment? Come with me.'

We were walking along Broad Street but he turned us both round by gripping my shoulder and spinning on his heel. 'Our lab is not far, just past Wadham on Parks Road. There's always someone working late.'

And so I saw my second dead body. As a third-year student, Merryfield had his own key to the laboratory. He was right, there were two other students working there still. The place was freezing.

It was a cold November night, but I surmised the place was kept cool by some clever artificial means.

The cadaver Merryfield showed me was that of an old man. He was kept packed in ice in a steel cabinet. Merryfield opened the door to the unit and slid the body out on a narrow tray. I glanced down at the forlorn figure on its metal bier. His skin was yellow and as wrinkled as a dried prune. 'He was seventy-seven when he died,' Merryfield commented.

'But how do you obtain your specimens?' I asked. 'Is there still a trade in grave-robbing?'

Merryfield looked greatly offended. 'No, there is not, Sandler!' he snapped. 'We are morally minded students, just like you. The dead bodies we use are all officially accounted for and their passage from the workhouse, the prisons and the hospitals is documented in triplicate.'

'I'm sorry, I . . .'

'Burke and Hare went out of business a long time ago,' he added.

I held my hands up and made a very fine show of trying to pacify my 'friend'. The fact was, of course, that I was greatly amused by his reaction, though I could not let him know that. 'So how on earth do you preserve the corpses?' I said, quickly putting Merryfield back into a position where he could do his best to impress.

'Well, that's actually a very good question,' he said, his ill temper evaporating. 'It's not at all easy. Have you heard of refrigeration?'

'Yes.'

'That's what we do here. We have a gas generator at the back of the building which keeps the room cool. You must have noticed?'

'Yes, I did,' I retorted with a shiver.

'The body is embalmed with a special chemical called glutaraldehyde and packed in ice in the box there.' He pointed to the dead man's steel tomb. 'The glutaraldehyde has turned Franklin's skin yellow.'

'Franklin?'

'That was his name. A murderer, apparently. Killed two small children.'

I stared down at the sinewy naked form and could not visualise it as ever having been a living thing, let alone a person possessing the passion to kill.

Later Merryfield and I walked back to Broad Street together. After arranging a date and time for my first extra-curricular anatomy lesson with him, we parted on good terms. He wandered off to his room in Lincoln College and I walked slowly along Turl Street towards Exeter. But I knew even then that I would not sleep until I had spent some more time with Franklin.

I waited for three hours, watching the clock on my mantelpiece until the hands reached one. We were all supposed to be tucked up in our rooms by ten at night, and the curfew was strictly enforced. But, as you will have gleaned, I've never been an entirely conventional fellow. Within twenty-four hours of arriving at Exeter I had found at least three different ways to avoid the Bulldogs. It was a simple matter to slip unnoticed past the head porter, Mr Cooper, as he read the *Oxford Times* and sipped tea in the porters' lodge. I could move with great stealth and almost completely silently. As a precaution, I had put on black clothes, smeared my face with paint and pulled a hat tight down over my head.

Another useful skill I had acquired years earlier was the ability to pick locks. To this day there is still not a lock that has defeated me . . . and, believe me, good lady, I have picked a few.

I have a near-perfect memory and could recall every detail of the inside of the lab. Another useful skill of mine. You have to admit, I am a rather clever chap. The room was black, but there was a gas lamp close to the door. I pictured the layout of the room: the wooden and metal benches, the chairs, the sinks and the metal 'tombs'. I made my way in the dark straight to the part of the room where Merryfield and I had been talking the previous evening. I lit the gas mantle, turning the tap to produce the palest, most sallow light.

The memory of it all is as clear as crystal in my mind today. Most people would probably have felt uncomfortable in that place. The cold was biting, my cheeks felt numb and my fingers were freezing. I could see my own breath in the air. But aside from these discomforts, I felt remarkably relaxed. The dead have never scared me, and in this dark, frigid room, I felt absolutely at home. And so I set to work.

I shall not describe precisely what I did. Let us just say I was searching for something. I always had been. This was in the days when I believed there was still something to find inside the human body. A time before I realised there was nothing there. Before I gleaned the real truth.

I haven't really explained this so far, have I? Perhaps I should. My parents' religious zeal repelled me, this much is undeniable. I had no time for myths and legends, and I certainly did not believe in a benevolent God. But at the same time, I could not come to terms with the idea that this meagre existence on Earth was the end of the story. I realise now that it was just my ego making me think this. After all, it is human ego that drives all religious faith, and like most people I needed to believe in the existence of the soul. As far back as the days when I'd vivisected rats and frogs, I was searching for a physical manifestation of it. I knew it had to be in there somewhere. That is what I was doing that night in Merryfield's lab. I was hunting for tell-tale signs that the dead murderer's body had once hosted a soul, that traces of it somehow remained. I realise the futility of it now, dear lady. But I was young once.

Anyway, I digress. I half-expected something concerning my nocturnal adventure to appear in the local paper, but, disappointingly, nothing was ever reported. It seemed the University hushed up everything. No blame was ever placed upon Merryfield because he shared the cadaver with at least a dozen other students. He told me there had been a discreet enquiry into the episode and that he had been questioned at length. I put on a wonderful show of shock and disgust when, after swearing me to secrecy, he told me what had happened. None of the medical students or teaching staff could quite understand why a hard-to-come-by corpse, employed for serious research, had been so comprehensively and systematically eviscerated, each organ ransacked, every inch of flesh diced and pulverised.

For my part, I'm just as mystified as to why Merryfield never showed the slightest suspicion that the destruction of Franklin's dead body had been in any way linked with our visit the previous night, or that it was anything to do with me. Either he was a very naïve chap or I am an even better actor than I give myself credit for.

Chapter 15

Stepney, Friday 23 January, 8.30 a.m.

The morning sun was trying to break through heavy dark cloud as Pendragon and Turner drove through grey morning streets. Pendragon was sipping coffee, the sergeant at the wheel.

'Did you learn anything from Chester Gerachi?'

'Nah, just confirmed what that bird Selina said.'

'About Arcade?'

'Yeah, and Berrick leaving with Hedridge.'

'Where did Gerachi go after the private view?'

'Got a cab home. He lives in Bermondsey. I checked with the cab company. They dropped him there just after one-thirty.'

Pendragon nodded and took another sip of coffee. 'Which doesn't entirely rule him out. He could have made it back to Stepney in time to bump off Berrick.'

'I thought the same thing. He's clear though. His girl-friend was waiting up for him.'

They pulled up outside a large Victorian terraced house on Glynnis Road, close to Whitechapel tube station. Half a dozen rings on the doorbell brought no response, so Turner leaned on the ancient brass bell push until the front door was finally opened a crack. Through the narrow opening they could see a man's face, eyes crinkled to slits. His long, spiky hair was almost comical, like the much-maligned cat in a *Tom and Jerry* cartoon after he's had his paw jammed in a plug socket. Pendragon pushed his ID up to the crack. The young man glanced at it and went to close the door again, but Turner had his foot in the opening. There was a brief sigh from the other side of the door and it swung open a little.

Francis Arcade lived in a bedsit on the first floor. It consisted of one large room with a minuscule bathroom and a galley kitchen. Windows in the main room looked out over the grey street, parked cars, ragged, leafless trees and Stepney grime. It was a high-ceilinged room with elaborate cornicing. It would once have made a fine master bedroom. The floorboards were bare and painted black. The walls were painted dark grey. A bare bulb hung from the centre of the ceiling. It cast a bright, stark light over the dark surfaces. In one corner stood a narrow bed. It was the only piece of furniture in the room.

The rest of the space was taken up with canvases laid flat on the floor or leaning against the walls, an easel, boxes of paints, and pots stuffed with brushes of all sizes. One wall was covered with advertisements from magazines and newspapers. The canvases, a good dozen of them, were identical, flat black, featureless surfaces. Arcade caught Turner staring at them.

'A new series,' the young man said. 'Shades of white.'

Turner made to reply but a glance from Pendragon stopped him. 'Mr Arcade, we're from Brick Lane Police

Station. My name's DCI Pendragon and this is Sergeant Turner. May we ask you a few questions?'

Arcade was tall, two or three inches over six foot, but incredibly thin. He could not have weighed more than seventy kilos. He had obviously just rolled out of bed. He was bare-foot, dressed in a pair of black baggy trousers that flapped about his feet, and a ripped T-shirt through which one pale nipple could be seen. About his neck was a grubby red kerchief. He had large hands, long fingers, filthy nails. His mop of jet-black hair was a mess, spiked up with gel. He had the remnants of black mascara about his large eyes, black pupils, a long, shapely nose and a sensuous wide mouth. Given a bath, a haircut and a few good meals, he could have been a good-looking kid.

Pendragon recalled what he knew of Francis Arcade from the record. He had been reported for two relatively minor offences, disorderly conduct and petty theft. No charges had been brought on either count. He had studied at St Martin's and had once been considered a promising young artist. There had even been an article about him in *Paint*, which had trumpeted that Arcade was *the* young artist to keep an eye on. Then it had all gone wrong. He had been kicked out of college, a remarkable feat in itself. Officially it had been because he had slandered the school in an interview in the *Big Issue*, but Arcade had claimed he had been victimised and that they had used the interview as an excuse to get rid of him. Whatever the truth, it marked the start of a rapid slide in his fortunes. He was soon ostracised by the painting fraternity, and his few friends deserted him. He had taken to attacking the London art world at every opportunity, but each attempt to deride or upset those who pulled the strings had backfired, and now he was perceived by most people in the scene as an object of ridicule.

'I take it this is about the stiffs?'

'If by that you mean the two men whose deaths we are investigating, then, yes.'

'That's cool. I'll tell you anything you'd like to know about the fuckers. I hated the air they breathed. Very good riddance, as far as I'm concerned.'

'That seems a strange thing to say at this juncture, Mr Arcade.'

The young man shrugged. 'Innocent until proven guilty, I was always told. Has that changed suddenly?'

Pendragon stared at him. 'Can you account for your movements early on Wednesday morning?'

'Yes, I can actually. I was at the Lemon.'

'The Lemon?'

'A club, sir,' Turner said.

Pendragon screwed up his mouth and nodded. 'And what time did you leave . . . the Lemon?'

'About four, I think. You could ask them at the door. They saw me arrive about midnight. There were quite a few people at the club who could vouch for me. I was on the floor the whole time. Didn't stop . . . except to take a piss a couple of times.'

'What about early yesterday morning?'

'Was that when my dear departed friend Noel Thursk died? I thought he hung himself.'

'Just answer the question, please.'

'Am I a suspect suddenly?'

'You're helping with our enquiries, Mr Arcade. If you

would prefer to come down to the station, we have nice warm interview rooms there.'

Arcade bit on a dirty fingernail. 'I was at the Lemon then too.'

'Two nights in a row?'

'I've been in a dancey mood.'

Pendragon looked around the room before staring hard at Arcade. 'You knew Kingsley Berrick and Noel Thursk well?'

'Better than I would have liked. Berrick was a breadhead, nothing more. He had no real interest in art. When he looked at a painting or a sculpture, he saw pound signs. And Thursk? A seedy little charlatan. All he was interested in was digging the dirt on the people around him. He was a crap artist and a crap writer. No great loss, really,' Arcade concluded, screwing up his face in a mock smile.

'I assume you blame these two men for your recent problems,' Pendragon replied.

Arcade's smile dissolved, to be replaced by a stare as black as one of his new canvases. 'And what would those "problems" be, Chief Inspector?'

Pendragon felt Turner staring sidelong at him from where he stood a few feet to his left. Arcade gave a short laugh. 'You don't really understand anything, do you?' he said. 'There are two types of people in the art world, Chief Inspector. There are the creators and the spongers. Berrick and Thursk are . . . sorry, *were* . . . spongers, parasites who fed off the spirit and the soul of artists. For me, there are no "problems", as you call them. There are only opportunities . . . opportunities to create. I learn from everything that happens to me. Each new experience in my life feeds my work. Because of that, I don't have *problems*. I'm immune.'

Pendragon glanced at Turner then back at Arcade. He wanted to argue, to point out that he was contradicting himself, for if there were no problems, then Berrick and Thursk had not been problems. If they were simply fuelling his creativity, they had been doing him a favour; no reason to hate them therefore. 'Tell me about Tuesday evening,' he said instead.

'What? The sickening display of pomposity and backslapping at Kingsley's gallery?'

'An event to which you weren't invited.'

'Wouldn't have gone if I had been.'

'So gatecrashing was just a display of frustration? Or was it performance art?'

Francis Arcade spun round to face Turner. 'Oh, man, your boss is a comedian.'

Turner stared at the young man, his face impassive, and Arcade looked back at Pendragon. 'So, what? Is "performance art" a new phrase you've picked up, Mr Plod? It's got fuck all to do with anything like that. I gate-crashed because it amused me.'

Pendragon gave Arcade a doubtful stare and then looked sidelong at Sergeant Turner. There was a sudden stillness in the room. Arcade walked past the two officers and stopped at his easel. He picked up a palette covered with black paint and began to dab at the canvas. To Pendragon it felt as though a switch had been thrown and Arcade was no longer with them.

Chapter 16

'Have to say, guv, these artistic types are a bloody odd bunch,' Turner said as they walked across the street to the car.

Pendragon was deep in thought.

'I mean, that bloke hated Berrick and Thursk and made no bones about it. Doesn't he care what we think?'

'Clearly not, Sergeant. Which may strengthen the view that he had nothing to do with the murders.'

'Or it could be a double bluff.'

Pendragon exhaled through his nostrils and shook his head. 'I think you've been watching too many American crime shows, Turner. Check out Arcade's alibis for both nights as soon as you get back to the station. But, I can guarantee, they'll stack up. And while you're about it, see how Grant and Vickers are getting on with the CCTV footage. Give me a call if they've found anything.'

'Where will you be?'

'I've got to see a man about a book.'

Ten-thirty on Friday morning, and the only people milling around Soho Square were shoppers wrapped up against the biting wind and laden down with spoils from the January sales. Pendragon turned into a side street and

94

headed towards a stucco-fronted building close to the end of the narrow road. Steps girded by black railings led to a large black-painted door. He pushed a button on the wall and a voice distorted by electronic noise came through the intercom speaker. 'May I help?'

'DCI Pendragon. Here to see Mr Lewis Fanshaw,' he replied. There was a momentary pause and the door clicked open.

A narrow hall with a vaulted ceiling led through to a broad reception area. Pendragon introduced himself again and the receptionist gestured towards a line of leather-covered chairs around a low table piled with literary magazines and publisher's catalogues. Pendragon was trying to find something interesting in an article about yet another great Indian saga due to be unleashed upon the world when a beefy man in his mid-forties appeared from the hall, one huge hand extended, a smile on his face. He was wearing a crumpled blue jacket and grey slacks, a white open-necked shirt and a very bright waistcoat.

'DCI Pendragon,' he said. 'I'm sorry to have kept you waiting. Please, come in.' He placed one hand on Pendragon's shoulder and waved the other towards his room.

Lewis Fanshaw's office was large and square. A pair of sash windows opened on to a narrow courtyard surrounded by dark brick walls. On the ledges stood two window boxes, the plants inside them dead, their crumpled leaves glazed with frost. Fanshaw sat down behind a handsome old mahogany desk. To each side of it stood piles of manuscripts, some contained by rubber bands, others spilling out haphazardly. Fanshaw sat in a modern cloth-covered swivel chair and leaned back, right leg over left knee, one Hush Puppy and one Donald Duck sock on display with a strip of pink flesh just visible above the sock. He placed his interlinked fingers on his crossed knee and said, 'So, Chief Inspector, you must be here about poor old Noel. Did Margaret get you a coffee or a tea, by the way?'

'That's fine,' Pendragon responded. 'Yes, that's why I'm here. We're treating Mr Thursk's death as murder.'

Fanshaw blanched. 'Murder? But I was told . . .'

'Suicide? That appears not to have been the case.'

'I see. Well, of course, Chief Inspector, anything I can do to help . . .'

'We're beginning to suspect that Noel Thursk's murder may be closely linked with that of Kingsley Berrick. The two men knew each other, and, well, there are connections between the murders which I cannot go into at this time.'

Fanshaw was nodding. 'No, of course not. So how may I be of assistance?'

'I understand that you were going to publish the book Noel Thursk was writing.'

Fanshaw raised his eyebrows and sighed. 'Yes, well, that was the theory.' Pendragon gave him a puzzled look. 'We signed the book over four years ago. Delivery dates came and went several times. I'd begun to lose heart. Now, of course . . . I'm sorry, I didn't mean that to sound callous. I liked Noel. He was a strange, very reserved man these past few years. Never used to be. We were at college together, you know. He was a lot of fun in those days. I think he had the stuffing knocked out of him. The winds of fate, and all that?'

'What do you mean, precisely, Mr Fanshaw?'

'Sadly, Noel was one of those people whose ambition outstretched his talent by some considerable degree. He was a good artist, don't get me wrong, but not exceptional. And his style was deeply, deeply unfashionable. He could not adapt. People stopped taking him seriously a long time ago. Eventually he accepted it and crossed the tracks, as it were, to write about painting rather than actually being a painter himself. But it damaged him. He made the transition, but he relinquished a major part of himself along the way.'

'What was his book to be about?'

Fanshaw uncrossed his legs and shifted in his chair. 'It was provisionally entitled *The Lost Girl*. It was about Juliette Kinnear.'

Pendragon gave him a blank look. 'I'm sorry . . .'

The publisher smiled and sat forward, elbows on the desk in front of him. 'It's okay, Chief Inspector. I'm not surprised you don't recognise the name. I think this book would have brought the subject to a much wider audience. Juliette Kinnear was an artist. She was one of the Biscuit Kinnears, you know who I mean?'

Pendragon nodded. 'I've heard of them. A very wealthy family.'

'She was enormously talented. Indeed, I would say she was the most talented female artist of her generation. If she had lived, she would have been world renowned by now, I'm sure of it.'

'What happened to her?'

'Oh, she suffered from some mysterious mental disorder and committed suicide in the mid-nineties. A terrible waste.'

'And Thursk's book was a biography of her?'

'No, it was actually a lot more than that. It was really an exposé, with Juliette's story as its cornerstone. Noel was digging deep, very deep, into the London art world. He was extremely well connected, you see. Basically, he knew everyone. And everyone's guilty secrets.'

'Ah,' Pendragon intoned.

'So there you have your motive, I imagine, Chief Inspector.'

Pendragon nodded. 'Although it doesn't quite explain the connection with Kingsley Berrick.'

'Maybe the connection is spurious.'

'I don't think so, Mr Fanshaw. But I'm most grateful for the information. Now, would it be possible for me to have a copy of Thursk's manuscript, as far as he wrote it?'

Fanshaw drew a deep breath and screwed up his face. 'I'm afraid, that's just it, Chief Inspector. Noel hadn't delivered a single word.'

Chapter 17

Brick Lane, Stepney, Friday, 1 p.m.

Pendragon was in a foul mood as he came through the doors of the station, head down, barely looking where he was going. The duty officer turned to a young constable beside him and raised his eyebrows as the DCI stormed past them. Just beyond the main desk, Pendragon almost knocked Jimmy Thatcher off his feet. The young sergeant was holding armfuls of papers, half of which flew across the corridor.

'Damn it!' Pendragon exclaimed, and crouched down to help. Straightening, he passed a large sheaf of paper to Thatcher and apologised. 'Sergeant?' he added. 'You tied up with paperwork?'

'Yes,' Thatcher said mournfully.

'Well, take a break. Get over to Noel Thursk's flat. Forensics have been through the place. I want you to bring in the man's computer and any disks or . . . what are those things? . . . USB drives you can find. Pass them all on to Turner. Then you can get back to the paperwork.' And he nodded at the untidy pile in the sergeant's arms.

'Anything from Grant and Vickers on the cameras?'

Pendragon asked as he strode into the Ops Room, pulling off his overcoat as he went.

Turner was seated at one of four desks arranged in a vague semi-circle. 'Nothing, sir. But I've stumbled on something you might find very interesting.'

'Arcade's alibi?' Pendragon asked as he approached the desk. Turner was staring intently at a flat screen and tapping at a keyboard. 'Nah. A podcast.' Turner looked up at his superior's blank expression. 'You have no idea what I'm talking about, have you?' the sergeant added.

'None at all.'

'A podcast is a broadcast over the internet. You can stream it on an MP3 player or any computer if it's online. Audio, visual . . . It's a bit like TV or radio, but you pick it up with a computer.'

'So what sort of *podcast* have you found?' Pendragon asked. The way he said it sounded as though he couldn't quite grasp the concept or why the world needed such a thing.

'I was doing a search on Francis Arcade. Got the standard Wikipedia stuff and a few art sites he's mentioned on, then this popped up.' Turner clicked the mouse and the screen changed. Photographs of two faces appeared, those of the murder victims, Kingsley Berrick and Noel Thursk. Written across the faces were the words *TWO DEAD MEN: A Post-mortem Podcast*. The sergeant clicked again and a two-and-a-half-minute video played. It was shot using a single camera. The jerkiness showed it was almost certainly hand-held. The setting was the Berrick & Price gallery the previous Tuesday. It featured the two dead men of the title in conversation with others at the event. The camera moved around the room. Snatches of conversation could be heard – Berrick deliberating on some aspect of commercial art, Thursk nodding as he listened to a woman telling him an anecdote. He smiled and replied with something inaudible.

The podcast ended as abruptly as it had started and the screen turned black.

'Before you ask, guv, this was only put online a couple of hours ago.'

'Shame,' Pendragon said.

'So what do you make of it?'

The DCI shook his head and lowered himself into a chair. 'I'm at a loss. It's almost as though the man wants us to pin the murders on him.'

'You want to go back for a second visit?'

'No, Sergeant. I think this time we get Mr Arcade in here.'

As Pendragon spoke into the digital recorder, Arcade sat perfectly still on a metal chair pulled up close to the table in Interview Room 1. The Chief Inspector concluded by saying that the suspect, Mr Francis Arcade, had declined the services of a lawyer.

Pendragon stared at the young man and remained equally still, equally silent, for more than two minutes. The only sound in the room came from the electronic ticking of the wall clock. Finally he pulled a plastic folder towards him across the shiny metal surface of the table. 'I watched your wonderful piece of work,' he began. Arcade did not stir. 'Who filmed it?'

Arcade returned Pendragon's intense gaze. 'Michael Spillman, a friend.'

'We might need to talk to him.'

'I wouldn't bother. He flew to New York early Wednesday evening. Besides, he was just doing me a favour. Made a copy of the videotape and emailed it over. Berrick and Price had commissioned a recording of the evening. It was all above board. Ask your mate Jackson.'

'It's a rather obvious message, isn't it?'

'A few days ago these two men were alive and well. Now they cannot speak or move, and soon they'll be ash. Haven't you ever wondered at recordings of someone who has since died? Are they really still alive? Were they always dead? I sometimes wonder if isolated tribes who have no understanding of the camera are right to fear it. Perhaps it does leach away our souls. But then, perhaps it's good that it does, for how else may we be kept alive when memory fails?'

'Very profound. Very Damien Hirst,' Pendragon replied tonelessly. 'Where's the artistic merit to it?'

'I thought this was a murder investigation. Why are you so interested?'

Pendragon shrugged. 'Humour me.'

Arcade gave a wan smile. 'I don't spare a moment's thought for artistic merit and nor should you, Chief Inspector. But . . . if you want me to humour you.' He tilted his head to one side for a second. 'It's about intent. My friend supplied the material just like an art shop provides paints and canvases. I edited the film. But much, much more important is the intent behind the work. The conceptualisation, if you like. In this case, the mystery of the after-image. The only possible form of Life After Death.'

'Why?'

'I'm an artist. That's what I do.'

'Oh, come on! That's a glib remark and you know it, Francis.' Pendragon allowed a look of disappointment to flicker across his face.

'It's the truth.'

'It's boring.'

Arcade could not hide his surprise.

'You're provoking us, deliberately positioning yourself as the prime suspect. Why?'

The young man shrugged and stared fixedly at a point on the wall behind Pendragon.

'I think I know what you're up to. This is all about publicity, isn't it?'

'Hah! You sound like Berrick,' Arcade exclaimed. 'That's the sort of shit he was so concerned about. *The oxygen of publicity*,' he added in a pompous tone.

'But it makes sense, doesn't it?' Pendragon moved a hand across the space between their faces. '"Failed Artist Seizes Opportunity to Get Noticed". Perfect.'

'You surprise me, Chief Inspector. I was beginning to think you weren't quite as thick as some of the other pigs.'

Pendragon paused for thirty seconds, letting the silence grow uncomfortable. Then he placed the plastic folder upright on his lap and opened it so that Arcade could not see the contents. 'I imagine, as an artist, you are quite accustomed to seeing extreme images, Francis.' Pendragon stared into the young man's eyes. 'This is Mr Berrick, though I'm not sure you'll recognise him.' He removed a glossy from the folder and pushed it across the table. It spun round and stopped a few centimetres away from

103

Arcade. It was a close-up of Kingsley Berrick's disfigured head taken by the police photographer at the gallery on Wednesday morning.

Pendragon could just about discern a flicker of something in Arcade's eyes, but was not sure what that something was.

'Perhaps not as you remember him.'

Arcade slid the picture back. 'You're right, DCI Pendragon. I *am* accustomed to extreme images.'

Pendragon plucked the photograph from the table and replaced it in the folder. Then he removed two more glossy prints, turned each so that Arcade could see them and moved them across the table. The first one showed the flattened body of Noel Thursk, pensile over the tree branch in the cemetery. The second was a picture taken in the Path Lab from a camera placed high above the remains. With nothing else around it to offer perspective, the body looked like an amoeba under a microscope.

'Recognise him?'

Arcade stared silently at the picture.

'Looks a little peaky, I admit. But do you really not know who this poor fellow is? It's your old friend Noel Thursk.'

Arcade looked up. His mouth moved as though he were about to say something, but he let it go. Then he gave a brief smile. 'Quite something, Pendragon. I'd say you should be looking for someone with a dead Surrealist fixation.'

This time, Pendragon could see nothing slipping from behind Arcade's mask, but he was sure it was a mask. 'Very well,' the Chief Inspector said calmly. 'If that's the way you want to play this, you give me no alternative but to place you under arrest. See if you still feel so relaxed after twenty-four hours in a cell. That's how long I can hold you without charge. Meanwhile I'll obtain a warrant. Shouldn't take long. Then we'll go through your studio with a fine-toothed comb.'

Arcade did not flinch.

Chapter 18

Friday, 7.30 p.m.

Pendragon's mobile rang as he fumbled for the key to his flat. It was Turner. 'Towers and Mackleby have just come back from Arcade's studio,' he said.

'And?'

'Nothing really, sir. The place is clean . . . a couple of joints, some rather ordinary porn, but nothing relevant.'

'No tapes?'

'Well, most cameras use memory sticks . . .'

'Okay, Turner . . . no *memory sticks*?'

'No, guv. Zilch.'

'Turner? Why do you insist upon using such ridiculous . . . oh, never mind. So Towers and Mackleby have got nowhere?'

'I didn't say that, sir.'

Pendragon sighed.

'When they found nothing at Arcade's studio, they went straight to the gallery to see Jackson Price, see if he had the original of the film taken at the private view.'

'That's surprisingly enterprising. And?'

'He did, and he was very co-operative, apparently.'

'Well, that's good,' Pendragon said. 'We'll watch it

y

106

first thing tomorrow. Get in early, Sergeant.'

He clicked shut the phone, slotted the key into the lock and pushed on the door.

He had moved into this two-roomed apartment over six months earlier with every intention of using it as a stopgap until he found somewhere better, but now the place was growing on him and he was finding himself less and less inclined to move.

He had come to London from his old job in Oxford where he had worked for the best part of two decades. His wife Jean had left him for another woman and he had departed the force for a short time, only to be lured back by the chance of returning to the place where he had grown up and which he had visited only occasionally since his early-twenties. Oxford had become his home, but he no longer wanted to live there; it was tainted for him. His and Jean's daughter, Amanda, had disappeared five years earlier. She had been nine at the time, and simply vanished on her way home from school. Jack had not only suffered the horror of losing his daughter, he had had to endure the pain of professional impotence – a cop whose only daughter had been abducted. Amanda's disappearance had been a major factor in the collapse of his marriage. His twenty-year-old son, Simon, was a post-grad Mathematics genius at the University. Pendragon saw little of him now but they were only fifty miles apart, a sixty-minute drive down the M40.

The flat was tatty and had been neglected, first by the landlord and more recently by Pendragon himself. But only a week earlier he had decided to decorate, buy some decent furniture. It was a form of acceptance, an acknowledgement that he had moved on, left Oxford behind, and that this place, Stepney, East London, where he had been born almost forty-seven years ago, was again his home.

And he really did feel at home now. After a shaky beginning, his colleagues and subordinates had accepted him and he had grown in confidence. It was a fresh start and he was out of the blocks. He had even enjoyed a brief romance since arriving at Brick Lane. He and Dr Sue Latimer, a psychologist, had been neighbours – she had rented a flat on the ground floor. They had got on well and Pendragon had even dared to imagine the relationship might actually lead somewhere when Sue had broken the news that she had accepted a job in Toronto. She had left six weeks ago, and he was still feeling sore from the loss.

The door to the flat swung inwards and he stepped across newspaper taped to the floor. When he flicked on the light, the room came alive – white ceiling, white skirting and doorframes, half-painted walls. Pendragon strode over to the kitchen worktop at one end of the room, tossed his briefcase and overcoat on to the Formica surface and leaned back to appraise the shade of light brown he had chosen. On the shade card it had been called something ridiculous like 'elm bark brown' and now it covered the top half of two walls. He was about to get on with the rest, but suddenly felt hungry. He opened the fridge door and sighed. A can of lager and a piece of old cheese sat there. Leaning on the door, he tried to decide what to do.

In a moment, he was pulling his coat back on and heading towards the hall outside the flat, checking he had some cash in his wallet. There was a half-decent deli around the corner and an off-licence a few yards beyond that. While the deli owner warmed up a *panino*, Pendragon went along to the off-licence. There was a queue and he was forced to spend ten boring minutes reading and re-reading labels on wine bottles and signs around the shop informing him of cut-price bulk buys. Leaving with a bottle of South Australian Shiraz, he picked up the *panino* and headed back to the flat.

At the kitchen worktop, he poured himself a generous glass of wine and surveyed the walls he had painted. Fifteen minutes later, the deli wrapper was in the kitchen bin and the wine glass recharged. Pendragon had changed into a pair of old jeans and a T-shirt, put his favourite Wes Montgomery LP, *Smokin' at the Half Note*, on the stereo and had a roller in his right hand.

Painting was a mild anaesthetic, he decided. It seemed to guide the mind into a mellow groove whereby you could perform the physical process, but at the same time you could think about, well, anything. Whatever flooded in, flooded in. He had spent most of the afternoon poring over art books. The local library had a surprisingly good selection. While Turner Googled and searched through blogs and websites, Pendragon did one of the things he did best – he stared at ink on paper, just as he had done as a student at Oxford, just as he had done throughout most of his career. All the secrets of the world could be unravelled with ink on paper. He would always believe that. Although he had lost faith in many things, this was one principle he would never doubt.

'So, what do we have?' he said aloud to the empty room as he prised open a fresh tin of paint. 'René Magritte:

Surrealist artist, born Lessines, Belgium, 1898. Came to prominence in the late twenties, early thirties. Creator of a style defined as Magic Realism in which he used ordinary objects but placed in unreal situations and juxtapositions. His work exhibited a great sense of humour, a certain contrived and deliberate dislocation from perceived reality.

'And Salvador Dali: a close contemporary of Magritte's, six years younger. Born in Figueres, Spain, May 1904. Named after a brother who died nine months before the painter's birth, he was told by his parents that he was the reincarnation of his dead sibling. Rose to prominence at about the same time as Magritte. The two men knew each other and spent time together first in Paris in the late-twenties and then at Dali's Spanish home in the thirties.' He paused for a moment and lowered the roller into the paint tray, watching the sponge soak up the paint.

'Any other associations? Each man lost his mother when he was young. Magritte was fourteen, Dali seventeen. Anything connecting the two painters to the two murders – other than the fact that in each case the body was set up in a pose reminiscent of their most famous work?'

Pendragon picked up the roller. 'No,' he said aloud. 'No connection that I can see.' Perhaps Francis Arcade had been on the money when he remarked that they should look for someone with a dead Surrealist fixation. There seemed to be nothing to connect the murders other than the painting style of the two artists whose work had been travestied.

'Okay,' he went on, and pushed the roller back into the paint tray. In the background, Wes Montgomery was playing sweetly, an elaborate riff in B-flat minor. 'Obviously the killer is trying to tell us something. But what? Are they a frustrated artist, ignored and angry? In other words, just like Arcade? Or is it someone who is setting up the murders to make us *think* the murderer is a frustrated artist? Is the killer someone in the arts community . . . or are they trying to make us think along those lines, to throw us off the scent?'

The door buzzer went and Pendragon placed the roller carefully on the rim of the paint tray, walked over to the door and depressed the switch on the intercom.

'Yes?'

'Sir? It's Turner. Can I pop up for a minute?'

Surprised, Pendragon pushed the button to open the front door. Thirty seconds later the sergeant had reached the top of the stairs, slightly out of breath. He had a leather satchel slung over his left shoulder. 'Evening, guv. I'm sorry to disturb you.' He couldn't resist a half-smile, seeing DCI Pendragon in jeans.

'Come in, Turner. It'd better be something very interesting.'

'Doing a spot of DIY then, sir? Looks good.' Turner went over to the kitchen worktop and off-loaded the shoulder bag, placing it carefully on the Formica top. 'It's to do with Noel Thursk,' he said, unzipping the bag and pulling out a laptop.

'What about him?'

'Thatcher got back with this just after you left.' He nodded towards the laptop. 'It's Thursk's. It didn't take long to get into it.' He looked at Pendragon for approval. 'Password was peanuts to figure out. Ninety-nine per cent of people do the bleedin' obvious, even though they're always being told not to.'

'The obvious?'

'NT0658.'

'Initials, then month and year of his birth?'

'Correct. It was the second attempt because some people use the day of the birth month. Anyway . . . I've gone through the machine. Nothing. I've searched every disk and every USB drive in Thursk's flat. Nothing on those either. No notes, no rough drafts. The only thing on there is the original proposal, which the publisher has anyway – a ten-page outline that gives the bare bones of the book.' He brought it up on the computer. Pendragon read from the screen and scrolled down. It told him very little, merely making reference to Thursk's long and close association with key players in the London art world. As the publisher, Lewis Fanshaw, was an old friend of his, he would have needed little convincing of Thursk's credentials.

'Not a great help.'

'No, sir. But I dunno, I had a sense something wasn't quite right. Just an instinct, I s'pose. So I ran a piece of software through it called Re-Search. It scans the computer and can find traces of files that were once on the hard drive and have since been deleted. It's to do with binary markers that . . .'

'Yes, all right, Sergeant. Get to the point.'

'The point is, Thursk deleted a whole load of files from the hard drive very recently. You can see here.' He pointed towards the screen. A list of processor files appeared. Six of them had been greyed-out. 'I checked all the disks and external drives and found the same thing on one of the USBs.'

'Amazing. And you can retrieve them?'

''Fraid not, guv.'

Pendragon paused for a moment, lost in thought.

Turner surveyed the tiny apartment. He had been here on two previous occasions, but each time had barely stepped beyond the door.

'Okay, well, that's progress of a sort. It tells us three important things.' Pendragon counted them off on the fingers of his right hand. 'One: Thursk knew he had some pretty incendiary material – why else would he be so secretive? Two: he must have been worried someone was after him – why else would he erase the files just before whoever it was caught up with him? And three: he wouldn't have destroyed all traces of his work. He would have made a backup that he's hidden somewhere.'

Chapter 19

Stepney, Friday, 10 p.m.

The killer was quoting aloud to no one while packing equipment into a shoulder bag: '"Before I start painting I have a slightly ambiguous feeling . . . happiness is a special excitement because unhappiness is always possible a moment later." Mmm . . . one of Francis Bacon's better comments, and very apt,' the killer said. 'And tonight . . . I shall *be* Mr Bacon.'

Mr Bacon duly left the building, pacing through the gloom and mist, face obscured by a hoodie and sunglasses. It was a long walk to the church, but the last thing Mr Bacon wanted was the attention of a CCTV camera offering up an incriminating registration plate for some clever copper to jump on. No, Mr Bacon had important work to do.

The church was open, of course; the Lord protects, no need for locks. It was dark, Evening Mass over. Mr Bacon walked slowly towards the altar, the only illumination coming from the street beyond the stained glass. The vague light picked out sharp lines of gold: a giant crucifix in the centre of the altar, orderly strands of glinting thread tumbling to the stone floor, one corner of a portrait of a gasping Christ.

At the door to the vestry, Mr Bacon paused, took several deep breaths and lowered the shoulder bag to the floor. Next to the door stood a fine wooden chair, a throne of dark wood trimmed with gold and mother-of-pearl inlay. It was a prized piece, donated by a wealthy benefactor years earlier. Mr Bacon smiled and turned away, then with a sudden burst of violence, he smashed open the door and charged in, Mace spray in hand. The elderly priest, Father Michael O'Leary, was folding the evening's vestments and turned just in time to receive a faceful of noxious, blinding vapour. Falling back in shock and pain, he stumbled over a stool and landed in a heap on the floor. Mr Bacon was on him in a second, ramming a knee up into the priest's groin with so much force his testicles became lodged in his abdomen. O'Leary screamed.

Mr Bacon bent down and twisted the man face round. It was pale and contorted in agony. His eyes were streaming. 'Do you really not recognise me, priest?' Mr Bacon said.

The injured man tried to focus, staring up uncomprehending, terror and pain overwhelming him. 'Look closer,' Mr Bacon spat, peering down at him. 'Ah, yes, you are beginning to remember . . .'

Father O'Leary went limp, his face now a white drooping thing, his eyes like coals dropped on snow. Trying to understand what was happening, he struggled to pull himself up, survival instinct overcoming his agony. But Mr Bacon moved a hand to the priest's throat and gripped it tight. O'Leary caught a glimpse of a hypodermic with a nine-inch needle. He began to kick and struggle, but Mr Bacon was fit and strong and the priest was old, his body a mess. Mr Bacon brought the needle round the back of O'Leary's skull. He tried to move his head, but the combination of shock, Mace and the pain raking his aged body made him no match for Mr Bacon.

The needle began to penetrate the soft flesh at the nape of the neck. 'An interesting fact . . .' Mr Bacon said matter-of-factly. 'According to some historians, the term "tenterhooks" comes from a form of execution popular in the fourteenth century. The condemned were left to hang on a metal hook passed through the nape of the neck. Very painful, apparently.'

Mr Bacon pushed the entire length of the needle through the priest's skull. Father O'Leary shuddered, and as the plunger was levered down, releasing heroin into his brain, began to shake violently. He froze, then died.

Lowering the body to the floor, Mr Bacon stepped out of the vestry, grabbed the arms of the ornate chair positioned against the wall and dragged it across the stone floor. Levering the door open and keeping it in place with one foot, it was just possible to manoeuvre the chair through the opening and into the vestry.

Inside the shoulder bag lay a bundle of clothing. Taking it out, Mr Bacon unrolled the fabric. Papal vestments: a white surplice, purple cope and purple hat. Placing these carefully over the back of a chair, the murderer stripped the dead man to his underwear, discarded his clothes and dressed him in the papal garments. When the body was ready, Mr Bacon heaved it on to the seat of the wooden and gold chair. It was a struggle, but empowerment came from the incredible thrill of the moment, the sweet nectar of cold, cold revenge, pure *Schadenfreude*.

Inside the shoulder bag was a folded steel rod. This Mr Bacon unravelled then placed inside the back of the papal cope to keep Father O'Leary's dead spine straight and upright. Rope was then removed from the bag and tied about the waist and chest, pinning the priest's corpse to the chair. More rope secured the arms, while the hands were draped over the throne's sides.

Now there was just the face to attend to. From the bag came two lengths of clear surgical tape. Peeling back the priest's eyelids, Mr Bacon applied the tape to the soft skin and stuck the other end to the man's forehead, pinning open his sightless eyes. Lastly, from a pocket in the hoodie, came a clear plastic sphere the size of a tennis ball. This was rammed into the priest's mouth, behind his teeth, forcing open O'Leary's mouth. Next the corpse's lifeless lips were folded back, exposing the teeth. The entire ensemble created the look of a man screaming and grasping the arms of the throne, as though he were being electrocuted.

Mr Bacon stood back to appraise the evening's work and nodded appreciatively, then stepped out through the door, locked it and pocketed the key.

Chapter 20

To Mrs Sonia Thomson
13 October 1888

So, when was it that I stopped searching for the thing that is not there, the thing Christians call a 'soul'? When was it that I started to treat human beings as playthings . . . materials for my work? I have one special individual to thank for that revelation, a most singular man, and I think, dear lady, I should explain how he crossed my path.

My little experiment to see what life would bring me as an actor in all my daily actions proved remarkable. People flocked to me, men and women. I seemed to be irresistible, and my life at the University became a whirlwind of socialising. So much so, in fact, it was a minor miracle that when it came to scholarly concerns I managed to appease my professors at all.

I was quick to learn that the best fun was to be had from mixing with those for whom three years at Oxford was a time in which to indulge their every whim. There were two types who fitted this bill. The less interesting of the two were the genuine artists, the poets, painters and philosophers who ignored most conventions, kept within few bounds and believed they were on a mission to experience 'real life' in order to fuel their artistic ambitions. They could be entertaining, but they were strangely predictable. Nevertheless through them I grew close to two Oxford legends, William Morris and Edward Burne-Jones. They were each in their fifties when I was introduced to them and had already gained the status of gods within the artistic community. They spent little time in Oxford except that each of them delivered a special annual lecture at the Faculty of Arts. I found both men surprisingly open to the ideas of youth, and, again, perhaps it was down to my talent as an actor and mimic, but they took to me.

The other group were the immensely wealthy sons of the aristocracy, children of stalwarts of the House of Lords, themselves future peers. These young men whored, gambled, drank and took every drug known with complete abandon, as though their wealth made them immortal and immune from bodily corruption . . . the fools! They acted the way they did not from any high ideals or aesthetic imperatives, but simply to have a good time before having to submit to a more conventional existence. The problem about associating with these types was that one needed money to do so.

I circumvented this initially by sponging off others. I used my considerable charm and thespian talents to wheedle my way into the cliques that seemed to be the most high-living. But even my charisma has its bounds, and eventually I was forced to find money from somewhere. Father provided me with an annual allowance, which, as you may imagine, was pitifully meagre. To fund my escapades, I found gainful employment as a Society artist. I was in my final year at Oxford and had something of a reputation as an up-and-coming young painter. I even managed to procure a letter of recommendation from Morris himself. What wealthy businessman or lady of leisure could resist?

It was an altogether loathsome experience. The women were, without exception, pampered snobs gone to seed. The worst aspect to it was the sexual opportunism I was obliged to endure. Perhaps one in three of the gracious ladies would proposition me at some point, and I would find it a challenge to keep myself from vomiting over them. Needless to say, such experiences did nothing but exaggerate my hatred for everyone alive.

Ironically, it was through the artists rather than the fun-loving aristos that I met the man who would set me on the correct path. That man was Magnus Oglebee. No, you probably have not heard of him, my dear lady, but then very few have. He was something of an enigma by intent. He guarded his privacy jealously and trusted only a select few. But when he did place his trust in you, you felt very special.

It was Burne-Jones who invited me to Oglebee's

soiree in May 1888. Oglebee held these events at irregular intervals and only the elite of Oxford were welcome. As you may imagine, I was delighted. The party was at Oglebee's mansion close to Boars Hill, outside the city. It was a cab ride there, and I arrived just as the sun was setting over the Neo-Gothic towers of the enigma's grand home, Clancy Hall.

It was a magnificent house, set in splendid gardens. The grand hall was dominated by a mahogany staircase that swept up to the first floor then split to left and right before sweeping round in two great curves. The main dining hall was lit with literally hundreds of candles held in crystal chandeliers. I was told the owner of this palace shunned gaslight and would only illuminate his home with the natural glow of candles. It was a breathtakingly beautiful affectation.

No one knew how Oglebee had made his fortune. No one seemed to have a clue what he actually did in the world, or even how he spent his days. And, of course, this set tongues wagging among those few who even knew the man existed. I remember there was some fevered speculation that he was a vampire who only came out at night. Absurd, of course, and a notion most probably fuelled by excessive quantities of opium. But certainly a flattering piece of gossip, nevertheless.

There were just twelve guests that night. Oglebee made it a happy thirteen. Morris and Burne-Jones were there. The author Charles Dodgson arrived late, fretting comically. And I saw at least two well-known politicians, one from the Upper House, men whose faces are often seen in the pages of *The Times*. We dined early, an exquisite meal of oysters, salmon and game followed by a wonderful dish I had never before experienced, a thing called *crème brûlée* which was originally called Cambridge Burnt Cream, a delicacy from 'the other place'. I'll send you the recipe sometime.

After the meal, we were invited into the vast library. Servants supplied us with cigars and brandy. I perused the books, staggered to find such delights as first editions of de Sade, Rochester, Byron, Keats, and a host of other luminaries. As well as these, I found books on alchemy and necromancy, the titles of which I had never heard of before, but all lovingly bound in the softest calf-skin.

I had still not been formally introduced to Oglebee when I felt a gentle tap on my shoulder. I turned to see the man himself standing rather uncomfortably close. He was an exuberant host and I'd had many a chance to observe him during the course of the evening. In an oddly high-pitched, reedy voice, with a mild, indefinable accent, he had held forth at dinner upon a range of interesting subjects and regaled his guests with a succession of wonderful anecdotes. He was small, barely passing my shoulder, and had a bird's face: pinched nose, and small black eyes that darted quickly from side to side as he spoke. And when his eyes were occasionally fixed straight ahead, he had the rather unnerving habit of seeming to look straight through you. He exuded immense confidence, almost disturbingly so, and I am happy to admit that, with him, I immediately felt I had to up my game. The acting skills that had served me well with the common herd of humanity, even with Oxford dons and artists, suddenly seemed insufficient. Oglebee, I realised, was a man apart.

'Come,' he said. 'Entertainment has been arranged.'

He beckoned to the others and we all followed him into a large room adjoining the library. We began chatting amicably, and perhaps a little drunkenly. At dinner I had been careful to imbibe little, surreptitiously tipping most of what I had been given on to the carpet. Some instinct told me I needed to keep a level head.

The room already lay in deep shadow, but then a team of servants appeared and began quenching the remaining candle flames. This cast us all into absolute darkness. The sound of music sprang from some hidden source. It was music such as I had never heard before. I could not imagine how Oglebee had managed to bring it into the room without any visible performers, but I quickly forgot how strange this was for suddenly a line of six lights appeared. They moved across the room, and as the glow grew brighter I realised they were candles in gold holders each carried by a young woman. Their naked bodies were painted gold and each woman had blonde, waist-length hair. They began to dance exquisitely.

I felt a wooden object pushed into my hand. I could barely see it in the half-light, but as I bent close I could make out a pipe. I went to push it away, but saw that it was Oglebee sitting next to me, offering the contraption. He nudged it back and nodded. I could not refuse. I took a child's drag on the pipe's ebony tip. Oglebee laughed and poked an elbow in my ribs. 'Oh, stop pretending, young man,' he said. 'I thought you were . . . an *artist*!'

There is an unpleasant void in my memory. It lasts from soon after I took a deep draw on that pipe to a point in time where it seems a veil was drawn aside and I slowly surfaced into some form of normal consciousness. I detest losing control, or worse still, being forced to lose it. But that must have been what happened, for the next thing I recall is seeing a pair of breasts swaying in front of me and feeling a burning sensation in my groin. I remember pushing out my arms and pressing against soft flesh. I knew I was naked. I clambered to my feet a little unsteadily and took a deep breath.

It was dark, and several moments passed before my eyes began to adjust. I found a robe of some sort. Ignoring the cries of the girl I had pushed away, I staggered towards a source of light. I almost collided with the edge of a door as I pulled it towards me and stepped into a wide corridor. Light spilled from under a line of doors to either side of me. I could hear strange animal sounds: grunts, a scream, something falling, a heavy object crashing to the floor and shattering.

I reached the end of the corridor. The walls were sliding away. I knew I was still intoxicated, but I felt drawn onward. There was another door, with a large brass handle. I clutched it in my hand, turned it clockwise, pushed the door open and fell forward.

I lay sprawled on the floor for what seemed an age. Then, slowly, I pulled myself to my feet. I felt a stabbing pain in my side and did my best to ignore it. I looked around. Light seeped in at a window in the far wall. In front of this I could make out the shape of a chair and a man sitting in it, straight-backed. I took a step forward, and then another. I saw Oglebee. He was facing me in a large, throne-like chair. He was wearing a white robe smeared with red. The head of a young woman lay in his lap, her long blonde hair draped to the floor. He was stroking her hair. Her eyes stared at me, sightless. Utterly dead, of course.

I would be lying if I said I was not shocked. I was, but it did not last long and it was rapidly replaced by an intense ripple of excitement, a thrill I had only rarely experienced in my life up to that point. I smiled at Oglebee.

'I thought you would enjoy it, William,' he said. 'I understood what you were the moment I set eyes on you.'

'You did?' I said, genuinely puzzled. I kept being drawn to the dead girl's sightless eyes. After a moment, Oglebee lifted the head, still dripping blood and gore, and laid it carefully on the floor beside his chair.

'Of course, young man. You are not the first and you will not be the last.'

'Oh, I rather supposed I was unique,' I said quietly, staring into his small black eyes.

He chuckled. 'What is it that drives you?'

'I could ask the same of you, Mr Oglebee.'

'Yes, you could. But I asked first. *Humour me*.'

I said nothing for a moment, staring at the man, trying to read his face and failing utterly. 'I realised some time ago that I'm searching,' I began. 'Searching for something very difficult to find.'

'In a way we are all searching, are we not? Even the brainless masses are searching. It's just that they don't actually realise it.'

'Does that mean you are searching too?'

He chortled again. 'Oh! Believe me, William, I searched assiduously. But then I realised the thing I sought did not exist.'

'So you stopped?'

Oglebee glanced down at the head resting on the floor. He nodded towards it. 'I stopped searching, if that is what you mean. Now I'm happy to *entertain* myself. You see, you are a very fortunate young man.'

'I am?'

'Yes, because you have great talent. Your friends praise you very highly.'

I stared at him, expressionless.

'You don't really understand what I'm talking about, do you?'

I did my best to call his bluff, but it was useless.

Employing all the skills I had learned proved of little value to me at that moment. Oglebee knew me, he really *knew* me. He seemed to know everything.

'It is time, William, for you to move on. What you seek is not there. It's time for you to have some fun instead . . . to deploy your talents fully. I cannot tell you what to do. I can only guide and advise you. Think about combining your natural instincts with your natural talents.'

I was still confused, but realised I should at least make a pretence of understanding, in the hope that, later, I really would comprehend. I realised that Oglebee would miss nothing, that I would not be fooling him in this way, but I could think of nothing else to say or do.

'How do . . .' I began, but Oglebee raised a hand to stop me.

'I cannot tell you what to do. I've said that already, William. It is for you to work out what I am trying to explain to you. However, I will give you one small piece of advice to help you on your way.' He fell silent for a moment. The room was utterly silent, unnaturally so. It felt as though we were floating in space. 'To move on,' he said, 'you must eradicate your past. You must begin again. Shed your skin. Become someone new.'

I was still not entirely convinced. After all, I had been searching for a long time and I had dwelt on the matter of the soul since childhood. But I knew Oglebee was right about two things at least. It was

127

time I had some fun, and it was time to expunge the past.

I took some time away from my studies using the excuse that my father was ill and that I needed to return home for a few days. No one seemed to care. I caught an early-afternoon train and had the carriage all to myself for the entire journey. I changed trains in London and arrived in Hemel Hempstead just as it was getting dark. I was travelling light, with just an overnight bag, and so I walked the mile or so from the station to Fellwick Manor. It was a clear night, unusually warm, the stars out in all their chaotic profusion. I've never liked the stars.

There was a light on in my father's study at the front of the house. I could see it through a small gap in the curtains. My shoes crunched on the gravel. I pulled the bell and waited, listening to the sounds of my father hauling himself up from his chair in the study and walking across the floor. I had chosen the servants' half-day for this return home. Then came the familiar creak of the loose floorboard near the front door. Another pool of light appeared as Father lit a second lamp. Through the stained-glass panels of the front door, I watched the distorted sphere of yellow pass along the hallway.

'Who is it at this hour?' my father called.

'It is I, Father. William.'

'William? What the devil . . .'

I heard him place the lamp on a table near the door and then came the rasp and scrape as he undid the locks and slid the bolts. Finally, the door opened and we stood face to face.

I had been back here only rarely since going up to Oxford. I hated this place and I did not wish to refresh my memories of the years I was forced to live in Fellwick Manor. I wrote to my father only very occasionally, and when I did filled the letters with the sort of utter tosh and lies I knew he would want to read, so as not to deter him from paying me my allowance. I had known for as long as I could remember that the man detested me. Always had done. Always would. Furthermore, he had no glimmer of understanding as to why I should wish to waste three years studying Fine Art. But that said, Father was civil enough upon my arrival. He did not send me back to town to find a lodging house, at least. He offered me some food. Cook had left a plate of cold meats in the pantry. What I wanted most was a stiff whisky, but I knew that that would be entirely out of the question, and so I settled for cocoa, which I insisted I made, while Father sat nearby and asked me inane questions about life at Oxford.

The drug took only a few minutes to work. The first sign was that he started to slur his speech, as though he were drunk. Then he began to stare at me with a slightly glazed expression. 'Good Lord,' he said, running his fingers over his bald pate. 'I feel most odd.'

'That would be the morphine, Father.'

He stared at me unsteadily, his eyes wandering off target, then he looked puzzled.

'I put morphine in your drink.'

He did not have the energy to move or even to alter his facial expression. It was really very amusing, dear lady. I did not waste a moment. I knew I had to move fast because I had only used a tiny quantity, so it would soon wear off. I wanted its effects to evaporate, but not until I was entirely ready.

I walked around the back of Father's chair and pulled him to his feet. He could barely walk, but I managed to half-carry him to his study. As we reached the room, I could tell he was already beginning to shake off the effects of the drug, but I had a firm grip on him. I pulled two short lengths of rope from my pockets and swiftly bound his wrists and ankles. Then I positioned a chair in front of the desk, spun my father round and pushed him so that he fell face forward across the desk, with his knees on the chair.

'Have you . . . go . . . gone . . . ma . . . mad?' he managed to splutter.

'Most probably, Father,' I retorted. I pulled off my cravat and wrapped it around his head, pulling it tight between his lips so that he could no longer move his jaws. The best he could manage was a low grunt, which I found quite hilarious. I stood back to survey my efforts, then took a step forward to tear away the back of his shirt. I then undid his trousers and yanked them down to his ankles, exposing his scrawny backside. Spinning round, I reached into the cupboard for the cane. It was there, just as it always was.

I walked around the other side of the desk and crouched down to twist my father's head round so as to face me. His eyes were wild with fear and fury. Saliva ran down his chin because in this position he could not swallow.

'Well,' I said, 'this is what the novelists call a reversal of fortune, Father. For many years I've fantasised about doing this. I've had very pleasant dreams about it. The only pity is that your bitch of a wife is not here to see it too. That would have been a truly delicious experience.'

He grunted and struggled to slide off the chair, but he was not the man he once was, and I was no longer a little boy he could overpower.

I returned to the other side of Father's desk, raised my hand and brought the cane down with that old familiar 'whoosh'.

I cannot tell you for how long I beat my father, each stroke more frenzied than the last. I lost all track of time. My arm began to ache from the exertion, but I did not let that deter me. I was panting; sweat ran off me. At length I felt a terrible pain in my chest and almost passed out. That was when I stopped.

Slowly, I lowered my arm to my side and dropped the bloodied cane to the floor. It fell silently on the rug. My father had stopped making any sound some indefinable time earlier. There was little left of his skin. The flesh was flayed, blood-smeared, grey; a few vertebrae lay exposed.

I seemed to snap back to myself then. I untied the

ropes, letting Father's body tumble to the floor. Then I slipped the ropes back into my pocket, crouched down and removed my cravat from his distorted mouth. His face was blackened and bruised from where it had slammed against the desk. His horrible moustache was bloodied. His eyes were closed. Turning, I picked up the cane and broke it in two, tossing the pieces to opposite sides of the room.

In the outhouse, I found a can of paraffin. I opened the top and sniffed, coughing as the fumes hit me. Then I paced around the ground floor of the Manor with the can tilted, the liquid sliding out and over the floors. I started the fire in the study by tossing the oil lamp on to the floor beside my father's body. Staying inside the house just long enough to get the stink into my clothes, I blackened my face and shirt with soot. As I ran out on to the road beyond the Manor's grounds, the flames really started to catch hold. I heard the voices of neighbours running towards me. Putting on a performance that would have made Sarah Bernhardt proud, I staggered along the path, weeping and screaming for assistance. Deep inside me, I felt the old William Sandler, son of Gordon and Mary Sandler, vaporise like my father's blood spilled on the study carpet.

Chapter 21

Brick Lane, Saturday 24 January, 6.30 a.m.

The station was quiet. It usually was at this time of the weekend, a relatively mellow stretch between the chaos of late-Friday night and early-Saturday morning, when the holding cells were emptied and the drunks booted out. Jack Pendragon nodded to the duty sergeant at the front desk and paced down the corridor towards his office. Glancing into the Ops Room, he saw Turner sitting at a terminal. The sergeant looked up, bleary-eyed.

'You look awful,' Pendragon said, stepping into the room.

Jez yawned loudly, placing a hand over his mouth. 'Thanks, guv. But at least I don't look as bad as some of this lot.' And he pointed to the screen.

'What is it?' Pendragon came round the desk and leaned on Turner's chair.

'It's Jackson Price's film of the knees-up on Tuesday night. Some right old characters.'

'Have you seen anything interesting?'

'No. I've been through the whole thing. Just about the most boring two hours I've spent in my life. On my second run-through now.'

Pendragon pulled up a chair and studied the images on the screen. The film was shot in fashionable Gonzo-style. The cameraman, Michael Spillman, passed through the room casually interviewing people. Sometimes he would merely ask how they were; at others he was more mannered, offering faux-philosophical questions. 'Do you think the creator of a work has a controlling stake in the outcome?' he asked one guest. The reply was inaudible and he moved on to a tall woman in dungarees. 'If there's an afterlife,' he posited, 'what would be God's commission?'

'I've done some Google searches on a few of the characters on the guest list and matched them up with the video,' Turner said. Then he pointed to the screen. 'There's Berrick.'

A solidly built man came into view holding a champagne flute. In his mid-fifties, he was jowly, hair dyed black, with a confident, proprietorial air about him. 'The woman he's talking to is Meg Lancaster the actress.' Pendragon nodded. 'And there's Noel Thursk,' Turner added, tapping the screen. A slightly built, white-haired man appeared from the right-hand edge of the monitor. He was wearing a black suit, a collarless white shirt and grey waistcoat.

'Who's the woman there?' Pendragon asked, pointing to a tall brunette in a stylish black evening dress. She looked to be in her mid-thirties, with a stunning figure that could only have come from a combination of great genes and hours spent in the gym. The strapless dress clung to her like a second skin. Her hair was styled in a dramatic bob with a straight, high fringe. She was smiling sexily over her glass at two men who appeared to be fawning over her.

Turner consulted his notes. 'That's Gemma Locke. She's an artist, apparently. Never heard of her, but she ain't bad-looking, is she, guv?'

Pendragon stared at the screen. 'That's Gemma Locke?' the DCI said, fascinated. 'I've seen her work. Who're the two men she's talking to?'

'No idea,' Turner replied. 'Couldn't find anything on 'em.'

'So how far through the tape is this?'

The sergeant consulted the timer. 'About twenty minutes in.'

'Rewind it. I want to watch the whole thing.'

Turner's face dropped.

'It's all right, Sergeant. I'm not that cruel. Get hold of Inspector Grant. He was following up on any CCTV from around St Dunstan's on the morning of Thursk's murder. See what he's turned up . . . if anything. And when you've done that, go through the files and try to find a picture of Juliette Kinnear.'

'Who?'

'Remember? I told you – the girl who was the subject of Noel Thursk's book . . . the young artist.'

'Ah, yeah.'

Pendragon took off his coat, folded it over the back of a chair and dropped into Turner's seat. He faced the screen and pushed the Play button. Turner was right, it was incredibly boring. It reminded him of his student days watching one of Andy Warhol's movies, *Empire* or perhaps *Sleep*. Either way it had been interminable, and he had only managed to sit through it because he was interested in the girl who had dragged him to the cinema. In a similar way to the Warhol movie, this film had a soporific effect and he had to force himself to stay alert. But after two hours spent watching people chatting and wandering around the gallery with only the brief distraction of Francis Arcade's rather lame attempt to crash the party after one hour and seventeen minutes, he felt utterly bored and disappointed. Pushing the Stop button, Pendragon stood up, stretched and leaned forward, his palms on the desktop.

Turner popped his head around the door and then came in. He was waving a print in front of his face. 'Juliette Kinnear,' he said, coming over. 'Took some searching out.'

It was a professionally taken, posed photograph and showed a girl of about seventeen wearing a floral dress. She had shoulder-length blonde hair, parted to one side, a round, chubby face and thin lips. She was a plain girl. Her best feature was a pair of deep blue eyes, but even the effect of these was nullified by thick brows. At first glance she looked quite prim. It was only when he looked closer that Pendragon noticed the tattoo of a rose on one side of her neck, close to her shoulder. 'Strange,' he said.

'What? The tat?'

'Yes. Completely incongruous. She looks every bit the rather plain daughter of a wealthy businessman posing for a family portrait, except for that tattoo.'

'Yeah, but knowing what we do about young Juliette, it's not that weird, is it, sir? She obviously had a rebellious streak. I bet there was a right barney over her wearing a dress that exposed the rose tattoo!' Turner concluded with a laugh.

'Yes,' Pendragon replied quietly, still staring at the photograph. 'Maybe.' Then he looked up. 'Anything from the CCTV?'

'Yep,' Turner replied, suddenly remembering. 'Grant's found something.' He withdrew a DVD from his pocket, slid it into the machine and pulled over a chair beside Pendragon's.

The screen lit up with a frosty pre-dawn grey sky. At the top ran a line of trees. A narrow tarmac path wound through them and then followed a vertical line down the centre of the image.

'That's the park close to the church,' Pendragon said. 'What's a camera doing there?'

'It's a Parks Department camera. They've just finished some maintenance work and put the CCTV up to deter vandals.' As he finished explaining, a green vehicle appeared among the trees and drove towards the camera through the gloom. Its lights were off, and in the semi-darkness it merged with the landscape, taking shape only gradually. It was a boxy machine perched on four small wheels: a cherry-picker. Dominating the front of the vehicle was a rectangular metal cage attached to a concertinaed steel arm that was folded up tightly. Inside the cage lay a cylindrical grey object. At the rear of the vehicle was a small, low-roofed cabin. They could just see someone seated inside it, guiding the cherry-picker along. But in the dark, it was impossible to make out any further details.

'Can you enhance that?' Pendragon asked.

'I'll try,' Turner replied, and ran his fingers over a control panel to one side of the desk. The picture vanished for a second. When it reappeared it was clearer.

'Good. Close in on the figure in the cabin.'

Turner let the film run for a few seconds then rewound it, finally settling on the best frame. He pushed Pause again and turned a dial on the control panel. The image of the cabin grew larger, but as it did so it lost clarity. Turner fiddled with other controls and the image cleared a little. He zoomed in some more.

'That's about the best I can do,' he said after a moment.

The image was indistinct. They could still see a figure in the cabin but it was completely featureless, little more than a grey blob.

Pendragon's mobile rang. 'Dr Jones,' he said. 'Yes. When would be a good time? Excellent. See you then.' He stood up and pulled his overcoat from the chair back. 'Come on,' he said to Turner.

'Where're we going?'

'The Forensics Lab in Lambeth. Jones and Newman have put their heads together and apparently have some interesting news for us.'

Chapter 22

The traffic was appalling. Pendragon's parking permit bought them a space but it was a hundred metres from the Forensics Lab along Lambeth Road. Even running through the freezing drizzle, by the time they reached the front of the three-storey modern building, they were wet and chilled to the bone.

'Did you know, sir,' Turner remarked, wiping his forehead and following the DCI to the reception desk, 'there's a theory that running in the rain gets you wetter than walking?'

'Really, Turner? How incredibly fascinating.' Pendragon turned to the receptionist and showed his ID. The girl printed them each a pass which she slipped into plastic wallets. The policemen attached them to their jackets. 'Dr Newman is working in Lab B103,' the receptionist said. 'Probably best to take the stairs.' And she pointed towards a row of lifts and a broad stone stairwell to their left.

One flight down, the stairs opened out on to a wide corridor painted a calming shade of green. Anaemic pictures of flowers and birds hung along one wall. The other was taken up by a row of double doors spaced about twenty feet apart. Each was painted dark green with a number at head-height; 103 was around the first bend in the corridor. Pendragon depressed a buzzer to the right of the door. A few moments later, Colette Newman appeared and ushered them into the lab.

It was a huge room, brightly lit and dominated by a large stainless-steel bench at its centre. The two policemen crossed the echoing floor. Pendragon nodded to Dr Jones who was leaning over the remains of Noel Thursk.

'We use this lab for special cases,' Dr Newman said. 'And I think you'll agree, Chief Inspector, that this is definitely a special case.'

Pendragon stared down at the flattened corpse. He had seen it in the grounds of St Dunstan's and when it had been brought down from the tree, but here, in the harsh neon glare and placed on a square, steel-topped bench, it had somehow lost the last vestiges of humanity he had associated with it. That helped. Turner, meanwhile, was standing very quietly beside him, unable to take his eyes from the gruesome sight.

'So what have you found?' Pendragon asked the two experts.

'Well, as you can see, the body has been reduced to something amorphous, which means any normal procedures are pretty redundant,' Jones said, rubbing his beard. 'But fortunately Dr Newman has some very sophisticated machinery which is perfectly suited to studying flattened bodies,' he concluded.

'We did a succession of hi-res X-rays,' she explained. 'And then used a type of MRI, similar to the procedure employed in neurology units in hospitals.' She led the three men to the far wall, depressed a switch, and a panel two metres long and a metre high lit up. She then removed a sheaf of transparencies from a drawer and pinned them to the light screen. 'These are the detailed X-rays,' she said, pointing to a collection on the left. 'And these are the MRI stills.' She indicated a clutch of rectangles on the right.

Newman stepped back and Jones ran his fingers close to the images. 'You'll notice that although the body has been flattened to a thickness of a couple of centimetres, the arrangement of the internal structure has been retained.' He pointed to an image of the entire corpse. 'Here are the arms, legs and torso.' The body parts were only vaguely recognisable, the bones shattered into hundreds of pieces or powdered completely, organs flattened and stretched obscenely.

'So what does that tell us about the way it was done?' Pendragon asked, turning first to Newman and then to Jones.

'It's clear from these images that the flattening was not done by a pounding machine or a large punch.'

'How do you know that?' Turner interjected.

Dr Newman pointed to the periphery of the image Jones had referred to. 'There are no overlapping edges,' she said. 'Try to visualise someone placing a body on a punching machine – something like the devices they use in factories to knock out metal shapes from steel sheets, for example. Every time the punch lands, it makes an edge. We would see an irregular arrangement of those edges around the periphery, here.' She indicated the extremities of the body with her finger. 'It would be a bit like kneading dough. You'd get a repeat pattern around the edge. But this body was worked flat either by being passed through a set of rollers or by being run over repeatedly with a steamroller.'

Newman led them back across the room to a bench dotted with test-tube racks filled with coloured liquids. At one end stood a cluster of electronic devices. 'We've also conducted a battery of chemical tests,' Jones explained as they approached the bench. 'Combining these with the images, we've been able to extract a few samples that may throw up some leads.'

On the bench lay three Petri dishes. In the first two were flakes of coloured material; the third contained a few threads of fabric.

'We found these – paint in two different colours. The green we've narrowed down to what our universal palette catalogue calls "Cider Apple Green". The other is plain white, but it comes from a metal surface. We've isolated traces of pressed steel. Almost certainly paint from a motor vehicle.

'The grey fibres in the other dish are treated cotton. Under the microscope we can see a water-resistant wax coating on the threads. It's most likely fibre from a tarpaulin.'

Pendragon looked admiringly at Dr Newman. 'That's very clever,' he said. She reddened slightly.

Jones coughed. 'There's more, Pendragon.' He picked up a sheet of paper from the counter and handed it to the DCI. Jones leaned in and pointed to a series of graphs. 'The arrangement of spikes, there,' he said, 'indicates a large quantity of heroin.'

'Heroin?' Pendragon exclaimed, staring at the pathologist.

'Even more interesting is this,' Jones said, and handed him another sheet covered with a series of coloured lines.

'What's this?'

'An analysis of Kingsley Berrick's blood. Same spikes. An almost identical heroin level.'

'You think the two victims were junkies?' Turner asked.

'A fair assumption, Sergeant, but no. These concentrations of heroin would kill instantly.'

'So it was the means of dispatching them?' Pendragon commented, studying the charts.

'Remember the needle wound in Berrick's brain?' Jones said. 'I thought he died from a massive haemorrhage. But it seems clear now that the hole was caused by the introduction of the drug. If Thursk still had a brain, or come to that a head I could study, we might find a similar mark.' Then, after a moment, Jones added, 'There's one other interesting result.'

'Oh?' Pendragon said, looking from him to Colette Newman.

'Dr Newman suggested we did a rape test on Berrick's body.'

'A rape test?'

'It didn't occur to me back at the Path Lab, but . . .'

'It struck me as being prudent in light of, well . . . Mr Berrick's sexual orientation.'

'Okay,' Pendragon said doubtfully.

'Berrick had intercourse shortly before he was murdered. We ran DNA tests.'

'And?'

'We found traces of Noel Thursk's DNA.'

Turner suddenly laughed, then put his hand to his mouth and rolled his eyes. Pendragon glared at him and turned to Dr Newman. 'Wheels within wheels,' he said, running his fingers over his forehead.

Chapter 23

The rain had stopped by the time they left the Forensics Lab. Pendragon tossed the keys to Turner. 'You drive.'

They pulled out into the heavy traffic and almost immediately ground to a halt again.

'It's hard to imagine how anyone could actually have performed those murders,' Turner said, glancing over at his boss. 'I mean, to have a steamroller and nobody see you using it. And Berrick, you'd need some sort of electronic press to do that to his head, wouldn't you, guv?'

'Yes, I think you're right, Turner. I've been wondering the same thing and I've just thought of someone who might be able to give me some answers.'

Turner dropped Pendragon outside the Blind Beggar on Whitechapel Road. The rain was coming down harder now and the DCI made a dash for it between two market stalls selling knock-off saris and pirated Bollywood DVDs. Inside, the pub reminded him of a cave. There was subdued light from cheap plastic chandeliers fitted with green bulbs, dark wood panelling around the bar, heavily patterned wallpaper, and a carpet that had so much beer rubbed into it, it was impossible to tell what colour it might once have been. The place stank of alcohol and detergent.

The pub had just opened and he was one of only three customers. The other two sat at separate tables, each nursing a beer and staring silently towards the windows on to Whitechapel Road. Pendragon ordered a pint of bitter and sat in the corner furthest from the other patrons and well out of earshot. These days, the Blind Beggar was something of a tourist attraction. It had once been a favourite of the notorious Kray twins, who had run the most powerful crime cartel in the district back in the sixties and seventies. It was in this pub in 1966 that Ronnie Kray shot dead George Cornell, an associate of a rival gang, the Richardsons.

Pendragon saw Sammy Samson pass the window and enter the pub. He gave him a discreet wave. Sammy smiled and strode over to the table, extending one hand as Pendragon stood up. He was wearing an ancient double-breasted suit with stains down the front, the shoulders and elbows shiny with wear. His shirt was off-white with a ragged blue tie keeping the collar almost closed. He had shaved, but badly, leaving lines of half-shorn stubble here and there and a trail of bloodied nicks.

'Pendragon, old boy,' Sammy said. 'It's been a while.' His voice was brandy-cracked and ravaged by tobacco and God knows what else, but Sammy still spoke the Queen's English like the old Etonian he was. Pendragon indicated he should sit and called Sammy's order to the barman before turning back to look at the man in front of him.

The Hon. Sammy Samson was the stuff of legend and Pendragon knew he should only take notice of a fraction of what was said about the man. What had passed through the DCI's filter was that Sammy was a genuine aristocrat, the son of an earl who had lost the favour of his family decades earlier and been cut off without a penny. Back in the late sixties he had fallen into the drug culture, survived a spell managing a couple of bands, and then become a full-blown junkie. His father had expelled him from the family and none of his siblings would talk to him.

By that time, he was already enamoured with what had to him become a charming alternate reality: the East End and the ordinary lives of ordinary people. Even in his early twenties, he had felt more at home enjoying a pint of brown ale and a knees-up at the local boozer than back on the playing fields of Eton or at Royal Ascot. Rejection by his own family had strengthened these feelings, and with surprising ease he had become part of the Stepney scene. Later, he had fallen in with the gang lords, worked as an accountant for the Krays, spent five years in jail, and then simply turned to a life of wandering around the East End, day after day, week after week, decade upon decade.

As a boy, Pendragon had seen Sammy Samson around Stepney. Even then, the lapsed aristocrat had been a local celebrity. So it was perhaps not surprising that when Jack took the job at Brick Lane, Sammy had been one of the first people he had asked after. When he discovered the man was very much alive and an active police snout, he had reached out to him. Sammy always kept an ear to the ground, and what he did not know about the goings-on in the East End crime world was not worth pursuing. Now in his mid-sixties, Sammy looked seventy-five. He was pretty much broken beyond repair, surviving from day to day. Pendragon liked him a lot.

'So what may I do for you, Pendragon?' Sammy asked, knocking back his drink in one. 'Might there be value in my enlightened observations on recent unhappy goings-on?'

'I think you've hit the nail on the head, Sammy. You always were an astute man.'

'Ah, my dear boy, flattery will get you everywhere.'

Pendragon signalled to the barman, and a few moments later another brandy appeared at Sammy Samson's elbow. 'Very gracious of you,' the old man said and raised the glass, downing only half its contents this time.

Pendragon looked around. They could not be overheard here. 'To be specific,' he said as Sammy eyed the rest of the brandy, 'we're trying to piece together a *modus operandi* for our local killer. I can't go into details, but the murders don't take place where we find the bodies. In fact, I'm looking for a large work space the killer is using. I don't think it's their home. I'm pursuing the idea our man is renting somewhere anonymous but near here.'

Sammy considered Pendragon with intelligent eyes. 'An office? Something of that nature?'

'No. Larger. More industrial.'

'A derelict factory or school?'

'Maybe, or a warehouse perhaps.'

'I see,' Sammy said slowly, leaning back in his seat and crossing his legs. Pendragon noted the holes in the soles of his decades-old handmade brogues. 'I will have to give that some thought,' he said. 'Ask around. What . . . er . . . what sort of remuneration are we thinking of, Pendragon? Only, you understand, I'll have expenses to consider.'

He gave the older man a brief smile. 'Don't worry, Sammy. I've always looked after you, haven't I?'

'Indeed you have, dear boy. Indeed you have. While we're on the subject of Mammon, I may already have some snippets of information concerning the case under investigation.'

'Snippets of information?' Pendragon gave him a crooked smile.

Sammy nodded and a glint came to his eyes. 'I should remind you I was once given the epithet "the eyes and ears of Stepney".'

Pendragon laughed and shook his head. 'Honestly, Sammy, you're worth every penny for the sheer entertainment value.'

Sammy's ravaged face broke into an indignant expression. 'Well, I suppose I must consider that a compliment.'

'What have you heard?'

'That depends. How entertaining have I been?'

Pendragon sighed, withdrew his wallet from his inside pocket and pulled out a £20 note. Sammy took it and pushed his glass forward an inch. Pendragon nudged it back. 'Let's hear it first, Sammy.'

'Well, how should I put this? Your first victim, the gallery owner . . . he was very friendly with the descendants of my former associates.'

Pendragon fixed the old man with his eyes. 'Kingsley Berrick had gangland connections?'

Sammy Samson nodded.

'What sort of connections?'

'That's the limit of my current knowledge on the subject, Chief Inspector.'

'Come on, Sammy.'

'God's honest . . . as my local friends would put it.' And he held his hands up, palms out.

Pendragon gave him a sceptical look. 'So you're telling me you've just heard it through the grapevine? No details?'

'You now know everything I do.'

Chapter 24

Brick Lane, Stepney, Saturday

'All right, Jack. Let's have an update.'

They were in the Super's office. Jill Hughes sat at one end of the leather sofa, Pendragon at the other. Hughes was nursing a cup of tea. The door was closed, keeping out the noise from the station. The clock on the desk told them it had just passed midday.

'Well, so far we've got a miscellaneous collection of facts. All useful, but none of it seems to fit together.'

'Explain.'

'First, we have the forensics and path reports. Turner and I had a thorough debriefing from Jones and Newman over at Lambeth this morning. Appears that both victims died from a massive heroin overdose. No,' Pendragon added quickly, seeing the Super's expression, 'I don't think either of them was an addict. The heroin was injected straight into their brains. That's what killed them. They also found Thursk's DNA in Berrick's remains.'

Hughes looked suitably surprised. 'So they were obviously well acquainted,' she said dryly. 'And Berrick's business partner, Mr Price, reckons that Berrick and Norman Hedridge were a couple at one time?'

'Yes.'

'So you're leaning towards this being a sexually motivated murder? A jealous ex-partner, perhaps?'

'No, I'm not. I don't think there's anything in that idea at all.'

'Why not?'

'The murders are all too elaborate, ma'am. Too staged. I think the killer is clearly warped, but my gut tells me this has nothing to do with sex.'

'The Surrealist link?'

'Yes.'

'Couldn't it be some sort of in-joke? A very black joke? Maybe the motive has something to do with the sexual relationships between these men, but they were each involved in the art world, remember.'

'Well, it's possible, but I'm a great believer in Occam's razor.'

'That the truest answer is always the one based on the fewest assumptions?'

Pendragon nodded.

'Okay. What else do we have? What other assumptions can we make?'

'Newman and Jones found some fibres of tarpaulin and some flecks of paint in two colurs, green and white. We're thinking a van or other motor vehicle for the white sample but the green . . .'

'The cherry-picker. I was shown the CCTV footage earlier. And the tarpaulin would have been used to wrap the flattened remains of Thursk. That's the cylindrical object you can see in the cage of the picker.'

'I think that's correct,' Pendragon said. 'The killer must

have bumped off Thursk with the heroin jab, mutilated the body, then used the cherry-picker under cover of dark to get the remains to the tree and into position. One person could do it.'

'Dr Newman's hunch that the murders were carried out some distance from the place the bodies were found looks spot on. With Berrick's murder they used a wheelchair to transport the body through the gallery, and with Thursk they drove the cherry-picker. I don't suppose you've found any CCTV footage of a vehicle close to the gallery on Wednesday morning?'

'Afraid not. There're no cameras close by. Whoever committed the murders must have transported Berrick's body to the gallery in the early hours, but I don't think it would help much if we could get some footage. The person responsible for these crimes wouldn't let anything slip. The number plate would be obscured. They would be disguised.'

'So what about this Francis Arcade character?'

'Yes, him. I'm pretty convinced he knows a great deal about what's going on, but he shows no interest in sharing anything with us.'

'Could he be our killer?'

'I don't think so, ma'am, though he certainly hated the two victims. He's never disguised that fact. You've seen the podcast?'

'Yes. Pretty incriminating if you ask me.'

'He has an alibi.'

'And it checks out?'

'Unfortunately, yes.'

'In that case we'll have to let him go.'

'I know. I'll leave it to the last second, though. There is one other thing. I had a chat with Sammy Samson.'

'That old wreck? I don't understand why you bother with him.'

'Actually, he's been pretty useful before now,' Pendragon said defensively.

'Okay, Jack. I'll take your word for it. What golden nugget has he given you this time?'

Pendragon gave the Super a wan smile. 'He tells me our Mr Kingsley Berrick was involved with the local gangs.'

'And you believe him?'

Pendragon paused for a moment and took a deep breath. 'I think it's worth following up.'

Hughes looked intently at him and decided to concede the point. 'Yes, you're right, Jack. We can't leave any stone . . .' She was interrupted by a rap on the door. It was Turner. He looked excited.

'Sorry to interrupt, ma'am,' he said, looking directly at the Super. 'Just had a call. We've got another one.'

Chapter 25

To Mrs Sonia Thomson
14 October 1888

June was a very busy month. I was obliged to organise my family affairs in Hemel Hempstead, bury my father, and help the authorities with their investigation into the fire at Fellwick Manor. I was aware of a few suspicious voices being raised, but nobody came out with any clear accusations and there was no evidence to incriminate Yours Truly. Naturally, I played the role of grieving son beautifully. My father had few friends and we had no remaining family connections. His unmarried elder brother had died of cholera some ten years ago, and Mother, like myself, had been an only child. I inherited everything.

After an appropriate length of time I was able to escape to Oxford where I had still to attend to the matter of satisfying my professors that I was worthy of a good degree. You may wonder why on earth this would matter to me; but, you see, I'm one of those people who, once something has been started, likes to finish it in style. This I succeeded in doing, and in June, I was ready to make my farewells to the university town that had opened up so many new opportunities for me.

But, for some reason, I could not quite bring myself to board the train. I lingered for two days. Most of the students had left and the place began to feel unnaturally quiet. Before dawn on the third morning, as I lay in bed, I realised what it was that was holding me back. I packed a bag with some bread and a bottle of ale, and headed south past Christ Church and over Folly Bridge.

The sun had been up for an hour by the time I reached Boars Hill and the day was already warming up. After leaving the track at the edge of the city and passing into the fields close to Boars Hill, I neither saw nor heard another soul. The only sound was the buzzing of insects. Clancy Hall was surrounded by a fence on three sides and a wall on the other. The driveway was gated but I found a way over the wall to the east of the gate, close to a copse of trees, and traipsed across a patch of knee-high grass that led me to the edge of the carefully manicured gardens close to the house.

I sensed the place was deserted long before I reached the double front doors and tried the bell. The windows were shuttered; the driveway empty and freshly raked. I tried the bell a few more times without really knowing why and then took a few paces back to the far edge of the driveway, to stare at the blank walls and shutters.

I was crossing the lawn to leave when I saw a solitary figure some fifty yards away: a gardener working on one of the flowerbeds. He was wearing steel-capped boots and had thrust his spade into a heap of soil stacked high in a wheelbarrow. Arching his spine, he pushed back his cap, wiped his weathered face with a scrap of cloth and turned to watch my approach.

'Good day,' I said.

He gave me a suspicious look, his thick grey eyebrows knitting together. 'Sir,' he said, touching the front of his cap.

'I'm a friend of the owner,' I said, and nodded back towards the house. 'My name is Mr Sandler.'

'Pleased to meet you, sir.'

'I was surprised to see it all boarded up.'

'Well, perhaps you haven't been around for a bit, sir,' the gardener said mildly. 'Been this way for a while now.'

I was about to reply, but checked myself. I wiped my own sweaty brow with the sleeve of my jacket. 'Any idea where Mr Oglebee has gone?' I asked, staring the gardener directly in the eye.

'Mr Oglebee?'

'Yes, man,' I snapped. 'Mr Oglebee.'

The gardener shook his head slowly and I could feel the anger building up inside me. He clicked his tongue. 'Don't know about a Mr Oglebee, sir. Clancy Hall is owned by Lord and Lady Broadbent. Or at least it was. They died a few years back. Their son Charles is master of the estate now. But he lives in South Africa. Hasn't been back for, oh . . . at least three years.'

I looked into the old man's eyes, trying to see if there was any trace of artifice, but there was none. I simply thanked him, turned and walked back to Oxford.

Later, following the porters out through the gates of Exeter College and on to the Turl, I could not snap out of the puzzled reverie I had found myself in since leaving Clancy Hall. There was no one in Oxford to whom I could put the conundrum, and something inside told me that even if I were to mention what I had discovered, I would receive no satisfactory form of response. It was a little while later, as I sat alone in the train carriage allowing myself to be lulled to sleep, that I began to see the funny side of it and to accept what an amusing *divertimente* the whole thing had been. Oglebee, I realised, was even more of an enigma than I had suspected.

I had been to London on several occasions prior to that, always with my father. They had been solemn affairs; silent train journeys with me obediently tagging along. All those trips were to the more salubrious parts of the capital, on visits to lawyers and meetings with Father's religious brethren. My plans now were very different.

The train pulled into Paddington Station with its usual cacophony and billows of steam. I followed the porter through a concourse milling with early-evening travellers. We stopped at Left Luggage and I gave the man a good tip. He doffed his cap and strode off with his trolley to find another customer.

In the gentlemen's conveniences I changed, swapping my tailored suit for a pair of rough workmen's trousers, an old collarless shirt, a flat cap and steel-tipped boots. Folding my smart clothes into one of my cases, I removed a ripped canvas bag and stuffed it with a few essentials. I also removed a black leather bag which contained my paints and materials as well as a collection of knives and a newly sharpened saw. After putting my two cases into storage, I headed out through the main doors on to the busy street.

It was hot and sticky still, the air heavy and cloying. A storm was brewing. I went to hail a cab and found myself discombobulated. The cab slowed, but then the driver took one look at me and whipped on his horse. I had to smile at the efficacy of my own disguise. Turning, I walked a few yards back along the road and found another hansom waiting for passengers from the station. When I approached the cab driver and told him where I wanted to go, he gave me a puzzled look and was about to pull away without a reply when I told him I would pay double in advance.

'Show us it then, matey boy,' he said.

I pulled out half a crown and handed it to him. 'Righty-ho, sir,' he said. 'Jump in.' He flicked his whip and we were away.

I sat back as the cab wove a course through the busy streets, and simply soaked up the atmosphere of this incomparable place. London . . . the greatest city in the world by far. This was a city the Emperors of Rome would have envied. I know, dear lady, that you have yourself been to London many times. Your husband told me this. But I also know that you have led a rather cloistered life in the Berkshire countryside, so you must indulge me in my recollections of my sense of rapture upon finding myself here a free agent at last. Here I was, newly graduated from Oxford, a young man with very clear ideas of what he was about to do. No wonder I was excited.

The storm broke as the cab bounced over the cobblestones of Tottenham Court Road. From inside my cab, I could see pedestrians scatter for cover as thunder hamméred overhead and lightning ripped open the sky. I heard the driver seated on his box behind me yelling at the horse and then his whip crack above the beast's rump.

The journey seemed interminable. Even my enthusiasm for the place began to wear thin. I had arranged my accommodation already, contacting a landlord through an advertisement in the *Oxford Times*. I wanted something in the heart of Whitechapel and had no qualms about the sordid condition of most of the dwelling places there. In fact, the filthier it was, the better I would consider it to be. I was quite confident that I could look after myself. As we approached the address of the lodgings, I asked the cab driver to pull over to the side of Whitechapel Road. I did not want the neighbours to see me arriving in a hansom. I jumped down, pulling my bag over my shoulder, and headed over the uneven, rubbish-strewn cobbles with my hat tugged low over my face and my head down against the still driving rain. The weather was on my side, I thought.

My new lodgings were on Wentworth Street. I rented a single room above a corn-chandler's shop. The shopkeeper, a Mr Girthwright, owned the building. His shop was crammed full of bird cages, broody hens, baskets of eggs, seed and corn. It was more farm than shop, and the stink of bird excrement and rotting straw seeped through the ceiling into the rooms above.

The room itself was wonderfully squalid. Just what I was looking for. I needed to soak up the atmosphere, melt into the crowd, become part of the local landscape. I was priming myself, making ready for my project, my grand work, the one that would make my name immortal.

It was a mean room, a low ceiling surmounting brown walls that had been papered last when Victoria was a young woman. The floor was of bare boards. There was a narrow bed, a rusted gas mantle, no form of heating. A single ornament hung on the wall above the bed: a crucifix. But, as crude and unprepossessing a place as this was, I knew from my studies of the area that this house was one of the better lodgings to be found here. It was not uncommon for four families to share a place this size, and the exorbitant price demanded for it – three shillings a week – was justified if I were to have my privacy. That was the last thing I could afford to sacrifice. I dropped my bag to the floor and sat on the edge of the bed, looking around my new home, feeling immensely pleased with myself.

By the time I left the building, the sky had turned russet, casting a striking light across the buildings and the still-wet streets. The rain had passed and the stink of the place was reasserting itself. It was a smell I had never before experienced, a blend of so many odours: soot, tar, rotten food and human waste. There was also a salty tang to the air, the southerly breeze wafting into the narrow streets the stench of the river.

I had not visited a place even remotely like this, and it thrilled me inordinately. I knew all the stories about this part of London. How the poor had been expelled from the Rookeries around St Giles to the west of the City, their old slums razed. The countless, faceless hordes of bedraggled humanity had swept eastward just a few miles and turned the East End of London into the cesspit it now was. It was, dear lady, Hell on Earth, a place Londoners refer to as 'the Stew', and I loved it immediately.

How do I begin to express its unique atmosphere, especially to one so well bred and closeted as your good self? I've tried to convey the smell, but really this was just one element in the overall experience. Indeed, one could almost describe the process of walking out of my lodgings and on to the street as something of an overloading of the senses, for everything about it piqued and challenged my perceptions.

Immediately outside the door to my lodgings, a pieman had set up. He had placed a small box-shaped container on short metal legs on the cobblestones. On top of this lay a row of meat pies kept warm by a small fire burning inside the box. The pieman wore a short jacket and a dirty kerchief. His top hat was pushed back at a rakish angle and he wore a brown-smeared apron about his waist. A woman stood beside him. She looked ill, with pinched cheeks and dark hollows beneath her eyes. Immediately in front of the pie stand stood a young boy in a cloth cap, calling for customers. He was crouching on one knee and held a pair of coins in his hand which he tossed into the air. 'Toss and buy,' he called, inviting customers to have a turn at guessing which way the coins fell while they waited for their pie.

It was the time of the evening when the streets were beginning to fill. The few residents who had jobs were returning from their labours, and others, the prostitutes or 'brides' as I knew they were called by the locals, were just about to start their evening's work.

The workmen looked particularly bedraggled. I saw a young man, his face as pale as death, hair already thinning, eyes hollow. He almost knocked my shoulder as he swayed, half-drunk, along the narrow pavement. I caught the stench of him, fish and brine, and I knew that he was a waterman, one of those who pulled corpses from the Thames in the hope of finding something valuable, be it a farthing sewn into a seam or a gold tooth pulled from a corpse.

Crossing a lane that led on to Whitechapel Road, a group of four exhausted figures passed by. These were paupers on their way from the labour yard where those without any gainful employment spent twelve hours a day breaking stones and rocks for a few pennies. Then a more colourful sight: a 'budgerigar man', a slight fellow in an off-white top hat standing behind a hastily erected table covered with a frayed cloth. Four budgerigars perched along his outstretched arm. On the table top lay four cards. 'Guess the card and win yourself a night out!' the man called as I approached. I ignored him, but watched fascinated as a young couple stepped up.

The girl was giggling as her male friend offered the budgerigar man a farthing. 'Which one would the lady like to choose?' the man behind the table quizzed, ogling her. 'Could be your lucky night, my darlin'.' The girl tittered stupidly and nuzzled up to her beau. The young man chose for her, second from the left. The budgerigar man pocketed the money and lowered his arm to allow one of the birds to hop on to the table. The budgerigar paraded importantly up and down next to the cards, then stopped and pecked at one of them: the second from the left. The woman squealed and threw her hands to her mouth. I walked on, wondering how many times the budgerigar man would let the couple win before he turned the tables on them.

Now, dear lady, you must not think me a

completely idle fellow because this little exploratory trip was serving a definite purpose. I was heading somewhere and I knew exactly where it was. My destination was the Pavilion, or the 'Pav' as the locals preferred, a music hall of the most wretchedly sordid kind, but an entirely suitable place of entertainment for the residents of Hell.

How do I begin to conjure up a clear portrayal of the Pav? It would be much easier for me to paint the place. But I will try. I want you to have every detail.

The front of the building gave no clue as to what went on inside. It looked like a simple, decent theatre. But beyond the doors, the place was a haven for the lower orders. Great rough wooden tables ran the entire length of the main hall, and upon either side of these stretched benches. By nine each evening every single space on the benches was taken, beer mugs were constantly refilled with cheap, watered-down ale, and the venue burst into life.

As you may gather, I went to the Pav on many occasions. Indeed I purchased a box there for no less than five guineas. I was captivated by the place that very first night of my new life in London. Before I had slept a single night in the Stew, I had made myself at home at the New Royal Pavilion Theatre, to give it its proper name. What was it that I loved so much there? I hear you ask. I think it was the sense of barely masked hopelessness, the ludicrous lengths to which people go in order to forget temporarily the vileness of life. Thomas Hobbes once wrote: 'Life is solitary, poor, nasty, brutish and short', but any nascent realisation that the average person may have of this may be dispelled with enough beer down their throat; enough rowdy music, sly innuendo and double-entendre; enough time with a whore on their lap. Or, for the richer desperadoes, enough opium in their blood. But it's all a ridiculous falsehood, all a pretence, and it amused me enormously to watch the faces of the cattle at the trough, trying to make all that is bad in the world go away. Only one thing makes that disappear, and it is not something you find in a music hall. At least, not directly. At least, not until Yours Truly arrived in the neighbourhood.

But, dear lady, forgive me, I digress again. I seem to have something of a penchant for it, do I not? Let me get back to the point. There were two very important consequences to my sojourn along Whitechapel Road and my trip to the Pav. First, it led me to the women I was later to slaughter. And second, it was the place in which I was to meet your husband, Archibald, a man who ended up playing a significant role in the events which were to unfold during the late summer and autumn of this year.

I've not mentioned Archibald before this point. This was not, of course, due to any desire on my part to save your feelings. You must know me better than that. But now I come to the part of my story when Mr Thomson makes his first appearance.

No doubt you knew one face of the man. I knew several. We would doubtless agree that Archibald was a hard-working, intelligent, industrious and quaintly ambitious fellow. These things will be said at his funeral. Goodness, I wish I could be there! But there were other aspects to your husband, about which I imagine you had little inkling.

The Pav, that wonderful establishment, was not merely a music hall. The owners earned a tidy sum from all the four-penny pieces handed over at the admissions desk and the half-penny a pint they charged for the slops they passed off as beer, but they, like all of us, were greedy men who knew a captive audience when they saw one. Imagination not being their forte, the theatre owners turned the floor above it into a brothel.

I discovered this on my second visit to the Pav and was thrilled by the revelation. I had spent all of twenty-four hours in Whitechapel, and in my mind had already started to sketch in the details of my planned endeavour. I had decided that there would be four women. Why four? Symmetry perhaps. Four suits to a deck of cards? Four sides to a square? Four Horsemen of the Apocalypse? Actually, none of these ideas crossed my mind. Some, I understand, after the event, tried to find connections between my work and the doings of the Freemasons, the Anarchists, even members of the Royal Family, for Hell's sake! None of these things were in my mind in July. I admit, I played around a little, leaving false clues, but these were for my own amusement and had no foundation in political or, the Devil help me, *spiritual* reflections. So why four? It just felt right.

Four women. I had given some thought to the methods and procedures, but had yet to select my candidates. And I did feel the need for structure here, some element of form. Because all art has form, no matter how loose it may be. When I learned of the brothel above the Pav, some of the pieces of the jigsaw fell into place. I now had a fitting source for my human materials.

Now, dear lady, you may already have surmised an important fact about Yours Truly. That is, I have no desire for women. Indeed, I have no sexual drive whatsoever. I don't know why this is, and I don't care. It is not something I ever dwell upon. I know that for generations to come learned men will postulate and ponder, they will probe what they believe to be my mental make-up. But they will not know me as I know myself, no matter how clever those men may be. They will suggest all manner of sexual aberrations, but really, you have to believe me, there is nothing to that theory. And, quite frankly, I could not be more pleased, for what a terrible waste of energy sex is. What purpose does it serve? If you gain no pleasure from it, it is merely an act of procreation, and the last thing the world needs is more children. So I was not in the brothel for the usual reasons. I was there to paint, and to select.

Soon after I stumbled upon the existence of the brothel above the Pav, I made it my business to explore the place. Exploration is key to what I do, an essential discipline that enables me always to keep one step ahead of the police. Careful not to draw attention to myself, I rapidly learned how the upper rooms were laid out and how some of them interconnected. I soon discovered a clever little network of secret passages and escape routes built into the shell of the building.

Now back to Archibald. I met him some two weeks after arriving in Whitechapel. I had been making nightly excursions to the Pav and its brothel. To the girls, I was known as 'The Painter', and they all seemed to like me because I never touched them, just sketched. It was a Friday night, growing late. My model was becoming impatient, even though I had paid her twice her normal fee and all she had to do was recline decorously on a chaise. I too began to tire, not of work, but of the woman's sighs and restlessness. Dropping my pencil on the sketchpad, I tossed her the robe she had arrived in and told her to get out. Angry now, I put the pad and pencil on to the bed and lit a cigarette. Pulling myself up from the chair and shaking my head irritably, I paced over to the door, stepped out on to the broad landing and leaned over the balcony. I could hear the noise from below, every note of the penny opera. It lurched to screeching halt and the Master of Ceremonies bellowed to the crowd: 'What now, ladies and gentlemen? What now?'

I had seen and heard it all before, of course. I could picture the scene. The Pav's favourite, Marie Lloyd, would be ready in the wings. I could hear her entrance music. I could picture her striding on to the stage with her umbrella. It would jam and she would declare: 'Oh, Gawd! I ain't 'ad it up for ages!' And there, on cue, came the roar of laughter from the baying crowd. Oh, what simple things can please.

Then I heard a succession of new sounds. A crash, a scream, the blast of a whistle . . . a police whistle. Peering over the balcony, I caught a glimpse of two constables charging through the main door to the theatre. I turned on my heel and dashed for the door to the room I had rented. Except, in my startled frame of mind, I went for the wrong one and fell into the room next to mine.

I picked myself up and received another surprise when I saw the figures on the bed. Yes, one of them was your beloved husband, my dear lady. He was unaware of the commotion below, lost in his own lusts. But when I charged in, I made such a noise he jumped up, a look of horror on his face. The stupid trollop on the bed, one of the girls I knew, Catherine Eddowes, pulled a sheet up over her scrawny frame.

'What the hell!' Archibald blustered.

Ignoring the pair of them, I dashed across the room. Reaching the wall to the right of a small window, I felt along the cheap, lumpy wallpaper. Archibald pulled on his trousers and plucked at his jacket.

'What's going on?'

I didn't even turn round. 'Coppers,' I hissed.

'Oh, fuck!'

Crouching, I found the leading edge of the hidden

door in a notch in the skirting. Running one finger up to waist-height, and, a few inches to the left, I found the latch, tugged it and let the door swing out. In a flash, I had crawled into the opening and was about to shut the door again when Archibald pushed himself in after me, almost crushing me against the back wall of the narrow concealed passageway behind the bedroom wall. He just managed to yank the door shut before a loud bang told us the police had reached the landing outside.

In the dark, behind the door, we held our breath. Then, using for cover the noises coming from the room – the door crashing open and the squeals of the prostitute – I groped my way along the hidden corridor. Three steps on, I reached a stone wall and felt the rungs of a short ladder screwed to the masonry. I pulled myself up in the darkness and with my left hand felt above my head for the escape hatch. My hand touched rough wood and I recoiled as a splinter slid under one fingernail. Ignoring the pain, I pushed on the trapdoor and levered it up.

Pulling myself through the opening, I found myself on the roof, the cool night air very welcome after the stifling, airless escape route. I slumped back, panting, against a sloping section of tiles. Archibald's stocky form appeared, silhouetted against the light from a yellow half-moon. I had forgotten he was behind me. He stumbled upright and took two steps towards me before leaning back against the same section of the incline and pulling a silver cigarette holder from his trouser pocket. I could see his face in the moonlight: round and sheened with sweat, and those black dog-like eyes of his. 'I think I owe you a drink,' he said.

Chapter 26

Stepney, Saturday 24 January, 2.30 p.m.

St Aloysius's Church on Buckhurst Street, just north of Mile End Road, was a modern concrete building. Pendragon sighed as he stepped out of the car and glanced up at the irregularly shaped stained-glass panels in the window over the entrance. He tilted his head slightly in an effort to understand what the images represented. Giving up, he glanced over at Turner. 'Not exactly Rheims, is it, Sergeant?'

'If you say so, sir,' Turner replied.

'But isn't it odd how our ancestors could construct wonderful buildings to honour their God, while today we get monstrosities like this?' The DCI waved one hand at the church.

'All about money, I expect, guv.'

'Yes, Turner. And, of course, the Catholic Church is *so* poor.' He shook his head and walked under the low concrete canopy that projected from the bunker-like façade, through a set of double doors and on towards the central aisle. He could see a gaggle of people standing close to the altar, and the door to the vestry stood open inwards. Inspector Towers appeared as Pendragon and Turner arrived at the altar.

'Another weird one, sir,' he said.

'Who are these people?'

'Members of the Church Council, sir.'

There were two men and two women in the group. The women were sobbing and one of the men was comforting the elder of them. The other man saw Pendragon and stepped forward.

'I'm the Churchwarden,' he said. 'Malcolm Connolly.' He was a tall, slender man in his fifties, bald but for the tufts of white hair to either side of his head. He was wearing a checked shirt and a brown tie under a tweed jacket with leather elbow patches. He smelled of pipe tobacco. Connolly offered Pendragon his hand, and the DCI introduced himself. 'I found the body, with the Old Father,' the Churchwarden added.

'The old father?'

'Sorry. Father Lionel Ahern, retired. He was parish priest here before Father Michael.'

Pendragon nodded. 'I see. Well, if you could wait here a moment, I would like a word after I've seen the crime scene.'

The room was no more than three metres square, wood-panelled and windowless, with two ornate wall lamps illuminating the space. It smelled of incense and the mustiness of the recently deceased. The chair in which the dead priest had been propped up stood in the centre. Mackleby and Vickers were to one side. Dr Jones was leaning over the victim, shining a small torch into the dead eyes.

'Another fetching tableau to add to the collection,' he said, without even looking round. '*Study after Velázquez's*

Portrait of Pope Innocent X, I do believe, Pendragon.'

The DCI stared at the corpse. 'This is getting repetitive,' he said quietly. 'So now we have a Francis Bacon to add to the list of dead Surrealists. Marvellous.' He took a step closer. 'What have you ascertained?'

'What? In the ten minutes I've been here, Pendragon?'

'Yes.'

Jones exhaled through his nostrils. 'Victim is male, aged about fifty-five . . . sixty. He has a mark on the back of his neck, same as the others.'

'Time of death?'

'At least twelve hours ago.'

Pendragon turned to Towers. 'What's the victim's full name?'

'Father Michael O'Leary.'

'He's been dead for twelve hours. How come? When did that chap Connolly get here?'

'He was only found an hour ago by the retired priest, Father Lionel Ahern, and the Churchwarden.'

'Where is Father Ahern now?'

Sergeant Mackleby stepped forward. 'He's in hospital, guv.'

Pendragon gave her a blank look.

'He's in his eighties. Turned up this morning to have his weekly coffee with Father O'Leary but found the vestry door locked. He also noticed that the chair,' she nodded towards the throne-like seat in which O'Leary's body was arranged '. . . was missing from its usual place outside. It took him a while to get help from the Churchwarden. He had a spare set of keys and together they found the priest.'

'And the old man?'

'Collapsed on the spot. Heart attack. Rushed to the London Hospital.'

Pendragon shook his head. 'This is turning into a farce,' he said, exhaling loudly. 'Okay, Sergeant. I'll talk to Connolly now.'

Turner and Mackleby interviewed the other members of the Church Council while Pendragon led Malcolm Connolly to one of the pews. 'Talk me through finding the body,' he began.

Connolly wiped a bead of sweat from his forehead with a white handkerchief he had pulled from the top pocket of his tweed jacket. 'Sorry,' he said. 'This is all a bit of a shock.'

Pendragon grimaced. 'I understand.'

'Er, right. Father Ahern knocked on my door about midday. He was in a confused state, the poor chap. He had turned up here at ten, apparently. He has coffee once a week with Father Michael. It's been a regular date for years, since the new parish priest arrived in 2004. Anyway, he found the vestry locked and noticed that the chair had been moved. He loved that old chair. It was presented to him back in the fifties. He brought it with him to his new church.'

Pendragon nodded.

'Well, the Old Father is getting on. He went home and sat in front of the fire for a while, trying to work out what had happened and what to do. Eventually he called on me and we came back here together.'

'I see. You keep the spare keys, I take it?'

'Yes. Look, Inspector, what is this all about? Michael

O'Leary was a good man. He never hurt a soul. Why would anyone do such a thing to him? And why this way? What does it mean?'

'I'm afraid we don't yet know, Mr Connolly. But I can assure you, we'll do everything in our power to find whoever did this.'

Connolly said nothing, just stared at the crucifix hanging above the altar.

'How long had you known Father O'Leary?' the DCI asked.

'Since he arrived here. I started as a Churchwarden at St Aloysius soon after it was built in the late eighties. Moved here from Hong Kong with my late wife. I worked in the Civil Service over there.'

'Would you say you knew Father O'Leary well?'

'I suppose so. We saw each other almost every day. I'm retired so I devote a lot of my time to the church. Father Michael was very popular here. Everyone liked him. That is what I find so bizarre. It couldn't have been an opportunistic murder, could it? This was planned. Father Michael was picked out.'

Pendragon nodded but refrained from comment. 'Well, thank you for your time, Mr Connolly. My officers may need to ask you a few more questions once they've had a chat with the others on the Church Council.'

'And you will keep us informed, won't you, Inspector?'

'We will,' Pendragon said, and walked back to the altar where Mackleby and Turner were still questioning the three other members. He turned as Jones emerged from the vestry.

'Usual thing, Pendragon,' the pathologist said. 'Get him over to me as soon as the lovely Dr Newman has finished dusting and poking around.' He nodded and slumped off down the central aisle.

'Sorry to interrupt,' Pendragon said, cutting into Turner's questions. The sergeant was talking to a short, ginger-haired man with very pale skin and a face spattered with freckles. 'Sergeant, I'm heading back to the station now. When you've finished questioning everyone, come and find me in my office. I have a feeling there's a long paper trail ahead of us.'

Turner nodded. 'Okay, guv,' he said, and carried on with his next question. Pendragon spotted Inspector Towers and called him over. 'Check out the car park and the main road for any CCTV. You never know, God may send us a miracle.'

Ken Towers gave him a smirk.

'I want a full report on my desk by four o'clock,' the DCI added, and the inspector's face fell.

Pendragon walked slowly towards the main doors. The voices of those standing at the altar reverberated around the room, amplified by the acoustics of the place, but they were nothing but a jumble of disconnected words. He tuned out and tried to focus on the new facts that had presented themselves. He was so lost in thought that as he emerged from the doors of the church into the car park he almost walked straight into a man wearing a greatcoat and a Chelsea FC bobble hat.

'DCI Pendragon, no less,' the man said.

Pendragon looked up, startled for a second, and sighed when he saw the face of the journalist Fred Taylor, his would-be nemesis from a local rag, the *Gazette*. He was a short, tubby man with a naturally ruddy face coloured further by the cold. He had a large nose that today was also tinged red and he wore round tortoiseshell-framed spectacles. Six months earlier, when Pendragon was dealing with his first case, a serial killer at large in Stepney, Taylor had taken an instant dislike to him and had done everything he could to discredit and embarrass the new DCI, including running a near-libellous piece about how Pendragon's wife had walked out on him. It had also delved pruriently into the fact that the DCI's own daughter, Amanda, had disappeared five years before. Beside Fred Taylor was a taller man in an expensive-looking leather coat buttoned up against the cold. He had a Nikon digital camera on a strap about his neck.

'God help us if good old Jack here's been put in charge of catching the Modern Art Murderer,' Taylor exclaimed, turning to his colleague.

'Hah!' the younger man snorted.

'What did you say?' Pendragon snarled.

'God help us . . .'

'No, Taylor, after that.'

The journalist grinned. 'What? The Modern Art . . .'

'Yes.'

'Well, I wouldn't be much of a journalist if I didn't know what was going on in my manor, now would I, DCI Pendragon?'

'And how did you know . . . ?'

'About the latest horror, here at St Aloysius?' Taylor tapped his nose. 'A little birdie.'

Pendragon took a deep breath. 'I see.'

'So, if you don't mind, DCI Pendragon, Mickey and I would like to get the latest info and a few snaps for tomorrow's edition. My boss has been holding us back like we were a couple of mares on heat, to be honest. But with the third one . . . Well, I think even she will agree it's high time we got the story out there.'

Just at that moment, Turner and Inspector Towers came through the double doors. They took one look at Taylor and his friend and stepped over to back up the DCI.

'Excellent timing,' Pendragon said. 'These two gentlemen wanted to go barging into the church. I don't think the Council members would like that, do you?'

'Definitely not, sir,' Towers responded immediately.

'So I think we ought to ask them to lock the doors, don't you?'

Turner immediately spun on his heel.

'Wrong decision, Pendragon,' Fred Taylor hissed. 'Thought you would have learned from bitter experience not to get in the way of legitimate journalism.'

Pendragon gave him a sweet smile and walked away.

Chapter 27

'DCI Pendragon, please.' The caller's plummy tones were immediately identifiable.

'Sammy,' Jack responded.

'Dear boy. I hope I find you in good health.'

Pendragon smiled to himself. 'Perishing cold, but that aside . . .'

'I have some information for you. Oh, blast it . . .'

Pendragon heard fumbling and the clink of coins.

'You're in a call box?'

'There . . . Yes. Don't believe in mobiles. What was I saying?'

'You had some information.' Pendragon glanced to left and right as he crossed Buckhurst Street and headed towards Mile End Road.

'May have found what you're after. Got the address here.'

A rustling of paper.

'What's suspect about it?' Pendragon asked after Sammy had read out the address.

'My source tells me it's been unused for years, but was rented out last week . . . for one week only.'

'One week?'

'Correct.'

'Names?'

'A paper chase with no satisfactory conclusion so far. The owner is Westbrick and Co. They have a representative in Docklands . . . Sunrise . . . listed in the book. The unit was rented in the name of Rembrandt Industries. That's all I have.'

'Okay. Thanks, Sammy. It's a warehouse, I take it?'

'Believe so. Down on West India Quay.'

'Right,' Pendragon responded. 'I know it.'

Sergeant Turner was waiting for Pendragon at the reception desk of Sunrise Properties, the London representatives of Westbrick and Co. 'Hi, guv. Only got here a couple of minutes ago. The manager's in.' He glanced at his notebook. 'A Mr Derrickson.'

'Have you found anything on Rembrandt Industries?'

'A phone number, disconnected. An email address, also disconnected.'

'Banks? How were funds transferred?'

'Through third and fourth parties, an entity called Gouache and another called Cubist and Co.'

'Very amusing,' Pendragon retorted. 'I think our murderer's messing with us. Anything on these damn intermediaries?' he asked bitterly.

''Fraid not, sir. Their numbers and email addresses have also been disconnected. The financial transactions went through a branch of Lloyds in Reading. Accounts have been closed . . . of course.'

'And, naturally, no trace of the person who set up the accounts and closed them down?'

At that moment, a tall, bald man in his mid-thirties

appeared from the corridor ahead of them. The receptionist nodded to the two policemen and the man walked over, right hand extended, a serious but not unfriendly expression on his face.

Derrickson's office was an ultra-modern, minimalist affair with a Mac, a phone and a notepad on an otherwise empty metal and glass desk.

'So, gentlemen. How may I help?'

'We would like access to one of your properties.'

'I see.'

'17A, Knox Lane, West India Quay. Apparently, it was let for one week only and we believe it may be useful to us in furthering a criminal investigation.'

'Okay,' said Derrickson, concerned. He tapped on his keyboard and looked up. 'Yes. Rembrandt Industries.'

'Is it unusual for companies to rent warehouse space for so short a time?'

'Yes, it is, Inspector. But the client offered to pay for three months. I'm amazed you know about it.' Derrickson looked straight into Pendragon's eyes.

Jack ignored him and glanced at Turner before returning Derrickson's gaze. 'All traces of the company who leased the warehouse have been erased,' he said. 'You were paid and then the account was closed.'

Derrickson looked surprised. 'Odd.'

'So, you see, we have grounds for suspicion.'

'What exactly are you investigating, Inspector?'

'I'm afraid the details are confidential, but it is a homicide matter.'

Derrickson nodded. 'Right. So what would you like from us?'

'We want to see inside the property.'

'Ah, that's delicate as the client has paid upfront.'

'But relinquished the lease.'

'Even so . . . .'

'All right, Mr Derrickson. We can proceed in one of two ways. You can grant us unrestricted access and we go about our business quietly. Or I return in sixty minutes with a search warrant, lights flashing and sirens blaring, for all your neighbours to see. It's entirely up to you.'

Derrickson looked down at the shiny surface of his desk, his fingers interlaced on the glass. Then he spread his hands. 'Okay,' he said, and picked up the phone.

The Victorian warehouse faced the water on West India Quay. It stood in the middle of a row of similar buildings. Each unit was used as a medium-term storage facility for importers. The blank façade was a windowless expanse of carefully restored brickwork. To one side was a wide roller door big enough to drive a bus through. On the other stood a smaller door with a security lock activated by a keypad.

Inside, Pendragon flicked a switch and a bright yellow light snapped on and off twice before staying on to illuminate a single, square high-roofed space. The floor was of bare concrete, the walls entirely unadorned. It was really just a gigantic storage box, with one incongruous feature: a cluster of heavy machinery in the centre of the room. Pendragon and Turner headed straight for this, their shoes echoing on the concrete.

'Fascinating,' Pendragon commented as they stopped two feet before a metal press. Beside it stood an electric roller. On the floor, in the harsh fluorescence, they could make out spots of blood and gobbets of grey matter.

They took separate tours around the machines. The metal press was about seven feet tall and three wide. It comprised a steel framework supported on three sturdy metal feet. In the centre of the framework was a two-foot-square opening. Poised above this was a punch about six inches in diameter. It was suspended about a foot from the base of the opening. Pendragon tilted his head to look at the underside of the cylindrical metal punch and noticed a streak of dried blood.

The roller was a very modern, high-tech version of a steamroller. It had three forward gears and a reverse, and consisted of a heavy steel drum and a sprung seat for the driver. On the floor nearby, between the metal press and the roller, stood a box of miscellaneous tools: a power drill, a hedge trimmer, an assortment of blades, lengths and coils of wire, clips and a roll of gaffer tape.

The two policemen met up on the far side of the roller and stood silently staring at the floor. A strip of red flecked with grey stretched ten feet from the roller towards the back wall of the warehouse. The strip was about two metres wide. Pendragon squatted down at one edge and looked closely at the stain. Up close, he could see small lumps of fleshy material. 'A veritable Chamber of Horrors,' he remarked, pulling himself upright. 'Dr Newman is going to have a field day, but I bet she won't find a fingerprint or a single trace of suspect DNA.'

Chapter 28

'What can you tell me about the murder of Father Michael O'Leary?' Pendragon asked, staring down at the disfigured face of the dead priest lying on Neil Jones's slab.

'A carbon copy of the first two,' the pathologist replied. 'At least, the cause of death is. A needle straight into the centre of the brain and a hefty dose of heroin. Of course, after that the killer got his jollies in a different way. Eyelids taped back, mouth stuffed with this plastic ball.' He held up a tennis-ball-sized clear plastic sphere: 'All very theatrical if you ask me, Pendragon.'

'Any other marks on the body?'

'No, the assailant appears first to have stunned O'Leary with Mace. There are traces of Trimyristin, its main component, around the eyes.'

'What about the man's physical condition?' Turner asked.

'What? Other than the fact that he's dead, Sergeant?

Pendragon sighed and Jones turned to him. 'Jack,' he said with surprising familiarity, 'the humour comes free. Relax.'

Pendragon looked down at his shoes and then at Turner. 'What shape was O'Leary in *before* he was killed?'

'A typical sixty-year-old male. Liver a bit over-used. He obviously liked a drink. Not particularly overweight. No signs of serious injury either old or recent. A bit of rheumatism. Why?'

'We're just trying to establish who O'Leary is . . . was. He doesn't seem to match up with the first two vics at all, but there must be a link because of what you refer to as the theatre of it all.'

'I'm afraid I can't shed much light on that, Pendragon. But I'll send my report over to Lambeth, and I trust Dr Newman will reciprocate. I find working with her rather rewarding.'

Pendragon raised his eyebrows. Turner was just closing his notebook when Jones stepped around the mortuary table. 'Hey, Sergeant,' he said. 'I have a joke for you.'

Turner stared at the pathologist, tilting his head slightly to one side.

'How many Surrealists does it take to change a light bulb?'

Turner shrugged.

'Fish.'

'What?' Turner said, completely bemused. He glanced at Pendragon, who couldn't stop a smile spreading across his face as he headed for the door.

Chapter 29

Stepney, Monday 26 January, 12.10 p.m.

Pendragon had heard of the grand old tradition of East End funerals, but had never before experienced one. When he was a child growing up in Stepney he had been too young to attend such events. His uncle Stanley had died when Jack was seven, but he had been kept at home, watched over by a distant cousin from the other side of the family. He could still remember the sense of pantomime surrounding the occasion, the buzz of something grandiose happening which he did not quite understand and from which he was shielded by the mourning grown-ups.

Uncle Stanley had been a pillar of the community and much loved locally. Pearly King of 1953, no less. It all seemed to have happened a long time ago and in a very different East End, Pendragon thought as he arrived at the service for Kingsley Berrick. Today's big show for the art dealer seemed completely incongruous. Berrick had certainly been a flamboyant character: a man who loved to party, loved to make money; a man who, according to some, loved art. But, most of all, he seemed to have loved his own image, and this was never clearer than in the way he had planned his own farewell to the world.

But Berrick, the record made clear, had been born in Surrey and had only arrived in the East End after setting up his gallery in the late-1980s, first in Shoreditch and then in Whitechapel. He was no more cockney than Liberace, but now here he was, lying in a ridiculously ornate coffin surrounded by flowers spelling out his name. Outside the church, a carriage drawn by two black mares in black feather headdresses stood waiting with an escort of no fewer than six professional pallbearers in black top hats and tails.

The service was long and drawn-out with speeches from a host of luminaries of the British art scene. It was finished by a eulogy from Jackson Price, in which he claimed his friend had been one of the most influential people in his field.

Pendragon mingled with the mourners as they slowly emerged from the church on to Clyde Street close to Whitechapel Road. Much of the snow of the previous week had turned to slush. But now, early on Monday afternoon, it had begun to snow again, huge, fluffy flakes tumbling gracefully from a leaden sky, settling on the tops of cars and the roofs of the surrounding buildings.

Pendragon was about to take the steps down to the street when he felt a tap on his shoulder. Turning, he was confronted by a tall woman wearing an ankle-length fake-fur coat and Russian-style fur hat. She had fine cheekbones and large brown eyes. Her lips were full and coloured crimson, slightly parted in a faint smile. Her gloved hand was extended towards him. He looked at the woman's face then down at the hand and took it before he finally recognised her from the film of the private view at Berrick & Price, just before the first murder.

189

'DCI Pendragon,' she said.

'Ms Locke.'

The woman's smile broadened. 'How polite. It's Gemma. I saw you in the paper,' she added as Pendragon gave her a puzzled look. 'Quite a spectacular affair, isn't it?' She gazed around. 'Typical Kingsley. Always the showman. Had to be the centre of attention . . . even in death.'

'You knew him well?'

'Oh, I had known him for a long time. But I wouldn't say we were close buddies.' She paused for a moment and looked around again. A middle-aged couple squeezed past and joined the other mourners on the pavement. 'Inspector, I read the piece in the local rag. I took a lot of it as standard hyperbole, but it struck me you do have a nasty mystery on your hands, and clearly three murders linked by some bizarre artistic connection.'

Pendragon looked at her and it suddenly struck him that Gemma Locke was not simply striking in the way many women are at first sight. She was a rare beauty, almost too perfect for words, a face not merely crafted from a fortunate combination of genes but one that was animated and alive, expressing an inner radiance and energy. He had only seen a woman like her a handful of times before this, and in nearly every case it had been in a movie. The thought suddenly occurred to him that Gemma Locke bore a striking resemblance to Greta Garbo in her prime. He realised then he hadn't said anything for a long time and that Gemma Locke was staring at him, a faint smile playing across her lips as though she found him inexplicably amusing.

'Sorry,' Pendragon said. 'Yes, um, we do have a mystery. I haven't read the piece, but I think hyperbole is pretty standard for that paper. We made an official statement yesterday providing as much detail as we care to divulge at this time. The *Gazette* obviously used that, especially the information about the most recent death – the murder of the priest.'

'I'd be happy to assist if you have any questions of an artistic nature. Anything I can do to help catch the person who killed my friends.'

Pendragon felt surprised for a second, then glanced at his watch. 'Would later this afternoon be okay?' he asked. 'Say two o'clock?'

At that moment the funeral carriage started to move off slowly towards the cemetery two hundred yards along the road.

'Do you know Alberto's on Pandora Lane, off Stepney Green?'

'I'll find it,' Pendragon said, and watched the artist turn away into the throng and descend the stairs carefully.

'I was terribly shocked,' Gemma said, staring straight into Pendragon's eyes as she lifted a coffee cup to her mouth. She took a sip and settled the cup back in its saucer. 'We all were. Kingsley could be a pig . . . a tough negotiator. There were times I wished he represented me,' she added with a laugh. 'But, deep down, he was a nice man and absolutely committed to the cause of art.'

'I've heard others say that,' Pendragon replied. 'But I've also heard the opposite.'

'Oh, don't tell me . . . Francis.'

Pendragon nodded and drank some coffee.

'I imagine you have him high on your list of suspects.'

'We did. Brought him in for questioning, as a matter of fact, but he has a water-tight alibi.'

'He's also a baby, Inspector. Hardly the type to kill anyone, especially in the way these people were killed.'

'Can you help fill out some details about Berrick and Thursk?'

'I'll try.'

'Did you know Mr Berrick had underworld connections?'

Gemma Locke looked surprised and was about to say something when she seemed to change her mind. There was silence for a moment, then she said, 'I didn't know that. But actually, come to think of it, it's not that unexpected.'

'It isn't?'

'No. I think that on some level the world of the art dealer and that of the gangster are not so far apart. I think you'd be surprised just how seedy things can be on the art scene.'

'Illuminate me.'

'Argh! I don't have precise facts and figures, Inspector,' Gemma laughed, and took another sip of coffee. 'I'm an artist. Oh, God! That sounds pretentious, doesn't it?'

It was Pendragon's turn to laugh. 'Not really. You *are* an artist.' And he drained his cup.

'I just hear stories. We all do. I think it takes a specific type of person to sell art. It's a difficult business at the best of times – shark-infested waters.'

'Yes, I can imagine.' Pendragon nodded to her cup.

'Another?' He called the waitress over and ordered two more coffees.

'What about Noel Thursk? Can you imagine any connections between him and Berrick, apart from the obvious?'

'What would you call obvious, Inspector?'

'Look, if I'm going to call you Gemma . . .'

'You must be Jack?' She laughed, and Pendragon nodded and found himself giving the woman a flirtatious smile. He only realised after he had done it and felt suddenly ridiculous. But then he concluded that Gemma Locke hadn't noticed anyway.

'Noel and Kingsley had known each other a long time. I think they were occasional lovers. But then, if I tried to work out the labyrinthine sexual relations between all the gay men I know, I would soon be lost. I know they had frequent fallings-out. But again, nothing unusual in that. They were on friendly terms when I saw them last . . .' And her voice trailed off as though she had suddenly remembered that the two men were dead.

'Did they clash over the book Thursk was supposed to be writing?'

Gemma looked up sharply. 'What book?'

It was Pendragon's turn to be surprised. He had assumed Thursk's associates would have known about it. 'His projected book about Juliette Kinnear?'

'Oh, that!' Gemma shook her head dismissively. 'I'd forgotten about it. But then, I think Noel had too, bless him. It was a bit of a joke, wasn't it?'

Pendragon shrugged. 'You tell me.'

The coffees arrived and Gemma Locke leaned forward

193

to blow gently across the foam on top of her latte. 'He started it years ago,' she went on. 'Interviewed everyone. All very serious. He never stopped spouting off about his big book deal. But then everyone seemed to lose interest, Noel especially. I assumed the whole thing had been quietly dropped.' She stirred the coffee and lifted the cup a few inches above the saucer. 'Anyway, Jack, I thought you wanted to ask me some more technical questions.'

'Yes,' Pendragon said. 'I'd love to pick your brain, learn some more about contemporary British art. But somehow I'm not convinced it will bring me any closer to the killer.'

'But with the third murder, it's obvious there's a strong link.'

'Well, yes, but that was already pretty clear after Thursk's body was found. I don't think there are any clues to the murderer's identity in the choice of painting or even artist, other than the fact they're all modern painters. I suppose you could vaguely label the three of them – Magritte, Dali and Bacon – Surrealist, couldn't you?'

'Yes, but those tableaux were all particularly gory examples, weren't they? Not all modern artists paint such striking themes. There are plenty of calmer, more peaceful images.'

'But they would not be so readily adaptable by our murderer.'

'It might still be early days.'

'Oh Lord! Don't say that!' Pendragon exclaimed.

'I'm sorry. That was insensitive of me. It's just . . .'

'Just what?'

'Well, the sheer violence of this killer. I get the feeling

that whoever they are, they're motivated by some deep-rooted fury. It must have taken an awful lot of effort to create the tableaux described in the newspaper. The murderer is either driven by a manic sense of revenge and hatred, or else they want to make a big point with the killings.'

'Showing off?'

'I guess so.'

'And your suggestion is that, either way, it doesn't look like they've finished the job just yet,' Pendragon concluded grimly, drinking down his coffee and pushing away the empty cup. He beckoned the waitress so he could get the bill, and started to rummage in his pocket.

'Let me,' Gemma said.

'Certainly not. You've been offering useful information to the police – definitely my shout!'

She laughed. 'Well, if you put it like that.' Then she paused for a second, clearly weighing up whether or not to say something.

'What?'

'How about I return the favour?'

Pendragon gave her a questioning look.

'I have two tickets to a concert – tonight, at the Barbican.'

Pendragon could not disguise his surprise. 'Well, yes . . .' he stumbled.

'Don't you want to know what's on first?' Gemma laughed.

'No . . . well, yes.'

'It's a theremin performance.'

'Oh . . . interesting.'

She gave him a sceptical look, tilting her head to one side.

'No, really,' Pendragon said quickly. 'I like all sorts of music. And the theremin is . . . unusual.'

Gemma clapped her hands together. 'I never know when to believe you,' she said. 'I quite like that. Okay, how does seven-thirty sound? I'll pick you up at your place if you give me the address?'

'Sounds good to me.'

Chapter 30

Pendragon was staring into space, his feet up on his desk, chair tilted back. Outwardly, he might have been recalling a favourite holiday or reliving some other fond memory, but in fact his mind was churning over the facts of his current investigation. For him this was a pleasurable exercise, in spite of the gruesome details. Naturally, he wanted to solve the puzzle as quickly as possible. He had Superintendent Hughes breathing down his neck for a start, and she would have her boss, Commander Ferguson, breathing down hers, but Pendragon had become a policeman primarily because he loved solving puzzles. For him the thrill of what he did lay in the intellectual exercise, the chase. But there was no denying that this case was proving frustrating, to say the least.

Three murders, each incredibly contrived . . . the most contrived he had ever experienced, in fact. In spite of what he had said to Gemma Locke about the choice of paintings, he couldn't get out of his head the idea that there was some sort of message in the way the bodies had been arranged. Why would anyone do this? That was the question underlying the whole investigation. But all he had to go on were scraps, a few of the jigsaw pieces, and so many others were still missing. The solution seemed to be receding rather than becoming clearer. The first two murders had been linked in more ways than their gory scenarios. The two victims had known each other, intimately. It had even seemed possible then that the killings were somehow linked to the personal relationships within the relatively small group of artists and dealers in the East End. But then Pendragon had been thrown two curveballs. The first was the fact that Kingsley Berrick had gangland connections, and then, more importantly perhaps, the fact that the third victim, Michael O'Leary, had been a priest with seemingly no connection whatsoever to the art community.

Pendragon pushed back his chair and swung his legs off the desk. He leaned forward and punched in the number of a local pub, the Duke of Norfolk. It was Sammy Samson's favourite and he could usually be found there at most times of the day. Jack spoke to the landlord, Denny West, who had always been civil towards the DCI, and in a few moments Sammy was on the other end of the line.

'Jack, old boy. What may I do you for?'

'A little more digging, Sammy. If you're up for it?'

'Always happy to help.'

'Good. I'm after any information you can find on a company called Rembrandt Industries . . . Yes, as in the painter. It was the one who rented the warehouse in West India Quay, remember? My lads are doing their bit, but I wondered if you'd heard anything about the firm on the grapevine.'

'Can't say I have, dear boy. But that doesn't mean I won't . . . if there's anything to find out. What sort of thing do you want to know?'

'Well, they seem to be a fly-by-night operation. I'd be particularly interested if any of your associates had had any dealings with them, anything at all.'

'All right, leave it with me.'

Pendragon put the phone down and dialled Colette Newman's number at the Lambeth Forensics Lab.

'Inspector,' she said, 'we must have a telepathic connection. I was just about to call you.'

'Oh?'

'I've found something I think you might be very interested in.'

'A DNA trace?'

'Can you come over?'

'Absolutely. I'm putting on my coat as we speak.'

Pendragon strode along the corridor. It was quiet and he realised he had lost all track of the time. Glancing at his watch, he was surprised to see it was only five o'clock. He nodded to Terry Vickers who was on duty at the front desk and stepped out into the freezing evening. The traffic was building up, but he felt unusually calm as he drove along the slushy streets. It was good to be alone, without even Turner in the seat beside him. He had always been a private – even occasionally isolated and closed-off – man who enjoyed his own company, but for the past six months, he had been unusually busy and it was only at moments such as this that he realised how claustrophobic and intense his London life was. He suddenly felt the press of people all around him.

He'd had an active, busy professional life with the Thames Valley Police, and had enjoyed his work there, but it had not been quite so full-on. Although he had not realised it at the time he was working in Oxford, he had been ready for a big change. Then Jean had left him, forcing him into a life-altering situation, and, strangely perhaps, that change had energised him, kick-started something that was long overdue.

He still only vaguely understood his reasons for returning to the place of his birth. Intellectually, it was obvious. He was trying to reclaim the security of childhood, hoping to return to a simpler, more innocent time. But, on an emotional level, he could not quite come to grips with this thought. He was far too much of a rationalist to do that. He could recognise emotional frailty in others, but found it inconceivable that the idea could apply to himself.

The streetlights flashed by; the icy slush off the road slapped against the underside of the car. From far away, he could hear a siren and glimpsed the flashing light of an ambulance down a side street. By the time he reached the Forensics Laboratory on Lambeth Road, he felt himself engulfed in an almost Zen-like calm he had not experienced in years.

'Inspector,' Dr Newman said, opening the door on to the corridor outside her office. She waved him to a chair and handed him a read-out. He tried to decipher it as he sat down. Colette Newman perched herself on the edge of the desk. She was wearing an unbuttoned white lab coat with, underneath this, her usual ensemble of knee-length skirt and pristine blouse.

'We found some strands of waxed cotton and paint that match those from the cherry-picker,' she told him. 'Also, samples of blood and tissue from both of the first two victims, Berrick and Thursk. But the most interesting thing is this read-out.' She handed the DCI a single sheet of paper that had been lying on the desk. 'There were half a dozen hairs on the floor close to the metal hole punch in the warehouse,' she said, coming straight to the point. 'Long blonde hairs, so clearly not from any of the three victims. It was a bit touch and go getting a usable DNA sample from them, but we managed it.'

'So it's a question of hoping we can get a match from the national database?'

'It's done.'

'What?' Pendragon looked astonished, then shook his head. 'Fantastic.'

'Sort of.' Dr Newman tapped at her keyboard and turned the screen so they could both see it. 'Here.' And she positioned her index finger a millimetre from the screen. 'We have ten matching markers linking the sample from the hairs in the warehouse with this individual on the database, number 3464858r.'

'Well, that's pretty conclusive, isn't it?'

'Oh definitely. There's no doubt that the hair belongs to this person. That wasn't the problem, but the "r" in the designation was. It stands for "restricted".'

'Ah.'

'Yes, ah. Naturally I got on to the database administration centre right away. But they knocked me back. Seems there are levels of "r" ratings in the database designation system. The highest level "r" is given to politicians, senior civil servants and top military brass. But until the rules were tightened up in the late nineties, it was also awarded to a few very wealthy private citizens.'

Dr Newman saw Pendragon's disappointed expression. 'However, I am nothing if not dogged,' she said quickly and raised her eyebrows. 'I contacted a senior colleague at Cambridge University who has a Level Three Civil Service clearance, and owes me one. He had the identity of our restricted individual within half an hour.'

Pendragon exhaled loudly through his nose. 'Okay. Who is it?'

'A former female patient at Riverwell Psychiatric Hospital in Essex.'

'Former? When did she get out?'

'Depends what you mean by "getting out", Inspector. Number 3464858r died in 1996. Her name was . . .' and she flicked through three pages of notes on her desk '. . . Juliette Kinnear.'

Chapter 31

To Mrs Sonia Thomson
14 October 1888

I have to admit, dear lady, that your husband Archibald always did his best to be a most entertaining companion. He seemed to take an immediate shine to me. He told me all the things about himself that you would, of course, know already: his middle-class upbringing in Shropshire, his reading English at Cambridge, and his earliest forays into the world of journalism. He described how, by the age of forty, he had become the editor of the *Daily Tribune*, and had then made the momentous decision three years ago to set up a paper of his own, the *Clarion,* in partnership with a fantastically wealthy patron named Lord Melbourne.

'My vision, Harry, is to drag newspapers into the modern era. I think journalism should be stronger, more graphic. And I would love to use photography, though it's all so damn complicated, and expensive,' he told me the evening we first met, over that promised drink which he bought me in a seedy pub called the Duke of Lancaster.

I had spun an interesting background yarn for him. I told him my name was Harry Tumbril – you'll have to forgive me; this little touch of black humour came to me on the spur of the moment. As Harry, I was an artist from South London. I had, according to my tale, just recently returned from France and a spell living in Paris. I was currently living in Whitechapel to prepare the sketch for a commission I had received from an English family who now lived in Lyons. It came to me as I said it, almost as though the words and story had materialised in my mind from some external source. Archibald did not question it, and why should he have?

'Can I see some of your sketches?' he asked.

I handed him my pad, filled with images of scantily clad prostitutes and music-hall performers, and he flicked through it. Stopping only to order another round of drinks, he turned the pages and studied my work with care. 'Very good,' he said slowly, without lifting his eyes from the page. Then, looking up, he added, 'You are *very* talented.'

I smiled and offered him a nod of thanks.

'You could make some money from these, you know, Harry. I have contacts in some of the less salubrious areas of the publishing business.'

I plucked the sketchpad from his fingers. 'Thanks, but no.'

'Well, if you ever change your mind.'

I stared at him, and for the first time really

studied the man. I have no need to describe him to you, of course, but as I write this I can't shift from my mind a very clear image of him as he was that first night we met. Archibald was a big, beefy fellow, was he not? Not fat, just chunky, with a huge head, a mop of brown-grey curls, ruddy cheeks, and what I earlier called those dog-like eyes. He was dressed quite ordinarily as would befit a trip to the Stew, and was a little dishevelled from our eventful escape from the Pav. He had lost his hat and his jacket was covered with dust at the shoulders.

I immediately had the feeling with Archibald that he too was something of an actor. Not in the way I performed, of course, but I couldn't help thinking that he led something of a double life. As I have already said, you, dear lady, probably saw just one side to him, I the other. He was, to a large extent, what I would call a man's man, and was immediately open to expressing his own vision of the world. At home he was almost certainly a perfect gentleman, but I saw straight away that Archibald was a man who took his pleasures very seriously.

I declined his offer of a third drink, but he ordered three more for himself in quick succession. Meanwhile he talked, not a word of it slurred, his mind remaining focussed and sharp. He told me of his love of sex, and of his adventures in the opium dens of London and elsewhere. He was perfectly frank about these things and, oddly, I did not find myself repulsed as I had previously been by the carnal and hedonistic impulses of the sheep milling around me everywhere I went. Perhaps it was because no one had ever really talked to me with such honesty before, or perhaps it was simply that I saw Archibald as in many respects superior to the dullard masses with whom I shared the fetid air.

Archibald was intelligent . . . no, he was *very* intelligent . . . ambitious, probing, inquisitive, acquisitive and energetic. I can't say I ever liked him, I don't really understand the word 'like', but I found I had an odd, grudging respect for him. He was almost seductive, in a funny sort of way. He was a man in love with the world; a man completely at home within his own skin and in the city in which he lived. Archibald Thomson was what Mr Darwin would describe as a creature that had found its niche.

But, you know me. After we'd waved goodbye on the corner of the street, I forgot all about him. Returning to my lodgings, I spent a few quiet moments cleaning my knives and oiling the saw, then I flicked through the sketches I had made earlier that night.

It was with some surprise that when I arrived at the Pav the following evening, I found myself accosted by a young servant who ran up and handed me a cream envelope with the name 'Harry Tumbril' written across it in an elegant, but obviously masculine, hand. It was a brief note from Archibald, inviting me to lunch the next day at the offices of the *Clarion*, Pall Mall.

No more than six miles from my new home in Whitechapel, Pall Mall was a different world entirely, more reminiscent of the one I had visited with my father years earlier. It was as though all the wealth and sophistication, all the things that people consider clean and virtuous and wholesome, had been sucked out of the East End and deposited on the western side of the city, to form an atmosphere of cloying smugness.

Even the sun had come out after days of overcast weather. God truly is a capitalist, I thought, as I turned into the newspaper office's doorway and pulled on the bell next to a pristine, freshly painted scarlet door. A servant ushered me in and led me up a broad staircase. I could hear sound spilling out from the rooms above: urgent, self-important voices, bells ringing, the stamping of feet. We emerged on to a sun-splashed landing and I followed the servant through a door, along a corridor and then through another door, whereupon I found myself in a large room packed with men sitting at desks.

The air was filled with the clatter of typewriters, the smell of cigarette smoke and sweat, and constant shouting as news flew around the room like some real, corporeal thing batted from man to man. Without breaking his stride, the servant marched towards another, smaller room. It was walled in glass, though the door was closed. I could see Archibald on the other side of the glass. He held a strange contraption against his ear. Turning towards us, he beckoned me in. The servant bowed and vanished.

Archibald indicated a seat but then, ignoring me, started to speak into the contraption held close to his head. Then I realised what it was. I had read in *The Times* about these things. Of a sudden he was finished. With a curt, 'goodbye', he replaced the device, a cylindrical black object, on a squat rectangular box in front of him on the desk.

'Damned accursed things,' he said, standing up and offering me a hand. 'Alexander Graham Bell should be taken out at dawn and shot,' he went on. 'A telephone, Tumbril. Seen one before?'

I shook my head. 'No.'

'Can't hear a damn thing most of the time. And when I do, all I get is demands from my financiers. We're the only people who have the bloody things ... millionaires and harassed newspaper editors! Still, I suppose that's progress for you. I'm told that one day every home will have one.' And he laughed. 'Come on then, Harry. Let's go to lunch. I'm famished. Reform Club all right with you?'

It was a short walk. Archibald marched along as though the seconds were passing faster than they actually were and he was trying to fit more into the day than was possible or reasonable. At the Reform Club, he nodded to the doorman and slipped him a shilling before ushering me into the cool, cavernous interior.

As we ascended the grand marble staircase, we could hear voices coming from one of the rooms on the first floor; a peal of laughter followed by the clink of cutlery. A waiter in white tie and tails met us at the top of the stairs and led us into a vast room with huge windows offering a view over St James's Park. We sat at a table to one end of the room close to the windows and Archibald ordered a bottle of claret. 'It's not half bad here, Harry,' he said. 'Quite a decent wine list.'

I gazed around me at the opulence and inhaled the scent of wealth and privilege. I was used to such things, had mixed with company far beyond my social standing at Oxford, and there was nothing the Reform could offer that I had not previously experienced at the Oxford Union or High Table at Christ Church. I could tell, though, that Archibald was enamoured of it all. He was a clever, educated man, but had only recently come into money after working his way up the slippery pole to mix with those who ran the country. He confessed to me once that at Cambridge he had been forced to keep to himself and had got by on a meagre allowance because his father was struggling financially at the time.

'Don't look round, but we have rather a decent turnout today,' Archibald said matter-of-factly.

I gave him a puzzled look.

'Quite a broad spectrum of the great and the good. Over there is Henry James the novelist.' And Archibald nodded discreetly to a point beyond my left shoulder. 'Oh, and Henry Irving the actor. Overrated if you ask me. And, well, well, well, what a surprise . . . there's Dilke.'

I gave him another puzzled look.

'Charles Dilke? The politician?'

I nodded and looked down at my menu.

'I'm astonished the man has the cheek to show his face so soon after the scandal. Oh, well. And . . . oh, goodness.'

I looked up and frowned. 'Who now, Archibald? The Queen?'

'Almost, Harry. Gladstone. God, he looks positively prehistoric.'

I turned at this and saw a very old man sitting at a corner table, two much younger men accompanying him. He was eating a bread roll with such tiny bites I could not imagine how he would ever finish it, let alone make it to the soup course. When I looked back, Archibald was still staring. I gave a brief cough and he broke away.

'Why have you invited me to lunch?' I asked.

He was about to reply when the waiter appeared to take our orders. The wine waiter then topped up our glasses, and Archibald raised his. 'To fortunate meetings,' he said, and there was a silence for a moment as we savoured the fine claret. 'A bit too sharp at the top end,' Archibald said judiciously. I searched his face for a moment, thinking he might be making a joke, but he was perfectly serious. I felt a sudden wave of nausea, took another sip of my wine, and it passed.

'I appreciate the gesture,' I said. 'But why did you invite me here?'

'To offer you a job of course, Harry.'

I was genuinely surprised, and Archibald laughed. 'Is it really so improbable?'

I shook my head slowly.

'Let me explain,' he went on. 'I want my news-paper to be modern.' He almost hissed the last word. 'These fellows,' and he waved a hand towards the famous men seated around the room, 'most of them are yesterday's men. They are rooted in the nineteenth century, while I am a man of tomorrow. I'm already thinking like a man of the twentieth century, Harry.'

I studied his face in silence. I was not interested in a single word he was saying, but I had lost none of my ability to fool others.

'I intend to be radical,' he went on. 'Not so much in the political sense, although my convictions do lean that way, I'm thinking more about the style of the *Clarion*, Harry. The way we report. I want my paper to epitomise the coming age, not pay lip service to an era that is passing.'

'Forgive me, Archibald,' I said. 'But I don't understand what that has to do with me.'

The first course arrived as he was about to reply. It did not slow him down. Between mouthfuls, he ran on. 'I've seen your work. I like what you do. You have guts. You're not afraid to represent reality. I want you to be my number one illustrator.'

'But you already have artists.'

'I do. But none of them has your eye.'

'I'm flattered,' I lied.

He looked at me eagerly, with that ridiculously

enthusiastic expression of his, and I felt like retching again. 'All right, Harry. Let me make it clear. This city . . .' And he paused, wiped his mouth and swept out one hand to encompass the view visible through the windows. 'This city is a most wretched place. Every day we report at least one terrible murder – vile acts from every level of society. I want to let our readers see the reality. I'm tired of pussyfooting around with euphemism and innuendo.'

'But you must have rules and guidelines to follow?'

'We do, but there is leeway, my good fellow. The written word is one thing, but I want to capture the true nature of our modern world using the skill of men like yourself. All my artists are competent draughtsmen, but none of them has your sense of realism.'

I was not sure what to say. I studied Archibald's face and realised for the first time that the man was most probably insane, or at least heading along the road to insanity. He was perfectly able to function and may yet have much to offer the world, but he was becoming unbridled, losing track of himself.

'What about photography?' I said after a long silence. 'Surely that's the modern way to proceed?'

He exhaled loudly and shook his head dismissively. 'Have you seen how long photographers take to set up their equipment? And have you seen the quality of their work when they have? No, Harry, the future is all about ideas, not gadgets. It's like that damned telephone, it's a gimmick. No, it's up here,' he proclaimed, tapping his forehead, his cheeks flushed with excitement and claret. 'It's up here. That's where the future is made. Ideas, Harry, ideas.'

I was about to point out to him that gadgets came from ideas, when, out of the corner of my eye, I noticed movement. Archibald turned, a puzzled look on his face, and then his expression relaxed. The head waiter appeared at our table. Beside him was a young man in a cheap, ill-fitting suit. He had a light fuzz of hair in the middle of his chin, very pale skin and small brown eyes.

'Sir, this fellow says he has a message for you.'

'Yes, thank you, Cartright,' Archibald said, standing up. 'Please leave us.'

The man took two steps backwards and then turned with a flourish, called over an underling and strode towards the kitchen.

'Harry,' Archibald said to me, returning to his seat and indicating to the young man that he should sit for a moment, 'this is one of my lads from the office – James Shallworthy.' He turned to the young man. 'What is it, Jim?'

'I'm sorry to . . .'

Archibald waved his hand again. 'Just get on with it.'

'Sir, there's been an 'orrible murder.'

Archibald shot me a glance, then fixed the messenger with a stern stare. 'Where?'

'Just down the road in Charin' Cross, sir.'

*

It was a double murder. You must have read about it in the newspaper, dear lady; your husband's newspaper, in fact. It was not an incident to be easily forgotten. A double killing: of the actor Donald Peters and his lover and co-star Mildred Nantwich. The murderer, Mildred's estranged husband Norman Nantwich, was imprisoned the same evening when he turned up at Charing Cross Police Station to confess to the murder, his hands, face and coat still covered with blood.

Archibald sent his assistant back to the newspaper office and hailed a hansom on Pall Mall. We were at the murder scene within a few minutes. The deed had been done in Donald Peters's dressing-room at Toole's Theatre on William IV Street. There was a hubbub in front of the venue with police escorting away theatre-goers who were angrily waving tickets for the cancelled matinee performance.

'We'll take the back entrance,' Archibald said as we alighted from the cab. 'I know the owner, John Toole, very well.'

Archibald also evidently knew his surroundings, because within a few moments we were inside without a single person preventing us. He led the way through a maze of corridors and up a flight of stairs. At the top a corridor led to the actors' dressing-rooms.

We could hear sounds coming from one of the rooms on the left, and then two policemen emerged. Immediately behind them appeared a tall, well-built man with a massive handlebar moustache. He was

heavily jowled and greying. 'But this is preposterous!' I heard him say, his voice little more than a
growl.

Archibald strode along the passageway towards
them. I stood where I was, just watching,
intrigued.

'Toole, old chap,' I heard Archibald boom.

The two policemen and the theatre-owner turned
as one.

'Thomson?' the man responded. 'What the
devil . . .?'

One of the policemen stepped forward with his
hand held out to prevent Archibald's approach. 'I'm
afraid, sir . . .'

'Oh really, officer,' he snapped. 'I'm a newspaper
editor.'

'I don't care who . . .'

'Look here, Thomson. This really isn't the time,'
Toole interrupted.

'There *has* been a murder here, has there not?'

'Well, yes, but . . .' the theatre-owner blustered.

'Sir,' the policeman said again. He stepped
forward and placed a restraining hand against
Archibald's chest. The newspaper man simply
looked down at it and then gave Toole a hard look.

'If you want an accurate report on this incident
written by a friend, John, I would suggest you let
me in.'

Toole gazed back at him. From where I stood, I
could see the lines of strain on the theatre-owner's
face, and his eyes looked wild. He was clearly

struggling to contain his panic. I could sense the fear in him. It was quite a heady sensation, actually.

'Officer,' Toole said, 'the gentleman has my permission to remain.'

'That's not really the point, sir,' the policeman began, but Archibald was already in the room. In all the commotion, I too approached the door to the dressing-room, completely ignored, and stepped inside.

I shuddered and must have made a sound because Toole noticed me then.

'And who the hell are you?' he snapped.

'He works for me,' Archibald interceded.

I ignored them all, intent on soaking up the scene. It was a beautiful thing to behold. Both victims had been stabbed. The woman lay over the dead man. A knife was still embedded in her back. She was wearing a petticoat stained red. The walls were splashed with blood, the mirror over the dressing table was crimson-spattered, as though an artist had taken a brushful of paint and flicked it randomly. It took me only a moment to record the entire scene in my mind, every detail noted.

Toole was shaking his head. 'All right, Thomson,' he was yelling, 'that's quite enough, old chap.'

One of the policemen grabbed me by the arm and I saw the other take a grip on Archibald's shoulder.

'You really should talk to me, John,' Archibald insisted as he was turned towards the door.

I caught a glimpse of Toole as I was escorted through the doorway to the corridor. He had lowered himself on to his haunches in the corner of the room, his head in his hands, sobbing quietly.

It was growing dark by the time I reached my lodgings on Wentworth Street. I lit the single gas lamp, moved my table directly beneath it and began to sketch.

I was so absorbed in my work that I completely lost track of time. When I pulled out my watch and looked at it, I was amazed to find that it was past midnight. It was only as I returned to the real world that I realised how cold and hungry I felt. But I was indifferent to my own condition. Staring into space, I relived the delicious scene at Toole's Theatre. The sketches of it were very good. I was pleased with them. And then I began to think about Archibald, and our conversation at the Reform Club. Suddenly it all seemed to fall into place. What glorious serendipity it had been that I should meet your gracious husband, dear lady. What delectable good fortune that he should have seen my sketches from the Pav, and liked my work. What a splendid coincidence that he should want to have an artist working on his newspaper in the way in which I worked. He had unwittingly put me in the perfect position to facilitate my plans. For, during the course of the two days between meeting Archibald and going to lunch with him, I had drawn up my list of victims. I had catalogued their movements; ensured that they would each be suitable models for my work. And now, thanks to my new friend, the half-mad newspaper proprietor, I had a perfect excuse for being at the scene of any murders that might – by pure chance, of course – start occurring in and around Whitechapel. What a splendid prospect that was.

Chapter 32

London, Monday 26 January, evening

The theremin concert was held in one of the smaller halls of the Barbican. It was sold out. Pendragon had been secretly sceptical before the event, but after a few minutes he found himself enjoying it. He had heard of the theremin, though he knew very little about it. He remembered reading once that it was the only instrument played without any physical contact being made between the musician and the instrument itself. Instead, the performer moved their hands close to a pair of antennae, which modulated both sound and volume. But, not wishing to seem ignorant, he had done his homework in a spare five minutes at the station, reading what Wikipedia had to say about the instrument – how it had been a spin-off from a Russian government-funded experiment into proximity sensors. The instrument had become quite popular in the 1930s then fallen out of fashion, though Robert Moog, inventor of the synthesiser, had attributed his youthful fascination with the theremin as a key influence on his own innovation.

Tonight's theremin player was the leading proponent of

the art, a French woman named Françoise Guillaume. It helped that she was strikingly beautiful with long blonde locks and what was obviously, even from eight rows back, a magnificent figure. But the repertoire was also brilliantly eclectic – versions of Mozart, Grieg, Miles Davis and Jimi Hendrix, which were all perfectly recognisable but cleverly altered.

Leaving the theatre, Jack said nothing. He waited for Gemma to break the silence, but she seemed to be lost in thought, only turning to him when he suggested a drink at a little wine bar he knew on Beech Street. Outside, it was freezing and they pulled their collars up against the biting wind and strode through the car park and on to the main road. The wine bar was busy, but they found a quiet corner away from the theatre crowds where they could at least hear each other speak.

'So, what did you think, Jack?'

'I have to confess, before it began I was sceptical, but I really enjoyed it.'

'Good. It's healthy to push yourself outside your comfort zone occasionally.'

Pendragon nodded and took a sip of his wine. 'When you get to my age, it's all too easy to play it safe.'

'Listen to you! "When you get to my age"! You're what? Early forties?'

'Yes, Gemma,' he mocked.

She looked at him, serious-faced.

'Actually, it'll be my birthday in a few days. I'll be forty-seven . . . God!'

'Well, you look very well preserved.'

He smiled and inclined his head in thanks.

'As an artist, I'm all for people staying young – mentally, anyway.'

'You live for art, body and soul, don't you, Gemma?'

She looked a little surprised, but admitted, 'Well, yes, I do.' She drank some wine and added, 'Quite simply, it's the most important thing in the world.'

'I once knew a painter,' Pendragon said. 'An old girlfriend actually . . . at Oxford. She said to me that if she could choose between a Titian or the invention of the wheel, she would pick the Titian.'

Gemma sipped her wine and placed the glass back on the table. 'I'm right there with your old girlfriend on that,' she said. 'No question. The thing is, the wheel provides the world with a practical advance, but the Titian feeds the soul.'

'Fair enough, but if you can't eat, you can't appreciate art. And if the wheel had not been invented, we wouldn't have got far as a race, now would we?'

'So what? It's a chicken and egg situation with technology. Humans invent the wheel and so civilisation evolves. Life becomes more comfortable. Then more people come into the world needing food and transport. And so on it goes. Art is above all that.'

Pendragon looked at her thoughtfully and swirled the wine in his glass.

'It's all about Truth-seeking,' she went on. 'Whatever form of art we're talking about, it only has value if the creator is trying to represent Truth. Ninety-nine per cent of what's created is worthless because it is not honest, it's just entertainment. Think of all the horrible pop songs you hear, with their fake sincerity and ersatz emotion. Art isn't about painting cute kittens, nor is it about romantic stories in which the heroine is swept off her feet by a tall, dark stranger who treats her mean. None of that is Truth. Titian is Truth. Dylan is Truth. Dostoyevsky is Truth.'

'All right,' Jack responded. 'But what about the ego of the artist? There's always that to consider, is there not? There must always be that element of the individual putting themselves into what they create.'

'Naturally, Jack. We're talking about human beings. Artists are rarely anything else!'

He laughed. 'Fair enough. But there's a thornier problem. Truth can't be pure because the way it is perceived by the artist or the creator is not necessarily faithfully represented by them, is it? Theirs may be a distorted vision of the Truth. Which means that, sometimes, the end result is pretentious rubbish, no matter how honest the artist is being.'

'Sure,' Gemma agreed. 'But that's because of the other imperative of the artist.'

He gave her a puzzled look.

'The need to innovate. An artist has to seek Truth, but also represent it in a new way.'

'Which is what the Surrealists were doing, for instance?'

'What all real artists have done, down through the ages.'

'Yes, but I was thinking specifically about the case I'm working on now and the artists who have been imitated.' And he caught himself gazing into space. 'I'm sorry.' He shook his head. 'Talking shop . . . thinking out loud.'

Gemma smiled. 'I think we need more wine.' And she held up her empty glass.

Chapter 33

Brick Lane, Tuesday 27 January, 7.30 a.m.

Pendragon was sitting in silence watching Superintendent Hughes flick through his latest report on the investigation. After a few moments she lifted her head, placed her interlocked fingers over the pile of paper and let out a pained sigh.

'So, we have a potential murderer who's been dead for over fifteen years? Excellent. An arrest should be easy.'

Pendragon met the superintendent's eyes, his face expressionless.

'Theories?' she enquired. 'Anything at all?'

'Oh plenty of theories, Super,' Pendragon responded. 'But they are just that – theories – unsubstantiated by anything like a single fact.'

Hughes looked at him, keeping her silence, forcing Pendragon to talk on.

'There are three possibilities for us to consider. One: there was some mistake with the DNA. But Dr Newman assures me that is not an option. There are so many matching markers that it is a six billion to one chance the DNA does not belong to the deceased Juliette Kinnear. Two: the woman isn't in fact dead. We got on to Riverwell in Essex straight away. They emailed over a single sheet of facts and dates. Turner did some additional checking. Juliette Kinnear drowned during a hospital excursion to Maldon. The incident was witnessed by a Riverwell nurse, Nicolas Compton. The body was found two days later and identified by a family member. The girl was cremated. Full police records are extant.'

'All right,' Hughes said wearily. 'The third option better be good, Jack.'

Pendragon ran one palm over his forehead. 'I wish it were, ma'am,' he said. 'The only conclusion we can draw is that the murderer planted the DNA.'

'Planted it!'

'To throw us off the scent. It wouldn't be the first time it had been done.'

'Yes, Jack, it's been done once before – the Mettlin case in Manchester, right?'

He nodded.

'But that was very different. The planted DNA was from another gangster, an erstwhile "friend" of the real culprit, a living person who might easily have committed the crime if he hadn't been beaten to it by the real killer, Johnny Mettlin. That was also eight years ago when DNA analysis was not so sophisticated.'

'I know the facts, ma'am,' Pendragon responded. 'But the two scenarios are not that different. Hair may easily be preserved.'

'But the owner of this DNA has been dead for fifteen bloody years!'

It was Pendragon's turn to stay silent.

'Okay,' Hughes said after an uncomfortable thirty

seconds. 'What does Newman think about this scenario?'

'That it's certainly possible the sample could have been planted.'

'Can she not tell if the hair has been preserved in any way?'

'No. That was the first thing I asked her when the first two options were written off.'

'So, what now?' The superintendent looked exasperated. 'We have three murders in under a week. A possible perp who has been dead a long time. No witnesses to any of them. Little in the way of other forensics. We don't have a lot to go on, Inspector.'

'I've contacted Riverwell. Turner and I have an appointment with the Chief Administrator there, a Professor Martins, at two o'clock. We need to get some more detailed background on Ms Kinnear.'

'What about nearer to home?'

'Inspector Towers and Sergeant Vickers are trying to find out as much as they can about the cherry-picker used in the second murder as well as ascertaining where the murderer set up shop after vacating the warehouse on West India Quay. Grant is following up on the background to the murdered priest. We're particularly interested in trying to find any link at all between him and the first two victims.'

Hughes was looking down at her desk and nodding.

'And I've got Sammy Samson sniffing around.'

She looked up. 'God help us.'

'He led us to the warehouse, and from there to the DNA,' Pendragon reminded her.

'Yes, I suppose we should be thankful for small mercies, shouldn't we?' Hughes said coldly. 'All right. Report to me the moment you get back from Essex.'

Pendragon stood up and walked to the door. As he turned the handle, the super added, 'And, Inspector, come back with some good news, okay?'

Chapter 34

The Riverwell Psychiatric Hospital was a small, private establishment three miles inland from the coastal town of Maldon. At any one time it accommodated no more than thirty-four patients, and according to the hospital's website offered exclusive pastoral care for those with chronic conditions.

Jez Turner was reading through the hospital's glossy brochure as Pendragon pulled the car up before a guarded gate set in ten-foot-high ornate iron railings enclosing the hospital grounds. Turner whistled suddenly, making Pendragon glance away from the uniformed gateman who was examining his ID through the open window.

'Get this, guv,' the sergeant said. 'Riverwell is world renowned as a centre of excellence for the care and comfort of patients with medium to severe conditions. Annual full board and treatment fees come in at just under seventy-two grand.'

Pendragon raised an eyebrow. 'More than I earn in a week,' he responded dryly, nodding to the guard and driving forward as the barrier was raised.

The building ahead of them looked more like a boutique hotel than a psychiatric hospital. It was brick-built with high gables in a steeply sloping roof, topped off

227

with a stocky chimney placed roughly in the centre of the roof. Pendragon guessed the original building had gone up in the first decade of the twentieth century, but he noticed that there had been many newer additions over the years and it had been extended so much these now made up the majority of the floor space. The grounds were pristine, and white with a hard frost.

They were met at the main door by a rotund man in his mid-fifties. He was wearing a pin-stripe suit, waistcoat and grey tie. He had a neatly trimmed white beard, small dark eyes and narrow lips. At first glance he looked like Santa after a make-over. 'Welcome,' he said in a rich baritone. 'I'm Professor Martins . . . Nigel Martins.' He stepped forward to offer his hand first to Pendragon and then to Turner. 'Good journey, I hope. It's not too far from the sound of Bow Bells, is it, Inspector?' His face creased into a smile.

He led them through a reception area where a pretty blonde at a flat-screen Mac ignored the new arrivals. They followed the professor along a wide corridor. It was softly lit, the floor covered with a sumptuous, pale green carpet. The walls were hung with what looked like expensive paper. A cream dado rail ran along them at waist-height, and there was elaborate ceiling cornicing overhead. They passed an open door and saw half a dozen patients sitting bunched together on a pair of sofas, facing a bulky old TV set high up on a shelf on the far side of the room. At the end of the corridor, they took a right, then a left, and Martins stopped before a heavy oak door with an engraved brass plaque bearing his name. The professor removed a bunch of keys from his jacket pocket, unlocked the door and held it open, gesturing to the two policemen to enter. Martins bustled in after them and indicated a pair of leather chairs. 'Gentlemen, please.' He turned as an elderly lady in a black skirt and white frilly blouse appeared in the doorway.

'Ah, Madeline,' Martins said. He looked enquiringly at Pendragon and Turner. 'Tea?'

Turner glanced at the DCI who was nodding. 'That would be very welcome,' Pendragon said. 'Milk, no sugar.'

'Same for me,' Turner said.

'Okay, that's the essentials out of the way,' Martins commented, lowering himself into his chair. 'Now . . . could you just run through what it is you're here for, Inspector? My secretary gave me a brief summary, but . . .'

'We're following a lead in a multiple homicide,' Pendragon replied, coming straight to the point.

'I see. Well,' Martins sighed, 'I'll obviously do everything I can to help, but what possible connection can there be with Riverwell?'

'Did your secretary mention that we were particularly interested in a patient who was here in the mid-nineties, a young woman named Juliette Kinnear?'

'No, she didn't. Good Lord, Juliette Kinnear! Now that's a name I haven't heard for a long time.'

'You were working here then?'

'Yes, I was. I transferred from Luton in 1993. Juliette arrived in . . . I think it was 'ninety-five. I'll get her file.' Martins touched a button on his desk phone. 'Selina, could you track down the file on Juliette Kinnear, please? She was a patient here in the mid-nineties. She'll be under

Archive K. If you could print out two copies and bring them in ASAP. Thanks.' He turned back to Pendragon. 'You'll know, of course, that Juliette is dead.'

'It happened on an excursion from the hospital, didn't it?' Turner put in.

Martins turned to the sergeant and sat back in his chair, arms folded across his chest. 'Yes,' he said. 'It was a terrible tragedy. We thought we were getting somewhere with Juliette. We still have no idea what really happened down at the jetty.'

'Can you talk us through it?' Pendragon asked.

Martins looked at the DCI for a moment and screwed up his mouth. 'Well, yes,' he said. 'It was quite a day. Certainly not one I'll easily forget.'

There was a short rap on the door then and the tea arrived. Madeline passed around the cups and withdrew without a word.

'It was a warm spring day in April 'ninety-six. Juliette had been here for about a year. When she first arrived, she was in a terrible state. We kept her away from the other patients for the first three months. She was anorexic, belligerent, never spoke. But gradually we got her to eat, and she slowly began to accept where she was. She was on some pretty strong medications, but was improving in herself. At least, we thought she was.'

'It seems she had come a long way . . . from when she was first admitted to the hospital. Being trusted to go on an excursion, even if was only to Maldon,' Pendragon remarked.

'Well, as I said, Juliette did make a fairly rapid improvement and we were feeling confident about her.'

'This trip to the town,' the DCI asked. 'What was the reason for it exactly?'

Martins shrugged. 'We believe it's important for our residents to leave the confines of Riverwell when they are able. As part of the rehabilitation process.'

'But surely Ms Kinnear was still a long way from leaving here permanently?'

'Yes, of course, but she was supervised and it was only a small group.'

'How many people were in it?' Turner asked.

Martins thought for a moment. 'Let's think . . . There were six patients and three staff.'

'Can you recall any names?'

He recited a list of staff members and Turner jotted them down in his notebook. 'I'm not sure of all six patient names,' the professor continued. 'But I can check and get back to you on that.'

Pendragon glanced at the list Turner had written down. 'Are all three members of staff still here?'

'No. Stacy Franklin is a senior nurse now, in London. Dr Roger Napier – who was supervising that day – left in 'ninety-eight. Last I heard, he was working in Melbourne. The other man on the list . . . Nick Compton . . . was a junior nurse. Sadly, he passed away a few months after Juliette's death.'

The two policemen looked startled to hear this. 'What happened?' Pendragon asked.

'Suicide. Poor Nick hanged himself.'

'Can you give us some further details, Professor?'

'It compounded the tragedy. Nick Compton always blamed himself for the accident. He was with Juliette,

231

you see. Had been left alone with her for a few minutes when . . .'

'There must have been an investigation into the incident?'

'Of course there was, Inspector,' the professor responded, a little testily. 'A very thorough investigation, as a matter of fact. I can get you full documentation.'

'That would be useful.'

'Obviously Dr Napier too came under close scrutiny. He was the most senior staff member present and Juliette was his patient. He was investigated for any possible negligence, and fully exonerated. He gave a very detailed account of the lead-up to the accident. One of the patients . . . Helen Weatherington, I seem to recall . . . had felt sick. The two nurses were otherwise occupied, and Napier had taken the girl to a washroom. Nick Compton had been supervising Juliette who decided she wanted to take a walk along the jetty. It was getting late and had started to rain. Nick tried to dissuade her from going, but the whole excursion seems to have fallen into chaos by that point. Nick was inexperienced and easily persuaded by Juliette, who was a very forthright and intelligent girl.'

'She went over the railings?'

'Yes. The police were called. Nick went into the water to try and find her and was almost drowned himself. There was no sign of her.'

'But the body was found some time later?' Turner commented.

'Yes.' Professor Martins looked ashen. 'Severely decomposed.'

There was a gentle tap on the door and they all looked

up. Selina came over to the desk with a sheaf of papers. 'Thanks,' Martins said, without looking at the blonde girl, and she retreated. The professor handed Pendragon a dozen printed pages. There was a picture of Juliette Kinnear, taken probably a year before her death. She looked thinner than in the picture Turner had found. The DCI glanced through the material with Turner reading over his shoulder.

'Juliette was rather an exceptional girl,' Martins said after a moment. 'She had been a promising young artist and also dabbled in writing and music. An all-rounder.'

'Do you have any idea what precipitated her mental collapse, or was it simply a gradual process?'

'Well, Inspector, it's a complex matter, as you'll appreciate. In Juliette's case, her breakdown appears to have been brewing for a while unnoticed. Then, you could say, the dam burst. It's a fairly common scenario.'

'Can you elaborate?'

'Juliette was a talented artist, there's no doubt about that, but probably not as good as she thought she was. Consequently she was not receiving the recognition she thought she "deserved". She experimented with drugs – we got some of the details out of her during group therapy. She believed she could enhance her artistic abilities and achieve success by taking the right cocktail of stimulants. When that failed, her mental stability began to slide, a decline exacerbated by the narcotics she continued to use. She was living with her father, John Kinnear, at Ashcombe Manor, near Braintree – about ten miles from here. He's dead now. Mrs Kinnear had died a few years before when Juliette was fourteen or fifteen. John hadn't remarried.' Martins paused for a moment then added, 'The family were biscuit manufacturers.'

'Yes, I know,' Pendragon commented.

'When I interviewed Mr Kinnear on Juliette's admission he recalled the way his daughter would lock herself away for days. She wouldn't eat, talked to no one, painted and painted and then destroyed the canvases in a fit of rage. She caused a small fire in the house while trying to burn her latest collection in her bedroom studio.'

'And no one thought this odd?' Turner asked.

'Well, yes, they did, Sergeant. But John Kinnear feared the embarrassment of Juliette's condition becoming public knowledge. He was worried about his business interests.'

The DCI raised his eyebrows. 'Naturally,' he said with a weary sigh.

'The tipping point came when she attacked the gardener.'

Pendragon had just reached the part of the report which described the incident, so was not too surprised. He looked up, scrutinising the professor's face. 'How serious was the attack?'

Martins swallowed and looked away for a second. 'The poor man was stabbed, Inspector.'

Pendragon glanced down, looking for a police report.

'There was no investigation.' Martins anticipated his question. 'John Kinnear managed to keep it quiet.'

Turner glanced at Pendragon. The DCI was staring blankly at the professor.

'Money talks,' Martins said matter-of-factly.

'He paid off the gardener?'

234

The professor nodded and shrugged. 'But Kinnear realised his daughter was seriously ill and she was sectioned.'

'And the gardener?'

'Macintyre, Jimmy Macintyre. He was a patient here for a short time after he was attacked. He's still alive, lives alone – in a housing estate in Braintree, a short distance from Ashcombe Manor.'

'We would like his address before we leave, if you have it?'

Martins nodded and leaned forward on the desk, hands clasped together over the report. 'Inspector, I fail to see the connection between Juliette Kinnear and your current investigation.'

'Well, we'll keep you informed of any developments there, Professor,' Pendragon said crisply, and stood up. 'Thank you for your time and co-operation. I take it we can have this,' he added, waving the report, and before Martins could say another word, had turned towards the door. 'The address for Mr Macintyre . . . I imagine your secretary would have that on file?'

Chapter 35

'Bloody odd,' Turner commented as they strode across the gravel driveway back to the car.

'Which part?'

'Well, all of it, actually. But how did the Kinnears get away with covering up a serious assault?'

'As Martins said, money talks.' Pendragon tossed him the car keys.

'So, what now?' the sergeant asked.

'We pay Jimmy Macintyre a visit.'

The country road taking them north-west towards Braintree was icy and treacherous. They drove slowly and stopped for a late pub lunch at a place called the Knight and Garter that was surprisingly good: a traditional ploughman's and beer, rather than Korean, Ethiopian, or the other exotic cuisines favoured by so many pubs made over by their brewery.

They found the address extracted from the archives at Riverwell without too much trouble, and pulled up outside a tiny brick-and-slate council house. Its red-painted front door had faded to a fleshy pink; there were traces of snow on the roof, frost on the windows. The garden had been left untended and was overgrown with weeds. As they approached, the policemen noticed the door was badly cracked and the letterbox simply a rectangular hole.

Pendragon rang the bell. The house remained silent. Turner stepped back on to the path and looked at the upper storey. There were no lights on, the curtains were all drawn. Pendragon rapped his knuckles on the door. Still no reply. He stepped back to join Turner and the sergeant had another go, leaning on the bell. Eventually they heard some shuffling sounds coming from the hall.

'Who is it?' The voice was frail, that of an elderly man.

'Police officers, sir. Is that Mr Macintyre?'

A silence. Then the sound of the man clearing his throat. 'What ya want?'

'My name is DCI Pendragon. We'd like to have five minutes of your time.'

'Why?'

'We wanted to ask some questions about Juliette Kinnear. The woman who attacked you.'

A longer silence.

'Mr Macintyre?'

'Go away.'

'Sir, we just need to ask you a few . . .'

'I said, go away.'

Pendragon looked at Turner, who shrugged.

'We've come a long way, sir,' Pendragon said gently, giving it one last try. 'Could do with a cup of tea.'

Silence.

'Sir?'

Silence.

Pendragon let out a sigh and turned towards the path. The sergeant hovered close to the door for a second and

237

then retreated. They had just reached the end of the path when they heard a sound. Pendragon spun round and saw that the door had opened a crack. They caught a glimpse of Macintyre, one hand extended, beckoning them in.

Jimmy Macintyre hung back behind the door as Pendragon and Turner stepped into the dark hall. 'Straight through. On ya right,' he said.

It was very dark inside the house and it grew darker as Macintyre closed the front door. A faint red glow was the only illumination, produced by daylight filtering through flimsy crimson curtains. The place stank of rotting food and urine. There was no carpet, just grimy ripped old newspapers forming a trail from the hall into what passed for a living-room. They could just make out a tatty armchair, the foam stuffing protruding at half a dozen points along each arm. Beside this was a metal-framed dining chair.

'Grab the chair from over there, young fella,' Macintyre said to Turner as he lowered himself into the armchair. The sergeant did as he was told, removing a pile of newspapers from another spindly metal chair. Pendragon sat down to the left of Macintyre.

Gradually their eyes adjusted, but they could still make out little in the room. Macintyre fidgeted in the armchair. He had a walking stick, which he placed against his left leg. He sat back, looking down at his lap. 'So, what do you wanna know?' he asked, then coughed suddenly, a raspy, guttural sound that seemed to go on for a long time.

'We've just come from Riverwell Hospital,' Pendragon began.

'Ah, I see. So you know the Kinnear girl is long dead.'

'Yes, Mr Macintyre. We were given the outline of the story. About her disappearance in 1996 on a day trip.'

Macintyre coughed again, noisily.

'We also learned that Juliette Kinnear had attacked you, and how that led to her being sectioned.'

The old man said nothing. He just kept looking down at his lap. All they could see of him was a dim outline.

'For a lot of people, 1995 was a long time ago,' Macintyre said, his voice little more than a whisper. 'Not for me. It was the thirtieth of November 1995, but it still feels like yesterday.'

'Are you able to talk us through it, sir?' Turner asked, trying to see a page of his notebook by holding it a few inches from his face. After a moment, he gave up and lowered it to his knees. He thought of asking if he could put on a light, but concluded it might upset Macintyre too much.

'I ain't spoken to anyone about it since I left the Kinnears' employ.'

'They paid you off?'

'Oh, yes. I didn't see much point in fighting 'em,' Macintyre responded quietly, still staring down. 'The girl was put away. They hoped she could be cured. I knew it would be in my own best interest to take "early retirement", so to speak, and to keep me mouth shut. Officially I wasn't stabbed, just had a bit of an accident in the grounds of the 'ouse.'

'I see,' Pendragon said. 'Do you feel able to tell us more about the attack? What might have provoked it, for instance?'

Macintyre looked up sharply. 'Provoked it? Nothin'

239

provoked it,' he snapped. 'I did nothin'. Absolutely nothin'. The Kinnear girl was mad. Didn't need no provocation.'

Pendragon let the man calm down, allowed him to go at his own pace.

'I was working on one of the flowerbeds. It was unusually mild that autumn. A busy time of year for a gardener, clearing away the leaves, turning the soil . . . Anyway, there I was behind the greenhouse. I knew the girl well. She used to come and talk to me sometimes. She was a strange kid, even before . . . She would paint in the garden. Crazy pictures, if you ask me. She'd paint the house and the gardens but the pictures looked nothing like anything I could see. Modern, I s'pose. Some folk seemed to think she was pretty good, but I could never see it meself.

'Anyhow, that Sunday she comes out into the garden and sits on the wall to talk, just like she often did. I thought she looked a bit odd. The pupils of her eyes were huge. I know now, of course, that she had been taking something. Suddenly she says, "Mac . . . Would you let me paint you?" I laughed. "What the 'ell would you wanna paint me for?" I said. "Anyway, I reckon it wouldn't look much like me when you'd finished." She laughed with me at that. Then she jumped off the wall.'

He fell silent again.

Turner glanced over at Pendragon, but even though his vision had begun to adjust to the darkness he could barely see his boss. Pendragon waited patiently.

'I saw a flash of something at the last moment. Didn't realise it was a bread knife, of course. Not exactly expecting it, was I?' Macintyre's voice had become almost inaudible. He seemed to realise this, shifted in his chair and cleared his throat. 'Fourteen wounds,' he said matter-of-factly. 'Lost pints of blood before a delivery boy just happened to notice me on the path. No one in the house had heard my screams.' He let the final word trail away. Pendragon and Turner could hear the old man breathing heavily. 'Sergeant?' he said after a moment. Turner could tell Macintyre was looking at him, but could see almost nothing more than the vague shape of his face. 'Could you please open those curtains a fraction?'

Turner glanced towards Pendragon, but could not make out his expression. Standing up, he picked his way through the gloom towards the red haze of the window, arms extended like a blind man. Then he felt the waxy fabric of the curtains between his fingertips, stopped and searched for the edge. Taking two steps to his left and running his hands along the fabric, he grabbed a fistful of curtain, and pulled it to his right.

Light flooded into the room. Turner spun on his heel, shading his eyes. He could see Pendragon with a hand at his brow and then lowering it before turning towards the hideously disfigured face of Jimmy Macintyre.

'Fourteen wounds,' the man said, his upper lip bisected by a scar that ran from where his left eye had once been, twisting it into a grotesque facsimile of a leer. 'All of 'em to the face.'

241

Chapter 36

To Mrs Sonia Thomson
15 October 1888

Now, Sonia . . . I hope you won't mind my being so informal, dear lady. It's just that, well, I feel we have grown to know each other quite well. I learned much about you from your loquacious husband, and you know more about me than anyone else ever has. Anyway, I have come to the part of my story in which I was finally able to put my ideas into action.

There is almost always a moment before beginning a new work in which there is a flutter of anxiety, a brief tremor of uncertainty. Can I do it still? Can I create? I'm sure I'm not the only artist or writer who has ever experienced such a thing. But, strange to report, on the morning of 31 August this year, less than two months ago, I felt no such trepidation. Indeed, I was so involved with my plans, so excited by the prospect of beginning my masterpiece, that I experienced none of the nervousness I might have expected.

I considered my notes and preliminary sketches.

The first victim: Mary Ann Nichols. Forty-three years old, five feet two inches, dark hair, grey eyes. A mother of four. Separated from her husband William. Well known locally as a 'bride' of no fixed abode. I checked my watch. It was 1.34 a.m. I pulled on my overcoat, picked up my bag and stepped out into the rain.

Heading straight for the Pav, I found the streets quiet. The music hall was closing up, but the brothel was open still. I took the stairs slowly and waited in the anteroom. It was empty and quiet. I picked up a newspaper and started to read. I knew Mary Ann worked here three nights a week. I had studied her routine and knew what to expect. At 2.15 she emerged from one of the rooms along a corridor to my left. As she strode by, I looked up. She was shorter than I had remembered and looked sick, malnourished. She eyed me lasciviously and paused beside me. 'Just finished tonight, darlin',' she said, smiling, her pale lips pulled back over crooked incisors, the front two upper and lower teeth missing. 'But I could spare time for you, sweetheart . . . if you're interested?'

I shook my head and returned to the newspaper.

'Suit yerself.'

She headed for the stairs and I heard the clink of coins as Mary Ann tossed them merrily in the air as she walked. She was clearly pleased with her evening's work. Perhaps she had made enough to cover the fourpence she needed for a bed in the lodging house she frequented at 18 Thrawl Street.

I waited a moment before I carefully folded the newspaper, stood up and followed her down the stairs. Emerging on to Whitechapel Road, I just caught sight of my prey as she turned a corner into a narrow side street. I had an idea where she was headed. I quickened my pace and reached the corner just in time to see the woman duck into a narrow doorway that I knew led to a drinking den run by a tough Irishman named O'Connor, whom I had already had the misfortune to meet during the course of my research.

I decided to wait in the narrow street, standing silently in the shadows. There was only one way in and out of O'Connor's place, and so I knew Mary Ann could not slip away without my seeing her. Thankfully, the rain had stopped and I was so charged up with excitement and expectation that the time seemed to pass quickly. And, sure enough, after half an hour the woman reappeared with a man on her arm. She was giggling drunkenly. The man looked more sober, but a little jumpy. He was young, pale-faced, with large, nervous eyes. I watched the pair turn into the lane in the opposite direction to Whitechapel Road. Keeping to the shadows, I followed as silent as a mouse.

I was soon lost in the back lanes, a maze of narrow streets and alleyways where the houses crowd in and shut out the sky. I had been in the East End for several weeks by this time, but was still unable to stomach the horrendous stench of the place. In these confined parts, where the roads ran with excrement and rats larger than some cats I've seen dashed through the shadows, the smell was almost overpowering.

It was also very dark. The only light came from the moon high overhead. But that was little more than a pallid, sickly yellow semi-circle streaked with cloud. My senses were heightened by excitement and honed by my many previous nocturnal adventures. I could hear the couple a few yards ahead of me, their breathing and the few words they exchanged.

They stopped and so did I. I heard the rustle of clothing. From the shadows, I could just make out two indistinct shapes. Mary Ann was leaning against the wall, her hands above her lowered head. Then came a few muffled groans. Words of encouragement from Mary Ann followed by a low growl. More rustling of clothes, a giggle, and then footsteps retreating along the passageway. Very quietly, I slipped my bag to the floor, unlatched the clasp and withdrew an eight-inch blade.

The cloud over the moon broke, and for a moment, the cobbled lane was lit up. I could see the woman adjusting her skirts. She looked up as the sliver of moonlight cast its tawdry gleam over walls wet with rain that had fallen earlier. I caught a glimpse of the side of Mary Ann's pale, pock-marked face. She had no idea I was there until I grabbed her from behind. With my left hand at her throat, I pulled her head back and drew the edge of my knife over her skin. As it slid from left to right, I pulled the metal back towards me, scything into flesh, right down to the vertebrae.

I have no recollection of the journey from Buck's Row, the alley in which I had dispatched my first whore, to my lodgings on Wentworth Street. No matter how hard I try, I cannot visualise anything from the moment Mary Ann's body slid to the floor until I found myself washing my hands and face in a bowl of water I had filled before leaving the room hours earlier. I recall gazing at my reflection in the tiny chipped mirror I used to shave with, which stood propped up behind the bowl. My blondish hair was plastered to my forehead, cheeks flushed. My eyes peered back at me, unnaturally black, the pupils huge. I glanced at the red water, and for an instant I was no longer in the filthy, low-ceilinged room over a corn-chandler's shop in Whitechapel. I was a small boy again, bent over a desk in my father's study, my mother's crimson handkerchief an inch from my nose. I found my face in the mirror again and produced a grin as wide as a Cheshire cat's.

I could not sleep. Instead I sat close to the window, listening intently to the sounds of the neighbourhood awakening to a new day, waiting for the first indications that the prostitute's body had been found. Around six o'clock I heard a commotion, the shriek of a police whistle. Checking myself in the mirror, I straightened my tie, pulled on my hat, tucked my sketchpad under my arm and stepped out into the breaking dawn.

There were two men in black suits crouched down beside the body and a policeman standing a few inches away from the dead woman's head. The officer looked up as I turned into Buck's Lane, and as I approached the two men beside Mary Ann's corpse turned to me in unison.

'And what can I do for you?' the policeman asked. 'This is a crime scene. Were you not stopped by one of my men?'

I produced a piece of folded paper from my jacket pocket and handed it to the officer. It was a letter of introduction from Archibald. 'I'm a newspaper artist,' I said. 'Harry Tumbril.'

The policeman glanced at the letter and sniffed. 'All right,' he mumbled. 'Keep out of everyone's way.'

I nodded and strode along the side of the narrow lane to get a better view. They had turned the woman over on to her back. The gash in her neck looked unnaturally red in the morning light. The blood at her throat had dried. It was now thickly encrusted, like a crimson rope or some bizarre necklace. Her skirt was up and her undergarments rent. I could see two deep cuts along her torso.

'How long has she been dead?' I heard the policeman addressing one of the other two men.

'A few hours, I would say. She's as stiff as a board.'

I pulled out my sketchpad and started to draw.

'My God! The poor unfortunate young woman,' Archibald exclaimed as he held the pad at arm's

247

length. We were standing in his office on Pall Mall. 'But that said, these are quite wonderful, Harry.' He looked me up and down, his face full of admiration. 'It's just . . . I don't know, old man. It's so damned hard to imagine what sort of bastard would do this, don't you think?'

I nodded. I was beginning to feel tired. Glancing at a clock on the wall, I noticed it was almost midday. I had not slept for more than twenty-four hours. The huge excitement I had felt, and which had kept me going, was fading. I still felt exhilarated, that much is irrefutable, but the heart-pounding thrill of standing beside those foolish plodders in Buck's Row as I sketched my victim and they pondered the manner of her death was beginning to give way to fatigue.

'So what do you say we pop along to the Reform? Have a glass or two?'

I shook my head. 'Not today, thank you, Archibald. Have to say I'm a little weary.'

He frowned and then his expression slid into a smile. 'Quite understand,' he said, and placed a hand on my shoulder. I shuddered involuntarily, but Archibald did not seem to notice. Squeezing my shrinking flesh, he added, 'You get along home. Have a good rest, Harry. I'll get these pictures into the evening edition.'

I felt uncommonly tired. Once I'd reached Wentworth Street I simply collapsed on to my bed and slipped into a dreamless, undisturbed sleep. When I awoke it was dark outside and quiet. I pulled my watch out and was staggered to see it was almost ten in the evening.

Now, if you'll please excuse me, Sonia, I must explain a few more things before I proceed with my story. I need to say a word or two about how an artist works. For I realise I have been steaming ahead, forgetting that you are but a simple woman who knows nothing of such things.

The fact is, an artist must employ a structure. By this I mean that for a work to be successfully executed, there have to be rules, guidelines. There must be discipline. Without this, art is mere anarchy and therefore valueless. I would go so far as to say that what distinguishes a true artist such as myself from a mere dauber is the way in which one such as I approaches each piece: with rigour and intelligence. And this was certainly how I approached my masterpiece. I had decided before initiating a single stroke of the knife that I would kill four women, and had developed a detailed plan of campaign. I had the names of my victims and a sizeable dossier on each of them gathered from weeks of research. I knew their movements and their habits. I knew their associates, and I knew a fair amount about the background of each of the ladies. I also knew exactly how I was going to arrange the representation of their corpses on canvas and what the incidental details captured in the pictures would be. Lastly, I had selected the colours I would be using. I had prepared the paints and the canvases. I knew exactly what I was doing.

Now, having said all that, art, be it painting, sculpture, music, even the written word, is not an automatic process. It is not a rigid, inflexible thing. It is organic, alive, ever-changing, vital and unpredictable. The crucial element of the unexpected is what makes the role of creator so satisfying. So, I had my plans . . . only to see them dissolve and be washed away by the irresistible force of spontaneity. Perhaps I was overwhelmed by the thrill of it all. Maybe I had begun to loosen my creative control. It doesn't matter. The simple truth is that as I woke up in that fleapit of a room I felt the unquenchable desire to kill again . . . and right away.

I deliberated over my disguise. It was essential to get it just right, not only for my own protection but because I wanted everything to be correct and precise in order to satisfy my artistic sensibilities. I had procured a black wig which fitted snugly over my own hair. I exchanged my usual suitably ragged top hat for a fashionable brown deerstalker. I applied colour to my face to darken my naturally pale complexion, and glued on, with great delicacy, a black-and-grey-flecked beard and moustache. Looking in the mirror over the wash bowl, I spent a few extra moments perfecting the line of the beard around my lower lip and positioning the deerstalker just so. At length, smiling at my reflection, I felt ready for anything.

Elizabeth Stride was to be my second victim. She was forty-seven, five foot tall and plump. A mother of three, she was a stereotypical Whitechapel whore who was fond of her drink and had ended up separated from her husband, estranged from her children, and living in a doss house in Spitalfields. I knew just where she would be that night. Just where she was every Tuesday and Thursday evening: on the corner of Hanbury Street and Spital Street.

I walked north along Osborn Street. A hansom passed me, splashing water over my boots, but I barely noticed. Turning into Hanbury Street, I saw Elizabeth some fifty yards ahead of me. She was leaning against a brick wall. She had a small bag in her hands and was swinging it: left, right, left, right. Coming closer, I could hear her voice. She was singing something I half-recognised from the Pav, a silly musical hall ditty. '*Oh! Mr Porter, what shall I do? I want to go to Birmingham. And they're taking me on to Crewe. Send me back to London, as quickly as you can. Oh! Mr Porter, what a silly girl I am!*'

'Good evening,' I said.

She seemed startled. My approach must have been quieter than I had realised. But then I could see she was drunk and caught the tang of gin on her breath. She pushed herself away from the wall and gave me a practised solicitous smile, an action she could perform no matter how drunk she was. 'Well, good evenin' to you, guvna,' she slurred. 'And what may I be doin' ya for?'

I gave her a brief encouraging smile. 'Well, I have a vivid imagination.'

'Lovely,' she replied, and, taking my hand, pulled

me along a few paces until I found myself in a narrow alley that stank of fish and cabbage. 'Over 'ere,' Elizabeth said, and I felt her fingers slip from mine. I could only just make out her shape in the gloom. But then her silhouette appeared with a sallow light behind it from a gas lamp set in a tenement window.

It started to rain and I felt water spatter my face. 'Over 'ere, darlin',' I heard the woman say, and her fingers closed around my privates. I gasped and felt a sudden wave of nausea. I reached my right hand into my jacket and extracated my favourite knife.

Elizabeth glanced down, saw the steel glinting in the dim light. 'Oh, no!' she mumbled, and then her face froze as I covered her mouth with my left hand and slid the metal between her legs. Pulling the blade away, I spun her round and brought the knife up to her throat, ran it across her neck and let her slump back as her warm blood ran over my fingers and down my wrist.

I had plenty of time, having decided days earlier exactly what I was going to do with the *material* at my feet. In the event, it did not take as long as I had anticipated. I made the incisions across Elizabeth's face, cutting the shape of a triangle on each cheek. I then set about the torso, opening her up and removing her womb. I draped a length of her intestine over her left shoulder and took out the right kidney. Pocketing this last item, I checked that no one was close by. I heard nothing. Standing up from my crouching position, I stretched, releasing the tension in my back. It ached rather. Removing a piece of chalk from my trouser pocket, I walked over to the brick wall a couple of yards from where Elizabeth Stride's feet lay. On the wall I wrote a message: 'The Juwes are not the men that will be blamed for nothing'. Stepping back, I surveyed my evening's work in the pale glow cast from the tenement.

I was back on Osborn Street in a moment. Pulling my hat low over my brow, I strode along the wet street, heading south towards Whitechapel Road. Within two minutes, I was at the corner of Wentworth Street, turning towards my lodgings on the left no more than twenty yards down the road.

Two police officers were walking towards me. I don't know why, but I overreacted. Perhaps it was simply the fact that I had just dispatched a woman and ripped her open. Or maybe it was because I had one of her kidneys in my pocket, oozing blood into the fabric of my coat. I turned as casually as I could and walked back towards Osborn Street, then, dodging the passing carriages, I reached the far side and afforded myself a glance backwards. The policemen were nowhere to be seen.

I was on Old Montague Street. I knew it well from my researches. Twenty yards beyond the busy junction with Osborn Street there was a narrow lane on the left that led to Finch Street. I ducked into the inky dark, letting the sounds of the late-night revellers, the braying of horses and the splashing of water on brickwork fall behind me.

Ten yards along the lane, I could barely see my hand when I held it in front of me. I crouched on the ground close to the left-hand wall of the lane. Withdrawing the bloodied knife from my coat, I quickly gouged a hole in the filthy wet dirt. I used my fingers to scoop out the soil, then plunged my hand into my jacket pocket and pulled out the grey kidney. It felt like a fat sausage before it is placed in the pan. I let it fall into the soil and then used both hands to shovel the dirt back over it. I patted the ground flat, wiped my palms together and rose to my feet.

I walked back the way I had come, guided by the widening funnel of light between the lane's brick walls. Emerging on to Osborn Street, I kept my head down. A voice startled me. 'Watch out!' Glancing up, I was just in time to see a hansom cab bearing down on me. I reacted with amazing alacrity, stepping back and missing the oncoming horse's hoofs with barely an inch to spare. Water splashed my trousers and boots and I almost tripped over the high kerb.

Now, let me ask you this, dear lady: do you believe in serendipity? I always have. It is a mercurial force, but one that is nevertheless very real. Well, whether or not you believe it to be a part of the flux of Nature, I myself experienced a serendipitous moment as I caught my balance and steadied myself while the hansom rushed past me and the cabbie bellowed a malediction. The third woman on my list, Catherine Eddowes, was standing directly opposite me, on the far side of the street, soliciting for business.

Catherine, you may remember, worked at the Pav. She was, you will recall, the woman your husband was with the night I first met him. She was dressed in green and black, and on top of her long auburn hair wore a black bonnet trimmed with green velvet. She was clearly drunk, swaying unsteadily on the narrow pavement. I watched her as she tried her luck with a passer by. When the gentlemen rejected her, she swore at him, her voice muffled and lisping thanks to the fact that most of her upper teeth were missing.

Sauntering across the road, I stopped a few feet from her. She stank of booze. With a subtle nod, I indicated she should follow me down a narrow lane a few yards away along the street, another of the thousands of dark alleyways that splintered and dissected Whitechapel.

''Ang on, mithta,' came Catherine Eddowes's lisp from behind me. 'Let's thee ya money firtht.'

I turned slowly and she came right up to me, the gin stink oozing out of her. I looked down at her dirty face, a strand of frizzy hair escaping the bonnet to hang down over her eyes. She blew the straying hair away. I gave her a brief smile, pulled a shilling from my pocket and held it out in the palm of my hand. She gave me a furtive look and snatched the coin, before grabbing my collar. Giggling, she leaned back against the slimy brickwork, pulling me towards her.

'For thith, you get thpechial treatment, like,' she whispered and started to lower herself towards my groin.

'No,' I hissed. 'Up.' And swivelled her round to face the wall.

'Whatever you wanth, dar . . .'

The blade made a squelching sound as it split open her throat. Blood sprayed out of her, hitting the wall. A few drops caught me in the face and got into my eyes. I cursed and let her fall at my feet. Her bonnet slid to one side. Bending down, I turned her face towards me. Her eyes were glazed over and her mouth was moving silently. That was when I first saw the light, at the very edge of my vision. I spun round and could just make out the figure of a policeman holding his lantern at arm's length. The light from it illuminated his face – high cheekbones, bushy brows – his helmet with its silver badge, his voluminous cape revealed under the arm holding aloft the lantern. He saw me. I turned and ran.

There was a low brick wall at the end of the lane. The place was so dark I only saw the wall when I was almost upon it. Under normal circumstances, scrambling up the wet bricks would have been difficult, but I was fiercely energised, my heart racing, every muscle tensed. I heard the policeman blow his whistle, its shrill sound ricocheting from the walls around me. His lantern bobbed around, sending patches of light sliding here and there. I could see his silhouette as he crouched down beside Catherine Eddowes. In less than a second I was over the wall. I could hear his footsteps pursuing me now. He had reached the wall. 'Stop!' he screamed. 'Stop! Murderer!' He blew his whistle again. This time the sound was twice as loud. I heard voices, the beat of running feet, men answering the summons and looking for me. I sped off into the darkness.

Something crunched underfoot. I tripped, but just managed to maintain my balance. My outstretched hands came into contact with a large wooden object: a barrel of some sort. It fell to one side and clattered away. The whistle sounded again, and I sped through the narrow opening at the end of the alley.

A group of rowdy fellows was passing by. They were all extremely inebriated, swaying this way and that. I ducked past them and they remained completely oblivious to the commotion coming from the alley behind me. Sliding into a shadowy doorway, I gulped for air. It felt like the first full breath I had taken since slitting the throat of Catherine Eddowes. I noticed blood on my shirt. Pulling my jacket together at the front, I succeeded in covering up the crimson patch, and with my handkerchief wiped away the blood from around my eyes and drops of the stuff from about my mouth. I tasted a speck of it on my fingertip, relishing the iron tang. It was a flavour redolent of what the common herd would call 'sin'. But as you are, of course, by now aware, dear lady, I have little respect for prudish taboos.

I did not have long to linger. I peered out of the doorway and noticed that there were a number of people around. I decided to cross the street, and was about to turn down a narrow lane when I heard that dreaded sound again – the policeman's infernal whistle. I turned towards it involuntarily and there he was, at the end of the alley opposite, staring straight at me. I saw his mouth move and knew what he was about to yell.

'Murderer!' The bellow cut through the shuffling footsteps of drunks and silly giggles. After a second's pause I ran as fast as I could down an adjacent lane.

It was dark, as are all those lanes and byways, the alleys and brick passageways and foul-smelling gaps between tenements. I was becoming heartily sick of the place . . . and the zeal of its local constabulary! A narrow strip of light told me I was heading towards a main thoroughfare, but I had no idea where I was. I ran on and finally burst into the light of Whitechapel Road. I glanced back and, to my horror, saw two police lanterns bobbing along, approaching me fast.

I dashed left, past a shop, and then saw a chained-up door with next to that an opening above which hung a sign METROPOLITAN DISTRICT RAILWAY, WHITECHAPEL AND MILE END. I ducked inside, leaped over the gate to the platform and sped along an echoing tunnel straight on to the platform.

I had never before been in an underground railway station, and if the circumstances had been different I think I would have been quite fascinated. But not at that moment. Without breaking stride, I sped along the platform, barging past the few people waiting for a train. Some way along the platform, I heard the loudest sound I had ever experienced in my life. I thought for a moment that the earth was caving in and ready to fall around my ears; that by some great misfortune I had decided to dive into this subterranean world just as Whitechapel Station was about to collapse. But it was nothing so dramatic. It was merely a train roaring into the station. Like a bellowing, trumpeting demon from the pages of a horror story, it shot out of the tunnel in a burst of light and steam and smoke and fumes.

I had no idea if the enthusiastic members of H Division of the Metropolitan Police Force were still hot on my tail, and I was not about to wait around and see for myself. The train stopped and I jumped into the nearest compartment which happened to be First Class.

It was empty and I threw myself into a nearby seat, ducking down as best I could. The train started to move off and I felt a wave of relief sweep over me. Forcing my heartbeat to slow, I took deep breaths and looked around my new surroundings. The compartment was quite beautiful: brass fittings, mirrors on the walls, gas lights at the end of each row of seats. Then I heard the door at the end of the compartment start to open.

I thought I was immune to surprise, but when I saw the blue cape of a policeman appear at the edge of the door as it opened inwards, and then a domed helmet, I was confounded. I sprang up from the comfortable green leather seat and propelled myself along the central aisle towards the other end of the compartment. Reaching the door, I yanked on its handle. It gave and I plunged into the cool and the noise and the fumes and found myself on a narrow metal bridge between two carriages. I slammed the door behind me, jumped across the coupling and opened a door into the next compartment. It was another First Class carriage. The train lurched and I almost fell as I slammed the door shut behind me. There were just two people in the compartment. I ran along the aisle, hearing the door behind me open. Using the seat backs for additional impetus, I hurtled along the centre of the compartment with no thought for where I was going or what I hoped to achieve.

Standing on the footplate between the two carriages, I looked down and saw the walls slithering away. I sensed the vehicle starting to slow. I glanced back to the carriage I had just exited. There were two policemen running towards me, halfway along it and swaying with the movement of the train, grasping at the seats to steady themselves as I had done.

I stretched my hand towards the handle of the door to the next compartment, pulled down on it and pushed. It would not budge. I felt a spasm of excitement rush along my spine and smiled. I was enjoying myself. But what to do? I could run back and attack the policemen, but it was risky. Two against one. I had a knife, but they had truncheons. It would be a matter of percentages, and to be honest, dear lady, I was wondering if my luck was slipping through my fingers. I looked down again at the floor of the tunnel. The train had slowed considerably now, and as we approached a station light appeared in the tunnel. I turned to face the wall. There was a gap of perhaps a yard to either side of the train. Would it be enough? If I jumped, I could be caught under the wheels of the speeding train. If I did not, I would have to fight and would almost certainly lose. My heart was racing. I had never been in such a dangerous position and it was absolutely intoxicating. I knew then that if I survived, this would be a moment I would relive in my mind over and over again.

I took a deep breath and stared back at the police officers. The one in the lead – I was sure he was the man who had stumbled upon Catherine Eddowes – was almost at the door. I could see his eager face lathered with sweat, his truncheon raised. Turned back to the sight of the ground rushing by under my feet, my mind was filled with the roar of the train. Smoke blurred my vision. I took a step forward and jumped.

Chapter 37

Essex, Tuesday 27 January, early evening

Pendragon and Turner barely exchanged a word as they left Braintree and headed back to London. Turner drove and Pendragon reported in to the station as they pulled away from Macintyre's rundown council house. Hughes was in a meeting, but Rob Grant took down as many of the details as Pendragon was willing to offer over the phone.

It was overcast and snow had started falling again, melting to nothing as it hit the tarmac of the southbound dual carriageway. Each man was lost in his own thoughts, mulling over unanswerable questions, each trying in his own way to untangle the knotted threads of what they had learned today, a day that, by five o'clock, had started to feel interminable.

The ringtone of the car phone startled them. 'Pendragon,' the DCI said, after stabbing the green 'Incoming' button below the dash.

Expecting Hughes, he and Turner were surprised to hear Sergeant Roz Mackleby's voice. 'Sir,' she said, 'how near the station are you?'

Pendragon paused a moment. 'About twenty minutes, traffic permitting. Why?'

'I'm with Inspector Towers,' Mackleby replied. 'The Super's in a car behind us. We're on Johnson Road. We've got another murder.'

On any other day, the apartment on Johnson Road, Stepney, would have been considered beautiful, a place straight from the pages of a lifestyle magazine, but today it resembled a chamber from the depths of Hell.

A uniform stood at the front door leading from the marble-tiled hallway into the apartment itself. The door was listing slightly from where it had been knocked in. The lock was shattered. The PC nodded to Pendragon and Turner and continued to stare at the far wall as they followed the sound of voices coming down a wide passage from the living-room. Hughes saw Pendragon and paced over to intercept them. She took the DCI to one side.

'Jack.' She seemed relieved to see him. 'This is really not nice.'

He frowned. 'It never is. So, what do we have?'

'Definitely a fourth. Same MO. The vic is Chrissy Chapman. Quite a well-known artist, I believe.'

Pendragon looked stunned. 'Yes, she is. Very well-known.'

'But get this . . . Francis Arcade called it in. When we got here, he was sitting opposite her body, just staring at her. Hardly seemed to notice us when we forced the front door.'

'Arcade? Where is he now?'

'In the bedroom, under guard. He's out of it. In an almost trancelike state.'

Pendragon tilted his head and pulled a face. 'This just gets more ridiculous,' he said, starting along the hall.

Hughes took his arm gently. 'And, Jack,' she said, searching his face, 'Arcade's prints are all over her.'

A photographer was moving around one of two sumptuous sofas trying to get the best angles, and a forensics officer in plastic overalls was dusting for prints around a low walnut coffee table nearby. The victim, Chrissy Chapman, was propped up on the sofa. It was a pristine white. The woman's skin was just as pale as the sofa. She was dressed in a dark top, a scarf draped casually around her neck. Her dark fringe had been recently trimmed; some curls of hair lay on the scarf and scattered across the sofa. The face beneath had been hideously contorted, the flesh split under the hairline, the fine facial bones shattered, but the skin was still intact, heavily rouged around the cheeks and temples. Her features had been wrenched to one side, both her eyes were on one side of her face, her nose had been left behind, her mouth coated thickly with lipstick.

Pendragon felt a cold chill run down his spine. Turner had just appeared at his side and the DCI could feel a tremor run through the sergeant as the shock of what he was seeing hit him. 'Holy fucking Christ,' he said slowly and glanced at his boss, his mouth open.

Pendragon ignored him and took a couple of steps towards the obscene tableau of Picasso's painting of his wife Olga Khokhlova. It seemed so incredibly bizarre it was hard to believe the scene was real. But the girl sitting there had recently been a living, breathing human being; one who had been mutilated, violated with such malicious intent it was barely conceivable. It was one thing to take a life, Pendragon found himself thinking. This was act of an entirely different order.

He turned away and saw movement through the doorway into the bedroom. Inspector Ken Towers emerged. 'Sir,' he said. He looked tired and unusually jumpy. 'This fella Arcade . . . We have him in the bedroom. But he hasn't said a word.'

'Thanks.' Pendragon clicked his fingers in front of Turner's face and the sergeant snapped back to attention. 'I want you to go straight to Arcade's flat.'

'But it was searched, sir.'

'I know that, Turner. But I want it searched *again*. Take someone with you. Go over the place with a fine-toothed comb. Anything suspicious, anything at all, I want to know about it. Come straight to me after you get back to the station.'

Turner nodded and walked towards the front door.

The bedroom was large and brightly lit by a rash of powerful ceiling halogens. The blinds had been pulled down over a large window that took up most of one wall parallel to the bed. The decor was stark: white walls, white bedding, white rug over a polished concrete floor. On the wall opposite the bed hung an ornate French antique mirror, the only suggestion of anything other than straight lines and white in the room. Francis Arcade was sitting in a chair in the far corner. Uniformed policemen stood to either side of him. Pendragon flicked his head to indicate the constables should leave. They looked uncertainly at each other.

'It's all right, PC Flint,' the DCI said firmly. 'The Super's returned to the station. I'm back in charge, so skedaddle.' He closed the door behind them and walked back to face Arcade. The young artist simply stared into space, unblinking, hands held palms upwards and limp in his lap. He smelled unwashed. Pendragon lowered himself on to the corner of the bed a few feet from Arcade and leaned forward with his elbows on his knees.

'Francis, do you want to tell me what happened?'

The expressionless mask of Arcade's face did not change. Pendragon waited patiently for two silent minutes. 'You might feel better if you talk to me.' Still not a flicker.

The DCI studied the boy's face. He looked even more Goth than normal. He had not shaved for days and had dark patches under his eyes. His hair hung shapeless and greasy. There was something not quite right about all this, Pendragon thought to himself. Arcade had definitely not killed Berrick or Thursk. He was seen by scores of people during the timeframe for each murder. And he certainly had not killed the priest, Michael O'Leary, because at the time of that murder he had been in police custody. So why would he have killed this woman? A copy-cat murder? Another of the kid's cries for attention? That was hard to believe.

'Why did you kill her?' Pendragon said, completely without expression.

For the first time, Arcade stirred. He lifted his head and fixed the policeman with a look of complete clarity. 'I did not kill Chrissy,' he spat. 'I loved her.'

Pendragon felt startled for a moment but covered it well. 'Just because you loved her, that doesn't mean you didn't kill her.'

'I did *not* kill her,' Arcade yelled, and knocked his chair away as he sprang up.

The door burst open and one of the uniforms was there brandishing a truncheon. Pendragon glared at Arcade and the young man returned to his seat to stare down at the floor. The DCI raised a hand towards the police officer and flicked a look at the door. 'It's okay,' he said, and watched the door close again. He rubbed a palm over his forehead, suddenly feeling incredibly tired.

'Okay, Francis. Shall we start from the beginning?'

The boy looked up. A tear trickled down his left cheek. 'He killed her.'

'Who?'

'That bastard Hickle.'

'Hickle?'

'Chrissy's *boyfriend* Geoff Hickle. Dr Geoff Hickle. He killed her and disfigured her.'

'Wait a minute, Francis. Just slow down. What makes you think this Dr Hickle killed Ms Chapman?'

'Jealous. Jealous of me and her.'

'What evidence . . . ?'

'I just know,' Arcade hissed, staring straight into Pendragon's eyes.

'All right. Let's go back a few stages. What were you doing here?'

'Why shouldn't I be here? I love . . . loved Chrissy. She loved me. The doctor was out at work at the Royal London, saving lives. I came round to see her.'

'Had she called you?'

'No, that was the point, Inspector. She was supposed to ring me last night, but didn't. I was worried, but I didn't

267

want to seem uncool. And besides, I could only show when Dr Doolittle was away. It got to about four o'clock, though, and I couldn't bear it any more. Chrissy wasn't answering her mobile. The phone here just rang and rang. I did a quick check at the hospital and Hickle was there. He'd been in since eight this morning . . . apparently. So I came over.'

'You have a key.'

'Yeah. Don't tell Dr House, though.' And he pulled back his lips into a dark caricature of a smile.

'And you found Ms Chapman?'

Arcade looked away, fixing his gaze on the far wall over the bed. 'Yes.'

'What did you do? Your prints have been found on the body.'

He turned away from the wall and stared into Pendragon's eyes. 'I could not . . .' Another tear emerged from his eye. 'I still can't believe . . .' He swallowed hard. 'I sat beside her. I touched her face. It was cold. Then I sat on the sofa opposite and just stared at her. I must have called you lot. I don't remember doing it.'

'How long have you known Ms Chapman?'

Arcade seemed not to hear the DCI at first, or else he did not understand the question. Then he appeared to come round. 'Er . . . about two years. She was always saying she would leave Hickle, but he seemed to have some sort of hold over her. Every time I thought I was getting close to prising her away from him, she would flip back.'

Pendragon nodded, staring at the young artist and wondering if the frustration the kid felt could have been strong enough to push him to murder. He had seen crimes of passion before, triggered by messy love triangles and thwarted obsession, crushes that had spiralled into violence and mayhem. Could this relationship have been a delusion on Arcade's part? Perhaps the kid had slid into insanity, been tipped over the edge by rejection and a growing fury towards the world.

There was a crashing sound from outside and several raised voices. Arcade did not move, but Pendragon jumped up and dashed for the door. It swung open on to the living-room and Pendragon saw a tall woman in a faux-fur coat standing staring at the macabre murder scene. It was Gemma Locke, her face white as chalk. Her hands flew to her face and she seemed to stumble before regaining her balance. She lowered herself into a chair, a low moan emerging from between her gloved hands.

Chapter 38

Pendragon crouched beside Gemma Locke and handed her a glass of water he had just fetched from Chrissy Chapman's kitchen.

'I guess it's obvious you would have known each other,' Pendragon said gently, watching Gemma Locke take several small sips. She handed back the glass and he passed it to a constable standing close by. Then he stood up and pulled over a chair. Glancing towards the bedroom, he saw Arcade being led away in cuffs. The young man ignored Pendragon completely, and he and the two escorting officers passed behind Gemma's chair and out into the hall without her even noticing them.

'Chrissy and I were best friends, Inspector. We go back a long way – since I first moved to London.' Gemma shook her head and closed her eyes, a pained expression spreading across her face. 'I . . . I just can't take this in. It's crazy. Who would . . . Why?'

'What was Ms Chapman like?'

'Chrissy was a sweetheart. Everyone loved her, Jack. That's why this is so . . . ridiculous!'

'No enemies that you know of?'

Gemma Locke exhaled and shook her head again. 'No. Chrissy was destined for greatness. She was the best of us,

270

the most talented of our generation.'

'What can you tell me about her private life? She was serious about a doctor – Geoff Hickle, a surgeon at the Royal London, yes?'

She nodded. 'Yes, they had been together about . . . oh, a year, I think. But the relationship was turning sour.'

Pendragon raised an eyebrow. 'Oh?'

'Well, you'll find out before long, I suppose. Francis Arcade was pestering her.'

'Pestering her? I had the impression it was serious between them.'

Gemma Locke gave Pendragon a sceptical look. 'Hardly, Jack. Chrissy was ten years older than him for a start, and Francis is, well . . . not all there, to put it mildly. I'm sure he thought there was a serious relationship between them, but I can assure you there wasn't.'

'So, what was the problem with Dr Hickle?'

'Oh, classic really. He's a powerful figure in his world: a burns specialist at a top London hospital. Fancied himself as a real charmer and a bit of a medical hero. Big, big ego . . . huge. He was uncomfortable with the attention Chrissy was getting from the media. Felt he was living in her shadow. Didn't really fit with his self-image.'

'No. I can see there would be some conflict there.'

'But then, having said that. I can't see him as a killer.'

'No one's suggesting that,' the DCI retorted. 'Okay, look, I'm afraid you can't stay here. Forensics are going to be taking the place apart.' He helped Gemma to her feet and led her around the back of the sofa. She studiously kept her line of sight away from the dead woman.

271

'Are you okay?' he asked as they reached the hall.

Gemma took a deep breath and looked up at the ceiling. 'Yes, I'm fine.'

A few moments later, they were downstairs in the car park. The temperature had dropped dramatically as night had drawn in. Pendragon glanced at his watch. It had turned seven o'clock. He followed Gemma to her car. 'I'd like to have another chat with you,' he said as she reached into her bag for her keys. 'The questions just keep coming. But not the answers, unfortunately.'

'Sure. Give me a ring.'

He pulled his collar up and turned to go.

'Where are you headed?'

'Back to the station.'

'Jump in. I'll drop you there.'

The traffic was heavy with late-night shoppers and people on their way west. A fog had begun to descend on Stepney's frosty, neon-splashed grey. Music by Monteverdi that Pendragon half-recognised was playing softly. For a few minutes they said nothing, each lost in horrible thoughts. Then Pendragon looked away from the brickwork and the graffiti-stained walls. 'How well did you know Juliette Kinnear?' he asked.

Gemma Locke tilted her head slightly, but kept staring at the road ahead. A red light brought them to a halt. She turned towards Pendragon. 'Not at all. She was on the scene before my time.' Gemma looked back at the road for a second. 'But I do remember that she assaulted someone and wound up in a psychiatric hospital.'

'She committed suicide.'

'That's right.' Gemma flicked Pendragon a glance and

accelerated along Mile End Road. 'I remember now. I was in Athens. Doing the clichéd Inter-Rail thing. Must have been . . . what . . . 1996?'

'That's right.'

'I remember I didn't hear about it until over a week after she'd died. I was staying in a youth hostel. The only things to read were a dog-eared Jackie Collins someone had left and a week-old copy of the *Daily Mail*. I chose the paper!'

Pendragon saw Brick Lane ahead on the right. The car slowed for another set of lights. 'Do you know anyone who knew Juliette Kinnear?'

Gemma pulled a face as she thought about it. 'Don't think I do, Jack. As I said before, it was before my time. I didn't make it to London until 'ninety-eight. Actually, no, come to think of it, Jackson Price would have known her. He and Kingsley were already making names for themselves then. But Juliette Kinnear was never very successful, was she? A poor little rich girl, I thought.'

Pendragon shrugged. 'Conflicting accounts, of course. Some have said she was a great talent, her life cut tragically short. Others have suggested she was never as good an artist as she thought she was and that she committed suicide because she was sick of going unnoticed.'

'Guess we'll never know.' Gemma shrugged, turning the car into Brick Lane and slowing as they approached the gates to the police station car park. She drew to a halt at the foot of the steps in front of the station. When she turned to Pendragon, he saw her eyes were bright with tears. 'Please make sure you catch whoever did this terrible thing, won't you, Jack?'

Pendragon ran the fingertips of his left hand across his forehead. 'Thanks for the lift,' he said, and jumped out of the car. 'I'll call you.'

He was halfway up the steps when his mobile rang. The screen said 'blocked number'.

'Hello.'

'DCI Pendragon, please.'

'Sammy! I'd almost given up on you.'

'You should never do that, dear boy. I'm a man of my word.'

'So?'

'Rembrandt Industries. I could not write an article for the *Encyclopaedia Britannica* on them, to be honest, but I've got something that may help.'

'Fire away.'

'I asked around a couple of business associates. One of them said he'd heard of Rembrandt, but wasn't happy about it. He owns units all over the East End. He'd agreed to lease them a warehouse in Leytonstone. Rembrandt had booked it for three months, put down a small deposit and then done a runner after a week without paying any rent. He said things had picked up, though, because he'd since rented out two other places that had been empty for ages to a Titus Inc. They had paid up front for both places, one in Whitechapel and one in Bermondsey. I was about to call you about the first place in Leytonstone . . . hadn't thought much about the other two places my friend mentioned.'

Pendragon had reached his office. He pulled a pad of paper and a pen towards him across the desk. 'Why didn't you?'

'Well, it was only this evening, about an hour ago. I got waylaid.'

'Oh?'

'In the Duke of Norfolk. But . . . ssh, Pendragon! It was fortunate that I did.'

'Really?'

'Yes, Jack. And actually, when you hear how clever I've been, I think you'll agree I should be on double time.'

'Do you now?'

'Yes.'

'Get to the point, Sammy.'

'All in good time, Inspector. I had a couple of drinks and was sitting there when it came to me. Rembrandt had a son. He painted the young man as a monk. Quite a famous portrait, actually. His name was Titus.'

'How on earth did you know that?'

'I *was* educated at Eton, Inspector.' Sammy sounded miffed.

'Okay, Sammy. A scholar and a gentleman.'

There was a short silence.

'So?' the snout said after a moment.

'Well, thanks,' Pendragon said. 'Can I have the addresses of all three places?'

'Can I have double time?'

Pendragon sighed and looked around the room. 'Yes. I suppose you deserve it.'

'I knew you'd see it my way,' Sammy Samson said.

Chapter 39

Turner eased open the front door to Francis Arcade's bedsit on Glynnis Road. Sergeant Roz Mackleby was a step behind him. When he flicked on the light, the main room was illuminated by a powerful yellow glow. Mackleby paced across the room to check that the bathroom and kitchen were empty. They did not want any unpleasant surprises. It took only a few seconds to confirm they were alone.

'I'll start in here,' Turner said. 'You go through the kitchen and the bathroom. And remember, Roz, every nook and cranny. I don't want to leave here empty-handed.'

The main room was as oppressive and as cluttered as Turner remembered it from his visit here four days before. The same canvases were stacked along the walls. The easel was empty now; the canvas Arcade had been working on was probably among the others but would have been indistinguishable. A bookcase stood against one wall. Turner walked over to it and began a systematic search, starting at the top left, removing a book, flicking through it and returning it, working his way down to bottom right.

A few minutes later, as he was halfway through the

collection of volumes, Sergeant Mackleby emerged from the bathroom. 'Nothing in there,' she said. Then stopped at the door to the kitchen. 'What exactly is it that we're looking for?'

'Not sure myself, to be honest,' he replied. 'But I'll know it when I see it.'

'That's a great help,' Roz retorted, and walked into the tiny kitchen.

Jez finished with the books, having found nothing. On the floor were pots of paint and containers sprouting dirty brushes. In one corner lay a rolled-up, paint-splashed sheet, and next to that a pile of old newspapers. Turner went through each pot, lifting the brushes clear of the cleaning fluid. He then emptied the liquid into a spare container, watching the oily paint residue swirl and form a filthy grey-brown mess. The containers concealed no secrets.

He walked over to the window. The tatty curtains were pulled back. He could see flakes of snow drift down, brush the window and dissolve. The road, the buildings and the sky were the colour of the mixed-paint residue. Then he saw himself and the contents of the room reflected in the glass. Beside his right leg, a canvas about two feet square was propped up against the side of the easel with its back to the window. Turner noticed that this one was stretched over a delicate wooden frame. He crouched down and lifted the painting, swivelled it, studied the back of the frame and ran a finger under the edge of the wood where the canvas wrapped around it. He could just get a finger into the gap. There was nothing there.

He put the frame down and picked up one from the top

layer of the collection leaning against the walls and the bed. He could hear Roz Mackleby in the kitchen, opening and closing cupboards and shuffling around cereal packets. It was not until the seventh canvas, just when he was beginning to lose heart, that Turner felt a metal object tucked between a wooden strut and the canvas. He managed to wedge another finger into the gap and pulled the object from where it had been nestling. It was a USB portable drive, smaller than his thumb. He lifted it to the light and read the lettering on one side side: Ciscom.Inc. 4Gb.

'Yes!' Turner said and smiled to himself.

'Okay, here we go,' said Jez Turner as he tapped at the keyboard in Pendragon's office. The DCI was leaning over his shoulder, staring intently at the screen. The USB drive opened and informed them that it contained two files: one entitled 'ms', the other 'investigations'. He positioned the mouse over 'ms' and double-clicked. 'Ah, password-restricted, naturally.'

'But you have the password Thursk used,' Pendragon said.

'Yeah, but will it work on these files?' Turner replied and started to tap in NT0658. The file opened. 'Very sloppy,' he tutted.

At the top of the first page, it read: *The Lost Girl: Life in the Demi-Monde* by Noel Thursk. Pendragon glanced at the foot of the page. The document was over fifteen thousand words long.

'Well, how about that,' Turner said triumphantly. 'Thursk had written something after all.'

Pendragon ignored him and scrolled down. The screen became a stream of words. He flicked the mouse and clicked the Print command. 'Okay, what's in the other one?'

This file also opened with the same password and a list of dozens of jpegs appeared. They were numbered in ascending order. Turner scrolled down. The last one was number 45.

'Start at the beginning,' Pendragon said, and Turner double-clicked the first on the list.

A picture opened on the screen. It was of Kingsley Berrick propped up as the figure in a Magritte painting. Pendragon leaned in and clicked jpeg 002. Noel Thursk's flattened body draped in the tree appeared. Jpeg 003 showed an equally graphic image of Michael O'Leary.

Turner looked round to Pendragon whose face was close to his, his eyes flicking from side to side as he took in the images on the screen a few inches away. 'I didn't think any of the police or forensics pictures had been released to the public,' he said.

'They haven't, Turner.'

Jpeg 004 showed the inside of the warehouse on West India Quay. The next was a close-up of the roller; 006 was a shot of the metal punch.

'Are these trophies?' Turner said, his voice icy.

Pendragon pulled himself upright and stood up, arms folded, staring at the screen. 'No,' he said as Turner spun round in the chair. 'They're something entirely different, Sergeant. And I don't want a word breathed about this until I'm ready. You got that?'

'Got it, guv.'

Chapter 40

To Mrs Sonia Thomson
16 October 1888

And so, an interlude. I had, I thought, done exceedingly well. There were certainly a few precarious moments, especially on the night of the double murder. I had seen the whites of the policeman's eyes before I jumped, and for a fleeting moment I half-believed I had reached the end of the road, with my skull crushed against the tunnel wall or my body shattered under the steel wheels of the underground train. But that was not to be. The worst I suffered was a sprained ankle and a few lacerations and bruises.

But I needed rest. And, to be honest, I wanted to observe at my leisure the repercussions from my adventures. For this was all part of the creative process. As I started work on the painting, building upon my experiences and my almost perfect recall, I sniffed the air, so to speak. I sensed and relished the rising panic and animal fear of the dumb herd around me.

The newspapers were full of it, of course, and I too

played my part, offering Archibald suitably sanitised renditions of the slashed bodies. I read with great amusement the inaccuracies and down-right fictions concerning what had been dubbed 'the Whitechapel murders'. There was even a copy-cat murder. A whore named Ann Chapman was dispatched by a rank amateur. I was irritated when I first heard of this, but after a moment's pause, I realised the truth of the adage that imitation is the highest form of flattery. Then, of course, some of the falsehoods had been initiated by Yours Truly. I was particularly proud of the graffiti I had daubed on the wall close to the body of Elizabeth Stride, and the removal of the kidney, which I had already dug up and used in the preparation of my paints. The message had conveyed a subtle suggestion that the Freemasons might be involved because of the vaguely ritualistic aspect to the murder. It had been another amusing little decoy, just to confuse the Old Bill, as the local ovine community call the noble guardians of the law.

Suspects were rounded up. One unfortunate fellow, a worker in a local abattoir, had the mis-fortune of being spotted close to the scene of Catherine's sad demise. He was given the nickname 'Leather Apron' because of the garment he wore at work. He was pulled in for questioning and held in the cells for a few days. But he was eventually released because the police had no real evidence with which to present a case.

The police were, by and large, completely

ineffectual, I'm pleased to say. I had chosen my theatre well, had I not, Sonia? After all, who gives a damn about a few repulsive, drunken whores? My work was conducted in a part of London which was, in the eyes of most people, beyond the pale. Wealthy gentlemen may have enjoyed visiting the Stew, dipping their toe into Hell and dipping their wicks into very rough receptacles, but that was merely the natural order of things. My victims were those who had fallen over the edge. If London had been portrayed by Hieronymus Bosch, Whitechapel would have been the lowest level of Hell, a place filled with barrels of pitch and fire and brimstone, the bodies of the useless tossed in at will to melt into the universal pit of nothingness. Why should a judge or a police commissioner, a university don or a bishop, care the slightest what happened there?

Inspector Frederick Abberline was the man at the centre of the investigation. And never a more plodding plodder have I encountered – again, I'm thankful, dear lady, if a little peeved, that I did not have a more interesting and challenging adversary. The police never really had a clue about me, and during the two weeks I spent lying low and painting, they called in for questioning literally dozens of nobodies.

It was at this point that I decided to become a little more playful. I started to write letters to the newspapers and the police. It was in the first of these, written in red ink – yes, I do confess this was a little melodramatic – that I introduced the nickname that will forever be associated with my work: 'Jack the Ripper'.

I can say in all honesty that I have no idea where the name came from. It just arrived on the page as I signed the letter to the Central News Agency. It was wonderful fun. I deliberately obfuscated the text, writing in the voice of a rather common, uneducated fellow, but nevertheless a man with a sense of humour. Here and there, I sprinkled the letters with tiny clues, egging on the police, trying to stir up a little fight in them. But to no real avail. The plodders continued to plod.

I spent a lot of time with your good husband during my fortnight's sabbatical. He was a curious fellow. The better I grew to know him, the more puzzling he became. Most striking was the fact that he was a man of both high and ridiculously low tastes. Now, you may say that many men are thus, but with dear old Archibald, it seemed this dichotomy was rather extreme. On the one hand, he delighted in frequenting the Reform Club and other such bastions of pretension and grandeur. He had high ideals, artistic integrity even. He wanted to make statements, to make his mark, to do something noble and worthy. In short, he had a great desire to encourage people to think; which is a quality I admire. But the corollary of all this well-intentioned public behaviour was the man's insatiable private lust for the low life. He had a seemingly limitless fascination with the seediest brothels, the worst pubs and drinking clubs. He took me to some of the most dangerous opium dens in London, places few people even knew existed, run by Chinese gangs – filthy, stinking rat holes close to the docks, where the air was so rank with opium fumes one barely needed to partake of the pipe to become intoxicated.

Together, during a three-night run of the dens in Limehouse, we witnessed two murders. One was a stabbing involving two Chinese dealers who dispatched a man who'd threatened to give them up to the police. The other involved the shooting of a young drugs runner. It was most entertaining. Although, I have to say, the high point of my nocturnal adventures with Archibald was the night he took me to the Mansion of Wonders, a fabulous misnomer if ever I heard one, because the venue was certainly no 'mansion' and the exhibits were some way short of 'wonders'.

The Mansion of Wonders was actually a couple of rooms to the rear of a shop at number 259 Whitechapel Road. Archibald informed me that until just two years before a famous grotesque, Joseph Merrick the Elephant Man, was on display there, and that the freak had been forced to sit in the shop window to attract the crowds. He is now in the London Hospital, of course. I'm sure, like most of the genteel classes in England, you have followed the strange man's story in *The Times*. But even with Merrick gone, there still remained plenty of interesting things to see at the freak show, although they were perhaps not in the same league. On the evening Archibald took me to the Mansion, we saw the Giantess of the Mountains, a woman no less than eight foot tall. She was more or less in proportion, though everything about her was laughably expanded. Her head was almost twice the size of mine.

In the next room sat the Siamese twins, a couple of elderly gentlemen joined by a six-inch strip of thick pink flesh along their sides. They had apparently been in the freak-show business for almost forty years. After we had enjoyed a good chuckle at the twins, they were taken away and Agatha, the world's hairiest woman, was brought in. For me, she was the oddest of the collection, because, if one were to ignore the fact that she was covered from head to foot with thick black hair, she was otherwise a normal human being.

Archibald was moved by the sight, I could tell. And I know why. It was the woman's eyes. They were perfectly shaped, large and dark brown, quite beautiful really. But the thing that must have stirred his emotions was the way those eyes peered out from that horrible globe of hair. They possessed an imploring stillness, an almost noble resignation. Archibald was deeply saddened by the experience whereas I felt a wonderful thrill. The woman's expression was so similar to that of Fred, the boy I had let drown so many years ago. Looking at Agatha, I felt something close to ecstasy. I wanted to laugh uproariously. It was only a sense of decorum that stopped me. I did not care about the sensibilities of those around me, but I did not want to draw attention to myself. At least not there and then.

After a while, I grew weary of Archibald's company and felt I was neglecting my work. I started to stay in my room most evenings as well as throughout the day, venturing out only to post letters from a variety of locations and to buy painting materials. I still went out with Archibald occasionally, and continued to supply him with drawings for the *Clarion*, but my heart was not really in it. I found I was becoming increasingly obsessed with my painting. Then, one evening at the beginning of this month, I suddenly knew it was the right time to move on, to claim my last victim and pass on to the final stage of my work.

It had grown chilly during the past few weeks, and I felt the cold even more because I had recently been closeted indoors for much of the time. I knew exactly where I was headed and who my victim was to be. It took me no more than ten minutes walking at a brisk pace to reach Dorset Street close to Commercial Road. Turning into the street, I checked my watch. It was 2 a.m. and there was not a soul around. Halfway along Dorset Street, I found the archway that leads through to a claustrophobic, cobbled courtyard surrounded by hovels. Mary Kelly, my last chosen victim, I knew to be staying in number thirteen.

It was very dark, the half-moon shrouded by thick cloud. Two narrow windows looked out from number thirteen on to the courtyard, and I could just make out a faint light behind them. From far off came an assortment of sounds. Close to, I could see that two of the panes of glass in the right-hand window were broken. It was obvious Mary had a man in there, so I kept to the shadows and waited.

The time passed slowly. I could not move around freely for fear of making too much noise, and the cold was creeping through my clothes. Eventually I heard the door to number thirteen creak open and a figure emerged into the freezing early morning. I caught a brief glimpse of him before he shuffled away into the alley leading back to Dorset Street. Approaching the door, I tapped quietly. When there was no response I tapped again. The door opened a crack and the face of a young woman appeared. She was tall, just a couple of inches shorter than me, and had a pretty if careworn face and long, blonde hair.

'I've finished work, love,' she said.

I looked down as though in resignation to distract her. Then, with a single shove, the door flew inwards and I grabbed Mary about the mouth. Dragging her across the room, I removed two pieces of rag from my pocket and tied one of them across her mouth as a gag. The other I used to bind her wrists. Guiding Mary to the bed, I pushed her so that she fell backwards. She writhed and tried to scream through the gag. Taking a length of rope from my bag, I tied her feet to the metal rail at the end of the bed. Pulling her bound wrists up over her head, I looped a length of rope over the rag binding and tied the other end to the head of the bed.

Ignoring Mary's efforts to break free, I surveyed the room. Even by the standards I had grown accustomed to in the Stew, the place was squalid beyond belief. There were piles of filthy clothes lying on the floor and thrown over the foot of the bed. The sheets were soiled and grey. The mean light I had seen earlier came from a gas mantle in the far corner. There was a fireplace in the wall nearest the door, but it was empty. The room was freezing.

Two rickety wooden chairs stood against the back wall, adjacent to the end of the bed. I extracted a box of matches from my bag and, finding some scraps of old newspaper on the floor, laid a fire in the grate. Grabbing a chair, I wrapped the legs in some of the repulsive clothes and rags scattered on the floor and smashed them against the end of the bed. The chair made a dull thud as it crumbled. I then yanked away the clothes and snapped the pieces of shattered timber until I had a nice pile of kindling for the fire. Within a few minutes, the flames were lapping and I could warm my hands in front of them.

'An extremely cold evening, I'm sure you'll agree, Mary,' I said to my prisoner.

She made some indecipherable sound through the gag, which I ignored. Then, satisfied my hands were warm enough, I set to work.

I did not sleep after returning to my room but began painting while everything was fresh in my mind. I knew that it would only be a matter of time before pandemonium broke out in the neighbourhood and the sheep started bleating.

I lost all track of time, but sure enough, around 11 a.m., I heard the sound of the police racing to the scene and the raised voices of shopkeepers in the street below my window. I felt a delicious sense of being anonymously at the centre of everything, behoven to none, a Master of the Universe, a god who could pull the strings of the little people and make them dance. It was utterly intoxicating.

Looking down at myself, I noticed my clothes were still soiled with streaks of blood and there was a small lump of tissue caught in one of the buttonholes of my waistcoat. Without further ado, I stripped, put the clothes into a bag, washed thoroughly, checking my appearance in the mirror close to the bowl, and changed into fresh things. By 11.30 I was at the entrance to Miller's Court watching, with concealed delight, the scurrying and the palpable distress.

Just before I approached the door to Mary Kelly's room, my attention was drawn to a policeman. His back was towards me as he bent forward in the shadows and vomited noisily against the wall. My goodness, how people overreact, I thought as I took a step closer to the door.

Two men emerged. One of them I recognised as Inspector Abberline. He had the complexion of a ghost, the blood completely drained from his face. He looked up suddenly and glared at me. We had met once before, the day after my busy night dispatching Elizabeth and Catherine.

'Mr Tumbril,' he croaked. 'How pleasant.'

I doffed my cap.

'I think even you would rather not go in there,' Abberline added with a slight flick of his head.

The policeman who had been vomiting appeared from the shadows wiping his mouth and looking embarrassed. He was about to speak, but when he saw Abberline's expression he straightened his jacket and retreated.

'These things are never pleasant, Inspector,' I replied as politely as I could. 'But I have a job to do.'

Abberline fixed me with a cold look, and then, without uttering another word, walked straight past me towards the alleyway and the main road beyond.

Inside, things were pretty much as I had left them. Mary was opened up from throat to groin. Most of her organs had been removed and placed around the room. The fire was burning and there was an oily deposit running up the wall above the grate – human fat that had reconstituted after vaporising in the flames.

A doctor and his assistant were at the scene studying the body. They ignored me completely and I stepped over to the far side of the room, pulled my sketchpad from my bag and began to draw.

It was then that my world changed. My eyes followed the lines of ruin in Mary Kelly's body, tracing the red and the grey lacerations along her thighs and across her devastated face. Her features were almost unrecognisable as ever having been human. It was at that precise moment I suddenly realised I was wasting my time. There was no need to draw, no need to paint, no need to *represent*. My art lay there on the bed, just as my other recent creations had lain on the wet ground of dark alleyways. Furthermore, this work was on a grand scale. In itself, each murder was a beautiful piece. But together . . . together they formed a *gestalt*, a masterpiece. The bit players, the Abberlines and the Archibalds, the plodding plodders and the doctors studying the inanimate flesh, they were all characters in the finished work, angels in the corner of a Michelangelo, foliage bordering a landscape. It was magnificent. *I* was magnificent.

In a delirium, I returned my sketchpad to my bag, turned and walked out of number thirteen Miller's Court. Unaware of anything going on around me, I swung into Dorset Street, weaving my way back to my room on Wentworth Street. Reaching the door at the side of the corn-chandler's shop, I turned the key in the lock, closed the door behind me and walked along the narrow hallway. Slowly, I ascended the stairs feeling as though the world could not become a better place. The conviction that I had broken through into a new form of perception was almost overwhelming.

Outside my door, I thought I heard a tiny sound from inside. I turned the key quietly and pushed the door inwards. I had left the curtains closed, but it was past midday and the sun was bright, casting a sparse light about the room. In my haste, I had left my collection of bloodied knives and a saw in my open leather bag. A bloodied cloth lay draped over the side of it. The entire arrangement sat beneath my latest painting. Standing a few feet from the bag and the canvas, close to the middle of the room, was Archibald Thomson.

Chapter 41

Brick Lane Police Station, Wednesday 28 January,
9 a.m.

Pendragon met Jimmy Thatcher at the entrance to the
Briefing Room. The sergeant was holding a low-sided
cardboard box filled with packets of sandwiches and cups
of coffee from the local deli.

'Good man,' Pendragon said, opening the door for
Thatcher and following him in. He picked a coffee and a
sandwich from the box and walked to the front of the room
to take a seat next to Superintendent Hughes. The whole
team had gathered. Pendragon glanced round the room and
saw how tired everyone looked. Some had been working
all night and the strain was beginning to show.

He thought it best to dive straight in. 'Okay,' he said,
standing up. Gripping the edge of a desk, he leaned
forward. 'We have a fourth murder and a suspect in
custody. But I have grave reservations about his possible
guilt.'

'Why? Hughes said, turning to him. 'Francis Arcade
was found at the murder scene and the dead woman had
his fingerprints on her face.'

'That's correct. But Arcade could not have killed the

first two victims. And he definitely did not kill O'Leary unless he slipped out of the cell, killed the priest and slipped . . .'

'There's no need to be sarcastic, Inspector.'

Pendragon checked himself. 'Yes, Arcade could have committed the latest murder,' he managed to say evenly. 'A copy-cat murder . . .'

'That is possible,' Grant interrupted.

Pendragon nodded and waited a moment before picking up where he had left off. 'It is possible. I've just come from questioning him a second time. Except I couldn't get a word out of him. He's clammed up again. He's almost catatonic.'

'Guilt? Sudden realisation of what he's done?' Hughes suggested.

'Possibly, ma'am. But I don't believe Francis Arcade is a killer. And . . .' he raised his voice a few decibels as the superintendent made to interrupt ' . . . even if he is, and even if he did kill Chrissy Chapman, who killed Kingsley Berrick, Noel Thursk and Michael O'Leary?'

There was a heavy silence in the room.

'We have more than enough to charge Arcade,' the superintendent persisted

'I know, ma'am, but I would advise against it.'

Hughes glared at the DCI then turned away.

'I've got a psych coming in at ten o'clock. We need to get Arcade talking. I don't believe he's a killer, but I do believe he knows a hell of a lot more about what's going on than he's admitting.' Pendragon took a gulp of coffee, straightened up and started pacing in front of the smart board and the usual wall of crime-scene photographs.

'Right, well . . . here we are again, and no nearer cracking this case.' Exasperated, he stopped for a second to look at his team. 'Let's run through the latest facts. Towers, have you and Sergeant Mackleby found out anything about Berrick's nefarious activities? If, indeed, there were any.'

'Well, guv,' Mackleby began, 'Kingsley Berrick was a promiscuous gay man, there's no doubt about that. I can list over a dozen regular partners, many of whom were at the private view at the gallery. Every one of them has an alibi for the time he is believed to have died.'

'And our friendly MEP, Hedridge?'

'They definitely had a relationship, whatever Mr Hedridge says, but he's in the clear. He spoke to his wife immediately after getting back to his flat. The call was logged at four minutes thirteen seconds, starting at three minutes past two in the morning. She was in New York for a few days. There is also CCTV in the reception of the apartment block where he lives during the week. It shows him arriving at one-forty. No one left the building until later that morning, at six-forty-three – a woman who lives along the hall from Hedridge's apartment.'

'Berrick did have connections with some of the local villains,' Towers commented. 'But nothing relevant that I can find. He had a liking for the old Bolivian marching powder apparently, and this led him to hook up with some unsavouries. He also did a bit of laundering, skimming off some of his profits to avoid tax.'

'You don't think he could have been bumped off because he got on someone's wrong side?' Inspector Grant asked.

'Nah. Don't make sense anyway. What about the others?'

Grant nodded and took a gulp of his coffee.

'All right, what about the cherry-picker?' Pendragon asked.

'Absolutely no other footage from CCTV.'

'And the machine itself?'

'Almost every cherry-picker in Greater London is owned by local councils or by private gardening firms, ones that specialise in the heavy-duty stuff – lopping trees, that sort of thing. None of the councils or the private firms has lost a cherry-picker.'

'What about hire companies?'

'There are hundreds scattered around the country, but only three in London. I had Vickers talk to them and go through their records. Between the three hire firms, eleven cherry-pickers have been rented out in the past three weeks . . .'

'I've accounted for all of them,' Vickers interrupted, wearily. 'So, then I checked sales of cherry-pickers around the country going back six bloody months.' He let out a sigh. 'I narrowed it down to green or white machines because of the paint flecks found by Forensics,' he added, and glanced at his notebook. 'Every machine was bought by a company – as you'd expect. I phoned all of them and they checked out, although . . .' he turned two pages and scanned his writing '. . . one's a bit iffy.'

'Oh?' said Pendragon.

'Yeah, green cherry-picker, model called a Finch, sold in October last year to a Dada Ltd, based in Maidstone. I tried to reach them by phone, but the number was non-existent. I emailed and it came back "undeliverable".'

'That'll be the one,' Pendragon said. 'Dada Ltd. God!'

How tedious.' He looked over at Hughes who was staring at him, puzzled. 'The killer has set up at least half a dozen phoney companies, each with a name in some way linked to art: Rembrandt, Gouache . . . Dada. It's becoming a little tiresome.' Then he turned to Sergeant Thatcher who was in his habitual pose, leaning against the back wall. Thatcher straightened up. 'I have some other companies I want you to chase up, and three addresses for warehouses that may have some bearing. I'll give you the list after the meeting.'

The sergeant nodded.

'So, victim number three Michael O'Leary,' Pendragon went on. 'Grant? What have you found out?'

Inspector Grant was at one of the desks close to the back of the room. He straightened and put down his coffee cup. 'Sergeant Vickers and I have interviewed everyone we know of linked with the priest,' he began. 'The Churchwarden, Malcolm Connolly, and the Church Council all said pretty much the same thing. Father O'Leary was a kind, gentle bloke, much loved by his flock.'

'Have you found anything to link O'Leary with Berrick or Thursk?' Hughes asked.

'Nothing at all. I'm pretty certain he never even knew they existed.'

'And what about the elderly priest who found the body? Father Ahern?'

'Yeah, the old boy's out of hospital and convalescing at his house close to the church. He's eighty-odd, and obviously finds the whole thing deeply disturbing, but he was quite coherent. He ran through the events of Saturday morning. All fits perfectly with what Connolly and the others said.'

'What about background?' Hughes asked.

'Ah, well, that's where it gets interesting,' Grant replied, and paused for a moment to glance around the room. Most of the team had turned to face him. 'I dunno, I got a bit sick of all the Church people saying what a wonderful geezer Father O'Leary had been. 'Course you'd expect them to, I s'pose. But anyway, I did a bit more digging. Before moving to St Aloysius, O'Leary had been the priest of St Luke's in Croydon. On a whim, I went there to interview the current priest, Father James Flannigan. He was a friendly guy, knew Father O'Leary vaguely. He was as keen as mustard to help us catch whoever had done this terrible thing to a fellow priest. Actually, he was a bit gabby, to be honest.' Grant smiled and shook his head. 'Or maybe it's just my natural easy-going manner . . .'

'Yeah, right,' said Inspector Towers, and glanced at the others, shaking his head.

'Well, long and short, Father Flannigan let slip that there'd been a couple of complaints made against O'Leary and this had prompted his move to Stepney. He wouldn't elaborate, but I dug a little deeper and found there had actually been a complaint to the local police too, suggestions of "sexual impropriety" as the report put it.'

'Really?' Hughes said, sitting forward.

Pendragon stopped pacing for a moment. 'Was there an official investigation?'

'Looks like it came to nothing. The Church did their usual job of keeping things quiet. Surrey police found no evidence and dropped it.'

298

'But then he moves to the East End,' Pendragon said half to himself. 'How long was O'Leary in Croydon?'

Grant flicked through his notes. 'Got there in 'ninety-eight,' he said, and turned another page. 'Before Croydon he'd been the priest of a small church in rural Essex, between Billericay and Braintree.'

'Braintree?' Pendragon and Turner said in unison.

Grant looked a little startled.

'Was he there for long?'

Grant looked back down at his notes. 'Yeah, fourteen or fifteen years.'

Pendragon stared at the gathering in silence.

'What is it?' Hughes asked.

'Juliette Kinnear grew up in Braintree.'

'Back to the Kinnear girl again, Jack?' Hughes sighed.

'Well, it might be a motive.'

'But she died fifteen years ago.'

'Yes, I know,' Pendragon answered and sat down next to the Super, folded his arms and looked out at the tired faces of the team.

'All right,' Hughes said, suddenly energised. She stood up. 'We have to make some headway with all this. The Commander is getting impatient, and so, quite frankly, am I. I realise everyone is working hard, but we are simply not getting anywhere.'

Pendragon made to interrupt, but Hughes carried on. 'There has to be a connection between the four victims. We're missing something, and we have to find it. Jack?' Hughes turned to face the DCI. 'What's the plan?'

Pendragon stood up again. 'I want everyone . . . and I mean *everyone* . . . connected in any way with Chrissy

Chapman to be interviewed – searching questions. I want to hear about any links with Berrick and Thursk that are out of the ordinary. Obviously, she knew both men well, but is there some subtext there? Anything, as the Super says, that we're missing?'

Pausing for breath, he looked down at the floor for a moment. 'I hate to sound like a pessimist, but I have a nasty feeling our killer hasn't finished yet. They are obviously working to a careful plan. The cherry-picker they used may well be the one bought by this firm, Dada Ltd. That was back in October. If it is the same one, it means these murders have been very carefully planned indeed. That would figure, considering the meticulously executed procedure, the attention to detail. We have to find a link between the four victims. I do not . . . I repeat *do not* . . . want a fifth body on our hands.'

Chapter 42

Brick Lane, Wednesday, 10.40 a.m.

The polarised glass window opened on to Interview Room 3 where two people sat at a table. A uniformed officer was standing motionless against the door to the corridor. There was a video camera mounted on a tripod in the corner, its 'record' light flashing red. Jack Pendragon and Jez Turner were standing in a narrow room behind the window. The DCI had his arms folded and he was staring intently at the two figures in the Interview Room. The person on the left was Francis Arcade; the other, seated across the steel table from him and adjusting a pair of spectacles to study a sheaf of papers stacked beside the A4 notebook in front of her, was Dr Rose Tremlin, the police psych from Scotland Yard. In her mid-forties, she was a tall, slender woman, her brown hair cut into a fashionable bob. She was wearing black flared trousers and a smart imitation Chanel jacket. She had a very large diamond on her ring finger.

Arcade was sitting stiff-backed in his chair. He looked terrible. He had been vomiting for most of the morning and his face had the pinched look of the deeply depressed. He stared straight at the psychologist, who looked up and started to speak. The scene had hardly changed for the past twenty minutes. Dr Tremlin would ask the young man a question, he would stare fixedly at her and say nothing in reply. The psych would then scribble in the notebook in front of her, occasionally adjust her glasses, and then, after a moment, start in again with another question. It was becoming wearing for Rose Tremlin as well as for the two policemen behind the glass. After three more questions, Dr Tremlin closed the notebook, placed the papers on top of it, pulled her chair back and stood up. Without another word, she turned and left the room.

'I'm afraid I can get nothing out of him,' she told Pendragon as he opened the door to the observation room behind the glass and ushered her inside. 'I would surmise it's too early. He's in shock. He's shut down.'

'You don't think he's faking it? Turner asked.

'No, I don't,' Dr Tremlin said with a dismissive air. 'That's not to say he is innocent. Some killers are shocked into this state after they commit their crimes. But, on the other hand, he could simply be an innocent witness who stumbled upon the mutilated body of the woman with whom he was infatuated. The short-term outward effects would be almost identical in each case.'

Pendragon looked through the glass at the forlorn figure in the Interview Room. 'Any suggestions?'

'He needs time.'

'I'm afraid, Dr Tremlin, that is a commodity in very short supply right now.'

She raised her eyebrows. 'Then there's little I can do. Please call me straight away if there is any change.'

Pendragon nodded and Turner opened the door for the

psychologist. Jack turned back to the room, studying Arcade's expressionless face. The only sound in the observation room was the ticking of the clock on the wall. Pendragon glanced at it. It had just passed 10.45 a.m. He stepped towards the door as Turner started to close it. A moment later, he was at the entrance to Interview Room 3.

'What you doing?' the sergeant asked as the DCI gripped the handle.

'I'm going to talk to him. You go next door.'

'But . . . don't you want me in there?'

'No. I'll talk to him alone.'

Pendragon pulled out a chair and sat down, legs outstretched, trying to look relaxed. Arcade continued to stare fixedly ahead.

'Francis,' Pendragon began, 'I know you're not our killer.'

The young artist did not react.

'Francis, look at me. I want to help you.'

Nothing.

Pendragon glanced down at his own fingers where he had them entwined on the desk. He suddenly felt incredibly weary. Then he heard Arcade's voice, and looked up, surprised.

'I loved Chrissy. I did *not* kill her.'

The DCI looked into Arcade's eyes. The boy had averted his fixed gaze from the back wall and was staring at Pendragon. For the first time since Jack had met Francis Arcade, almost a week before, the kid was presenting an unguarded, genuine face to the world. At that moment Pendragon could visualise the child beneath the surface, just below the abrasive, cultivated insouciance.

'Okay,' he said. 'I know that. But if you want my superiors to believe you, you're going to have to help me.'

Arcade glanced at the ceiling for a second, gathering his thoughts. 'I knew she was in danger.'

'Because you've been carrying out your own investigation? That's how you had photos of the murder scene . . .'

Arcade looked startled. Then his face relaxed. 'As it happens, I'm quite handy with computers, Inspector. Hacking into police files isn't that complicated. So you found the USB?'

Pendragon nodded. 'My sergeant did actually. But, yes, we have the files. So . . . care to explain?'

Arcade shook his head and looked at the table for a moment. 'It's a relief,' he began. 'I probably would have told you about it anyway before too long. Yeah, I've been investigating the murders, and I knew something nasty was going to happen, even before Berrick was killed. I was worried about my uncle.'

'Your uncle?'

Arcade let out a sigh. 'Yeah. Noel. He was my uncle.'

It was Pendragon's turn to be surprised. 'But you made such a fuss about how much you hated the man.'

Arcade allowed himself a brief smile. 'Well, I'm obviously a better actor than I thought I was! I wanted to throw you off the scent. I was conducting my own investigation. I didn't want you interfering. I wanted you to suspect me.'

'Okay. And your uncle also thought the situation was getting dangerous?'

'That's why he wiped his laptop and gave me the only

copy of the manuscript. He'd only written half a dozen chapters, but he had researched everything.'

'So he knew more than he put in the fifteen thousand words in the file?'

'Tons more, Inspector. But he kept it all up here.' And Arcade tapped the side of his head.

'So what you're saying is, you knew there was someone out there who was intent on shutting up your uncle?'

'Yes, but it was still a big surprise when Berrick copped it.'

'Because you thought Noel Thursk would be the first, perhaps the only, victim?'

Arcade nodded and looked away. Pendragon could hear the young man take several slow, deep breaths. 'It took me a while to see how the pieces fitted together. And it wasn't until the priest was murdered that I managed it. That's when I got really scared.'

'Why?'

'Why do you think, Inspector? I sussed out who had killed all three men, and why.'

Pendragon stared at him in silence. 'Okay,' he said after a moment. 'The stage is yours, Francis.'

'My uncle had only written about the early part of Juliette Kinnear's life, and her background, so I started to think that he was not taken care of for what he knew about her or any of the Kinnears. There was nothing salacious there. He hadn't even reached the part about Juliette stabbing the gardener. But you would have read the first bit by now, yeah?'

Pendragon nodded.

'Old Uncle Noel didn't pull any punches about the London art scene in the late eighties and into the nineties, did he?'

'No,' Pendragon responded. 'But no one is mentioned specifically by name.'

Arcade snorted. 'He didn't need to do that, Inspector. Everyone who was there at the time would know who was who. And . . .' Arcade put up a hand '. . . I know what you're going to say. So what? If they're all implicated and they all know who's who, but no one else does, what's the problem?'

Pendragon tilted his head as though to say: Very well, carry on.

'Perhaps you're at a disadvantage, Inspector. Because I had my uncle's confidence and I knew that he was working himself up to naming names later on in the book. Obviously, someone suspected this and decided to silence Noel.'

'So, you believe the killer is someone who was mentioned vaguely in the first part of the book?'

'I know it. And it was confirmed by murder number three.'

'Oh?'

'I just wish I had been quicker to realise that the murderer had also gone completely mad . . . that my darling Chrissy was in danger too. But I was so fixated with the sequence of murders, I thought I'd figured out who would be next, and it wasn't Chrissy.' He suddenly brought his hands to his face and wept. His shoulders shook. Pendragon waited for him to pull himself together.

'But you said you knew she was in danger?'

306

Arcade let his hands fall from his face. His eyes were red. 'Only after it was too late.'

Pendragon shuffled his chair forward and leaned his elbows on the metal table. 'So. Your big moment, Francis. Who is the killer?'

Arcade sat back and folded his arms. 'It was obviously someone mentioned in the first part of Noel's draft. Someone with a big secret to hide. Someone with a lot to lose. Someone with the skill to carry out such a series of murders and clever enough to make it seem like a serial killer hung up on some artistic theme. He was known as Jerome Travis in the early nineties. He was a young kid then, about the age I am now, a medical student who found a way to make a tidy little packet on the side to subsidise his grant.'

Pendragon shook his head.

'You know, don't you, Inspector?'

'Francis, don't you think you've become obsessed?'

'Obsessed?' Francis Arcade suddenly erupted. 'I'm *not* obsessed. I know the truth. And I will hate myself for the rest of my life for realising it too late to save the only woman I've ever loved. The only woman I will ever love.'

'But, Francis,' Pendragon spoke softly, trying to calm the boy down, 'where's your evidence?'

The young artist was gripping the table and taking more deep breaths. Pendragon could tell how important this story was to him, how he wanted to keep it rational, how he did not want to come across as crazy himself.

'Okay,' Arcade said, keeping his voice remarkably measured. 'These are the reasons I think Jerome Travis, aka Dr Geoff Hickle, has murdered four people.'

Chapter 43

Dr Geoff Hickle looked tired but perfectly composed. He was a well-built man and tall. His hair, although curly and thick at the sides, was thinning dramatically on top, and he had a dark shadow of bristle about his chin and cheeks. He had large brown eyes and heavy brows, thick, sensuous lips and fine teeth that had clearly seen a recent makeover. He ran a surprisingly delicate hand down the left side of his face.

They were in Interview Room 3, Hickle on one side of the metal table, Pendragon and Turner on the other. Pendragon had just finished recording the time and date and those present. '. . . Dr Hickle has declined the offer of a lawyer,' he concluded and let the silence hang in the room for a moment. Then he leaned forward with his arms on the table.

'Thank you for coming in, Dr Hickle. I appreciate this must be a very difficult time for you.'

Hickle gave a slight nod.

'How long have you known Ms Chapman?'

'We met about eighteen months ago.' His voice was a warm baritone, a comforting sound.

'How did you meet?'

'Oh,' Hickle sagged a little and then exhaled, 'I met Chrissy at a private view in Bath. A friend of hers, Jimmy Portine Della Rosa, the sculptor, had a show there. I was at a conference and a colleague dragged me along.' He smiled briefly, flashing those teeth. 'As you can tell, I'm not a big fan of art. Anyway, Chrissy was there, and . . . well, we hit it off straight away.'

'What was the conference about?'

'Sorry?'

Turner glanced at his boss and Pendragon ignored him. 'The subject of the conference in Bath?'

Hickle opened his eyes wide and flicked a glance to left then right, making it clear he thought it an odd question. Then he cleared his throat. 'Er . . . It was called *Skin Regeneration in Stage Three Burns Patients: A Post-operative Analysis*. Dr Fiona Wood . . . You know, the Australian researcher? . . . she was hosting it.'

Pendragon was nodding his head. 'Yes, Dr Wood.' He looked down for a moment then stared into Hickle's eyes. 'You're a burns specialist at the London Hospital, is that right?'

'It is,' Hickle replied.

'And you were working at the hospital at the time Ms Chapman was murdered?'

'I don't know, Inspector. No one has told me when they think the murder occurred.'

'Ah, I'm sorry,' Pendragon said, and glanced at Turner, who opened a folder and slid it across to the DCI. He took his time reading through the half-dozen lines of the murder report related to the estimated time of death. It had just been emailed over from Jones's lab. 'Early yesterday

309

morning. Between nine and ten.' Pendragon looked up at the interviewee.

'My shift began at ten-thirty. I'm pretty sure you've already checked that.'

Pendragon ignored the comment. 'So, pardon me if I appear blunt, Doctor, but can you account for your whereabouts yesterday morning?'

'The last time I saw Chrissy, I was leaving the flat, going for a run. She had been working late in her studio the night before, and was half-asleep. Must have been seven-fifteen . . . seven-thirty. I left her in bed. When I got back, the place was empty.'

'Wasn't that a bit strange?'

'No,' Hickle replied, shaking his head slightly and meeting Pendragon's eyes. 'Not at all. I go for long runs. I was out for an hour. I just assumed Chrissy had rushed back to the studio. She quite often gets . . . got . . . obsessed with her work and couldn't leave it alone. I thought it must have been one of those times.'

'What did you do then?'

'I took a shower, had breakfast, hung around the flat.' He shrugged. 'Went through some notes. Then I walked to work. I left the flat about ten, I think.'

Pendragon sat back. 'Okay, Doctor. Cast your mind back over the past week. Can you tell me where you were early Wednesday morning?'

Hickle looked down at the table and then lifted his head slowly. 'So, you do have me down as a suspect?'

'Well, I assumed you knew that.'

'Okay,' Hickle said slowly, his voice now devoid of its former warmth. 'Last Wednesday morning . . . Yes.

Wednesday is my early shift. I was at the hospital by five-forty for a six o'clock start.'

'And earlier?'

'Earlier? Well, I was asleep.'

'At Ms Chapman's flat, or yours?'

'Mine.'

'In . . .' Pendragon glanced at the notes again . . . 'Wilmore Terrace?' Pendragon continued to look at the report in front of him for a moment. 'And the following morning? Thursday?'

'When are we talking . . . one o'clock? Two?'

Pendragon looked up at him, his face completely expressionless.

'Between three and five.'

Hickle leaned forward, flashed Turner a black look and then stared back at Pendragon. 'I was asleep.'

The sergeant made to speak, but Hickle interrupted him. 'At Chrissy's place.'

'And Friday night, Saturday morning?'

'Chrissy and I had a quiet night in. But, of course, that can't be confirmed now, can it?'

Pendragon studied Hickle's face. The man was irritated, but he was remaining quite calm.

'It doesn't look good, does it, Doctor?' Pendragon said.

'Oh, nonsense, Inspector.' He flashed those teeth for a second, giving the policemen a slightly scornful look. 'There are many people within a mile of here who could not prove where they were on those four occasions. Doesn't mean to say any of them is your man.'

'No, you're right,' Pendragon replied. 'But I think the field narrows itself considerably if we only deal with

311

those who cannot prove where they were on those four occasions and who also knew *all* four victims.'

Hickle grimaced. 'What?'

'You knew Kingsley Berrick, Noel Thursk, Father Michael O'Leary and, of course, the final victim.'

'No, you're wrong, Inspector. I met Mr Berrick once. I believe I may even have been introduced to Thursk, but who was the third victim . . . O'Leary? I'd never even heard the name until I read the local paper the other day.'

'Well, all three men knew you. But probably not as Geoff Hickle. They would have been more familiar with Jerome Travis.'

Hickle looked genuinely surprised. 'Ah, I see. So it's about my student misdemeanours? That was an awfully long time ago!'

'I'm afraid there's rather more to it than that.' Turner passed Pendragon a second folder. 'Would you like me to refresh your memory of those far-off days?'

Hickle tilted his head. 'I don't think I could stop you.'

'You were studying medicine at St Thomas's from 'ninety-one to 'ninety-six. You're an Essex boy.'

Hickle gave the policemen a faint smile. 'You know what they say about taking the boy out of Essex . . .'

'Grew up in Billericay. Around 1994 you met Juliette Kinnear there during a summer vacation from college. She was seventeen and trying to break into the art scene. Through her family connections, she'd made the acquaintance of some of the younger movers and shakers in London, including Kingsley Berrick and Noel Thursk, who was at that time an aspiring painter himself.'

'This is an entertaining story,' Hickle said. 'But what relevance does any of it have to Chrissy's death?'

Pendragon ignored him. 'It was about this time that you realised you could make some serious money. You were fed up with living the student life on the breadline. Mum and Dad lived in a council house, so there was nothing to be had there. And this is where you got really lucky. You've always been a man of faith, haven't you, Doctor?'

Hickle nodded. 'Yes. Is that a crime now?'

Pendragon looked at Turner. 'Sergeant. You've done a lot of the leg-work. Perhaps you would like to continue the story.'

Turner cleared his throat, looked down at the information in front of him, intertwined his fingers over the papers and looked Hickle straight in the eye. 'Your family have been strict Catholics since your great-grandfather's time, and through the Church you met the local priest, one Father Michael O'Leary. Now, Father O'Leary is a . . . sorry, *was* . . . a very strange character. A priest, who was interested in little boys . . . Nothing very unusual there. But he also liked his recreational drugs. Somehow, and we haven't worked this out yet, he became very fond of cocaine. And cocaine, as you would know, Dr Hickle, is expensive. So, to finance his habit, our friend Michael O'Leary did a little dealing on the quiet. And when he met you . . . well, it was a marriage made in Heaven. If you'll excuse the pun.'

'Look,' Hickle said, turning from the sergeant to Pendragon, 'okay, I put my hands up for the crimes I committed . . . What? Almost twenty years ago? Press charges . . . ruin me if that gives you a kick. But it won't

313

bring Chrissy back, and it won't find you your killer.'

Pendragon looked down at the file. 'Dr Hickle, this is the situation. You knew all the victims. You must have discovered that Noel Thursk was writing a book about your old girlfriend, Juliette. You were concerned . . . no, very concerned, and justifiably so, that Thursk would destroy your medical career. It then occurred to you that there were others who knew all about your past and that they would back up Thursk's sordid little story. But the piece of information that really nails it is this.' And he passed a sheet of paper across the table to Hickle. 'As a man of science, you'll know what this is and you'll be able to interpret it.'

'It's a DNA analysis.'

'Correct. More precisely, it's a DNA analysis of hairs found on some machinery used to create your murder-scene tableaux. The DNA comes from Juliette Kinnear.'

'What?'

'Your old girlfriend, Juliette Kinnear.'

'But she died a very long time ago.' Hickle looked utterly lost, and for a second both Pendragon and Turner felt a twinge of uncertainty.

'But you were together for two years, were you not? A long time in which to acquire hair. What was it? Did she cut her hair on a whim and you preserved a clipping? Or did you swap locks as a romantic gesture?'

Hickle's face was grey. 'This is insane,' he managed to say. 'What sort of crazy story is this?'

'Do you deny knowing O'Leary?'

'No.'

'Do you deny knowing Berrick and Thursk?'

'No.'

'Do you deny having a relationship with Juliette Kinnear? Do you deny selling drugs to the artists you knew in the nineties? Do you deny being terrified by the prospect of Noel Thursk's book?'

'No . . . No . . . Yes!'

'Oh, come on, Geoff. Or should I call you Jerome?'

'Look, okay. I knew those people. But I had no idea this Noel Thursk guy was writing a book. And as for Juliette . . . it's absurd. Yes, we dated for a while, but . . . DNA, hair . . . oh, come on, Inspector.' Then, suddenly, Hickle seemed to bring his emotions under control again. 'You have nothing on me. This is all circumstantial.' He glared at Pendragon, studiously ignoring Turner.

Pendragon took a deep breath and looked at the papers in front of him. 'You're absolutely right, Dr Hickle. But it's enough to force you to give prints and agree to a DNA swab. And it's enough to keep you in custody while we find irrefutable evidence that you have killed four innocent people. Then we will most definitely have something on you.'

Chapter 44

'Jack, it sounds to me as though you're just dashing from one idea to another.' Superintendent Hughes was staring at him from behind her spotless desk. In front of her on the polished walnut top was a pad of paper positioned squarely with a black Mont Blanc pen placed precisely in the middle of the top edge of the pad. Her hands were clasped and resting on the desk.

Pendragon protested, 'I don't think that's entirely fair.'

'No?'

'No.'

Hughes folded her arms across her chest. 'Okay. So, what do we have? A dead girl's DNA planted as a decoy. A doctor who, over fifteen years ago, knew the victims and earned some pin money dealing ecstasy and cocaine.'

'He cannot prove where he was at the time of any of the murders.'

'Not enough, Jack.'

Pendragon stared off towards the blinds drawn over the window and the row of perfectly manicured cactus plants on the sill.

'Dr Geoff Hickle might once have been a student with a dodgy business plan, but he's now a stalwart member of the community,' Hughes went on. 'He is on two government advisory boards that I know of, chairs a very important charity, and he's an internationally recognised burns specialist.'

'All the more reason he would want to protect his reputation. He's worked hard to get where he is. How could he face losing it all if the truth about his past got out?'

'But you have no evidence.'

'I know.' Pendragon looked straight into his boss's eyes. 'Give me twelve hours and I'll have it. We'll nail the man.'

Hughes was shaking her head. 'I can't do it.'

Pendragon ran a hand over his forehead and looked up at the ceiling. 'We need to keep him in overnight. We can do that, surely?'

'He'll lawyer up and be out of here within an hour, no matter what we say or do,' Hughes replied. 'No, I'm sorry. Get me some real evidence and I'll move Heaven and Earth to help. But not until then.'

'Look, guv,' Turner said, meeting Pendragon's furious gaze. 'You can bang your head against the wall if you like, but all you'll get is a sore head.'

'Is that another example of your home-grown wisdom, Turner? Something your mum told you?'

The sergeant fell silent and looked away.

'I'm sorry,' Pendragon said quietly. 'That was uncalled for.'

'It's all right, sir.'

They were in Pendragon's office with the door closed. It was 9.15. The night shift had started two hours earlier and for the moment the station was relatively quiet. The troublemakers who would be in later were busy getting drunk in local pubs.

'At the risk of being snapped at again, it might be an idea to get some shut-eye, sir. I dunno about you, but I'm sick of the bloody sight of this place.' Turner sighed. 'The teams have drawn a complete blank trying to find any links between the friends and acquaintances of the victims. I know Jimmy alone has interviewed fourteen of Chrissy Chapman's buddies.'

'What about the units Sammy found?'

'Jimmy's getting on to those tomorrow.'

Pendragon sighed and rubbed his eyes. 'Yes, you're probably right, Sergeant. I think I should have a change of scene.' He stood up and they both saw Superintendent Hughes leading Dr Hickle past the office door along the corridor towards the main desk. He did not notice the two policemen watching him. 'Turner, I want someone outside that man's house all night. You take the first shift. I'll arrange for Vickers to relieve you in two hours.'

It took three rings before Pendragon surfaced from a deep sleep, and even then a couple of moments passed before he realised what the sound was. He reached for his mobile lying on the bedside cabinet and squinted at the number, noted the time – 2.02 a.m. – and opened the cover.

'Grant,' he said wearily. 'What's happened?'

'The nutter's struck again. We're on our way to the scene, a warehouse off Commercial Road.' Pendragon could hear the sound of rain and the beating of the squad-car wipers, then the tick of an indicator.

'Whereabouts exactly?'

'Thyme Street. There's a small industrial estate there. It's a warehouse Number 415b.'

'I'm on my way.'

Pendragon was out in under three minutes and pulling away from the kerb. The snow had vanished to be replaced by sleety rain. The pavements were clear, but soaked. It was a moonless night lit only by neon, and as he pulled away towards the end of his street he had a sudden stab of déjà vu. It was a similar call that had initiated him into the Brick Lane team just over six months earlier. He had just arrived from Oxford and was staying in a hotel for a couple of nights. The morning he was due to start work he had received a call from Inspector Grant at 3.05 a.m. telling him he was on his way to a crime scene on Mile End Road. It had been a rude awakening: a murdered labourer had been pushed through an air vent and crashed through the ceiling of an underground illegal dance club. That had been the start of a particularly intense investigation involving a cross-dressing psycho-killer and the discovery of a mysterious and ancient ring that had once belonged to Lucrezia Borgia.

Pendragon turned left and put his foot down hard on the accelerator. Just after two on a Wednesday morning, the streets were just about as quiet as they would ever be. He jumped the lights and turned left into New Road, pushing the accelerator to the floor. He slowed to turn into Commercial Road and then sped up again. Six minutes after leaving his flat, Pendragon was pulling into the industrial estate. He raced through a pair of opened gates, slowed, then pulled over to check the list of addresses on a huge metal sign. Turning back to the road, he saw an ambulance career around the next bend towards him. Its lights were flashing and the driver was just starting up the siren. Pendragon paused to let the ambulance pass. It churned up a deep puddle of murky water that splashed as high as the nearside windows of the squad car. Pendragon shot away again. A uniformed officer flagged him down as he approached the flashing blue lights of two police cars and a motorcycle parked outside a warehouse on the left.

The uniform held the car door open as Pendragon got out. A shutter door was positioned in the centre of the front wall of the warehouse, and displayed beside this, in artful chrome, was the number of the building. Inside, the large open space was lit by bright fluorescent strips hanging from a high ceiling. It took the DCI a second for his eyes to adjust, and then he saw Turner pacing towards him.

'That was quick, guv.'

'What's the situation? I just saw an ambulance.'

'Yeah, I think we might have saved this one.'

'What?' Pendragon stared past his sergeant at the scene in the warehouse. The front half was empty, nothing more visible than a painted concrete floor with a few pieces of newspaper blowing around it. Filling the back half were dozens of columns of wooden crates. They were stacked five high and in two groups, to right and left of the warehouse. A passage about three metres wide ran between them. Pendragon could hear voices coming from behind the crates and someone had set up a powerful floodlight creating shadows that played across the ceiling.

Turner led the way. 'We got a call about one-forty. A woman on her mobile. She's over there. Name's Vanessa French. She was hysterical, saying that her boyfriend, Gary Townsend, was being tortured. I got here first with Thatcher and Mackleby and saw Ms French outside the building. She was a complete mess . . . trying to keep quiet, but falling apart. Mackleby stayed with her and Jim and I went in. We could hear this horrible whimpering. We got to about here,' . . . and Turner pointed to the floor. '. . . I heard this scrambling sound.' We rushed forward. I caught a glimpse of someone in a protective plastic suit. You know, like the ones they use in bio-labs. We saw the vic on the floor. He was spread-eagled, tied down with ropes. I ran after the geezer in the suit.'

'I assume you didn't get a better look at him?'

'No, guv. They obviously knew their way around the place, had an escape route planned. A door at the back was open when I reached it, but no sign of anyone.'

They had reached the other side of the crates. It was a space about three metres square. In the middle of the floor there were four metal rings in the concrete. Lengths of cut rope were tied around these. There was a puddle of liquid at one end of the arrangement. Around the edge of the liquid, the concrete had started to dissolve. The puddle had been cordoned off with police tape. To one side stood two plastic barrels. Pendragon noted the stickers reading 'Corrosive' on one of them. Two uniforms stood to the right of the scene with Jimmy Thatcher and Inspector Rob Grant. To the left stood two spindly wooden chairs. Sergeant Roz Mackleby was in one, a young woman wrapped in an ambulance blanket was seated in the other.

Pendragon's mind automatically flashed back to the scene on Stepney Green six days earlier: Sergeant Mackleby comforting another woman in the back of an ambulance while close by a hideously mutilated body hung in a tree.

Jack walked over to the two women. 'Ms French, I'm DCI Pendragon.'

Vanessa French looked up, meeting his gaze. She was in her mid-twenties. Clearly undernourished, but pretty. Her shoulder-length hair hung loose. Her make-up was smudged and tear-streaked. She had a strong, intelligent face.

'Hello,' she said. 'DCI Pendragon, I really want to be with Gary right now.'

'I understand. But the medics will do everything they can for him and we can take you straight to the hospital from here.'

She looked at the concrete and then back at Pendragon. 'Okay. I've tried to describe what happened already. I imagine you would like to ask me to again.'

Pendragon found a faint comforting smile from somewhere. 'If you'll indulge me.'

'Where do I start? At the point where I crumpled into hysterical tears or before that?'

Pendragon said nothing, just waved a hand in front of her as if to say, You decide.

'God! I feel so utterly bloody useless . . . I should have stopped them.'

'No. You did the right thing.'

She took a deep breath. 'I thought Gary – that's my boyfriend, Gary Townsend – was having an affair. He's been going out late at night recently. He's Arts Editor for the *Daily Telegraph* – and, yes, I know getting out and about is par for the course in his job, but I was growing suspicious. So I followed him here.' She looked slightly embarrassed for a moment. 'Anyway, I got here about one-thirty, I suppose. The shutters were closed, but the side door was unlocked. I crept in. I could hear some weird sounds coming from around here at the back of the warehouse.

'I made my way between the boxes and hid just over there.' She pointed to the spot. 'And then I saw it.' She gasped suddenly and put a hand to her mouth. Mackleby leaned forward, but Vanessa French pushed her hand away gently.

'I'm okay,' she said and took a deep breath. 'Gary was bound, tied down. It was shadowy. I couldn't see properly. There was a figure in some sort of plastic suit and visor. He leaned forward with a plastic container, opened the top and peered down at Gary. Gary started to struggle. He was gagged, but I could hear him trying to shout, trying to scream. It was horrible.' She paused again then shook herself, trying physically to dispel the terror. 'The figure in the suit started talking, but his voice was distorted – like those voices you get on songs sometimes – do you know what I mean?'

Pendragon glanced at Mackleby, but she was concentrating her gaze on Vanessa French and did not see him.

'He said something like, "Now, my Edvard Munch . . ."' Then he just poured the contents of the plastic container all over Gary's face.'

Vanessa stopped and looked appealingly at Pendragon, then she pressed her hands to her face and dragged them slowly down her cheeks. Pendragon felt a cold chill run along his spine.

'Gary . . . Gary screamed. He screamed and he screamed.' Vanessa took a couple of very deep breaths. 'I was frozen to the spot . . . literally. I know it sounds like something out of a bad detective novel, but I did. I felt the world fall apart around me. I felt sick. Then . . . I ran.'

She stopped again and Pendragon searched her face. She was trying valiantly to keep control of her emotions.

'I got outside. I threw up. I was crying. My eyes were streaming – it must have been the fumes . . . Oh God!' She gasped and brought both hands to her mouth. 'Imagine . . . just imagine what Gary must have . . . .'

There was a long silence, broken only by the sound of a camera shutter. Pendragon glanced round and saw that the police photographer had arrived.

'That's when I called you . . .'

'Thank you, Vanessa,' Pendragon said, and leaned forward to take her hand. She jerked a little as he touched her, then looked up from the concrete to stare into his eyes again.

'Please get the fucking bastard, Inspector,' she hissed, and withdrew her hand.

'So you saw nothing on your shift outside Hickle's flat?' Pendragon said as he and Turner jumped into the car.

'No, nothing. Vickers rocked up about midnight. About an hour later we got the call to come here. I phoned

Vickers on my way to the warehouse. He reckoned no one had left Hickle's building.'

Pendragon negotiated the narrow road past the industrial units and out onto the main street. 'Hickle could have slipped out,' he said.

'It's possible I suppose, but not likely.'

'Well, then, if Hickle is involved he must have an accomplice.'

'Unless the guy is completely innocent, guv,' Turner said.

Chapter 45

To Mrs Sonia Thomson
17 October 1888

'So it was you!' Archibald exclaimed, his face pale as winter snow.

'It very much looks like it, old fellow,' I replied, throwing the bag containing my materials on to the bed.

'You killed those women.' He stared at me like a wax figure, so shocked, his eyes expressed no emotion. Just the corner of his mouth twitched. A nervous tic, I assumed. I had never seen Archibald nervous or even worried, not even during those dramatic times in the opium dens. He was always level-headed, self-confident.

'So now you know, Archibald,' I said quietly; and suddenly, he was rushing towards me, his fists balled.

As you know, he was a chunky fellow and strong. But he was at least fifteen years my senior and all that good living was hardly to his advantage. He threw a punch that went wildly awry. I extended my foot and he tripped, landing heavily on the floor close to the dining table where I had recently written my letters and planned my masterpiece. In an instant, I was on him. One hard punch to the back of his neck and Archibald was out cold.

I laid him on the bed flat on his back and looked down at his prone form. As I turned away the latest painting caught my eye. It sat there on the easel, untouched by our brief struggle. I approached and studied it carefully. It was a fine piece, and if I had decided to complete it, it would have merited every ounce of praise it would doubtless have received. But it was not to be. Looking down, I found my painting materials: a collection of jars with brushes poised at different angles, a tray of paints and a large bottle of thinner. Picking up the bottle, I opened the top, breathed in the rich odour and then poured the flammable liquid liberally around the room. From my coat pocket I extracted a box of matches and struck one, watching the flame grow and shimmer before my eyes.

The match landed on the carpet a few feet across the room and the thinning fluid caught immediately. Striding towards the bed, I pulled Archibald up and propped him over my left shoulder. On the way towards the door, I grabbed my bag of knives and implements and dashed for the stairs just as the fire started to take hold.

I had organised several escape routes and hideouts. After all, one of the most important aspects of any great creation is planning, and this could never be more true than of the form of art I have mastered.

It was an easy matter to get Archibald out of the building and along the street. In my adopted neighbourhood, semi-conscious drunks were more the norm than sober gentlemen. A quick turn into a nearby alley when no one was looking and Archibald and I were soon in the shadows at the rear of one of the tall buildings that fronted Whitechapel Road. I heard a couple of rats dash away from a pile of rubbish. Resting Archibald in a sitting position with his back to the brick wall of the building, I kicked away the nearby detritus until I could see the filthy stones beneath. I felt around in the dark. My fingers alighted on the metal ring in a drain cover. Pulling on it, I lifted the cover and the stench of the sewer below burst out into the narrow alley. I resisted the urge to vomit and turned away for a moment. I had a small lantern hidden beneath a pair of empty and rusted metal barrels close to the wall. I pulled it out, opened the window and lit the wick with a match. Returning to the drain, I yanked Archibald over to me by the feet.

Lowering myself into the hole via a short metal ladder, I plucked up my bag and dropped it inside before clambering after it with the lantern held aloft. I managed to reach the floor of the sewer only a few feet below the surface. I could not stand up straight, but I just managed to lever Archibald's legs into the hole and let him slither into the sewer on top of me, breaking his fall best I could with my arms and shoulders. He fell face first into the mess at the bottom of the tunnel and began to come round.

Before he could wake up properly, I grabbed his arms, yanked his wrists behind him and bound them with a length of rope I had taken the precaution of keeping in my bag. Then I slapped him to wake him up a little.

'Now, Archibald. You need to turn round,' I said. 'We're heading that way.' And I nodded to the black tunnel behind him.

'Ah, fuck!' he exclaimed. 'What is that stink?' And then he looked down to see in the dim light from the lantern that he was covered in human excrement.

'Move!' I snapped.

He glared at me. 'You'll pay for this, Tumbril. You will pay.'

I laughed at that. 'Archibald, my dear fellow, my name is not Harry Tumbril. It is William Sandler. Now, this is the last time I will say it, move!'

Bent almost double, Archibald shuffled along the tunnel. After twenty yards it opened out into a much larger channel some ten feet across, the tiled ceiling a little above head-height, the walls curved.

Along one side ran a metal pipe about three inches in diameter. There was a narrow gap between it and the wall, and it was fastened on to the tiles and the stone behind it with large steel clamps. I double-checked the rope around Archibald's wrists, then turned him to face me. He was clearly terrified, but he was also burning up with rage. He opened his mouth to say something, but I had grown bored. I punched him hard in the face and he stumbled back, hitting his head on the wall. Leaning over him, I checked that he was breathing. Then, standing up, I untied the rope about his wrists and reworked it about the pipe attached to the wall. I pulled it taut and stood back. 'Not exactly the Reform Club, is it, Archie?' I laughed.

And now, dear lady, I'm approaching the end of my tale. I took rooms at Claridge's, swapping the seediness of Whitechapel for the luxury and grandeur of Mayfair. To be honest, I felt I owed it to myself – a little reward for creating the most revolutionary piece of art since Giotto first popularised the use of perspective.

The hotel was entirely pleasing, as you would expect. Hot water, a luxurious bathroom, soft, clean sheets. I'm not one for hedonism, but it did make a favourable change from Wentworth Street. In room 325, I perused *The Times,* reading the most fantastical accounts of Mary Kelly's demise. And on pages four and six, I found two much shorter stories. One of these concerned a terrible fire in Whitechapel which had destroyed two shops and the rooms above them. Three charred bodies and dozens of roasted chickens were found among the wreckage. The other story concerned a certain newspaper editor who had disappeared without trace. Last seen at the Reform Club, Archibald Thomson had not returned to the offices of the *Clarion* on Pall Mall. The police had been notified, and the man's usual haunts visited by detectives. All to no avail. Mr Thomson seemed to have vanished into thin air.

I savoured Claridge's, but after two days told myself I had things to do. My first job was to purchase a one-way ticket to New York, first class. The ticket was for the White Star Line's ship *Oceanic*, which, according to the brochure, offered the ultimate in seagoing luxury. The ship was due to leave the following day, 6 October, on a two-week journey across the Atlantic.

That afternoon I returned to Whitechapel. Under cover of darkness, I crept into the passage where the drain was located, found the lantern which I had replaced behind the rusty barrels, and then retraced the steps I had taken with Archibald two nights before. Inside the narrow tunnel, the lamp cast a measly light, but I could see the dribble of excrement and the streak of unctuous mould. I crept along slowly and emerged into the larger tunnel. The light bounced around the discoloured tiles and illuminated the wretched figure of Archibald, just where I had left him.

Crouching down in front of him, I lifted his head. He was alive, but barely conscious. From my bag, I took a water bottle and brought it to his lips. He did not respond, so I slapped him hard about the face until he opened his eyes. He looked at me, but I could tell he could not make out who or what I was. I tried him with the water again and this time he sipped at it. The liquid seemed to invigorate him somewhat and he drank more, making small grunting sounds as the water trickled down his throat. Slowly he began to revive a little.

'I've brought you some things, Archibald,' I said. 'I'm going away now. But I thought I would leave you a few tokens to remember me by.'

From my bag, I withdrew my favourite knife, a fine steel eight-inch blade with a calf-skin inlaid handle. This I placed on the filthy floor about three feet away from where Archibald was bound to the metal pipe. Returning to the bag, I pulled out a parcel covered with cloth. Unbinding the wrapping, I lifted the gift to Archibald's face. In the gas light he could just see a box containing a round fruit cake, a ham, a large slab of chocolate and an opened bottle of red wine. More awake now, his eyes widened.

I lowered the box to the floor next to the knife, the whole assembly just out of reach. Then I placed the lantern close by so that the gifts would be illuminated after I left. Standing up, I looked down into his face. 'Look on the bright side, Archibald,' I said. 'It will all be over soon. Cheerio.'

So, dear Sonia, there we have it. I have to say that writing these letters to you has been a most interesting experience. I did not intend them to be so detailed, nor so long, but I got carried away. I would say that it was cathartic, but that would imply I needed to get something off my chest. A ridiculous notion, of course.

Do what you will with this information. I imagine you will want to find Archibald's body and to give him a decent burial. Each to his own. For me, this is certainly not the end of the tale, but the conclusion to the part in which we have shared a connection. I will be arriving in New York City in a few days, and from there . . . who knows? I have no fixed plans. I'll be glad to be away from London but shall doubtless, at some point, start to miss the place. I have a feeling I may never return to England. But anything is possible. Life is like art. Let your mind and your will run free, and who knows where fate may lead you? Farewell.

Chapter 46

The London Hospital, Thursday 29 January, 9.14 a.m.

It was a tiny explosion, barely enough to shake the bottles and boxes from the shelves inside the small room, but sufficient to set off the alarms and to send a plume of black smoke through the half-open door into the corridor. And it had taken no more than ten minutes to arrange: a short walk along the corridor disguised in an orderly's green plastic overalls, and then five paces past the door leading to Intensive Care. The chemicals were all there in the cleaner's storeroom – sulphuric acid, bleach and floor cleaner. Add to these some nail varnish remover, a simple pre-made circuit improvised from a small battery and the flashlight from an old camera, and . . . boom!

It worked perfectly. There was a loud thud from inside the store, followed by the high-pitched confusion of smashing glassware and the clatter of falling boxes. The alarm sounded and the corridor began to fill with smoke. The two nurses at the desk situated just inside the Intensive Care Ward ran out, followed a few seconds later by the only attending doctor on the ward. In the confusion, it was a simple matter to slip into the long, narrow room unnoticed.

The first job was to tamper with the alarm. The computer on the ICU sister's desk close to the door purred quietly. A few taps on the keyboard brought up the personal bleeper program. To change three of the parameters was straightforward. A tap on the 'Return' key completed the task.

Gary Townsend lay unconscious. Over the upper half of his body was a perspex canopy. He had three plastic tubes supplying him with different medications. A monitor bleeped and a screen displayed his vital signs. His face was a hideous mess, as though someone had taken a blow torch to a plastic doll's head. His hair had liquefied almost halfway back over his head, leaving random charred clumps. His eyes were shrouded with melted skin and there were deep furrows in his cheeks through which slices of stark white bone could be seen. Patches of diaphanous gauze lay across exposed stretches of the man's forehead and in strips down each side of his neck. He was barely breathing.

The canopy pivoted up on a pair of metal hinges. A quick glance round confirmed no one was coming back from the corridor. The cap of the hypodermic slipped off easily. Finding a vein was a little trickier, but then the needle slid into flesh, the plunger was pushed home and the heroin shot into Townsend's bloodstream. He was dead before the canopy had clicked back into place.

A steady walk back to the door, a turn right away from the scene of the diversion, remembering to look down turning the corner into the corridor covered by CCTV . . . and the job was done.

Chapter 47

Brick Lane, Stepney, Thursday 29 January,
9.45 a.m.

Pendragon had managed to grab a couple of hours' sleep.
At 3.30 a.m he had left the station and called Vickers
whom he knew would be on his way back to Brick Lane
from Hickle's flat on Wilmore Terrace. Vickers had told
him he had seen nothing of interest and that Thatcher was
now on duty. Less than six hours later, the DCI was back
in his office, checking on two other sergeants who had
done their stint observing the building in which Hickle
lived. There had been no sign of the man. Jack wanted to
check on Thatcher's progress with the warehouses
Sammy had mentioned, but knew the sergeant would not
be in for a few hours. Instead, he flicked on the coffee
machine and waited for it to warm up.

Turner knocked on the door and came in. He looked as
though he had not slept for a week.

'I think you need some of my extra strong Italian roast,'
Pendragon said as the sergeant lowered himself into a
chair the other side of the desk.

'That would be fantastic, sir.'

There was another tap on the door. A new recruit,

Sergeant Manners came in.

Pendragon turned away from the coffee machine. 'Sergeant?'

'Sorry to bother you, sir, but I thought you ought to know. Just finished on the duty desk, received a message about ten minutes ago, from the London Hospital.'

Pendragon raised an eyebrow. 'From whom?'

'A consultant in A and E. A woman was admitted early this morning after a mugging. She asked specifically for you. Name's Locke.'

'Gemma Locke?'

'Yeah.'

Pendragon came round the desk, holding the coffee scoop in his left hand. He watched Manners leave and ordered: 'Turner, you stay here. Chase up any of the warehouses Thatcher hasn't got to yet.'

'Where are you going?'

'To the London Hospital.'

'But, guv, the coffee . . .'

Pendragon ignored him and was out of the door before Turner's 'Oh, fuck' had left his lips.

The London Hospital never slept. At 10 a.m. it was abuzz with people. Ambulances rolled up or left the main bay at the front of the building, using the narrow slipway on to Mile End Road. The reception area was a throwback to Victorian times. Very little natural light reached it. Chipped marble columns and scuffed walls covered with noticeboards added to the sense of claustrophobia. A rather sorry excuse for a gift shop stood in the corner furthest from the main doors.

Pendragon made his request and flashed his badge to the young girl at the desk who started to tap on the keyboard of her computer. 'Yes, Ms Locke,' she said, between chews on her gum, never meeting Pendragon's eyes. 'Down there.' She pointed to her left. 'After the second double doors, turn right.'

Pendragon strode down the corridor, ignoring the posters imploring everyone to stop smoking, cover up with sunscreen and get a flu jab. From all around came sounds of human activity. He heard a baby cry. A doctor in a white lab coat sporting a collection of pens in his top left pocket rushed past him. From further off Pendragon could hear drills and builders swearing. He pushed through the second set of doors and turned right, as instructed, to find another, smaller reception desk. He showed his badge again and the young male nurse pointed to a curtained area, the second bed on the left.

'Jack Pendragon!' Gemma Locke said, smiling as the DCI gingerly pulled back the curtain a little. 'You promised to call.' She was sitting on the edge of the bed reading a magazine. She had a bandage around her head and a row of steristrips on her upper cheek. Even without make-up, she still looked strikingly attractive. The bottom of her fringe protruded from the lower edge of the bandage around her forehead. Beneath it her dark eyes were as alive as ever.

'Apologies,' Pendragon said, suddenly remembering he had some flowers in his hand. He held out the small bouquet.

'Oh, Jack! That's very thoughtful of you.'

'Well, you look like you've been in the thick of it,' he replied.

Gemma touched the bandage and nodded towards a chair beside the bed. Jack lowered himself into it. 'I don't think it's as bad as it looks,' she said. 'They gave me the all-clear after a check-up about eight o'clock this morning. Came back about half an hour later to give me a painkilling jab.' She pointed to her arm. 'The doctor told me it was a slow-release drug and that I should rest here for a couple of hours. He forbade me to operate any machinery, and said I should just read a book or something. I was about to call a taxi. But it's great to see you. You got my message, obviously.'

'Yes.'

'I thought I ought to report the incident, so I called my favourite copper. Actually, you're the only policeman I know!' Her face broke into a broad smile and then suddenly a pained expression. 'Ow!' she said. 'Make a mental note, Jack. Remind me not to smile.'

'What happened to you?'

'I was walking along Stanton Street about one this morning. Should have caught a cab, of course. That's what everyone will tell me.'

'One a.m.?'

'Yes, Jack,' she responded wearily and rolled her eyes. 'I'm an artist. I don't keep office hours.'

'Duly noted,' Pendragon replied lightly. 'I'm a copper, I don't do nine to five either. Go on.'

'I didn't hear anyone approach. Just felt this pain in my head and felt . . . I don't know how to explain it . . . puzzled isn't the right word. But, well, yeah, it'll do. Puzzled. What could be hurting me . . . you know? That's it. I woke up on a bed a bit like this one.'

'I take it you were robbed too?'

'Oh yes. Phone, cards, a bit of cash.'

'Well, sorry to be predictable but I'll have to be the first to say you should have caught a cab.'

'Oh, you're way too slow. The doctor has already said it.'

'So you're free to go now?'

'I am.'

'Well, the least I can do is to put you in a cab.'

'All right,' she responded. 'But only on condition you let me make you a coffee at my place.'

Pendragon looked at his watch. 'Ah . . .'

'No deal then.'

Gemma Locke's fourteenth-floor apartment was in an exclusive new block in Wapping. It was very modern, but softened by a female eye for comfort as well as practicality. Where many a successful thirty-something single man would have furnished the place with black leather and chrome, Gemma had gone for a more subtle, feminine palette of burnt umber, ivory and unpainted plaster. It worked well with the urban view through a massive window opening on to Docklands. Canary Wharf was just visible, and beyond that the long twisting coils of the grey Thames. Great black clouds hung low over the scene, threatening more snow.

'I'm guessing you don't work here,' Pendragon said, surveying the beautiful space.

'Er . . . no!' Gemma replied. 'I have a studio in Bermondsey. I like to keep home and work completely separate. Or else I'd always be working.'

Pendragon insisted he made the coffee while she lay on one of the large sofas in the main space. He found everything where he expected it and brought over a tray, placing it on a mother-of-pearl inlaid Indian coffee table. Gemma pulled herself up, bringing one hand to her bandaged head.

'Hurting?'

'Not as such,' she replied. 'They gave me something the doctor said would make a mugged elephant feel better. I'm not sure I appreciated the allusion.'

Pendragon laughed.

'Do all coppers have such a good sense of humour?' she asked with a faint upturning of the lips.

'Some of them believe they do. My sergeant thinks he's very funny.'

She nodded and took a sip of coffee. 'Mmm . . . good.'

'So, now that you have my full attention,' Pendragon said. 'Perhaps you'll let me know some more about yourself. I Googled you.'

'Oh, God!'

'And you have an impressive website.'

'Pretty much *de rigueur* these days.'

'I imagine so. But they only scratch the surface.'

'What do you want to know? Am I being questioned?'

Pendragon shook his head and smiled. 'Strictly personal research,' he said, and drank some coffee.

'Well, that's a relief,' Gemma teased, eyeing him over her cup. 'Oh, the interesting stuff is all on the website actually. My life only really started when I got to London as a twenty-one-year-old, fresh out of art college.'

'You studied at the Berlin University of the Arts, I saw.'

'Yes. Dad was a colonel in the British Army. We moved around a lot – Cyprus, Gibraltar, even a less than glamorous spell in Belfast. I was about fifteen when we moved to Germany. Dad's regiment was stationed at Eberswalde, about thirty miles from Berlin. When I was seventeen, my father was offered a desk job and the family moved to Brussels. I stayed on in Berlin because I had just been given a place at BUA.' Gemma looked serious. 'Dad died a year ago, almost to the day.'

'I'm sorry . . .'

'No need to be. We were close when I was young, but we drifted apart. I'd hardly seen him during the two or three years before . . . maybe that makes it worse. Anyway . . .' She drained her coffee cup and placed it on the tray.

'So, your big break? That was . . .'

'*Freeways and Blood*.'

'I have to confess, I didn't really . . . well, get it. But it was undoubtedly clever,' Pendragon replied. In truth, he had not understood the piece at all. It was a rectangular box about two metres tall and a metre wide, divided laterally in two. On one side a video loop showed an aerial night-time view of a ten-lane freeway somewhere in America, the headlights of hundreds of cars running in ordered streams. Down the length of the right half of the box ran another continuous video loop of a magnified image of blood, showing the individual corpuscles bobbing against each other in a seemingly random flow.

'Oh, dear! Damned by faint praise.'

Pendragon held his hands up. 'No, not at all. I'm afraid

any shortcoming is mine. My tastes are a bit old-fashioned, I suppose.'

'Oh, please! Don't say the word "Monet".'

Pendragon frowned. 'Give me some credit!'

Gemma produced a small laugh, and winced.

'Look, I'm sorry,' he said, standing up. 'What am I doing, grilling you on art just after you get out of A and E?'

'It's okay . . .' Gemma began, and then yawned. 'Oops!' She started to get up, reached halfway and swayed. Pendragon caught her and helped her back to the sofa.

'Sorry,' she mumbled, and let her eyes close. 'Guess the doc was right about the elephant . . .'

'I'll see myself out,' he said.

Chapter 48

Pendragon was walking through the lobby of Gemma Locke's apartment block when the call came through from Turner. The traffic was gridlocked on Commercial Road, which meant it took over half an hour for him to reach the hospital. At reception, the same woman Pendragon had seen earlier that day directed him to the Critical Care Wing on the third floor. Turner met him at the swing doors into the ward.

The hospital administrators had gone into overdrive. The other four patients in Intensive Care had been moved to another building, and a dozen others in neighbouring rooms had been shifted to any available space beyond the doors into the ward. This included two elderly men who were forced to share a tiny room usually reserved for doctors needing a quick nap between shifts.

'Who else is here?' Pendragon asked, noticing Sergeant Thatcher and Inspector Towers. The two policemen were questioning a small group of hospital staff huddled in the corridor close to a workstation.

'Dr Jones has been delayed. But Colette Newman and an assistant are in the ICU.'

'And what's that smell?

'I dunno, sir. I noticed it as soon as we got here. It's like burned rubber.'

'Yes, and something else . . . I can't think what. Anyway, where's the ICU?'

'There.' Turner pointed to a door on the left towards the far end of the corridor.

The single bed containing Gary Townsend's body looked out of place alone in the room. Wires and leads hung from the wall at the other three bays. The machines still attached to Townsend stood mute. The monitor that had once recorded his shallow heartbeat now displayed a flat line. A plastic-suited forensics officer Pendragon did not recognise was dusting for prints along the rails and around the tubes on the far side of the bed. Dr Newman was crouching beside the bed, a test tube in one latex-gloved hand, a pair of tweezers in the other. She was wearing protective lab glasses and a paper mask over her mouth. Turning, she saw the two policemen approach, placed a stopper on the test tube, stood it in a rack inside a metal case on the floor beside the bed, and pulled the mask down to her chin.

'Well, Inspector, the bodies are piling up.'

Pendragon looked at the scientist with a pained expression then took a couple of steps to the side of the bed and peered down at Townsend's disfigured face. He let out a heavy sigh and turned back to Dr Newman. 'Any preliminary findings?'

'We've only been here ten minutes, but it looks like there're a lot of prints around the place . . . some hair . . . skin flakes. But then, you'd expect all those, wouldn't you?'

'How quickly can you analyse everything? I'm sorry to seem so damn pushy, Doctor, it's just . . .'

'No need to apologise. It will be our top priority . . . don't worry. Now, perhaps if you could . . .'

'Right,' Pendragon said awkwardly. He tapped Turner on the shoulder and pointed to the door.

Outside in the corridor, Towers was still talking to one of the nurses. The others had gone. Pendragon beckoned him over. 'What have you got?'

'Well, no one saw anything. Whoever got into the ICU set up a decoy.'

'What?'

'A homemade bomb. Feeble and crude, but enough to produce a bit of smoke and get people running around.'

'That explains the stink,' Turner said.

'The ICU sister, Agnes Daniels, insists she and her deputy were only away from the room for a couple of minutes. She got back and heard the buzzer on Gary Townsend's monitor going off. His heart had stopped. She immediately called a doc, but they couldn't revive him. Pronounced dead at nine-twenty-four this morning. She only realised over an hour later that someone had tampered with the computer at her workstation. They'd turned off the personal bleeper that warns her remotely of any patient distress if she's out of this room. She put two and two together, and immediately alerted Security. The call came through to the station about thirty-five minutes ago,' he concluded, looking at his notebook.

Pendragon strode over to Towers. The nurse he had been interviewing was walking away. 'Anything?'

'She was out here in the corridor. Heard a small bang from over there,' Towers pointed to a door a dozen feet away. It was ajar. Pendragon and Turner could just see inside. A forensics officer in a plastic suit was crouching down and prodding at something on the floor.

'They panicked a bit,' Towers went on. 'You know, what with terrorists here, there and everywhere. But then, when they realised it was a toy bomb, they decided it was probably some bloody idiot kids who'd got into the hospital. Security here dealt with it. Didn't bother reporting it to us.'

Pendragon was shaking his head. 'Understandable, I suppose. No one wanted the paperwork. So who else was here at the time of the explosion?'

Towers quickly scanned his notes. 'The Intensive Care sister, Agnes Daniels, and her deputy, Ungani Metubu, were in ICU. Two other nurses, Consuela Manito and . . . er . . . Ari Hullano, were out here at this desk.' He pointed to the now empty workstation along the corridor. A junior doctor was passing through on his way to J Ward. A Dr Imhrim Atullah. And there was a specialist due in at nine. But they didn't show.'

'Did they turn up later?'

'Not sure, sir.'

'Well, check then, Inspector!' Pendragon snapped, waving him away. 'Get the ICU sister . . . Agnes Davies . . . now!'

'It's Daniels, guv,' Turner said, and regretted it when Pendragon spun round on him.

'Sir, may I make a suggestion?' Sergeant Thatcher said, quickly defusing the situation. 'How about I talk to the

347

staff in the main reception area downstairs? See if they spotted anything unusual this morning around nine.'

'Yes, it's worth a try, Sergeant. And while you're about it, talk to any of the patients who were up and about or at least *compos mentis* around here this morning, to see if any of them saw anything out of the ordinary. And, you, Turner . . .' Pendragon went on '. . . can get all the CCTV tapes from the hospital. There must be cameras in some of the corridors, and there'll be plenty of them outside the building. Get the recordings back to the station and go through them, second by second, between nine and ten this morning.'

Pendragon turned and saw Towers approaching them. Beside him walked a tall, slender woman in dark blue uniform. Resting in the crook of her left arm was a clipboard. She could have been anywhere between forty and fifty-five, Pendragon decided. She had dark eyes, slightly sunken. She looked ill or else extremely tired.

'Sister Daniels,' Inspector Towers said.

The woman nodded brusquely to Pendragon. 'I understand you wanted to know about the specialist.' She had a deep, almost masculine voice and it sounded as tired as she looked.

'Yes, please.'

'He was due here at nine. Still hasn't appeared,' she said, a hint of contempt in her voice.

'I see. Do you have a name?'

She glanced at the clipboard. 'Yes, Dr Hickle. He was Gary Townsend's specialist. But I imagine it's pretty academic now anyway.'

348

Chapter 49

Whitechapel, 6 October 1888

'This bleedin' sack just gets 'eavier and 'eavier,' Eddie Morestone moaned. 'And stop fucking wrigglin' around, ya bastards!' he snapped, hoisting the sack a few inches above the slurry running along the floor. At thirty-two, Eddie was already an old man. The life of a tosher was a hard one, but he had come from a desperate family. His father and two uncles had been mudlarks whose work had involved finding anything of value they could in the sewage-filled banks of the Thames. At times their job had required them to pull a bloated dead body on to a barge or the sand banks, and to strip the poor soul of anything the waters had not aleady claimed: gold teeth, rings, crucifixes . . . anything that would fetch a profit. Eddie had worked on the river for two years but he hated the water and when a friend had suggested they go into partnership together as toshers, trawling through the East End sewers for rats that could be sold for baiting dogs in the gambling dens, he'd jumped at the chance.

The friend, Jimmy Grafter, had died five years

ago, a victim of cholera – 'the downside to the job' Eddie would joke darkly to anyone who would talk to him; anyone that is who could bear his stink. After Jimmy was taken, Eddie got himself a new partner, Quick Tom, a kid of twelve at the time who still deserved his nickname. He was already carrying the partnership, and Eddie's days down the sewers were numbered; they both knew it.

'Tom, slow down a sec, will ya?' he called into the darkness ahead.

'I wanna get 'ome,' the boy snapped back, keeping up the pace. He had his own sack of restless rodents to drag along. Then, out of pity, he stopped to let Eddie catch up. Sighing, he waited for the older man to slosh his way level, panting as he advanced. Tom was holding their only source of illumination, a small lamp poised just in front of his nose. It cast sinister shadows across his pox-scarred face.

'Cheers, son,' Eddie wheezed.

It was then that they heard the scraping sound.

''Ello,' Tom said, a grin appearing through the filth coating his face. 'Sounds like a big'un.'

'It's comin' from over there.' Eddie gave a brief nod towards a point further along the tunnel to their left.

They crept forward lightly. 'What the . . . ?' Tom exclaimed then.

'What is it?'

'It's a bloke!'

What?' Eddie sidled up and dropped his sack at his feet, ignoring the way it undulated with the movement of the angry rats inside it. 'Well, fuck me!'

Tom bent down beside the crumpled figure. 'He's been tied up, the poor sod.'

'Is he alive?'

'Dunno.'

Eddie crouched down and noticed the knife and a soggy box containing smears of something that looked like chocolate beside an opened bottle of wine. 'Somefink strange 'appened 'ere,' he noted. 'What're the knife and the bottle about?' Before Tom could reply, Eddie turned away and lifted the man's drooping head. Archibald Thomson's face was pale and a thick rope of dried vomit ran from his mouth, down his neck and across his shirt.

'He's breathin',' Tom said, and turned to Eddie with a glint in his eye. 'You finkin' what I'm finkin'?'

Eddie leaned forward and shook the man then tried to force open his eyes. Archibald shuddered.

'He's a gent,' Tom observed, studying the wretched figure's clothes. 'Check 'is pockets, Ed.'

Eddie thrust his hand inside Archibald's jacket and fished out a wallet. 'Weren't robbed then.'

'Nah. Anyfink in it?'

Eddie pulled out a handful of crumpled notes. 'Must be at least five pounds 'ere.'

Tom whistled. 'Nice one,' he said, pulling out a fob watch. 'Gold bleedin' chain and all.' He winked at Eddie. 'Come on. Let's grab the stuff and go. And don't forget the knife,' he added, nodding towards it where it lay a few feet away. 'Could be worth a bit.'

351

''Ang on.'

Tom looked at him, screwing up his eyes and tilting his head.

'Fink, Tommy, fink! Don't ya reckon there might be a reward out for this bloke? He's obviously a gent, and must be worth a bob or two. Someone should be very grateful we found 'im alive.'

Tom gave the older man a doubtful look.

Eddie could almost see the kid's mind ticking over. 'Well?'

'All right,' he said after a long pause. 'But we'll take the money on 'im. No one need be any the wiser, eh?'

Chapter 50

Brick Lane, Stepney, Thursday 29 January, 2.05p.m.

'Jack, this is the first breakthrough we've had.'

Pendragon listened to Superintendent Hughes's enthusiastic tone dispassionately. He was on his mobile hands-free in the car, heading back to the station.

'You don't seem very upbeat about it,' she commented.

'Well, I'm not. If Hickle is as clever as everyone thinks he is, he'll be a long way from here by now. He has almost three hours lead on us. He and his accomplice must have everything well planned.'

'Okay, we can't get into a time machine. But I've already got top-level support on this. I'll put road blocks in place. Close the ports. Get ID to the airport authorities. I'll even shut down the airports if I have to!'

Five minutes later, Jack was pulling the car into one of the bays outside the station, and forty-five seconds after that he was in Hughes's office.

'A team are due to arrive at Hickle's flat any moment now,' the superintendent said. 'I'm sure he won't be there but we have a warrant to search the place, see what nasty secrets the man's hiding.'

'They won't find anything.'

'Probably not.'

'What about Chrissy Chapman's place?'

'Grant and Vickers are on their way.'

'What do we do?'

'We wait.'

Pendragon forced himself to deal with the pile of paper-work that had been steadily building up all week, but he was finding it almost impossible to focus. Then the first of a succession of calls came in. It was from the team at Hickle's flat. The doctor was not there, and as predicted the flat had revealed nothing incriminating at all.

The second call was from Inspector Grant. They were driving away from Chrissy Chapman's place. Hickle was not there and the apartment was exactly how the police and cleaners had left it after Forensics, Pathology and the photography department had finished there the day before.

Pendragon had just looked at the clock displaying the time as 18.03 when the third call was patched through from the front desk.

'Inspector,' said Colette Newman.

'Interesting news, I hope, Doctor.'

'There were literally dozens of prints in the ICU, and a fair bit of DNA. I managed to get several good, clear prints of Hickle's as well as some skin flakes and hairs matching his DNA.'

'Well, that's all useful.'

'I guess so, but you realise, of course, that it doesn't mean that much. The doctor was often in the ICU. It

354

would have been more unusual if there had been no trace of his DNA or prints there.'

'Yes, I realise that, Dr Newman. But every bit of evidence helps. Thanks for processing things so fast.'

There was a rap on the door. Pendragon could see Turner's familiar outline and the door opened immediately. 'Sergeant,' Pendragon said. 'You have a DVD in your hand.'

Turner held it up and waved it in the air. 'Took a lot of persuading, I can tell you.'

Pendragon followed the sergeant into the corridor and through the third door on the left, the Media Room. Turner flicked on a few machines and pulled a chair close to a pair of monitors on the desk. Pendragon sat back a little, watching the computer boot up and the video analyser go through its litany of sounds as it analysed the DVD. Turner found the part of the film he was after. 'I haven't seen it myself yet,' the sergeant began. 'They have a master control centre for all the cameras – there're seventeen of them inside the hospital and another fourteen on the outside of the building. The operator gave me all the films from nine until ten, along with the numbers of the cameras that we'd be interested in – three of them inside and one outside. I can programme the analyser to search just those films. Shall we start with the camera nearest the ICU, sir?' he asked, swivelling in his chair.

Pendragon nodded. 'Probably best.'

Turner's fingers skittered over the control panel in front of the two flat-screen monitors and an image appeared on the left hand. It was a shot of the corridor leading from the main building into the area around the ICU administration desk. People passed in and out of shot. First, a nurse, then a pair of doctors. A patient using a Zimmer frame took several minutes to walk along the stretch of corridor covered by the camera. The clock in the corner of the screen clicked on. At 9.08 an orderly in a green hospital one-piece suit and tight-fitting cap appeared, head down, moving quickly along the corridor. As the orderly reached the edge of the camera's field, they lifted a clipboard to obscure their face even more. Then they darted through a door.

The clock ticked along. At 9.14 the orderly emerged from the room, clipboard again held in front of their face. They walked back along the corridor, and at that precise moment the improvised bomb went off. There was a dull thud through the speakers, and on the screen Pendragon and Turner could see smoke billowing out of the door the orderly had left ajar. Several members of staff ran quickly towards the source of the explosion. The only person moving in the opposite direction was the orderly. Glancing around furtively, they stepped into the ICU.

The clock moved on. At 9.17, the figure emerged from the ICU, clipboard held in front of them. Turning right, they walked quickly along the corridor towards the camera, head down. It had been obvious from the moment the orderly had appeared that it was not Dr Geoff Hickle. The person on the screen was slightly built and at least six inches shorter than the man they had suspected.

'Stop there, Turner,' Pendragon said. 'So this must be his accomplice.'

'Reckon so, guv.'

356

'I need some time to think. You must have some paperwork to be getting on with.'

The sergeant nodded.

'And, Turner, can you switch off the lights as you go out?'

Chapter 51

Bedlam Hospital for the Insane, St George's Fields,
Southwark, November 1888

The hansom passed through the imposing gates of
the Bethlehem Royal Hospital and Sonia Thomson
heard the cabbie whip the horse to make it speed up.
He had not really wanted to take her here in the first
place. 'Bedlam?' he had said. 'What d'ya wanna go
there for?' She had given him her chilliest look,
prompting him to mumble an apology.

The journey had passed in a blur. She was still
numb – the result of reading the batch of letters she
had received that morning. Arriving together from
America on the post steamer, they constituted what
was really a single, long missive. At times, it was
rambling and muddled, but it had shocked her,
terrified her, and, at some points, brought an inner
fury bubbling to the surface. She had always loved
her husband, always respected him, always
considered him to be brilliant, determined, hard-
working and dedicated, but she had also always
known that, in other ways, he was weak. Weak like
most men were. But the graphic way in which the

author of the letters, a certain William Sandler, had described Archibald's weaknesses, and had at the same time offered so much information about himself and his own evil-doing . . . Well, it had left her reeling.

She had as yet barely had time to absorb the contents of the letters, but a part of her – the logical, well-educated part, for she came from a long line of successful academics – had already started to ask some difficult questions. Foremost among them: What could or should she do with the information in her possession? It was clearly some sort of crazed confession, but was it genuine? Was it really a letter from Jack the Ripper? How could she be sure? True, the Whitechapel murders seemed to have stopped with the demise of Mary Kelly. And what of the description of how Archibald had ended up in the sewer? If the toshers she had paid off had told the truth, then William Sandler's version would have been entirely accurate. Even so, that did not mean Sandler – or Tumbril, as Archibald had known him – really was The Ripper. Those parts of the account could have been entirely fabricated.

But it was not this that preyed the most on her mind. Her most pressing problem was not the matter of who the author of the letters might be, but rather what she should do with them. She could not make them public without ruining her husband's name and reputation. Few people knew the truth of what had happened to Archibald. As far as the public were concerned, he was a kidnap victim abandoned and left for dead in a filthy sewer. The *Clarion* had gone to great lengths to report that their editor was recovering from the physical incapacity caused by his ordeal. She would do nothing to contradict that story. For what good would it do anyone to know that her husband had been so thoroughly duped by Jack the Ripper?

The cab drew to a halt and Sonia climbed down on to the gravel driveway. Walking slowly around the back of the cab, she approached the steps and found Dr Irvin Braithwaite, standing with hand extended in welcome. He was a tall, thin man, not unattractive in a scholarly, distant way. He wore black and his greying mutton-chop whiskers gave him an added air of distinction. He was the Head Physician at the hospital and had been caring for her husband for over two months. In this task he had been nothing but patient and considerate.

'Mrs Thomson,' the doctor said, squeezing her hand and bowing very slightly. He was such an old-fashioned fellow, Sonia thought, nodding back. 'Come, let us see your husband straight away.'

They passed between the portico's massive Neo-classical columns and moved on through the grand doorway and into an echoing entrance hall. Dr Braithwaite led them to the left, through some double doors and into a wide corridor.

'How is my husband?' Sonia asked.

'We are optimistic,' Braithwaite replied, guardedly.

She gave him a doubting look, which he studiously ignored. 'He has recovered well from the lobotomy and is responding to treatment with cocaine. He is much calmer now. I'm thinking of moving him on to a new drug, a substance called lithium carbonate. Some patients have shown great improvement with this. Ah, here we are.'

They stopped outside a metal door. Braithwaite produced a key and turned it in the lock. 'If you'll excuse me, Mrs Thomson, I would like to go first.' He opened the door slowly and peered in. Then he took two steps into the room and beckoned Sonia to follow him.

The room was small but looked surprisingly comfortable, with its barred window overlooking the manicured gardens to the front of the building. It was furnished with a bed, a side table and a couple of chairs. Archibald was sitting at the end of the bed, stiff-backed and staring straight ahead, his face utterly expressionless. He was wearing a dark brown dressing-gown over a crisp white nightshirt. His hair had been neatly combed. Sonia walked up to him and took his hand. It was icy cold, and he did not look up. She caught a whiff of carbolic.

When he had first been admitted to the London Hospital on Mile End Road, Archibald had been barely conscious. Over the period of a week, he had begun to mend. In some ways he had been remarkably lucky. He had suffered rat bites to his legs, but had thankfully not contracted any deadly disease from them. He was malnourished and dehydrated, but the physical ills had been relatively easy to treat. The problems had started just as he was growing physically stronger and begining to remember what had happened to him. Seemingly overnight, he appeared to lose his senses. He began to rant and rave, to shout incoherently. It had been possible to grasp a few words here and there, but nothing comprehensible. He had become violent, uncontrollably so, and as his mental state deteriorated, it became impossible to treat him in the hospital. That was when the decision had been made to move him to Bedlam. For his own good.

The doctors at the asylum had tried to calm Archibald. They had thrown him into a freezing cold bath, tied him to a bed and left him for twenty-four hours, and then tried spinning him at high speed in a chair for ten minutes. He had simply grown worse, ranting incoherently. Finally, with Sonia Thomson's permission, they had conducted a lobotomy. That had shut him up. Indeed, Archibald had now been silent for five weeks. He had not moved a limb by his own volition. Everything had to be done for him.

At the insistence of Dr Braithwaite, Sonia had stayed away until now. She received formal letters each week, detailing her husband's progress, or lack thereof, and she had done as the doctor advised. Then, upon the prompting of an Oxford Professor of Medicine who had been a close friend of her father's, she had written to Braithwaite telling him that she would be visiting Archibald in two days' time. The doctor could do little other than comply with her wishes.

'I'll leave you alone together, Mrs Thomson,' he said, and turned towards the door. 'A nurse will be outside should you require anything. Please come and talk to me before you leave.'

Sonia heard the door close behind him. She glanced at her husband. He stared back at her, unseeing. She gathered her thoughts. The friend of the family who had advised her to visit her husband had said she should simply talk to him as though nothing had changed. But at that moment, staring at Archibald's marble-still face, she realised that it was no easy thing to do.

'I thought you would like to know that everyone at the paper is thinking of you, my darling,' she began, swallowing back tears. 'They have been very kind. And . . .' She could no longer stem the tears and started to weep into her hands. Archibald did not react. After a moment, Sonia was able to pull herself together. She cleared her throat and dabbed at her eyes with a handkerchief. Then she removed a bundle of letters from her bag.

'I received some letters today, darling. The strangest letters from a man called William Sandler.' She looked into her husband's eyes to see if the name produced a reaction in him. 'I think you knew him as Harry . . . Harry Tumbril. Does that mean anything to you?'

Archibald stared at her. Silent.

Sonia felt a stab of fury. 'Archibald? Husband? Does this letter mean nothing at all to you?' She waved it in front of his face. He did not react.

She stood up and leaned over her husband. Grabbing him by the shoulders, she shook him hard.

'Archibald!' she shouted, and threw the letters on to the bed beside him. 'Archie . . . Archie.' She fell to her knees in front of him and started to sob again. Looking up, tears running down her cheeks, she grasped his chin in one hand and started to shake his head. 'ARCHIE!'

She heard a sound behind her. The door to the corridor had opened. A nurse was standing there.

'Is everything . . . ?'

Sonia ignored him and slapped her husband's face hard. His head rocked from the blow, but he simply stared straight ahead.

'Mrs Thomson!'

The nurse ran over and grabbed Sonia's arm just as she was about to hit Archibald again. 'Please, Mrs Thomson!'

Another male nurse appeared in the doorway, then strode in. Between them they turned Sonia away from her husband's blank stare, helping her to leave the room. They had almost reached the door when they heard a sound from behind.

'Tumbril.'

Sonia froze and the men tightened their grip.

'No. Please!' she cried. 'Please stop! My husband spoke to me.'

The nurses looked at each other.

'Please? He said something.' Sonia pulled away, turning back towards Archibald.

'Tumbril,' he said quietly. His lips moved, but his face remained frozen, staring straight ahead. The nurses took Sonia's arms again, lightly now. They too seemed to be transfixed by the sight of the patient speaking.

'Tumbril,' Archibald repeated, his face a blank mask. 'TUMBRIL!' The sound reverberated about the walls of the room, a deafening roar now. The three onlookers stared, petrified and powerless, as Archibald fell forward on to the tiled floor, his forehead hitting the hard surface with a dull thud.

Dr Braithwaite was yelling something incoherent as he ran into the room, a warder a step behind him. 'Out of the way!' he shouted, pushing them aside. He crouched down beside Archibald and, with the help of the warder, slowly turned him over on to his back. Sonia made a strange sound in her throat as though she were choking. The two nurses had let her go and taken a step back.

Dr Braithwaite checked Archibald's pulse and pulled up one eyelid. He let out a heavy sigh and his body seemed to sag. Standing, he walked over to Sonia. 'I'm afraid your husband is dead.'

'NO!' she cried. 'No! That's not . . . NO!'

She threw herself to the floor huddled next to her husband's body. Then she leaned back, pulling his bloodied head towards her breast and cradling it, sobbing and rocking. The others stood by in silence until Braithwaite crouched down, helped the widow gently to her feet and guided her from the room.

Chapter 52

Brick Lane, Stepney, Thursday 29 January,
2.05 p.m.

Pendragon sat in the swivel chair at the back of the darkened Media Room, the monitor casting a pallid blue haze all around. Apart from a scattering of red power lights, this was the only illumination. He sat back, resting his head against the back of the leather chair, and for a few moments ran through in his mind the first section of *The Inner Mounting Flame*, one of his favourite pieces of music.

An incongruous thought came to him. He was transported back twenty-six years into his rented flat in Oxford. He had graduated that summer. Now it was late autumn and he still had not decided what he was going to do with his life, but he had just suffered the greatest trauma he had yet known. He had discovered that Cheryl, his girlfriend of two years, had been sleeping with his best friend at college, Gareth.

It was 7 a.m. when Cheryl turned up at the flat they had shared. He had been up half the night waiting for her. He had opened the front door, saying nothing. When she tried to speak, he put a finger to his lips and pointed to a chair in the living-room. Then, with his mind in a numb, nowhere land, he had paced over to the record player, put on *The Inner Mounting Flame*, sat in another chair directly facing Cheryl, and insisted they both stay and sit and listen to the whole side of the LP. The moment the last notes died away, he had stood up, put the record in its sleeve and ignored Cheryl when she called his name. Still silent, he had walked into the bedroom, placed the record in his case of albums and picked up his two bags. Reappearing in the lounge with the sum of his possessions, he walked past her, through the door and out on to the pavement.

Now he sat up, lifted his head and saw the light from the blue monitor dominating the room. A single word had popped into his head – Eberswalde. Eberswalde . . . the town a few miles from Berlin. He had heard that name years ago. Yes, it was all coming back. Eberswalde . . . His uncle Sid had been a corporal in the 1st Armoured Division. He had been stationed in Germany in the late 1950s. Uncle Sid was always regaling Jack with stories from his halcyon days in the army. One of his favourites had been about the time he almost went AWOL because of a debauched weekend spent in the town of Eberswalde. There was *never* an army base in Eberswalde.

A cold chill ran down Pendragon's spine. He jumped up from the chair, yanked open the door of the Media Room and dashed into the hall. He strode towards his office. He could see it was empty and ran on to the Briefing Room. That too was empty. Retracing his steps, he went over to the main desk where Rosalind Mackleby was on duty. 'Sergeant, have you seen Turner?'

'Here, sir.'

Pendragon spun round to see Jez walking towards him munching a ham sandwich. 'Spot of late lunch,' he added, holding up the other half still in the packet.

'Turner . . . the film from the party at Berrick and Price? Can you get it – right now?'

'Sure. But . . .'

'Now!'

Pendragon was in one of the two chairs in front of the monitors in the Media Room staring anxiously at the machines when Turner came in with the DVD in his hand, his mouth crammed with bread and meat. He sat down and slid the disk into a slot in the front of one of the machines, on a rack perpendicular with the control desk. 'Give us a sec,' he said, and tapped at a couple of buttons. 'So, what's this about then, guv?' he asked, swivelling round to face the monitors.

'Take it to about ten minutes in,' Pendragon replied, grim-faced.

Turner touched the 'Fast-forward' button and the images on the monitor became a blur. He pushed 'Stop' then 'Play', and on the screen they could both see the gathering at the gallery over a week earlier, just before the first murder. The camera moved around the room.

'Go forward about sixty seconds.'

The sergeant depressed the control and the film rolled on, slower than the first time. When he pressed 'Stop' the picture froze, showing a small group of people talking. There were Kingsley Berrick and Noel Thursk, side-on to the camera. Between them, with her back to the camera, was Gemma Locke in her low-cut, black cocktail dress.

'Okay,' Pendragon said. 'Can you zoom in?'

'Yeah. Which bit of the picture?'

'Gemma Locke.'

Turner nudged a control and the image on the screen slowly expanded. He moved a toggle and the image shifted to the left as it grew bigger.

'Stop!' Pendragon said.

The entire screen was now taken up with the head and shoulders of Gemma Locke.

'Okay, Turner, nudge the film forward. She's starting to look to her left.' The film moved on a few frames at a time.

'Stop! Can you enhance that image?'

'Yes.'

A horizontal line shimmied down the screen and in its wake left a picture that was twice as clear as the original. Pendragon moved his face close to the monitor. He could just about see a dark mark on Gemma Locke's neck. 'Close in there,' he said, pointing to a spot on the screen. 'And can you make it any clearer?'

'I'll try.'

The picture shifted once more. The horizontal line again moved down the screen, leaving an enhanced still image of Gemma Locke's neck. In the centre of the image was a faint scar approximating a circle and a narrow vertical line of scar tissue leading downward. It was clearly the faint remnants of a tattoo removed by laser.

'That's the best I can . . .' Turner froze and then slowly looked round at Pendragon. 'Fucking hell!' he said.

Chapter 53

'Are you absolutely sure?' Superintendent Hughes asked, staring at the monitor in the Media Room.

'One hundred and ten per cent,' Pendragon replied, and told her about how Gemma Locke had lied to him about Eberswalde.

Hughes still looked doubtful for a second. She stared at the floor, concentrating, then suddenly snapped into action mode. 'Right. I'll get an armed squad mobilised immediately.'

Pendragon was nodding. 'As back-up, ma'am. Let me go in first. She knows me. And she won't be expecting us.'

'Inspector! The woman is insane and extremely dangerous.'

'I know. Turner and I will go together . . . armed. You can have the SWAT team ten seconds away.'

'Why, Jack?'

'I honestly couldn't tell you,' he replied, holding the Super's steady gaze.

'Very well. And you know where she is?'

'Oh yes,' Pendragon replied, recalling the Bermondsey address Sammy Samson had dug up. He suddenly had a clear image of Gemma Locke standing in her apartment the previous day, her face straight out of a Pre-Raphaelite painting, an image tarnished only by the thick swathe of bandage around her head. 'I have a studio in Bermondsey,' she had said.

Freezing rain was hammering against the road, coming down so heavily it was almost impossible to see the buildings only a few yards beyond the windscreen. Twenty-two units had been fabricated out of a vast complex of Victorian grain stores that backed on to the river near Tate Modern. Gemma Locke's stood at the end of a row, number eleven. It was a two-storey cube with at least two hundred square metres of floor space.

All the occupants of the other offices and units had been surreptitiously moved to safety. Pendragon and Turner donned Kevlar jackets and duty belts, each with a holster for the standard police issue Glock 17 pistol, a baton and a small tear-gas canister. They crossed from the car towards the rear of the units as nine highly trained officers from the Specialist Firearms Command, known as CO19, dressed in full body armour and armed with Heckler & Koch MP5 machine-guns as well as Glock pistols, took up position around unit number eleven.

Pendragon went ahead. Crouching low, he traversed the tarmac and pulled up against the back wall. The brickwork was sodden and had turned a dozen shades darker than normal. A gutter overhead had slipped from its bracket and freezing water in a sheet a metre wide cascaded down from the roof. As Turner reached the wall, Pendragon moved off towards the rear door. He tried the handle. It was unlocked and opened inwards.

Out of the rain it was suddenly eerily quiet with just the steady beating of water on the roof to dispel the stillness. Pendragon looked around. They were in a small lobby about eight feet square. A door in the far wall stood ajar. A strong smell, a blend of chemical cleaner, paint and linseed oil, pervaded the place. Jack leaned against the doorframe and pushed the door slowly inwards.

It opened on to a large space, considerably bigger then the ground floor of most suburban houses. The walls had been painted a creamy white, and the floor was of highly polished dark oak parquet. Two large windows set in one wall had been blacked out so there was no natural light coming into the room. Around the three other walls ran a balconied mezzanine level. A large chandelier holding dozens of lit candles hung from the centre of the vaulted ceiling and cast a surprisingly strong light over the room. But it was a strangely hollow light, a sickly orange hue. The chemical smell was stronger in here.

It took a moment for the two police officers to see the figure seated in the chair at the far end of the room. Pendragon walked carefully across the wooden floor, crouching and turning as he had been trained to do. He had the Glock gripped in both hands and was scanning the shadows in the far corners of the room, expecting the unexpected. Turner was a couple of paces behind him.

Dr Geoff Hickle was strapped to the chair, unconscious. He was dressed in a heavy green coat and a Russian-style fur hat. Pendragon had seen that hat before. His body was strapped so he was sitting back in the chair, but his head was slumped forward. His splendid teeth had been smashed and a pipe stuck into his ruined mouth. His right ear had been removed and placed in his lap. The wound had been wrapped in a bloodstained bandage pressed against the side of his head with a strip of adhesive gauze.

'Holy shit!' Turner exclaimed, coming up beside Pendragon.

Shocked, Jack leaned forward and felt for a pulse. There was one, but it was weak.

'So, what do you think of my Van Gogh?'

Pendragon and Turner spun round, their guns tracking the source of the voice.

'Oh, boys, put the guns down.'

Gemma Locke's face appeared over the rail of the balcony ten feet above their heads. 'I'm coming down now. I'm unarmed.'

She ducked out of sight. The policemen kept their weapons trained, listening, following the sound of the woman's shoes as she descended a set of spiral stairs they could just make out in the corner of the room. She reappeared a few seconds later. She was wearing a diaphanous white dress, her long bob swinging around her face and neck. She reached the bottom of the stairs and started to cross the floor towards them.

'Stop there,' Pendragon commanded.

'Oh, Jack, please. Put the silly guns down. I'm not going to hurt anyone. It's not in my nature.' She produced a shrill laugh that only succeeded in making both Pendragon and Turner tighten their grip on the weapons. 'Okay,' Gemma Locke went on, suddenly serious. 'Maybe I have been a little harsh with some of them. But . . .' and she screwed up her face . . . 'they were so . . . nasty to me, Jack. They were *soooo* nasty.'

'We need to get Dr Hickle to hospital, Gemma. The game's over.'

'Nearly over. I'm just putting the finishing touches to my masterpiece. Then the whole world will know what a great artist I am.' She took a couple of steps forward. Pendragon cocked the pistol. Gemma stopped and lowered her head. 'Okay, I see I'm going to have to explain.' Then she looked up quickly, a faint smile playing on her lips. 'It'll be a good rehearsal for the tabloids and the global networks who will be clamouring to hear my story. But where do I start?'

'Gemma, please. Stop this now. We need to get . . .'

'Shut up. Just shut up and listen!' Gemma Locke's eyes blazed in the oppressive gloom. Then she swallowed and seemed to compose herself. 'Yes, you can call me Gemma. I prefer it now. But as you have of course worked out, I was once Juliette Kinnear. Poor little Juliette.' Then she glanced at Dr Hickle. 'I made him my last victim because he broke my heart.' She turned back to the two policemen, an expression of contempt on her face. 'But you do understand, don't you? Revenge was simply an added bonus.'

'Why did you kill those people?' Turner asked, keeping his gun trained on her.

'I'm an artist. This is my masterpiece.'

'What?'

'Ms Locke believes that she has created art out of a series of murders,' Pendragon explained, his face rigid.

'The way you say it, Jack! Good God, show some respect! You have to admit, it is *damn* impressive.' She waved one hand in the air. 'Juliette started it. Well,

374

actually, no, my father started it. He was something of a bibliophile. Had a wonderful library, he was really proud of it. He was away a lot on business – selling biscuits! Mother died when I was fourteen. So, when I wasn't painting, or in London – with him . . .' and she flicked a glance at Hickle . . . 'I spent many hours on my own in the library. And then one day, I must have been seventeen . . . Yes, it was then, because I had just had a review of my first little exhibition in Chelmsford – a bad review from a young writer called Gary Townsend . . .'

'Townsend?'

Gemma Locke shrugged. 'Yes, I was annoyed when that one went wrong.' She sighed and looked down at the parquet floor for a moment before meeting Pendragon's eye. 'I had it all so carefully planned too. You've probably worked it out, Jack. I drugged Hickle. He could still walk. He was just, well, a little confused! I managed to slip out of a back entrance to his apartment block. Later, I met up with Townsend at the unit. I had convinced him to show by telling him I had a juicy story for his rag. But then his ditzy girlfriend followed him. I got away but I had to figure out a way to get to him in the hospital and divert any suspicion from myself. I faked the mugging, killed the bastard, and got you to come and see how poorly I was. Quite a performance, I thought. Especially the bit where I pretended to pass out at my apartment. You were so sweet.'

'What has your father's library got to do with any of this?' Turner asked.

'Oh, I found something there that changed my life, Sergeant. A journal. Well, a collection of letters really. I started to read them, and was astonished when I learned that they had been written by Jack the Ripper.' She stopped for a second. 'Don't believe me, Inspector? No, well, that's understandable. Anyway, it's irrelevant whether or not you accept what I say. The letters were an inspiration to me. They revealed that The Ripper had been a very talented artist who had chosen his victims to create a masterwork. The series of murders *was* the work.

'I was transformed by my discovery, though my first effort to apply the Ripper's concept did not work as well as I had hoped. As you know, I attacked our gardener, Macintyre. I was pleased with the piece – Jack, you should have seen his face. That combination of red and blackened flesh with a dash of brittle white bone . . . it was truly beautiful. But it landed me in a lot of trouble, and nobody seemed to understand what I was doing.'

'You attacked the man so you could paint him afterwards?' Turner asked.

Gemma Locke's eyes widened. 'Your sergeant's a little slow, isn't he, Jack?' She giggled.

Pendragon said nothing.

'The act itself was the work of art, Sergeant. I didn't do anything so crude as to *paint* the scene. I had moved way beyond such a commonplace approach. But, as I said, it didn't work out as well as I had hoped. I ended up in Riverwell. They drugged me, shocked me with their ECT and for a while it changed me. I never stopped wanting to get out of there, but the therapy quashed my artistic drive. So I faked my own death in Maldon. A nurse, Nick Compton, was besotted with me . . . a state of mind I had assiduously nurtured. He was complicit in the set-up on the seafront. I hid under the rafters of the pier, then crawled out and slipped away while the hospital staff panicked.'

'But the dead girl they identified?'

'Nick and I had killed her. He got me out of the hospital the night before the trip to Maldon. She was a young prostitute from Southend. Nick had a little dinghy. We dumped the body in the sea just off Maldon. We knew she would be washed up by the tide, but we weren't sure how quickly – that was the dodgiest bit of the plan, actually. But it all worked a treat. My father was too traumatised to make the ID at the morgue, and so his brother Lionel went along. But it was an irrelevance anyway. North Sea fish are fond of human flesh.' She smiled.

'And later you killed Nick Compton?' Pendragon asked.

'Yes. He knew too much and I was losing my grip on him.'

'Then you vanished.'

'I think of it more as a transformation. I went into a dormant phase, a chrysalis if you like. I was able to steal money from my father's accounts. I figured it would one day be my inheritance, I was just taking it early. I went to the States, underwent plastic surgery, bought some coloured contact lenses, several fake IDs . . . oh, and I had the tattoo removed.' She touched the side of her neck and smiled. 'I moved to London late in 1998 and gradually rebuilt my career under a new name. I wanted to prove to myself that I could succeed as a conventional artist. That if I had not had my original career stolen from me, I would be famous. Perhaps the most famous artist of our time. I knew I was that good.'

'But many years later something went wrong. Something recently led you back to the path of murder.'

'I don't consider it as "going wrong",' Gemma Locke said, matter-of-factly. 'No, two things coincided, Inspector. First, I began to doubt myself. That was Townsend's fault. The young journalist who had been writing for a local paper in Chelmsford was now the Arts Editor of a big national daily. He had no idea Gemma Locke had once been Juliette Kinnear, and he probably could not even remember giving the young Juliette a bad review for her fledgling exhibition in a lousy church hall. But he slammed my last show at the White Cube and it began a chain reaction in my mind.

'I started to wander into a different mental state, one I had experienced before. It was a joyous liberation. I felt free again, filled with creative energy and self-belief. I was so grateful I could almost have spared the bastard.' She produced a shrill laugh and looked from Pendragon to Turner. 'Oh, come on, guys. Don't you see the funny side? No? Okay . . . well, that's the truth of it. If it had been just that one bad review I might not have started a new masterpiece inspired by my old mentor, The Ripper. But then I discovered that silly little man Noel Thursk had unearthed some facts I would have preferred to be kept buried. I had known about his ridiculous book for years, but hadn't taken him seriously until then.' She threw her arms out and slapped her palms against her sides. 'Well, it was obviously a sign!'

'But why the others?' Pendragon asked, aware he needed to humour her until he could make a move.

'That's a good question,' she replied, warming to the subject. 'And one I want to explain at length to the media. From an artistic point of view, I wanted six tableaux. It's a matter of symmetry. Taken as one great piece, it's a beautiful composition. But the subjects were all on my personal hit-list anyway.' She lifted a hand and began to tick them off. 'Kingsley Berrick. That man did everything he could to keep me down and to promote other, far lesser, talents ahead of me.'

'Like Chrissy Chapman?'

'Precisely.' Gemma Locke beamed. 'My oldest, bestest friend. It wasn't Chrissy's fault that Berrick made her his poster girl over me. But it was her fault that she was on the verge of marrying *him*.' And she tossed her head towards the pitiful maimed figure tied to the chair. 'So, I thought I'd set up dear Chrissy in a way that would be in keeping with the others . . . and humorous as well.'

'Oh, I'm sure Chrissy Chapman's family are laughing their arses off,' Turner said, glaring at Gemma.

'Hah! You were right the other day, Inspector. Your sergeant does think he's funny.'

'And how did you manage to set up Ms Chapman in the way you did?' he replied keeping his tone even.

'Oh, it wasn't easy, I can assure you of that. But then, no great art comes easily. I trained as a sculptor under the Russian master Korentikoff when he lived in London during the early noughties. I also studied reconstructive surgery techniques privately. The internet is a wonderful thing. Anyway, Chrissy . . . I brought her here soon after Hickle left for his run. It was under the pretext that I had a surprise for her. I certainly didn't lie! I killed her quickly

– the same way as the others. Then I drained her of blood, smashed the bones in her face, and with liberal amounts of glue, spray-on skin and quick-setting plaster, was able to sculpt back her face to my liking.'

'And Father O'Leary?' Pendragon asked wearily, trying to draw the exchange to a close without tipping the woman over the edge. Lesson 101; psychopaths just love to talk about themselves.

Gemma Locke's face clouded over. 'That so-called priest abused me.' In the deathly silence, she breathed in sharply. 'Sexual abuse, DCI, the oldest trick in the book for many a Roman Catholic priest, God bless 'em. O'Leary was my local parish priest. My parents were religious, especially Mother. When I was thirteen, I was pushed into taking lessons in preparation for Confirmation.' She started to giggle again. 'I made sure Michael O'Leary realised who I was just before I dispatched him. But he died too fast. I was much too nice to him.' She suddenly leaned forward and took a step nearer Dr Hickle.

'Don't!' Pendragon snapped.

Gemma stood still then turned back towards them. 'Jack, you have to understand. I must finish my . . .'

'You're finishing nothing.'

Gemma Locke's hand slid into a pocket of her gown.

'Stop!'

'It's not a gun, Jack.'

'Bring your hand back into view . . . slowly,' Turner yelled.

She pulled her hand from her pocket. It was clasping a hypodermic.

'Put it down,' Pendragon commanded.

She ignored him and took a step towards Dr Hickle. A shot rang out, booming in the restricted, echoing space. Gemma Locke screamed in surprise. The hypodermic flew through the air and landed a few feet away. Blood spurted from a wound in her hand and she stumbled back, crumpling into a heap.

Pendragon dashed forward, his gun levelled at her head. Gemma Locke lay on her side in a foetal position, cradling her wounded hand. A line of blood spilled away across the wooden floor.

'Turner . . . call the paramedics,' Pendragon ordered.

He bent forward, keeping the gun pointed at Gemma's head, and pushed back her shoulder gently. She stared up at him, her smile sliding into a look of triumph.

'How perfect, Inspector. They'll have to add a new chapter to the textbooks, and it will be all about me.'

Chapter 54

Manhattan, December 1888

The man was known by many names. To some he had been William Sandler, to others Harry Tumbril, Cedric O'Brien, Norman Heathcote or Graham Harris. Although the name had never been used to his face, he had also acquired the epithet Jack the Ripper. Here, at the Broadway Central Hotel, he had registered as Francis Bettleman, a businessman from England, who was planning to invest in a road-surfacing company in Brooklyn.

He had been away from England for two months now and was itching to work again. On the voyage across the Atlantic he had spent many long hours in his cabin contemplating his next endeavour. But then, upon arriving in New York, he had been thrown temporarily off course. He had seen paintings of the city and some rare photographs, but the physical reality of the place was so overwhelming that, for a while, he had lost his sense of direction.

On the surface, the place reminded him of a very small London. It was grimy, dark, dirty, and filled with too many moronic humans. But in many other

ways it was an alien city. It was not so claustrophobic as London; the sky was huge, and so were
some of the buildings. Architects from across the
world were flocking here to flex their design
muscles and show off their expertise. It was a blank
canvas for them. And so it was for him too, once he
got his bearings. One had to be familiar with a
killing ground. Escape routes needed to be mapped
out, local customs understood. It would be so easy
to make a fatal error if he were not thoroughly
prepared. He could not contemplate such sloppi-
ness. He was a professional, a great artist. The
English might have calmed down now that their
notorious murderer had apparently stopped his
slaughter. But the New World was beginning to
wake up to his presence and he was revelling in the
delicious taste of fear and suspicion all around him.

His new work was to be another quartet. There
was something about the symmetry of the number
that pleased him. Two of the women had been
dispatched during the course of the previous three
nights. What had amazed him was that, although he
was in the 'New World', the sheep here were little
different from their English cousins. Everyone
reacted in exactly the same way. The silly whores,
the police, the public, the city bigwigs . . . and, of
course, the press. It was rather a disappointment,
but perhaps not entirely unexpected. After all,
people were people. Sheep were sheep.

Now, at 7 p.m. on a frosty December evening, he
was on his way to keep an appointment with Bessy

Munroe, a 'singer' in the music hall, an aspiring theatre actress apparently, who had come to New York from some God-forsaken farming town in the American interior. Bessy was a little further up the hierarchy of prostitutes than the ones he had known in London. A week earlier, Francis Bettleman had met her at Harry's Music Hall on Broadway, a short walk from his hotel. She had offered her services then, but the time was not right – he was busy planning murders one and two, Julie Grovenor and Helen Fritzle. Bessy was to be number three. And so he had waited until now.

Checking his watch, Francis stopped in the opulent foyer of the Broadway Central, nodded to the assistant manager behind his desk and headed towards the grand doors leading out on to Broadway. It was then that he experienced an odd sensation, a feeling that had come over him on several occasions during the past week. It was a tingling at the nape of his neck, the unmistakable sensation of being watched, being followed. He glanced round, but there was nothing to see. Either he was imagining things or the person watching him was very good at his job.

Outside the hotel stood a line of horse-drawn cabs. He jumped in the front vehicle, told the driver the address and sat back against the yielding leather of the seat as the cab bumped along the rough road. It took no more than a couple of minutes to reach his destination. Francis paid the driver, jumped down, and marched quickly into the music hall.

At the bar, he had a cup of coffee and waited. He was a little early, but all was going to plan so far. He looked around at the brass and marble of the bar and felt that familiar impervious self-confidence flow through his veins, energising him.

On cue, Bessy arrived and strode towards him. She was a very average-looking young woman, Francis thought, but with an air of self-belief about her that was almost attractive. It was a confidence he had found to be shared by many of the Americans he had met. It was as though they all considered themselves a part of something fresh and new and growing and purposeful. It gave them a sense of direction, a feeling they participated in something bigger than themselves. He found it at once laughable and piquant.

'Let's go somewhere else,' he said, draining his cup and turning towards the young woman as she made to sit beside him at the bar.

She merely smiled and let him lead her towards the door.

'So where do'ya fancy, Mr Bettleman?' Bessy said, taking his arm.

He removed her hand from him gently and ignored her puzzled expression. 'I have rooms close by.'

'Oh, do you now? I knew yous was a sophisticated man, Mr Bettleman.'

As they walked along the street, he suddenly realised Bessy was tipsy. That would make everything easier. 'Just down there,' he said, pointing to a narrow alleyway a few yards away on their right. She looked up at him and gave him a crooked smile, then hiccuped.

Bettleman stopped suddenly. It was that strange feeling again. He turned round. There were people walking close behind them along the edge of the busy street. He tried to blot out the sounds all around. Should he stop? Should he simply return to the hotel and change his plans? Come out another night? Then he felt a sudden surge of anger. No. He would not be controlled by anyone. He, and he alone, was master of his own destiny. He had proved that on so many previous occasions. He would not let this place, these people, intimidate him. He was better than any of them, infinitely better.

'What's wrong?' the prostitute asked, and then, seeing his deliberations started to giggle.

Francis looked down at her and felt a wave of nausea rise in him. He swallowed hard and drew in a gulp of cold air. 'Nothing,' he said after a moment. 'Nothing at all, Bessy. Come on.'

He took her arm now and guided her into the mouth of the narrow alleyway, beyond the hubbub. The noise of the busy street faded fast behind them. If it had not been for a full moon directly overhead, it would have been impossible to see anything in the alleyway. The moon cast a steely glow over everything.

'Where we going?' Bessy said, her voice edged with sudden anxiety.

'The door is just ahead,' Francis replied reassuringly. He put his hand into his jacket pocket to jangle a set of keys. It calmed the woman and she giggled again.

Twenty yards into the alleyway, Francis guided the prostitute towards the left then suddenly spun her round.

'Oh, Mr Bettleman,' she exclaimed. 'Can't you wait, sweetie?'

Francis plunged his right hand into the lining of his coat and felt for the handle of the eight-inch knife sewn into the fabric. The handle had been left to protrude from the lining. He grasped it and pulled it out, shielding it from view behind his coat. It caught the moonlight as he swung it free.

'Don't move!'

The voice that had spoken behind them was male, American. Bettleman froze. The prostitute looked up at him and screamed as she took in the scene: the knife still poised in his hand, the outline of a figure behind her customer, the new arrival's shadowed face, the pistol just visible in his hand.

'Drop the knife. Now!'

Bettleman stood rigid.

'Last warning, Mr Bettleman. Drop the knife.'

The weapon made a metallic sound as it hit the ground.

'You, young woman,' said the man with gun, and jerked his head back. 'Get.' She needed no further persuasion, scurrying away pressed to the wall. The man with the gun grabbed her arm as she passed him. The prostitute caught a glimpse of a pair of dark eyes over a scarf covering his mouth and nose. He was wearing a bowler hat pulled down low over his brow. 'Say one word and I will find you,' the man hissed, then let the woman go. 'Turn,' he snapped at Bettleman.

The Englishman started to and the man hit him across the left temple with the butt of the gun. Bettleman collapsed in a heap.

He awoke, moved his head, and a sharp pain shot across his forehead. He lay spreadeagled, tied by ropes at his ankles and wrists. He could just see that he was on some sort of platform or oblong table. The room was large, with a high ceiling. It was lit by tall candles on stands positioned at the corners of the room. He could just see in the far wall a massive window, and a glimpse beyond of slender, tall buildings beneath a sky lit by the bright orb of the moon.

'You must find it strange to be in the submissive position, Mr Bettleman.' The voice was coming from behind him, but he could not turn far enough to see who was speaking. Yet, there was something about that voice he recognised.

'You don't mind my calling you Mr Bettleman, do you? To me you were William Sandler. I know that with others you have used different pseudonyms.' The man took a step closer and Bettleman suddenly knew who this was.

'Oglebee! What the hell are you doing?'

'Very good, Francis. In Oxford, I affected an accent to disguise the American vowels of my youth. Being back here, in the place of my birth, I seem to have slipped into old ways.'

'Untie me, man,' Bettleman protested, trying to turn and identify Magnus Oglebee, the mysterious figure from the soiree at Boars Hill.

'Now why would I do that?' he replied, and walked slowly into view. He was wearing an immaculate dark suit with a gold watch chain hanging over his waistcoat. His shirt was wing-collared, slightly old-fashioned, and he had donned a grey cravat adorned with a large sapphire pin. His head looked dispro-portionately small above the starched collar, almost as though his head had shrunk. His tiny black eyes revealed a dark amusement with the situation.

'What is this all about?' Francis Bettleman said. He could not disguise the acid tinge in his voice. 'Is it one of your entertainments, Oglebee?'

'Yes, in a way, it is,' the man replied, perching himself on the edge of the table. 'But there's also a less frivolous side to it.'

'Would you care to explain? Only I'm beginning to grow a little irritated.'

'Oh, are you now, my friend?' Oglebee mocked.

'I'm not your friend,' Bettleman spat, unable to contain his anger any longer. 'I don't take kindly to being hit over the head and then bound like an animal.'

'No, I can empathise with that,' Oglebee responded. Then he gave a small shrug, pushed himself off the table and walked towards Bettleman's splayed feet. 'I've closely followed your exploits in London,' he went on. 'I have to say "Bravo". It was quite a performance. And . . .' he produced a vague smile '. . . I feel proud that you took my advice. That I was perhaps a source of inspiration to you. I always knew you had talent.'

Bettleman took several deep breaths to calm himself. 'Oglebee, can you untie me, please? I'm happy to chat, but this is not exactly . . .'

'No. I can't do that.'

Bettleman started to struggle but only succeeded in making the cords cut into his flesh. 'Oglebee!' he shouted. 'Let me go! Or I swear . . .'

Magnus Oglebee appeared at his side again. 'I take no pleasure in hurting you,' he said. 'But you of all people should understand that it is sometimes necessary. This is not some silly revenge I'm exacting. Far from it. I think your work has been fine. It's just that . . . well, time marches on, and what you've been doing is a little . . . how should I put it? . . . old-fashioned.'

Bettleman stopped struggling and fixed Oglebee with consternation in his eyes. 'What?'

'Let me explain, Jack. May I call you that? I think it's a good name for you – you chose it in good humour.'

Bettleman glared at the man, his fury almost palpable.

'When I met you in Oxford – goodness, it feels like ancient history, but it was only six months ago . . .

you told me you were searching for meaning, and then you found it in your creations. First you thought, naively, that you had to paint the murders you committed. Only later did you realise that a far higher art form would be to envision the collective acts of murder as, in themselves, the creation. It was a bold and intelligent step forward.' He paused for a second and drew close to Bettleman's face. 'I have to admit, I was a little jealous of your fecundity. I have never had any artistic talent and, as I explained to you in Oxford, had given up trying to express myself through murder. But then I made a most profound discovery.'

Bettleman was staring straight into Oglebee's tiny face, a strange feeling of dread growing in the pit of his stomach. 'Look, old boy,' he said, his voice surprisingly calm, almost melodious. 'Can we not discuss this sensibly? Man to man, over a brandy, perhaps?'

Oglebee ignored him. Straightening up, he began to walk back towards Bettleman's trussed feet. 'And, you know, although there is nothing new about the practical nuts and bolts aspects of what I'm doing, the principles, the concept . . . Well!' And he tapped his head with a flourish. '*These* principles, *these* concepts, are so perfectly attuned to this . . .' He swept his arms towards the view of Manhattan in all its nascent glory beyond the window. 'The artistic drive I have discovered is so new, so modern . . .'

'What are you talking about?' Bettleman screamed.

'The best form of explanation is action,' Oglebee said, and clapped his hands.

He disappeared for a moment. Bettleman tried craning his neck, but was pinned down on the table too tightly. Then the other man reappeared a few feet behind his head. Bettleman could not see him properly, but could just make out a dark boxy shape on spindly legs. It took him a few seconds to realise it was a camera being positioned on a wooden tripod.

Then he felt a current of air move close to his body. Twisting his head, he saw white shapes. Four women appeared around the table. They looked similar to the girls he had seen at the house in Oxford – willowy, tall and blonde. Their hair hung to waist-level and each of them wore a slender coronet of white flowers. At a signal from Oglebee the women took a step forward, so that they were all ranged close to Bettleman, two of them to each side of him.

Oglebee stood to the left of the camera, making a small adjustment to the contraption. Then he picked up a flash on a wooden pole. 'You see, Jack, I could never paint. But thanks to the technology of photography, I can capture moments, just like you do. And with this technology, I, like you, can express myself. I thought I would add a little humour to the piece. Four girls, one for each of your subjects in London. A nice symmetry, don't you think?' Then he walked round to the rear of the camera, made a final modification to one of the legs of the tripod, straightened up, and with the flash held out at arm's length, parallel with his head, took a deep breath. 'Ladies,' he said.

The girls turned slightly to look at Bettleman. He tried to focus on them, terror and confusion ripping through him, his stomach churning. He felt vomit rise up in his throat. He did not see the girls' hands move, did not see the blades until they were raised over his body. He made to scream, but nothing emerged, his muscles had seized in shock.

'On three,' Oglebee announced. 'One, two, three . . .'

And the flash burst, casting a white radiance across the room.

Chapter 55

Stepney, Sunday 1 February

Jack Pendragon felt more relaxed than he had been in a long time. If he had, during the previous week, found the time to imagine the end of the investigation into what the tabloids were calling the Modern Art Murders, he might have pictured things calming down pretty quickly. But that would have been far from the truth. In the three days since Gemma Locke had been apprehended, Pendragon had been the subject of media adulation. Much to Jack's satisfaction, Fred Taylor from the local rag had been the lone dissenting voice. And when the hack had refused to soften his line after the arrest, his editor had insisted he take a long-overdue vacation.

Gemma Locke was now in custody and undergoing extensive psychological testing. Geoff Hickle was on the mend. His ear had been reattached and was taking, but it would be a while before his glorious teeth would be back to their former state. A thorough search of Gemma Locke's flat had turned up the original collection of letters she had claimed were written by Jack the Ripper. Pendragon had held them between his gloved hands before bagging them for forensic analysis. After Dr

Newman had finished with them, he had contacted Professor Stokes, an eminent archaeologist and expert in the history of London at Queen Mary College. Six months earlier, Stokes had been instrumental in helping Pendragon solve the mystery of how a ring once owned by the Borgia family had ended up on an ancient skeleton found on a building site off Mile End Road. Pendragon knew that if anyone could authenticate the letters, Stokes could.

Jack looked up from the pages lying on his kitchen table, past piles of other books and papers, to survey the living-room of his flat. The walls were still multi-coloured, the grubby pale blue only partially covered by fresh paint; half the skirting boards were still to be sanded. Heaps of unironed washing lay on the sofa, and the sink was piled high with unwashed dishes. He had let the place go during the past fortnight, but did not feel bad about it. He had had more pressing matters to attend to. He would get back to the decorating and smarten the place up when he could.

Then his eye was drawn to the kitchen worktop and the solitary birthday card standing close to the kettle. He reached over and pulled it towards him. It was from his son Simon. It read simply: 'Dad, have a good one – 32 again? Love, Si'. Pendragon placed it back on the worktop and turned to his books, thinking that, after the chaos of the last two weeks, he really did not mind spending his forty-seventh birthday on his own, in the peace and quiet of his flat. He had never been one for parties and fuss.

The doorbell rang. He got up from the table and walked over to the intercom on the wall near the door. 'If it's

Jehovah's Witnesses . . . go away. Aren't you supposed to be in church?'

'Guv, it's me.'

'Turner? What is it?'

'Can I come up?'

Pendragon opened the door to his sergeant and showed him over to the sofa. He collected up two piles of clothes and strode through to the bedroom with them. When he returned, Jez was looking around at the half-painted walls.

'I know,' Pendragon sighed. 'Looks a bloody mess.'

Turner smiled. 'I think you have a good excuse.'

'Yes, well. What can I do for you?'

'I thought . . . well, as it's your birthday and all . . . I could buy you a drink?'

Pendragon ran his hand over his forehead, then folded his arms. 'That's very kind of you . . .'

'I guess you don't like to be reminded of birthdays any more.'

Pendragon produced a smile. 'No, haven't for a long time. But the drink . . .'

''Fraid I can't take no for an answer over that drink, sir. Looks like you've been slaving over a hot textbook. Thirsty work.'

Jack laughed. 'You've twisted my arm!'

'So, you discovered anything amazing from those letters?' the sergeant asked as they descended the stairs to the lobby.

'Professor Stokes has confirmed they do indeed date from the 1880s, but has to prepare them for some invasive analyses to see if he can find out anything more. To be honest, he's not very hopeful.'

They reached the ground floor and stepped out into the freezing early afternoon. There was a stiff breeze. 'Good God!' Pendragon exclaimed. It felt as though the cold was removing several layers of skin from his face.

'Yeah, a bit nippy,' Turner responded as they crossed the road. 'But Stokes gave you photocopies, right? I read most of them on Friday at the station.'

'More or less. He has some sort of scanner to duplicate delicate manuscripts without damaging them, and he was kind enough to pass copies on to me.'

'That's why the washing hasn't been ironed!'

Pendragon glanced at the sergeant. 'That and the constant demands from the media.'

'Oh, to be a celebrity!' Turner quipped. 'And, can you now answer the question that's troubled Ripperologists for over a century? Do you know who he was?' Turner looked genuinely excited.

'Oh, come on! Do you think if I did I'd be going to the pub with you now?'

'No, probably not, sir. So that would be a "no" then?'

'Sadly, nothing matches up. I think the letters were certainly written by a contemporary, and some details given about the murders prove almost conclusively that they were written by someone in the know . . . quite possibly The Ripper himself. But that's about as far as it goes.'

'Why?'

'The letters are a frustrating blend of truth and lies. There never was a Fellwick Manor in Hemel Hempstead, nor a Sandler family fitting their description living in the town. There was no William Sandler born on 10 August 1867, and no such student enrolled at Exeter College,

Oxford, under that name at any time between 1884 and 1886. But there was, and still is, a Wentworth Street, and there was even a corn-chandler's shop there that burned down in October 1888. But again, absolutely no trace of a Sandler or a Harry Tumbril ever living there. There was a White Star Line ship called the *Oceanic* which criss-crossed the Atlantic at that time, but there is no record of our quarry purchasing a ticket to New York. And, once he arrived in America, if indeed that was where he ended up, he simply vanished, never to be heard of again.'

'And what about the newspaper editor? Archibald Thomson, wasn't it?'

'He really did exist, and was abducted in late 1888. He was traumatised by the experience and died in Bedlam Hospital soon after.'

'How did you find that out?'

'Well, it was actually thanks to one of the most puzzling questions about all this – how did the letters get into Juliette Kinnear's hands?'

'Her father had them in his library.'

'But how did *he* get them?'

Turner shrugged. 'He collected books and manuscripts. I assumed he must have picked them up at an auction or a second-hand book shop.'

Pendragon gave his sergeant a sceptical look. 'Much more interesting, actually. I'd had them for at least a day before I noticed a very faint paragraph of writing on the bottom of one of them. It was written in a different hand from the author of the letters. It said, something like: "I cannot think what to do with these horrible things. I cannot destroy them, for that would somehow feel wrong.

So I entrust them to you". It was signed by Sonia Thomson.'

'Archibald's wife, the woman The Ripper was writing to?'

'Yes. I then traced back the Kinnear family tree. Turns out Juliette's great-grandfather, David Kinnear, had been the Warden of Bedlam Hospital between 1911 and 1914. Sonia Thomson must have left the letters at the hospital with one of David Kinnear's predecessors, and somehow they surfaced during his tenure. It seems it was David Kinnear who started the family library and sparked the bibliophilia in his grandson, Juliette's father John.'

They had reached the door to the pub and Turner held it open for his boss. They walked through the public bar, along a narrow corridor and emerged into the lounge bar. As Pendragon stepped into the room, a loud cheer went up followed by a tumultuous: 'HAPPY BIRTHDAY!'

Stunned for a second, he surveyed their faces – the entire team from the station were there as well as Colette Newman and Neil Jones. Behind them hung a paper banner with: MANY HAPPY RETURNS, JACK written on it. Jimmy Thatcher stepped forward, blowing a party whistle and holding out a pint of bitter.

Pendragon was so surprised he just stared at the gathering open-mouthed before grasping the glass of beer automatically. No one had ever thrown him a surprise party before and he could barely believe that it was happening now. He had not realised how much he had settled here, become part of the team. For a second he felt almost overwhelmed with emotion. Then he raised the glass and grinned from ear to ear.

Superintendent Hughes stepped forward with a gift wrapped in bright orange and red paper.

'For you, Jack.'

Pendragon looked at the gift and then back at the gathering.

'Come on, guv. Open it then,' Inspector Grant shouted from the back of the group, and they moved forward to surround him.

He looked around at all the smiling faces. 'Thanks,' he said, blushing. 'I didn't expect . . .' He pulled the ribbon and carefully peeled apart the edges of the paper. Inside it was a large coffee-table book with a blaringly colourful cover. He read the title aloud: *THE SURREALISTS*. Then he burst out laughing.

Equinox

Michael White

**A brutal murder. A three-hundred-year conspiracy.
A deadly secret.**

Oxford, 2006: a young woman is found brutally murdered, her
throat cut. Her heart has been removed and in its place lies
an apparently ancient gold coin. Twenty-four hours later, another
woman is found. The MO is identical, except that this time her
brain has been removed, and a silver coin lies glittering in the bowl
of her skull.

The police are baffled but when police photographer Philip
Bainbridge and his estranged lover Laura Niven become involved,
they discover that these horrific, ritualistic murders are not
confined to the here and now. And a shocking story begins to
emerge which intertwines Sir Isaac Newton, one of seventeenth-
century England's most powerful figures, with a deadly conspiracy
which echoes down the years to the present day, as lethal now as
it was then.

Before long those closest to Laura are in danger, and she finds
herself the one person who can rewrite history; the only person who
can stop the killer from striking again . . .

arrow books

The Medici Secret

Michael White

**An ancient mystery. A conspiracy of silence.
A secret to kill for.**

In the crypt of the Medici Chapel in Florence, palaeopathologist, Edie Granger, and her uncle, Carlin Mackenzie, are examining the mummified remains of one of the most powerful families in Renaissance Italy.

The embalmers have done their work well in terms of outward appearance. But under the crisp skin, the organs have shrivelled to a fraction of their original size, which means it is difficult to gather a usable DNA sample. Edie and Mackenzie both have serious doubts about the true identity of at least two of the five-hundred-year-old bodies.

And no one can explain the presence of an alien object discovered resting against Cosimo de' Medici's spine.

For Carlin Mackenzie, this is the most fascinating and the most dangerous discovery of his life. For Edie, it is the beginning of an obsessive, life-threatening quest . . .

arrow books

The Borgia Ring

Michael White

A weapon from the past. A secret that has survived the centuries. A deadly obsession.

When a blackened skeleton is unearthed on a building site in the City of London, no one can have the slightest idea of its extraordinary link to a plot to assassinate the Queen of England over 500 years ago.

But there is one very conspicuous clue. On the index finger of the body's right hand is a gold ring topped with a brilliant, round emerald.

DCI Jack Pendragon has just transferred from Oxford to Brick Lane police station – in part to escape his own past. Immediately, he finds himself investigating three particularly gruesome murders. And he will need all the experience he has acquired from two decades on the force to track down a killer for whom an eerie obsession has become total madness. A killer who draws his murderous inspiration from a Renaissance family whose power and cruelty remain a living legend.

arrow books